11.50

EIGHT

UNCOLLECTED TALES

OF

HENRY JAMES

EIGHT
UNCOLLECTED TALES
OF
HENRY JAMES

Edited With an Introduction by

EDNA KENTON

Short Story Index Reprint Series

Originally published by
RUTGERS UNIVERSITY PRESS
New Brunswick, N.J.

BOOKS FOR LIBRARIES PRESS
FREEPORT, NEW YORK

INTERNATIONAL STANDARD BOOK NUMBER:
0-8369-3915-8

LIBRARY OF CONGRESS CATALOG CARD NUMBER:
71-160936

PRINTED IN THE UNITED STATES OF AMERICA

Contents

Contents

INTRODUCTION

Introduction

BEFORE WE TAKE UP A SOMEWHAT UNCONVENTIONAL survey of these early tales of Henry James, far less as stories with "plots" than as foreshadowings of ideas and techniques that are basic in all of his later work, we shall make a brief preliminary survey of his short fictions through the period these uncollected stories cover.

From 1865 through 1876 James published twenty-eight tales of which he reprinted only thirteen; in *A Passionate Pilgrim and Other Tales* (1875), *The Madonna of the Future and Other Tales* (1879), and *Stories Revived* (1885). The remaining fifteen have come to be loosely known as the "uncollected stories." Except for stray references to them in old Letters and Memoirs of the '60's and '70's, till LeRoy Phillips listed their titles and dates in his first *Bibliography of the Writings of Henry James* (1906), they lay unknown in old files of the *Atlantic*, the *Galaxy* and *Scribner's Monthly*. Since by 1885 James could have undoubtedly resurrected any tale he chose to revive, we can safely say that for one reason or another he "rejected" these fifteen tales from any second printings. But to take it for granted that his rejections were governed by ordinary critical appraisal of them on their story values alone is to assume too much.

In 1919 Albert Mordell reprinted seven of this group of tales in *Travelling Companions*. The title story of 1870 was followed by "The Sweetheart of M. Briseux" (1873), "Professor Fargo" (1874), "At Isella" (1871), "Guest's Confession" (1872), "Adina" (1874), and "De Grey: A Romance" (1868). The other eight tales are in this volume, five of them reprinted here for the first time. At the end of this volume is a chronological list of the twenty-eight stories of this period, with serial and first book publication dates and with some later more accessible reprintings noted.

3

Of the three stories included here but reprinted before, "Gabrielle de Bergerac," first of the fifteen to be revived, was published in 1918 in a small edition now out of print. "The Story of a Year," James's first published fiction, was first reprinted in *American Novels and Stories of Henry James*, edited by F. O. Matthiessen (1947), and "The Ghostly Rental," last of the uncollected, had its first reprinting in *The Ghostly Tales of Henry James*, edited by Leon Edel (1948). The other five tales, as already noted, have their first reprintings here, and with Mordell's *Travelling Companions* this very special group of Henry James's stories is now complete in two volumes.

· *I* ·

The real interest attaching to these early tales is not in their "story" values, however significant these particular values may be. Orthodox canons of literary criticism therefore are not the standards used here. No plots are retold; no "Hawthornesque quality" is pointed out, no Eliot—or Turgenev or Sand or Hoffmann or Poe—influence. Orthodox literary appraisal is not made of these stories as good or bad, as romantic or realistic or psychological, or as studies of manners or morals or character. This kind of criticism applied to this kind of early James material is banal and footless, is not worth the labor.

If, however, we look at these stories in another light, that light strong or faint according to the degree of our knowledge of all of his work, and begin to discern in one and another of them ideas, subjects, themes, even incidents, treated elsewhere much later, they become exceedingly interesting. Through curious reading, through sharing work with the writer, we find indications of basic ideas even then in his mind that were later so highly developed. We find that his many technical variations of the First Person form of narration were almost all experiments of this early period. We find early and definite use of many of the later so famous Jamesian "terms," thus provably employed from beginning to end. We find foreshadowings of later tales, foreshadowing even of a great novel. Reading in this searching way, we begin to feel that James's rejection of some particular tale was not rejection of it as "bad" nearly so much as salvage of an idea or subject too good for its immature treatment, too fine to be wasted in premature exhibition.

4

In "The Story of a Masterpiece," for instance (first of James's many tales concerned with problems of painters and painting and first of a pair for the reader's comparison here—"The Sweetheart of M. Briseux" is the other), Baxter has painted "My Last Duchess," his "models" the figures of fancy and imagination sprung from his impression of a thing already done in art, and his recognition of a "type" in life painted in. "The picture," he says, "has been hanging about me for the last two or three years, as a sort of receptacle of waste ideas. It has been the victim of innumerable theories and experiments." Many of the ideas in this story, the finding and use of the figure, the type, the model, are in "The Real Thing," are notably in the Preface to *The Portrait of a Lady*. Even more is the idea of masterpiece as "exposure" used in a later tale, as even more is the process of transmuting real "identities" into art discussed in the Preface to "The Coxon Fund." In "The Story of a Masterpiece" Lennox, enraged at Baxter's exposure of Marian Everett on canvas, slashes and reslashes his sweetheart's portrait. Just so, twenty years later, Colonel Capadose of "The Liar" slashes away at Lyon's portrait of him for the same reason and with the same weapon (an Eastern poniard—or dagger) and with the same motion—a long downward cut through the face, then stabbings.

"De Grey: A Romance" has two such germinal ideas—these in mere sentences—developed much later elsewhere. Margaret, betrothed to De Grey, dares to revoke the ancient curse that the virgin love of a young De Grey spells death for its object. "I revoke the curse. I undo it. *I curse it!*" she says. Slowly she realizes that the curse may be shifted but not eluded. "But she blindly, senselessly, remorselessly, drained the life from his being. As she bloomed and prospered, he drooped and languished. While she was living for him, he was dying of her." (The Mordell text has a misprint here: De Grey was not dying "for" her.) This is a recognizable germ for *The Sacred Fount*, antedating by a full quarter century James's entry in *The Notebooks* of the same idea. The other foreshadowing of a later tale is Margaret's words: "My adventures? I have never had any," and De Grey's reply: "Good! that in itself is an adventure." This is exactly the idea of "The Story In It," discussed at some length in its Preface.

We cannot doubt that James himself actually invited us to look back at one of these early tales, for what end of his own or to what end for the reader is left for the reader to answer. In *Notes of a Son and Brother* he devotes seven pages (271-278) to a proffered "plot" for a story, pages all meaningless unless the reader matches plot with "Crawford's Consistency," unnamed there, or recognises its idea in a much later tale. James gives a three-page introduction to a letter of his father's "in the spring of '70" (it is really of March 4, 1873), his own reminiscences of his father's early friendship with the actor Forrest named at the letter's beginning. Then he quotes for four pages the letter in which the elder James gives his son the story of Matthew H. W., an early Albany friend, as "a regular Tourgénieff subject," and he follows the letter with no comment whatever. He did comment, however, three weeks later in a letter to his mother only recently published (Matthiessen's *The James Family*, p. 126): "Thank him [his father] meanwhile greatly for his story of *Mr. Webster*. It is admirable material, and excellently presented. I have transcribed it in my note book with religious care, and think that some day something will come of it. It would require much thinking out. But it is a 1st class theme." Its "much thinking out" took three years and, since the story of M.H.W. is almost exactly the story of Crawford, must have been over problems other than changes in plot.

What James *apparently* does in *Notes of a Son and Brother* is simply to drag up from the depths of forty years a charming proof of his father's active sympathy with his son's aesthetic career. He is apparently less interested in the proof—that is, in the proffered plot—than in his own memories of his father's early friendship with Edwin Forrest, player of roles and donner of masks. He is plainly not interested in naming the uncollected tale where he used the plot, is not interested even in intimating any use made of it ever. This is a typical instance of what is often called "ramblings" or "wanderings" in the autobiographies, even in the Prefaces. But this is where always an attentive reader of Henry James sits up and begins to take alert notice, for he has learned that special attention paid to such "ramblings" almost always brings a special reward. The elder James's plot *has* a commentary that precedes its text and "Crawford's Consistency" proves it. To the son's sense of the matter, his father knew two actors in his youth, one playing his roles in the temple of art itself, the other acting off stage. This conjunction of commentary and text makes us think irresistibly of another tale published some three decades later. In idea, in subject, "Crawford's Consistency" and "The Beast in the Jungle"

6

are of a *kind;* both of the so widely differing external plots illustrate the same figure. Examine John Marcher and Crawford as much as we like, turn them this way and that under whatever light or reflect upon them in darkness, in essential quality they are of a kind. And again we can feel with good reason that James "rejected" the earlier tale not necessarily because it was not "good enough" but because its fine subject was too good for its treatment.

Assuredly also James paints, and paints with some pains, into his *Small Boy* and the later *Notes* the incredibly early impressions that give "Gabrielle de Bergerac" its background. How early he realized the "sinister underworld" he describes in *The Princess Casamassima* has hardly yet been even suspected: the novel still seems to its critics alien alike to his interests and to his understanding. But we have no right to take his backward glancings here as vagrant, as anything indeed but deliberate.

He describes in *A Small Boy* (pp. 281-285) a journey by travelling-coach in June 1855 from Lyons to Geneva—he was then twelve years old. It was a series of impressions of manners gleaned at Lyons during a two-day stopover because of his illness—manners he was to know later as those of the *vie de province;* then impressions of a vista opening before him "in a village now nameless to me and which was not yet Nantua, in the Jura, where we were to spend the night," a vista giving on an object recognised with deep joy "as at once a castle and a ruin." (His vision of "castle" in America had been but the castellated villa with towers, "Ross Castle," on Staten Island the summer before; his idea of "ruin" came only from pictures in books.) He was "already somehow aware of a deeper note in the crumbled castle than any note of the solid one." He was aware that below it a woman in black bodice, white shirt and red petticoat was working in a field—"the effect of whose intervention just then is almost beyond my notation. I knew her for a peasant in *sabots*—the first peasant I had ever beheld, or beheld at least to such advantage." Supremely, he says, in that ecstatic vision was "Europe," sublime synthesis he was never to lose. Europe might not have been flattered, he adds, at his finding her thus "most signified and summarized in a sordid old woman scraping a mean living and an uninhabitable tower abandoned to the owls; that was but the momentary measure of a small sick boy, however, and

7

the virtue of the impression was proportioned to my capacity. It made a bridge over to more things than I then knew."

The bridge ended for A Small Boy at Boulogne-sur-Mer. In his final chapter James commemorates in especial (and especially "the upward cock of his so all-important nose") a schoolmate at the Collège Communal, C.-B. Coquelin, envied son of the town's principal pastry-cook, and he pays tribute also, for their manners and self-respect, to the toiling fishwives of Boulogne. In the later Notes, on his way from Bonn to Paris in 1860, he finds in the train chatter of servants attached to a noble French house the "first echo of the strange underworld, the sustaining vulgarity, of existences classified as 'great'," a sidewind of "the frenzied dance" through which a great régime was hurrying to its end.

No attention has been paid, in this connection, to the last pages of the Preface to The Princess, where James says that its scheme, calling for "the suggested nearness (to all our apparently ordered life) of some sinister anarchic underworld," meant meeting "the question of one's 'notes' " over the whole ground. He concludes that if one was to undertake to tell tales and to report with truth on the human scene, "it could be but because 'notes' had been from the cradle the ineluctable consequence of one's greatest inward energy: to take them was as natural as to look, to think, to feel, to recognize, to remember, as to perform any act of understanding. . . . Notes had been in other words the things one couldn't not take, and the prime result of all fresh experience was to remind one of that." In the autobiographies he gives us some of his earliest notes on the "underworld," and "Gabrielle de Bergerac" gives us his earliest use of them. This story is rich in foreshadowings that conspire after the fact "to haunt, to startle and waylay." No attentive reader of The Turn of the Screw is likely to escape an associational start over the final incident at the ruins of Fossy where the "governess" aunt and the small pupil stand at the foot of the higher tower with the tutor Pierre on its top waving his hat. Another like quickening is inevitable before the extraordinary conjunction of two names in this tale, Coquelin and Bergerac: it is almost prophetic foreshadowing of their conjunction in art a generation later.

The story of Gabrielle, told by the old Baron de Bergerac, her nephew, is of a summer in his ninth year, in pre-Revolutionary France, when his first tutor, Pierre Coquelin, takes over the young aunt's self-assumed governess duties. Coquelin, book-loving artist son of a village tailor, just returned from three years in the American Colonies where he fought with Rochambeau's troops against the British, kindles in the small Chevalier's childish breast "a little democratic flame which has never quite become extinct." Here are peasants at whose huts he and his pupil pause on long walks to buy bread and cheese and fruit. Here is Doré's illustration for Perrault's the Sleeping Beauty, the enchanted castle with its secrets in the far distance and below in the foreground the old woodcutters. Here are the ruins of Fossy, four leagues away from the Chateau de Bergerac, with its two great towers, one diminished by half, the other still "offering the sullen hospitality of its empty skull to a colony of swallows." Here at Fossy, "at once a castle and a ruin," the little Chevalier spent a day—"one of those long raptures of childhood which seem to imprint upon the mind an ineffaceable stain of light." Here Coquelin voices some of James's childhood "notes": "It's haunted with the ghost of the past. It smells of tragedies, sorrows and cruelties;" and again: "At the first glance we see nothing but the great proportions, the show and the splendor; but when we come to explore, we detect a vast underground world of iniquity and suffering." There is more, but here only this much of the notes taken in childhood and used at twenty-six years of age, on castle and ruin and peasant, on "underground world" and class against class.

· *II* ·

That Henry James began his writing career with some definite plan born of painstaking preparations is more than indicated by his early use of much later "famous" Jamesian terms. It is really startling to come on some of them in his first story, terms under and over which he wrote for fifty years. If we do not know James's terms we cannot know Henry James, and if that unqualified statement is doubted, James himself confirms it in a single sentence where he, then a man of sixty-five, bowed before them:

"What it would be really interesting, and I daresay admirably difficult, to go into," he wrote towards the end of his last Preface—to *The Golden Bowl*—"would be the very history of this effect of experience [the experience of "Revision"]; the history, in other words, of the growth of the immense array of terms, perceptional and expressional,

9

that, after the fashion I have indicated, in sentence, passage and page, simply looked over the heads of the standing terms—or perhaps rather, like alert winged creatures, perched on those diminished summits and aspired to a clearer air."

Readers of James know the value he put on "ideas" as against "things"—the factual gross detail of material existence; know his preference for the inner and private rather than the outer life; know his fondness for "the reverse of the tapestry"—or medal or picture; know his developed technique for "going behind." They know his concentration on "cases," on "center of interest," on "criticism of life," on "wondering," "curiosity," "inquiry," "observation," "impressions," "recognition," "feeling," "action," "experience," "adventure." They know his stressing of history and the saving sense of the past, of "types" and "antitheses" and the "reconciliation of opposites"; know his endless interest in art in its every connection, in subject and treatment, in representation, in fancy versus facts, in observation versus imagination. All these terms and a hundred others—they are not merely words, they are terms with definite meanings—are in the Prefaces, in the biographies and autobiographies, in the critical essays and travel sketches, in the novels and tales and plays. And somewhere in some way he defines them all till at the end the reader interested enough to do his share of the work may come to read James in James's own sense of the "immense array," some used from the beginning.

It is nonetheless amazing in "The Story of a Year," the first published tale, to find its young author throwing away "things," really the novelist's stock in trade. He refuses to follow his Civil War hero to the battlefield; for that record he refers his readers to the current public journals. "My own taste," writes this very young man of twenty-one, "has always been for unwritten history, and my present business is with the reverse of the picture." In "Osborne's Revenge" Osborne was "as certain of the bright surface of her [Henrietta's] nature as of its cold and dark reverse." "I have always had an eye to the back scene in the human drama," says the divinity student in "The Ghostly Rental." The narrator friend of "Crawford's Consistency" had never seen the reverse of Crawford's nature. "I had never got behind him, as it were; I had never walked all round him." "Reverse" in bewildering variations and shadings is one of James's great terms—in a very special sense perhaps

10

his greatest—and his Prefaces abound in overt and covert references to it and its techniques.

His first scene for his first story is set, therefore, not with "things" but with literal atmosphere, the "invisible ether" he uses in "A Passionate Pilgrim," the "cloud-scenery" he so oddly recalls in the *Notes* as hanging over the Charles during his brief student days at Harvard— "so extravagantly did I then conceive more or less associational cloud-scenery [of remembered English and Boulognese water-colours] to promote the atmosphere of literary composition as the act had begun to glimmer for me." He threw away the trumpet of brass, the charger of flesh, the cannon and blood of the battlefield. He placed his uniformed hero on a country road with his sweetheart beneath a sunset sky whose clouds in their imagery of moving mass and confusion were all of war. "There were columns charging and columns flying and standards floating,—tatters of the reflected purple; and great captains on colossal horses, and a rolling canopy of cannon smoke and fire and blood." We waste no labor in checking this passage for metaphor, originality, style and the like; we take it all simply as a most interesting hint of a first deliberate step on the long road of technique, the elimination of things for sake of better figuration of ideas behind them.

Criticism of fiction in fiction begins to play at once; his first paragraph is a tilt of the lance at the array of Civil War stories then, as later in other wars, overriding the fictional field. Its note is perhaps slightly ironic, almost slightly mocking, with its "Elizabeth (as I shall not scruple to call her outright)" quickly following. Jane Porter's *Scottish Chiefs* is the only book Elizabeth has read and she soon meets a Robert Bruce, designated her "Scottish chief," along with his sister Jane. If, in this contemporary tale of the Civil War, James was playing with Taine's theory of "the race, the medium and the time" as every serious writer of that day more or less began to play, he named his characters rather pointedly. Robertson, Robert, James, Elizabeth, John, are all family names. His paternal ancestry was Irish, his maternal, Irish and Scots, and the Scots nomenclature prevails in this tale. We can doubt that Elizabeth had her creator's self-admitted gift for putting people into books by very much the same turn of the hand with which he took them out, but the modern Bruce soon superseded the simple Lieutenant John Ford.

Books play all through James's writings; they are a part of his

11

famous "criticism of life." He never alludes for mere sake of alluding and it is never safe to take an even casual allusion as casual. A little attention here is also its own reward—to references as conventional even as those to Murray, Baedeker or Joanne upon whose pages James has been accused of leaning a little heavily in his travel sketches. As a matter of fact, these passing references are often light crutches offered the reader instead of a staff upon which the traveller leaned.

Browning's "My Last Duchess," for instance, is almost a protagonist in "The Story of a Masterpiece," Baxter's title as noted above for his portrait painted without a model. "I am ignorant," he says of the poem, "of whether it's an attempt to embody the poet's impression of a portrait actually existing. But why should I care? This is simply an attempt to embody my own private impression of the poem, which has always had a strong hold on my fancy. I don't know whether it agrees with your own impression and that of most readers." This is really criticism of poetized fiction within fiction, is really an invitation to read the poem again. If we do this we know afresh what Baxter was criticizing in his own medium as he painted, and we may thereby arrive at a more satisfying sense of his impression of it. If we gather up all the allusions to books in "Gabrielle de Bergerac" we are in possession of a veritable little mid-eighteenth century library. Pascal's *Thoughts* plays a lineless role in "The Ghostly Rental." "Pray keep this little book," says the divinity student to old Captain Diamond. "It is one I am very fond of, and it will tell you something about me." Perhaps its lines read by a curious reader will reveal more of the student than the story does.

In "Travelling Companions" Stendhal, Ruskin, Hawthorne and Murray figure more actively than lazy reading may suggest, but James is kind enough to say outright why Charlotte Evans read "Rappacini's Daughter" on her return from Padua. In "At Isella" there is a genial discussion of Alexandre Dumas round the Hospice table where the American tourist dines with its Prior and his monks, and we are frankly told why this talk of so unchurchly a writer. Dumas in one of his fictions "promulgated an inordinate fiction touching the manners and customs of the Hospice," and the reader who tracks down this old unnamed novel is likely to find his impression of the Hospice enriched by way of this suggested comparison of fiction with fiction. This

12

is in James's own particular sense "criticism of life"—the life of the mind.

Hence it follows that, since criticism feeds on and is fed only by wonder, curiosity, inquiry, imagination, and observation, these are among his great terms with acute differentiations between them. Elizabeth of the first story wonders, for instance, but how? "Her mental comfort lay in the ignoring of problems. . . . She was speculative without being critical. She was continually wondering, but she never inquired." This is far cry from the case of the small boy given in the autobiographies where all these terms play from first to last.

Observation is, to use a Jamesian adjective, an almost portentous term. It is the first term celebrated—is even personified—in the Prefaces, on the first page of the Preface to *Roderick Hudson*. "The art of representation," he says there, "bristles with questions the very terms of which are difficult to apply and to appreciate; . . . . Therefore it is that experience has to organize, for convenience and cheer, some system of observation—for fear, in the admirable immensity, of losing its way. We see it as pausing from time to time to consult its notes, to measure, for guidance, as many aspects and distances as possible, as many steps taken and obstacles mastered and fruits gathered and beauties enjoyed. Everything counts, nothing is superfluous in such a survey; the explorer's note-book strikes me here as endlessly receptive." For observation is the check on fancy, on unbridled imagination, to the end that they may take later flight from solid rather than quaking ground.

James paid this term the same tribute in "Travelling Companions" of 1870. The young narrator, just come down from Germany into Italy, finds that for the first time he really *felt* his intellect. "Imagination, panting and exhausted, withdrew from the game; and Observation stepped into her place, trembling and glowing with open-eyed desire." Then he and Charlotte Evans survey Tintoretto and Titian. As instance almost incredible of how the "immense array of terms" stretches through all of his work, in one of the *Transatlantic Sketches*—"From Venice to Strasburg," dated March 4, 1873—James compares these two painters from the standpoints exactly of observation and imagination, and defines the differences. We need hardly more than these two passages to illustrate the part that criticism played in his fiction—or the

13

part that his "fiction," for that matter, played in his criticism early and late.

But it is Miss Deborah of "The Ghostly Rental" who gives us a forthright system of observation. Miss Deborah, deformed little seamstress, never went out, sat all day at her window, stitching away. But her window commanded the whole town, the whole country, and knowledge came to her as she sat there. When the young student asked her how she had acquired her learning, she said simply, "Oh, I observe."

" 'Observe closely enough,' she once said, 'and it doesn't matter where you are. You may be in a pitch-dark closet. All you want is something to start with; one thing leads to another, and all things are mixed up. Shut me up in a dark closet and I will observe after a while, that some places in it are darker than others. After that (give me time), and I will tell you what the President of the United States is going to have for dinner.' "

So the divinity student begins to discover that passive wondering and active inquiry are two things sometimes irreconcilable; that observation is the mediator that may accomplish the "reconciliation of opposites." If this sounds a bit heavy it is nonetheless the problem that raised its head at Bonn in the summer of 1860 when Henry James was seventeen years old, and he expresses it in a few early pages of *Notes of a Son and Brother*. He was facing the problem of "the aesthetic, the creative, even, quite wondrously, the critical life," yet he felt them then as mutual opposites. He was to realize that neither was of the least use to him without the other, and the process of that realization was the process itself of their "reconciliation."

Even to suggest so reverberating a term as the theme for so simple a tale as "A Problem" would be to sacrifice it to "a stout stiff hardgrained underside"—otherwise the learning exclusively by books that then seemed to James the irreconcilable opposite of "impressions." Yet it is true that the year before this story appeared, he did posit a facet of this problem of opposites as a task for story-tellers. In an unsigned review of two historical novels (*Nation*, August 15, 1867), he made them the text for defining the seemingly irreconcilable differences between two dissimilar types of mind, that of the novelist and that of the historian. The historian works in the dark, with downcast eyes, on hands and feet as men work in coal mines, with a vast fabric of impenetrable fact over his head. The novelist, asking nothing but a subject and the basis of fact given, works under the open sky where nothing hinders the flight of fancy. "But," he continues (and let us not forget that he is but twenty-four years old), "there is no sufficient reason that we can see why the novelist should not subject himself, as regards the treatment of his subject, to certain of the obligations of the historian; why he should not imprison his imagination, for the time, in a circle of incidents from which there is no arbitrary issue, and apply his ingenuity to the study of a problem to which there is but a single solution."

Type, as James uses the term, is no commonplace word; it is often italicized, often quoted. "The Story of a Masterpiece" begins a long ruminative discussion that extends through the years on "type," on "illustration" of type and ethical use of type. "You know how a painter works—how artists of all kinds work; they claim their property wherever they find it," says Baxter when a resemblance is traced between his "Last Duchess" and Marian Everett. He had been feeling about for a "type" and when he found it he used it: "You see the resemblance is much more a matter of type than of expression." Crawford's path towards his recognition of type almost parallels Baxter's. "She is very fine in her way," he says of the vulgar young woman, seen first at the concert garden, who later became his wife. "My image of her was vague; she is far more perfect. It is always interesting to see a supreme representation of any type, whether or no the type be one that we admire. That is the merit of our neighbor. She resumes a certain civilization; she is the last word—the flower."

In this group of tales three special types are delineated with a good deal of youthful care, the "three men in the social system who," said the great lawyer Derville in Balzac's *Colonel Chabert*, "cannot respect the world—the priest, the physician and the lawyer."

In "Osborne's Revenge" the lawyer's story is told from his point of view; a single sentence emphasizes this: "But Philip, as a lawyer, naturally took a different point of view of the matter from Mr. Stone as a clergyman." So protected is Osborne in the telling that its third person form might become autobiographical first person almost without change, even to the charge that he "addressed a charming woman as if he were exhorting a jury of grocers and undertakers, and viewed the universe as one vast 'case'." All the misreading of Graham's character, all misapprehension of the whole situation that constituted his case against Henrietta is Osborne's own; and here is a first clear example of choosing and holding to a "central consciousness," James's "center of interest" from which later he consistently worked. "Case," by the way, is another famous Jamesian term, used here certainly in its broadest sense but used in this tale of 1868 as if he had already begun his remarkable collection of them. As indeed he had.

His first delineation of the physician type is Dr. ——, first person narrator of "Crawford's Consistency." We cannot go far afield in taking it for granted that for this Albany plot James's choice of physician, physiologist, and friend as reticent diagnostician of Crawford's "consistency" was deliberate. Dr. ——'s analysis of M.H.W. was not the elder James's. Dr. —— did not wonder with James Senior "what a heart and what a brain lay behind such a fortune," did not extol the "rare type of manhood," the "self-respect so eminent" of M.H.W. What Dr. —— felt in Crawford was oddly enough a certain actor quality. "Then I felt," he says, "how deeply he was attached to the part he had undertaken to play; . . . Even to me, his oldest friend, he would not raise a corner of the mask." In the jilting scene witnessed by Dr. ——, the heroine's father is like "the stage manager of a theatre," and the heroine, was she doll, consummate actress, or puppet? He continued to observe Crawford with interest, even with concern: "From this point onward, however, I do not pretend to understand his conduct. I was only witness of it, and I relate what I saw. I do not pretend to speak of his motives."

A similarity in mental process between Crawford and Baxter of "The Masterpiece" has already been noted. There is also an interesting identity of characteristic quality between Crawford and Marian Everett. Both have *equanimity* in common; they are companion pieces; they might flank each other on a mantel. Neither made claims or pretensions; each moved almost by cue. In face of all crises Marian retained her equanimity, "continued to smile and smile." At the end of Crawford's long martyrdom, "I cannot say," his physician friend concluded, "that this event restored his equanimity, for the excellent reason that to the eyes of the world—and my own most searching ones—he had never lost it." It is worth remembering that the earlier little study in "equanimity" antedated the elder James's letter by several years; in

16

other words, the idea that M.H.W.'s story illustrated was already in James's mind.

The "priest," otherwise the divinity student at Harvard "thirty years ago" who tells "The Ghostly Rental," is James's first study of this special type. There are constant reminders that the reactions to the general ghostly are those of a young man interested in theology but not yet divested of a saving light touch. "Half an hour before," he says of his first confrontation of the old Diamond house, "if I had been asked, I would have said, as befitted a young man who was explicitly cultivating cheerful ideas of the supernatural, that there were no such things as haunted houses. But the dwelling before me gave a vivid meaning to the empty words; it had been spiritually blighted." (As if the house were embodied mind; as five years before, in reverse figuration, the narrator of "A Passionate Pilgrim" said to Searle: ". . . you have lived hitherto in yourself! The tenement's haunted! Live abroad! Take an interest!") More easily, too, to priest than to lawyer or doctor, old Captain Diamond could say: "I killed my own child. . . . I struck her down to the earth and left her to die. They could not hang me, for it was not with my hand I struck her. It was with foul and damnable words." Here, starkly stated, is the life-in-death or death-in-life theme that with much "reverse" technique threads through many later tales.

· *III* ·

So far as I know there has never been a lively, interested and interesting study of Henry James's subtle use of "first person" in his story-telling—when, why, above all how and to what calculated effects on the reader. This is no place for a "study," and small space is left even for notes on its half-dozen recognised forms and James's variations on them. But we can float down the stream of the twenty-eight tales covering the writing period of this group and can return with these pearls of easy research: first, that ten of the uncollected fifteen and eighteen of the total twenty-eight are so-called "first person" stories; second—this is the larger pearl—that with one exception all these forms and variations (some extremely subtle shadings of the latter are used later) were experiments of these first eleven years. It is this sort of casual research that makes these early tales so very interesting; it so often confirms the conviction that from the beginning Henry James knew what he was "about."

To say, however, that ten tales of this uncollected group are "first person" stories is to use the term in its very loosest sense. True enough, ten tales are told by "I," but who "I" is and how introduced is another matter, for James's varied uses of first person differ essentially each from the other. It is a choice of what recording consciousness records a consciousness, and James is no haphazard selector.

The first person form may be the straight narrator of events in which he more or less actively participates, as in "Travelling Companions," "Guest's Confession," "The Ghostly Rental" (and, of the collected tales of this period, "A Passionate Pilgrim," "Eugene Pickering," even perhaps "The Last of the Valerii"). It may be the narrator of events impersonally observed, but here much depends on the role or the character of the narrator. He may be simply the "cordial observer" of "My Friend Bingham," the witnessing friend of "Crawford's Consistency," the mere chance spectator of "Professor Fargo," the more or less passive reflector of the emotions of others in "At Isella"—this particular reflector, be it noted, a would-be writer still merely fancying dramas and romances and love-tales. The passive reflector already become writer and creating his fantasy before us is the narrator of the collected "Benvolio."

Again, the first person form may be the diarist presumably writing only for his own eye. In the collected "A Light Man" of 1869 James uses the straight diary form for the first time, prefaced incidentally by a four-line quotation from Browning's "A Light Woman." The old-fashioned method of telling a story in a series of letters was not used till later and was soon abandoned. All of these first person forms are simple enough.

But first person narration, as James used and developed it, has forms far less simple—less simple, that is, for the reader so prone to forget the primal First Person Introducer of the narrator "I" who then takes the stage. He may be, first of all, the conscientious recorder, memorizer or note-taker—James explicitly indicates these several kinds—who sets down the story as it falls from the lips of another. In "Gabrielle de Bergerac," his first essay in this field, the primal I sets the scene—the Baron's little parlor, its paintings, its portrait of Gabrielle—and steps aside with: "I shall give, as far as possible, my friend's words, or the

18

English of them," for here the recorder is translator as well. He steps back at the end, as he steps back into "Master Eustace" of 1871, the second tale cast in this form. But never again does James risk a break in the reader's illusion: the primal I, serving his purpose at the beginning, becomes again and remains only the listening ear.

This is the passive technique used in "The Sweetheart of M. Briseux." The tourist I, recognizing in the single other visitor at the little picture gallery at M—— the original of "A Lady in a Yellow Shawl," meeting her later and falling into talk, drops out with: "I repeat her story literally, and I surely don't transgress the proper limits of editorial zeal in supplying a single absent clause," and the story ends on the note of the teller's voice. So in "Adina"—"We had been talking of Sam Scrope round the fire," it begins, and the recording I simply retells "our host's" addition to reminiscences after the other guests have gone. This same easy social device James had used the year before in "The Madonna of the Future": "We had been talking about the masters who had achieved but a single masterpiece," the recorder begins. "Our host" had shown a specimen of one and H—— is induced to tell the story of Theobald.

But this passive technique may not be passive enough—for the reader, that is, steeled against illusion and questioning lapses in memory or omissions in "notes" of verbal recitals. For this reader, then, James substitutes for the listening ear the moving hand that writes, and the recording I becomes mechanical medium for the written words of another. This technique was used very early, in "A Landscape Painter" of 1866, where a letter to an unnamed correspondent is followed by the "last hundred pages" of Locksley's diary. It was used twenty-five years later in "Sir Edmund Orme" where a manuscript selected from other papers has the prefatory assurance: "I have altered nothing but the names." "The Way It Came" of 1896—later retitled "The Friends of the Friends"—follows precisely the frame of "A Landscape Painter": here we are meticulously told that from "her" diaries the primal I has selected a single book whose contents "I have had copied out."

Yet here again the reader resisting illusion—the acutely questioning reader for whom James always wrote—may be too conscious of an active mind at work among papers, sifting, selecting *for* him; may doubt that he has the complete story or even the most interesting one.

For this reader, therefore, who will not be deceived, James contrived the ultimate of passivity by way of a single surviving manuscript and "from an exact transcript of my own" presented in *The Turn of the Screw* the whole of a case, and that case the reader's.

For the reader's case, from first to last, was Henry James's great concern. In his second writing year he had thought it out and had expressed it. In "The Novels of George Eliot," his first signed review (*Atlantic,* October, 1866), after criticizing *Adam Bede* as prolonged beyond its natural ending and so depriving the reader of the chance to deduce for himself a later, perhaps happier outcome, he says with a maturity far beyond his twenty-three years:

"In every novel the work is divided between the writer and the reader; but the writer makes the reader very much as he makes his characters. When he makes him ill, that is, makes him indifferent, he does no work; the writer does all. When he makes him well, that is, makes him interested, then the reader does quite half the labor. In making such a deduction as I have just indicated, the reader would be but doing his share of the task; the grand point is to get him to make it. I hold that there is a way. It is perhaps a secret; but until it is found out, I think that the art of story-telling cannot be said to have approached perfection."

This is the text for all of the foregoing on these early tales of Henry James. It is the secret too of the reader who "likes to read James"— his excited feeling of work shared with the writer. The secret of sharing is simple: "Attention of perusal, I thus confess by the way," James says emphatically in the Preface to *The Wings of the Dove*, "is what I at every point, as well as here, absolutely invoke and take for granted; . . ." What is this but allusion the most indirect to "the great empty cup of attention" that Sir Luke Strett on Milly's first visit sets between them on the table? The relation between physician and "case," established in Book Fifth of *The Dove*, almost parallels the relation between interested reader and yearning writer. James sets the empty cup of attention before us; all he has ever asked is that it be filled to the brim.

EDNA KENTON

NEW YORK
NOVEMBER 15, 1949

THE STORY OF A YEAR

The Story of a Year

"The Story of a Year," Henry James's first published tale, appeared in the Atlantic, *March 1865, just before his twenty-second birthday. It was reprinted for the first time in* American Novels and Stories of Henry James, *edited by F. O. Matthiessen (1947).*

Contrary to a general impression, James wrote a good deal about the Civil War, though not in his fiction: "Poor Richard" (1867) and "A Most Extraordinary Case" (1868) are the only other tales based on it. But those years touched the James family deeply. The two younger sons enlisted and through their letters from the front in Notes of a Son and Brother, *as well as from commemoration there and in* A Small Boy and Others *of three favorite cousins slain in 1863, we feel the War as a living presence in the James household. It plays all through the autobiographies and it is not too much to say that its influence largely determined the trend of James's whole later life work. Significant references to the coming War are in early pages of* A Small Boy: *his account of the Norcums, Fourteenth Street neighbors from Kentucky, is commentary also on North versus South; his first critical enlightenment was experienced before a dramatized version of* Uncle Tom's Cabin, *a work unrecognized then and rarely recognized now as our first "national" novel.* Notes of a Son and Brother *is filled with the sense of the War; from the closing pages of Chapter III (James is sometimes better read in sections than by cited lines), through some early pages of Chapters IV and V, some latter pages of Chapter VII, and all of Chapters IX, X, XI and XII. They are not all of the Civil War, but their background is what James calls somewhere here "that reviving consciousness of American annals" that the War was to quicken. Add to this roaming quest the chapters on Balti-*

23

more, Richmond and Charleston in The American Scene, *and we have a clearer impression of what the story of one of those years meant to Henry James.*

This first story was followed by "A Landscape Painter" (Atlantic, *February 1866) and "A Day of Days"* (Galaxy, *June 15, 1866), both reprinted in* Stories Revived, *Vols. II and I respectively (1885). Then followed the second of the uncollected tales.*

· *1* ·

MY STORY BEGINS AS A GREAT MANY STORIES HAVE BE-gun within the last three years, and indeed as a great many have ended; for, when the hero is despatched, does not the romance come to a stop?

In early May, two years ago, a young couple I wot of strolled home-ward from an evening walk, a long ramble among the peaceful hills which inclosed their rustic home. Into these peaceful hills the young man had brought, not the rumor, (which was an old inhabitant,) but some of the reality of war,—a little whiff of gunpowder, the clanking of a sword; for, although Mr. John Ford had his campaign still before him, he wore a certain comely air of camp-life which stamped him a very Hector to the steady-going villagers, and a very pretty fellow to Miss Elizabeth Crowe, his companion in this sentimental stroll. And was he not attired in the great brightness of blue and gold which befits a freshly made lieutenant? This was a strange sight for these happy Northern glades; for, although the first Revolution had boomed awhile in their midst, the honest yeomen who defended them were clad in sober homespun, and it is well known that His Majesty's troops wore red.

These young people, I say, had been roaming. It was plain that they had wandered into spots where the brambles were thick and the dews heavy,—nay, into swamps and puddles where the April rains were still undried. Ford's boots and trousers had imbibed a deep foretaste of the Virginia mud; his companion's skirts were fearfully bedraggled. What great enthusiasm had made our friends so unmindful of their steps?

24

What blinding ardor had kindled these strange phenomena: a young lieutenant scornful of his first uniform, a well-bred young lady reckless of her stockings?

Good reader, this narrative is averse to retrospect.

Elizabeth (as I shall not scruple to call her outright) was leaning upon her companion's arm, half moving in concert with him, and half allowing herself to be led, with that instinctive acknowledgment of dependence natural to a young girl who has just received the assurance of lifelong protection. Ford was lounging along with that calm, swinging stride which often bespeaks, when you can read it aright, the answering consciousness of a sudden rush of manhood. A spectator might have thought him at this moment profoundly conceited. The young girl's blue veil was dangling from his pocket; he had shouldered her sun-umbrella after the fashion of a musket on a march: he might carry these trifles. Was there not a vague longing expressed in the strong expansion of his stalwart shoulders, in the fond accommodation of his pace to hers,—her pace so submissive and slow, that, when he tried to match it, they almost came to a delightful standstill,—a silent desire for the whole fair burden?

They made their way up a long swelling mound, whose top commanded the sunset. The dim landscape which had been brightening all day to the green of spring was now darkening to the gray of evening. The lesser hills, the farms, the brooks, the fields, orchards, and woods, made a dusky gulf before the great splendor of the west. As Ford looked at the clouds, it seemed to him that their imagery was all of war, their great uneven masses were marshalled into the semblance of a battle. There were columns charging and columns flying and standards floating, —tatters of the reflected purple; and great captains on colossal horses, and a rolling canopy of cannon-smoke and fire and blood. The background of the clouds, indeed, was like a land on fire, or a battle-ground illumined by another sunset, a country of blackened villages and crimsoned pastures. The tumult of the clouds increased; it was hard to believe them inanimate. You might have fancied them an army of gigantic souls playing at football with the sun. They seemed to sway in confused splendor; the opposing squadrons bore each other down; and then suddenly they scattered, bowling with equal velocity towards north and south, and gradually fading into the pale evening sky. The purple pennons sailed away and sank out of sight, caught, doubtless, upon the

25

brambles of the intervening plain. Day contracted itself into a fiery ball and vanished.

Ford and Elizabeth had quietly watched this great mystery of the heavens.

"That is an allegory," said the young man, as the sun went under, looking into his companion's face, where a pink flush seemed still to linger: "it means the end of the war. The forces on both sides are withdrawn. The blood that has been shed gathers itself into a vast globule and drops into the ocean."

"I'm afraid it means a shabby compromise," said Elizabeth. "Light disappears, too, and the land is in darkness."

"Only for a season," answered the other. "We mourn our dead. Then light comes again, stronger and brighter than ever. Perhaps you'll be crying for me, Lizzie, at that distant day."

"Oh, Jack, didn't you promise not to talk about that?" says Lizzie, threatening to anticipate the performance in question.

Jack took this rebuke in silence, gazing soberly at the empty sky. Soon the young girl's eyes stole up to his face. If he had been looking at anything in particular, I think she would have followed the direction of his glance; but as it seemed to be a very vacant one, she let her eyes rest.

"Jack," said she, after a pause, "I wonder how you'll look when you get back."

Ford's soberness gave way to a laugh.

"Uglier than ever. I shall be all incrusted with mud and gore. And then I shall be magnificently sunburnt, and I shall have a beard."

"Oh, you dreadful!" and Lizzie gave a little shout. "Really, Jack, if you have a beard, you'll not look like a gentleman."

"Shall I look like a lady, pray?" says Jack.

"Are you serious?" asked Lizzie.

"To be sure. I mean to alter my face as you do your misfitting garments,—take in on one side and let out on the other. Isn't that the process? I shall crop my head and cultivate my chin."

"You've a very nice chin, my dear, and I think it's a shame to hide it."

"Yes, I know my chin's handsome; but wait till you see my beard."

"Oh, the vanity!" cried Lizzie, "the vanity of men in their faces! Talk of women!" and the silly creature looked up at her lover with most inconsistent satisfaction.

26

"Oh, the pride of women in their husbands!" said Jack, who of course knew what she was about.

"You're not my husband, Sir. There's many a slip"—— But the young girl stopped short.

" 'Twixt the cup and the lip," said Jack. "Go on. I can match your proverb with another. 'There's many a true word,' and so forth. No, my darling: I'm not your husband. Perhaps I never shall be. But if anything happens to me, you'll take comfort, won't you?"

"Never!" said Lizzie, tremulously.

"Oh, but you must; otherwise, Lizzie, I should think our engagement inexcusable. Stuff! who am I that you should cry for me?"

"You are the best and wisest of men. I don't care; you *are*."

"Thank you for your great love, my dear. That's a delightful illusion. But I hope Time will kill it, in his own good way, before it hurts any one. I know so many men who are worth infinitely more than I— men wise, generous, and brave—that I shall not feel as if I were leaving you in an empty world."

"Oh, my dear friend!" said Lizzie, after a pause, "I wish you could advise me all my life."

"Take care, take care," laughed Jack; "you don't know what you are bargaining for. But will you let me say a word now? If by chance I'm taken out of the world, I want you to beware of that tawdry sentiment which enjoins you to be 'constant to my memory.' My memory be hanged! Remember me at my best,—that is, fullest of the desire of humility. Don't inflict me on people. There are some widows and bereaved sweethearts who remind me of the peddler in that horrible murder-story, who carried a corpse in his pack. Really, it's their stock in trade. The only justification of a man's personality is his rights. What rights has a dead man?—Let's go down."

They turned southward and went jolting down the hill.

"Do you mind this talk, Lizzie?" asked Ford.

"No," said Lizzie, swallowing a sob, unnoticed by her companion in the sublime egotism of protection; "I like it."

"Very well," said the young man, "I want my memory to help you. When I am down in Virginia, I expect to get a vast deal of good from thinking of you,—to do my work better, and to keep straighter altogether. Like all lovers, I'm horribly selfish. I expect to see a vast deal of shabbiness and baseness and turmoil, and in the midst of it all

I'm sure the inspiration of patriotism will sometimes fail. Then I'll think of you. I love you a thousand times better than my country, Liz.—Wicked? So much the worse. It's the truth. But if I find your memory makes a milksop of me, I shall thrust you out of the way, without ceremony,—I shall clap you into my box or between the leaves of my Bible, and only look at you on Sunday."

"I shall be very glad, Sir, if that makes you open your Bible frequently," says Elizabeth, rather demurely.

"I shall put one of your photographs against every page," cried Ford; "and then I think I shall not lack a text for my meditations. Don't you know how Catholics keep little pictures of their adored Lady in their prayer-books?"

"Yes, indeed," said Lizzie; "I should think it would be a very soul-stirring picture, when you are marching to the front, the night before a battle,—a poor, stupid girl, knitting stupid socks, in a stupid Yankee village."

Oh, the craft of artless tongues! Jack strode along in silence a few moments, splashing straight through a puddle; then, ere he was quite clear of it, he stretched out his arm and gave his companion a long embrace.

"And pray what am I to do," resumed Lizzie, wondering, rather proudly perhaps, at Jack's averted face, "while you are marching and countermarching in Virginia?"

"Your duty, of course," said Jack, in a steady voice, which belied a certain little conjecture of Lizzie's. "I think you will find the sun will rise in the east, my dear, just as it did before you were engaged."

"I'm sure I didn't suppose it wouldn't," says Lizzie.

"By duty I don't mean anything disagreeable, Liz," pursued the young man. "I hope you'll take your pleasure, too. I wish you might go to Boston, or even to Leatherborough, for a month or two."

"What for, pray?"

"What for? Why, for the fun of it: to 'go out', as they say."

"Jack, do you think me capable of going to parties while you are in danger?"

"Why not? Why should I have all the fun?"

"Fun? I'm sure you're welcome to it all. As for me, I mean to make a new beginning."

"Of what?"

"Oh, of everything. In the first place, I shall begin to improve my mind. But don't you think it's horrid for women to be reasonable?"

"Hard, say you?"

"Horrid,—yes, and hard too. But I mean to become so. Oh, girls are such fools, Jack! I mean to learn to like boiled mutton and history and plain sewing, and all that. Yet, when a girl's engaged, she's not expected to do anything in particular."

Jack laughed, and said nothing; and Lizzie went on.

"I wonder what your mother will say to the news. I think I know."

"What?"

"She'll say you've been very unwise. No, she won't: she never speaks so to you. She'll say I've been very dishonest or indelicate, or something of that kind. No, she won't either: she doesn't say such things, though I'm sure she thinks them. I don't know what she'll say."

"No, I think not, Lizzie, if you indulge in such conjectures. My mother never speaks without thinking. Let us hope that she may think favorably of our plan. Even if she doesn't"——

Jack did not finish his sentence, nor did Lizzie urge him. She had a great respect for his hesitations. But in a moment he began again.

"I was going to say this, Lizzie: I think for the present our engagement had better be kept quiet."

Lizzie's heart sank with a sudden disappointment. Imagine the feelings of the damsel in the fairy-tale, whom the disguised enchantress had just empowered to utter diamonds and pearls, should the old beldame have straightway added that for the present mademoiselle had better hold her tongue. Yet the disappointment was brief. I think this enviable young lady would have tripped home talking very hard to herself, and have been not ill pleased to find her little mouth turning into a tightly clasped jewel-casket. Nay, would she not on this occasion have been thankful for a large mouth,—a mouth huge and unnatural, —stretching from ear to ear? Who wish to cast their pearls before swine? The young lady of the pearls was, after all, but a barnyard miss. Lizzie was too proud of Jack to be vain. It's well enough to wear our own hearts upon our sleeves; but for those of others, when intrusted to our keeping, I think we had better find a more secluded lodging.

"You see, I think secrecy would leave us much freer," said Jack,— "leave *you* much freer."

"Oh, Jack, how can you?" cried Lizzie. "Yes, of course; I shall be falling in love with some one else. Freer! Thank you, Sir!"

"Nay, Lizzie, what I'm saying is really kinder than it sounds. Perhaps you *will* thank me one of these days."

"Doubtless! I've already taken a great fancy to George Mackenzie."

"Will you let me enlarge on my suggestion?"

"Oh, certainly! You seem to have your mind quite made up."

"I confess I like to take account of possibilities. Don't you know mathematics are my hobby? Did you ever study algebra? I always have an eye on the unknown quantity."

"No, I never studied algebra. I agree with you, that we had better not speak of our engagement."

"That's right, my dear. You're always right. But mind, I don't want to bind you to secrecy. Hang it, do as you please! Do what comes easiest to you, and you'll do the best thing. What made me speak is my dread of the horrible publicity which clings to all this business. Nowadays, when a girl's engaged, it's no longer, 'Ask mamma,' simply; but, 'Ask Mrs. Brown, and Mrs. Jones, and my large circle of acquaintance,—Mrs. Grundy, in short.' I say nowadays, but I suppose it's always been so."

"Very well, we'll keep it all nice and quiet," said Lizzie, who would have been ready to celebrate her nuptials according to the rites of the Esquimaux, had Jack seen fit to suggest it.

"I know it doesn't look well for a lover to be so cautious," pursued Jack; "but you understand me, Lizzie, don't you?"

"I don't entirely understand you, but I quite trust you."

"God bless you! My prudence, you see, is my best strength. Now, if ever, I need my strength. When a man's a-wooing, Lizzie, he is all feeling, or he ought to be; when he's accepted, then he begins to think."

"And to repent, I suppose you mean."

"Nay, to devise means to keep his sweetheart from repenting. Let me be frank. Is it the greatest fools only that are the best lovers? There's no telling what may happen, Lizzie. I want you to marry me with your eyes open. I don't want you to feel tied down or taken in. You're very young, you know. You're responsible to yourself of a year hence. You're at an age when no girl can count safely from year's end to year's end."

"And you, Sir!" cries Lizzie; "one would think you were a grandfather."

"Well, I'm on the way to it. I'm a pretty old boy. I mean what I say. I may not be entirely frank, but I think I'm sincere. It seems to me as if I'd been fibbing all my life before I told you that your affection was necessary to my happiness. I mean it out and out. I never loved any one before, and I never will again. If you had refused me half an hour ago, I should have died a bachelor. I have no fear for myself. But I have for you. You said a few minutes ago that you wanted me to be your adviser. Now you know the function of an adviser is to perfect his victim in the art of walking with his eyes shut. I sha'n't be so cruel."

Lizzie saw fit to view these remarks in a humorous light. "How disinterested!" quoth she: "how very self-sacrificing! Bachelor indeed! For my part, I think I shall become a Mormon!"—I verily believe the poor misinformed creature fancied that in Utah it is the ladies who are guilty of polygamy.

Before many minutes they drew near home. There stood Mrs. Ford at the garden-gate, looking up and down the road, with a letter in her hand.

"Something for you, John," said his mother, as they approached. "It looks as if it came from camp.—Why, Elizabeth, look at your skirts!"

"I know it," says Lizzie, giving the articles in question a shake. "What is it, Jack?"

"Marching orders!" cried the young man. "The regiment leaves day after to-morrow. I must leave by the early train in the morning. Hurray!" And he diverted a sudden gleeful kiss into a filial salute.

They went in. The two women were silent, after the manner of women who suffer. But Jack did little else than laugh and talk and circumnavigate the parlor, sitting first here and then there,—close beside Lizzie and on the opposite side of the room. After a while Miss Crowe joined in his laughter, but I think her mirth might have been resolved into articulate heart-beats. After tea she went to bed, to give Jack opportunity for his last filial *épanchements*. How generous a

31

man's intervention makes women! But Lizzie promised to see her lover off in the morning.

"Nonsense!" said Mrs. Ford. "You'll not be up. John will want to breakfast quietly."

"I shall see you off, Jack," repeated the young lady, from the threshold.

Elizabeth went up stairs buoyant with her young love. It had dawned upon her like a new life,—a life positively worth the living. Hereby she would subsist and cost nobody anything. In it she was boundlessly rich. She would make it the hidden spring of a hundred praiseworthy deeds. She would begin the career of duty: she would enjoy boundless equanimity: she would raise her whole being to the level of her sublime passion. She would practise charity, humility, piety,—in fine, all the virtues: together with certain *morceaux* of Beethoven and Chopin. She would walk the earth like one glorified. She would do homage to the best of men by inviolate secrecy. Here, by I know not what gentle transition, as she lay in the quiet darkness, Elizabeth covered her pillow with a flood of tears.

Meanwhile Ford, down-stairs, began in this fashion. He was lounging at his manly length on the sofa, in his slippers.

"May I light a pipe, mother?"

"Yes, my love. But please be careful of your ashes. There's a newspaper."

"Pipes don't make ashes.—Mother, what do you think?" he continued, between the puffs of his smoking; "I've got a piece of news."

"Ah?" said Mrs. Ford, fumbling for her scissors; "I hope it's good news."

"I hope you'll think it so. I've been engaging myself"—puff,—puff —"to Lizzie Crowe." A cloud of puffs between his mother's face and his own. When they cleared away, Jack felt his mother's eyes. Her work was in her lap. "To be married, you know," he added.

In Mrs. Ford's view, like the king in that of the British Constitution, her only son could do no wrong. Prejudice is a stout bulwark against surprise. Moreover, Mrs. Ford's motherly instinct had not been entirely at fault. Still, it had by no means kept pace with fact. She had been silent, partly from doubt, partly out of respect for her son. As long as John did not doubt of himself, he was right. Should he come to do so, she was sure he would speak. And now, when he told her the matter was settled, she persuaded herself that he was asking her advice.

"I've been expecting it," she said, at last.

"You have? Why didn't you speak?"

"Well, John, I can't say I've been hoping it."

"Why not?"

"I am not sure of Lizzie's heart," said Mrs. Ford, who, it may be well to add, was very sure of her own.

Jack began to laugh. "What's the matter with her heart?"

"I think Lizzie's shallow," said Mrs. Ford; and there was that in her tone which betokened some satisfaction with this adjective.

"Hang it! she is shallow," said Jack. "But when a thing's shallow, you can see to the bottom. Lizzie doesn't pretend to be deep. I want a wife, mother, that I can understand. That's the only wife I can love. Lizzie's the only girl I ever understood, and the first I ever loved. I love her very much,—more than I can explain to you."

"Yes, I confess it's inexplicable. It seems to me," she added, with a bad smile, "like infatuation."

Jack did not like the smile; he liked it even less than the remark. He smoked steadily for a few moments, and then he said,—

"Well, mother, love is notoriously obstinate, you know. We shall not be able to take the same view of this subject: suppose we drop it."

"Remember that this is your last evening at home, my son," said Mrs. Ford.

"I do remember. Therefore I wish to avoid disagreement."

There was a pause. The young man smoked, and his mother sewed, in silence.

"I think my position, as Lizzie's guardian," resumed Mrs. Ford, "entitles me to an interest in the matter."

"Certainly, I acknowledged your interest by telling you of our engagement."

Further pause.

"Will you allow me to say," said Mrs. Ford, after a while, "that I think this a little selfish?"

"Allow you? Certainly, if you particularly desire it. Though I confess it isn't very pleasant for a man to sit and hear his future wife pitched into,—by his own mother, too."

"John, I am surprised at your language."

"I beg your pardon," and John spoke more gently. "You mustn't be surprised at anything from an accepted lover.—I'm sure you mis-conceive her. In fact, mother, I don't believe you know her."

Mrs. Ford nodded, with an infinite depth of meaning; and from the grimness with which she bit off the end of her thread it might have seemed that she fancied herself to be executing a human vengeance.

"Ah, I know her only too well!"

"And you don't like her?"

Mrs. Ford performed another decapitation of her thread.

"Well, I'm glad Lizzie has one friend in the world," said Jack.

"Her best friend," said Mrs. Ford, "is the one who flatters her least. I see it all, John. Her pretty face has done the business."

The young man flushed impatiently.

"Mother," said he, "you are very much mistaken. I'm not a boy nor a fool. You trust me in a great many things; why not trust me in this?"

"My dear son, you are throwing yourself away. You deserve for your companion in life a higher character than that girl."

I think Mrs. Ford, who had been an excellent mother, would have liked to give her son a wife fashioned on her own model.

"Oh, come, mother," said he, "that's twaddle. I should be thankful, if I were half as good as Lizzie."

"It's the truth, John, and your conduct—not only the step you've taken, but your talk about it—is a great disappointment to me. If I have cherished any wish of late, it is that my darling boy should get a wife worthy of him. The household governed by Elizabeth Crowe is not the home I should desire for any one I love."

"It's one to which you should always be welcome, Ma'am," said Jack.

"It's not a place I should feel at home in," replied his mother.

"I'm sorry," said Jack. And he got up and began to walk about the room. "Well, well, mother," he said at last, stopping in front of Mrs. Ford, "we don't understand each other. One of these days we shall. For the present let us have done with discussion. I'm half sorry I told you."

"I'm glad of such a proof of your confidence. But if you hadn't, of course Elizabeth would have done so."

"No, Ma'am, I think not."

"Then she is even more reckless of her obligations than I thought her."

34

"I advised her to say nothing about it."

Mrs. Ford made no answer. She began slowly to fold up her work. "I think we had better let the matter stand," continued her son. "I'm not afraid of time. But I wish to make a request of you: you won't mention this conversation to Lizzie, will you? nor allow her to suppose that you know of our engagement? I have a particular reason."

Mrs. Ford went on smoothing out her work. Then she suddenly looked up.

"No, my dear, I'll keep your secret. Give me a kiss."

· *II* ·

I have no intention of following Lieutenant Ford to the seat of war. The exploits of his campaign are recorded in the public journals of the day, where the curious may still peruse them. My own taste has always been for unwritten history, and my present business is with the reverse of the picture.

After Jack went off, the two ladies resumed their old homely life. But the homeliest life had now ceased to be repulsive to Elizabeth. Her common duties were no longer wearisome: for the first time, she experienced the delicious companionship of thought. Her chief task was still to sit by the window knitting soldiers' socks; but even Mrs. Ford could not help owning that she worked with a much greater diligence, yawned, rubbed her eyes, gazed up and down the road less, and indeed produced a much more comely article. Ah, me! if half the lovesome fancies that flitted through Lizzie's spirit in those busy hours could have found their way into the texture of the dingy yarn, as it was slowly wrought into shape, the eventual wearer of the socks would have been as light-footed as Mercury. I am afraid I should make the reader sneer, were. I to rehearse some of this little fool's diversions. She passed several hours daily in Jack's old chamber: it was in this sanctuary, indeed, at the sunny south window, overlooking the long road, the wood-crowned heights, the gleaming river, that she worked with most pleasure and profit. Here she was removed from the untiring glance of the elder lady, from her jarring questions and commonplaces; here she was alone with her love,—that greatest commonplace in life. Lizzie felt in Jack's room a certain impress of his personality. The idle fancies of her mood were bodied forth in a dozen

35

sacred relics. Some of these articles Elizabeth carefully cherished. It was rather late in the day for her to assert a literary taste,—her reading having begun and ended (naturally enough) with the ancient fiction of the "Scottish Chiefs." So she could hardly help smiling, herself, sometimes, at her interest in Jack's old college tomes. She carried several of them to her own apartment, and placed them at the foot of her little bed, on a book-shelf adorned, besides, with a pot of spring violets, a portrait of General McClellan, and a likeness of Lieutenant Ford. She had a vague belief that a loving study of their well-thumbed verses would remedy, in some degree, her sad intellectual deficiencies. She was sorry she knew so little: as sorry, that is, as she might be, for we know that she was shallow. Jack's omniscience was one of his most awful attributes. And yet she comforted herself with the thought, that, as he had forgiven her ignorance, she herself might surely forget it. Happy Lizzie, I envy you this easy path to knowledge! The volume she most frequently consulted was an old German "Faust," over which she used to fumble with a battered lexicon. The secret of this preference was in certain marginal notes in pencil, signed "J." I hope they were really of Jack's making.

Lizzie was always a small walker. Until she knew Jack, this had been quite an unsuspected pleasure. She was afraid, too, of the cows, geese, and sheep,—all the agricultural *spectra* of the feminine imagination. But now her terrors were over. Might she not play the soldier, too, in her own humble way? Often with a beating heart, I fear, but still with resolute, elastic steps, she revisited Jack's old haunts; she tried to love Nature as he had seemed to love it; she gazed at his old sunsets; she fathomed his old pools with bright plummet glances, as if seeking some lingering trace of his features in their brown depths, stamped there as on a fond human heart; she sought out his dear name, scratched on the rocks and trees,—and when night came on, she studied, in her simple way, the great starlit canopy, under which, perhaps, her warrior lay sleeping; she wandered through the green glades, singing snatches of his old ballads in a clear voice, made tuneful with love,— and as she sang, there mingled with the everlasting murmur of the trees the faint sound of a muffled bass, borne upon the south wind like a distant drum-beat, responsive to a bugle. So she led for some months a very pleasant idyllic life, face to face with a strong, vivid memory, which gave everything and asked nothing. These were doubtless to be (and she half knew it) the happiest days of her life. Has life any bliss so great as this pensive ecstasy? To know that the golden sands are dropping one by one makes servitude freedom, and poverty riches. In spite of a certain sense of loss, Lizzie passed a very blissful summer. She enjoyed the deep repose which, it is to be hoped, sanctifies all honest betrothals. Possible calamity weighed lightly upon her. We know that when the columns of battle-smoke leave the field, they journey through the heavy air to a thousand quiet homes, and play about the crackling blaze of as many firesides. But Lizzie's vision was never clouded. Mrs. Ford might gaze into the thickening summer dusk and wipe her spectacles; but her companion hummed her old ballad-ends with an unbroken voice. She no more ceased to smile under evil tidings than the brooklet ceases to ripple beneath the projected shadow of the roadside willow. The self-given promises of that tearful night of parting were forgotten. Vigilance had no place in Lizzie's scheme of heavenly idleness. The idea of moralizing in Elysium!

It must not be supposed that Mrs. Ford was indifferent to Lizzie's mood. She studied it watchfully, and kept note of all its variations. And among the things she learned was, that her companion knew of her scrutiny, and was, on the whole, indifferent to it. Of the full extent of Mrs. Ford's observation, however, I think Lizzie was hardly aware. She was like a reveller in a brilliantly lighted room, with a curtainless window, conscious, and yet heedless, of passers-by. And Mrs. Ford may not inaptly be compared to the chilly spectator on the dark side of the pane. Very few words passed on the topic of their common thoughts. From the first, as we have seen, Lizzie guessed at her guardian's probable view of her engagement: an abasement incurred by John. Lizzie lacked what is called a sense of duty; and, unlike the majority of such temperaments, which contrive to be buoyant on the glistening bubble of Dignity, she had likewise a modest estimate of her dues. Alack, my poor heroine had no pride! Mrs. Ford's silent censure awakened no resentment. It sounded in her ears like a dull, soporific hum. Lizzie was deeply enamored of what a French book terms her *aises intellectuelles*. Her mental comfort lay in the ignoring of problems. She possessed a certain native insight which revealed many of the horrent inequalities of her pathway; but she found it so cruel and disenchanting a faculty, that blindness was infinitely preferable. She preferred repose to order, and mercy to justice. She was speculative, without being critical. She was continually wondering, but she never inquired. This world was the riddle; the next alone would be the answer.

So she never felt any desire to have an "understanding" with Mrs. Ford. Did the old lady misconceive her? it was her own business. Mrs. Ford apparently felt no desire to set herself right. You see, Lizzie was ignorant of her friend's promise. There were moments when Mrs. Ford's tongue itched to speak. There were others, it is true, when she dreaded any explanation which would compel her to forfeit her displeasure. Lizzie's happy self-sufficiency was most irritating. She grudged the young girl the dignity of her secret; her own actual knowledge of it rather increased her jealousy, by showing her the importance of the scheme from which she was excluded. Lizzie, being in perfect good-humor with the world and with herself, abated no jot of her personal deference to Mrs. Ford. Of Jack, as a good friend and her guardian's son, she spoke very freely. But Mrs. Ford was mistrustful of this semi-confidence. She would not, she often said to herself, be wheedled against her principles. Her principles! Oh for some shining blade of purpose to hew down such stubborn stakes! Lizzie had no thought of flattering her companion. She never deceived any one but herself. She could not bring herself to value Mrs. Ford's good-will. She knew that Jack often suffered from his mother's obstinacy. So her unbroken humility shielded no unavowed purpose. She was patient and kindly from nature, from habit. Yet I think, that, if Mrs. Ford could have measured her benignity, she would have preferred, on the whole, the most open defiance. "Of all things," she would sometimes mutter, "to be patronized by that little piece!" It was very disagreeable, for instance, to have to listen to *portions* of her own son's letters.

These letters came week by week, flying out of the South like white-winged carrier-doves. Many and many a time, for very pride, Lizzie would have liked a larger audience. Portions of them certainly deserved publicity. They were far too good for her. Were they not better than that stupid war-correspondence in the "Times," which she so often tried in vain to read? They contained long details of movements, plans of campaigns, military opinions and conjectures, expressed with the emphasis habitual to young sub-lieutenants. I doubt whether General Halleck's despatches laid down the law more absolutely than Lieutenant Ford's. Lizzie answered in her own fashion. It must be owned that hers was a dull pen. She told her dearest, dearest Jack how much she loved and honored him, and how much she missed him, and how delightful his last letter was, (with those beautifully drawn diagrams,) and the village gossip, and how stout and strong his mother continued to be,—and again, how she loved, etc., etc., and that she remained his loving L. Jack read these effusions as became one so beloved. I should not wonder if he thought them very brilliant.

The summer waned to its close, and through myriad silent stages began to darken into autumn. Who can tell the story of those red months? I have to chronicle another silent transition. But as I can find no words delicate and fine enough to describe the multifold changes of Nature, so, too, I must be content to give you the spiritual facts in gross.

John Ford became a veteran down by the Potomac. And, to tell the truth, Lizzie became a veteran at home. That is, her love and hope grew to be an old story. She gave way, as the strongest must, as the wisest will, to time. The passion which, in her simple, shallow way, she had confided to the woods and waters reflected their outward variations; she thought of her lover less, and with less positive pleasure. The golden sands had run out. Perfect rest was over. Mrs. Ford's tacit protest began to be annoying. In a rather resentful spirit, Lizzie forbore to read any more letters aloud. These were as regular as ever. One of them contained a rough camp-photograph of Jack's newly bearded visage. Lizzie declared it was "too ugly for anything," and thrust it out of sight. She found herself skipping his military dissertations, which were still as long and written in as handsome a hand as ever. The "too good," which used to be uttered rather proudly, was now rather a wearisome truth. When Lizzie in certain critical moods tried to qualify Jack's temperament, she said to herself that he was too literal. Once he gave her a little scolding for not writing oftener. "Jack can make no allowances," murmured Lizzie. "He can understand no feelings but his own. I remember he used to say that moods were diseases. His mind is too healthy for such things; his heart is too stout for ache or pain. The night before he went off he told me that Reason, as he calls it, was the rule of life. I suppose he thinks it the rule of love, too. But his heart is younger than mine,—younger and better. He has lived through awful scenes of danger and bloodshed and cruelty, yet his heart is purer." Lizzie had a horrible feeling of being *blasée* of this one affection. "Oh, God bless him!" she cried. She felt much better for the tears in which this soliloquy ended. I fear she had begun to doubt her ability to cry about Jack.

· *III* ·

Christmas came. The Army of the Potomac had stacked its muskets and gone into winter-quarters. Miss Crowe received an invitation to pass the second fortnight in February at the great manufacturing town of Leatherborough. Leatherborough is on the railroad, two hours south of Glenham, at the mouth of the great river Tan, where this noble stream expands into its broadest smile, or gapes in too huge a fashion to be disguised by a bridge.

"Mrs. Littlefield kindly invites you for the last of the month," said Mrs. Ford, reading a letter behind the tea-urn.

It suited Mrs. Ford's purpose—a purpose which I have not space to elaborate—that her young charge should now go forth into society and pick up acquaintances.

Two sparks of pleasure gleamed in Elizabeth's eyes. But, as she had taught herself to do of late with her protectress, she mused before answering.

"It is my desire that you should go," said Mrs. Ford, taking silence for dissent.

The sparks went out.

"I intend to go," said Lizzie, rather grimly. "I am much obliged to Mrs. Littlefield."

Her companion looked up.

"I intend you shall. You will please to write this morning."

For the rest of the week the two stitched together over muslins and silks, and were very good friends. Lizzie could scarcely help wondering at Mrs. Ford's zeal on her behalf. Might she not have referred it to her guardian's principles? Her wardrobe, hitherto fashioned on the Glenham notion of elegance, was gradually raised to the Leatherborough standard of fitness. As she took up her bedroom candle the night before she left home, she said,—

"I thank you very much, Mrs. Ford, for having worked so hard for me,—for having taken so much interest in my outfit. If they ask me

40

at Leatherborough who made my things, I shall certainly say it was you."

Mrs. Littlefield treated her young friend with great kindness. She was a good-natured, childless matron. She found Lizzie very ignorant and very pretty. She was glad to have so great a beauty and so many lions to show.

One evening Lizzie went to her room with one of the maids, carrying half a dozen candles between them. Heaven forbid that I should cross that virgin threshold—for the present! But we will wait. We will allow them two hours. At the end of that time, having gently knocked, we will enter the sanctuary. Glory of glories! The faithful attendant has done her work. Our lady is robed, crowned, ready for worshippers.

I trust I shall not be held to a minute description of our dear Lizzie's person and costume. Who is so great a recluse as never to have beheld young ladyhood in full dress? Many of us have sisters and daughters. Not a few of us, I hope, have female connections of another degree, yet no less dear. Others have looking-glasses. I give you my word for it that Elizabeth made as pretty a show as it is possible to see. She was of course well-dressed. Her skirt was of voluminous white, puffed and trimmed in wondrous sort. Her hair was profusely ornamented with curls and braids of its own rich substance. From her waist depended a ribbon, broad and blue. White with coral ornaments, as she wrote to Jack in the course of the week. Coral ornaments, forsooth! And pray, Miss, what of the other jewels with which your person was decorated,—the rubies, pearls, and sapphires? One by one Lizzie assumes her modest gimcracks: her bracelet, her gloves, her handkerchief, her fan, and then—her smile. Ah, that strange crowning smile!

An hour later, in Mrs. Littlefield's pretty drawing-room, amid music, lights, and talk, Miss Crowe was sweeping a grand curtsy before a tall, sallow man, whose name she caught from her hostess's redundant murmur as Bruce. Five minutes later, when the honest matron gave a glance at her newly started enterprise from the other side of the room, she said to herself that really, for a plain country-girl, Miss Crowe did this kind of thing very well. Her next glimpse of the couple showed them whirling round the room to the crashing thrum of the piano. At eleven o'clock she beheld them linked by their finger-tips in the dazzling mazes of the reel. At half-past eleven she discerned them

41

charging shoulder to shoulder in the serried columns of the Lancers. At midnight she tapped her young friend gently with her fan.

"Your sash is unpinned, my dear.—I think you have danced often enough with Mr. Bruce. If he asks you again, you had better refuse. It's not quite the thing.—Yes, my dear, I know.—Mr. Simpson, will you be so good as to take Miss Crowe down to supper?"

I'm afraid young Simpson had rather a snappish partner.

After the proper interval, Mr. Bruce called to pay his respects to Mrs. Littlefield. He found Miss Crowe also in the drawing-room. Lizzie and he met like old friends. Mrs. Littlefield was a willing listener; but it seemed to her that she had come in at the second act of the play. Bruce went off with Miss Crowe's promise to drive with him in the afternoon. In the afternoon he swept up to the door in a prancing, tinkling sleigh. After some minutes of hoarse jesting and silvery laughter in the keen wintry air, he swept away again with Lizzie curled up in the buffalo-robe beside him, like a kitten in a rug. It was dark when they returned. When Lizzie came in to the sitting-room fire, she was congratulated by her hostess upon having made a "conquest."

"I think he's a most gentlemanly man," says Lizzie.

"So he is, my dear," said Mrs. Littlefield; "Mr. Bruce is a perfect gentleman. He's one of the finest young men I know. He's not so young either. He's a little too yellow for my taste; but he's beautifully educated. I wish you could hear his French accent. He has been abroad I don't know how many years. The firm of Bruce and Robertson does an immense business."

"And I'm so glad," cries Lizzie, "he's coming to Glenham in March! He's going to take his sister to the water-cure."

"Really?—poor thing! She has very good manners."

"What do you think of his looks?" asked Lizzie, smoothing her feather.

"I was speaking of Jane Bruce. I think Mr. Bruce has fine eyes."

"I must say I like tall men," says Miss Crowe.

"Then Robert Bruce is your man," laughs Mr. Littlefield. "He's as tall as a bell-tower. And he's got a bell-clapper in his head, too."

"I believe I will go and take off my things," remarks Miss Crowe, flinging up her curls.

Of course it behooved Mr. Bruce to call the next day and see how Miss Crowe had stood her drive. He set a veto upon her intended departure, and presented an invitation from his sister for the following week. At Mrs. Littlefield's instance, Lizzie accepted the invitation, despatched a laconic note to Mrs. Ford, and stayed over for Miss Bruce's party. It was a grand affair. Miss Bruce was a very great lady: she treated Miss Crowe with every attention. Lizzie was thought by some persons to look prettier than ever. The vaporous gauze, the sunny hair, the coral, the sapphires, the smile, were displayed with renewed success. The master of the house was unable to dance; he was summoned to sterner duties. Nor could Miss Crowe be induced to perform, having hurt her foot on the ice. This was of course a disappointment; let us hope that her entertainers made it up to her.

On the second day after the party, Lizzie returned to Glenham. Good Mr. Littlefield took her to the station, stealing a moment from his precious business-hours.

"There are your checks," said he; "be sure you don't lose them. Put them in your glove."

Lizzie gave a little scream of merriment.

"Mr. Littlefield, how can you? I've a reticule, Sir. But I really don't want you to stay."

"Well, I confess," said her companion.—"Hullo! there's your Scottish chief! I'll get him to stay with you till the train leaves. He may be going. Bruce!"

"Oh, Mr. Littlefield, don't!" cries Lizzie. "Perhaps Mr. Bruce is engaged."

Bruce's tall figure came striding towards them. He was astounded to find that Miss Crowe was going by this train. Delightful! He had come to meet a friend who had not arrived.

"Littlefield," said he, "you can't be spared from your business. I will see Miss Crowe off."

When the elder gentleman had departed, Mr. Bruce conducted his companion into the car, and found her a comfortable seat, equidistant from the torrid stove and the frigid door. Then he stowed away her shawls, umbrella, and reticule. She would keep her muff? She did well. What a pretty fur!

"It's just like your collar," said Lizzie. "I wish I had a muff for my feet," she pursued, tapping the floor.

"Why not use some of those shawls?" said Bruce; "let's see what we can make of them."

43

And he stooped down and arranged them as a rug, very neatly and kindly. And then he called himself a fool for not having used the next seat, which was empty; and the wrapping was done over again.

"I'm so afraid you'll be carried off!" said Lizzie. "What would you do?"

"I think I should make the best of it. And you?"

"I would tell you to sit down *there*"; and she indicated the seat facing her. He took it. "Now you'll be sure to," said Elizabeth.

"I'm afraid I shall, unless I put the newspaper between us." And he took it out of his pocket. "Have you seen the news?"

"No," says Lizzie, elongating her bonnet-ribbons. "What is it? Just look at that party."

"There's not much news. There's been a scrimmage on the Rappa-hannock. Two of our regiments engaged,—the Fifteenth and the Twenty-Eighth. Didn't you tell me you had a cousin or something in the Fifteenth?"

"Not a cousin, no relation, but an intimate friend,—my guardian's son. What does the paper say, please?" inquires Lizzie, very pale.

Bruce cast his eye over the report. "It doesn't seem to have amounted to much; we drove back the enemy, and recrossed the river at our ease. Our loss only fifty. There are no names," he added, catching a glimpse of Lizzie's pallor,—"none in this paper at least."

In a few moments appeared a newsboy crying the New York journals.

"Do you think the New York papers would have any names?" asked Lizzie.

"We can try," said Bruce. And he bought a "Herald," and unfolded it. "Yes, there *is* a list," he continued, some time after he had opened out the sheet. "What's your friend's name?" he asked, from behind the paper.

"Ford,—John Ford, second lieutenant," said Lizzie.

There was a long pause.

At last Bruce lowered the sheet, and showed a face in which Lizzie's pallor seemed faintly reflected.

"There *is* such a name among the wounded," he said; and, folding the paper down, he held it out, and gently crossed to the seat beside her.

Lizzie took the paper, and held it close to her eyes. But Bruce could

44

not help seeing that her temples had turned from white to crimson. "Do you see it?" he asked; "I sincerely hope it's nothing very bad." "*Severely*," whispered Lizzie.

"Yes, but that proves nothing. Those things are most unreliable. *Do* hope for the best."

Lizzie made no answer. Meanwhile passengers had been brushing in, and the car was full. The engine began to puff, and the conductor to shout. The train gave a jog.

"You'd better go, Sir, or you'll be carried off," said Lizzie, holding out her hand, with her face still hidden.

"May I go on to the next station with you?" said Bruce.

Lizzie gave him a rapid look, with a deepened flush. He had fancied that she was shedding tears. But those eyes were dry; they held fire rather than water.

"No, no, Sir; you must not. I insist. Good bye."

Bruce's offer had cost him a blush, too. He had been prepared to back it with the assurance that he had business ahead, and, indeed, to make a little business in order to satisfy his conscience. But Lizzie's answer was final.

"Very well," said he, "*good* bye. You have my real sympathy, Miss Crowe. Don't despair. We shall meet again."

The train rattled away. Lizzie caught a glimpse of a tall figure with lifted hat on the platform. But she sat motionless, with her head against the windowframe, her veil down, and her hands idle.

She had enough to do to think, or rather to feel. It is fortunate that the utmost shock of evil tidings often comes first. After that everything is for the better. Jack's name stood printed in that fatal column like a stern signal for despair. Lizzie felt conscious of a crisis which almost arrested her breath. Night had fallen at midday: what was the hour? A tragedy had stepped into her life: was she spectator or actor? She found herself face to face with death: was it not her own soul masquerading in a shroud? She sat in a half-stupor. She had been aroused from a dream into a waking nightmare. It was like hearing a murder-shriek while you turn the page of your novel. But I cannot describe these things. In time the crushing sense of calamity loosened its grasp. Feeling lashed her pinions. Thought struggled to rise. Passion was still, stunned, floored. She had recoiled like a receding wave for a stronger onset. A hundred ghastly fears and fancies strutted a moment, pecking at the young girl's naked heart, like sandpipers on the weltering beach. Then, as with a great murmurous rush, came the meaning of her grief. The flood-gates of emotion were opened.

At last passion exhausted itself, and Lizzie thought. Bruce's parting words rang in her ears. She did her best to hope. She reflected that wounds, even severe wounds, did not necessarily mean death. Death might easily be warded off. She would go to Jack; she would nurse him; she would watch by him; she would cure him. Even if Death had already beckoned, she would strike down his hand: if Life had already obeyed, she would issue the stronger mandate of Love. She would stanch his wounds; she would unseal his eyes with her kisses; she would call till he answered her.

Lizzie reached home and walked up the garden path. Mrs. Ford stood in the parlor as she entered, upright, pale, and rigid. Each read the other's countenance. Lizzie went towards her slowly and giddily. She must of course kiss her patroness. She took her listless hand and bent towards her stern lips. Habitually Mrs. Ford was the most undemonstrative of women. But as Lizzie looked closer into her face, she read the signs of a grief infinitely more potent than her own. The formal kiss gave way: the young girl leaned her head on the old woman's shoulder and burst into sobs. Mrs. Ford acknowledged those tears with a slow inclination of the head, full of a certain grim pathos: she put out her arms and pressed them closer to her heart.

At last Lizzie disengaged herself and sat down.

"I am going to him," said Mrs. Ford.

Lizzie's dizziness returned. Mrs. Ford was going,—and she, she?

"I am going to nurse him, and with God's help to save him."

"How did you hear?"

"I have a telegram from the surgeon of the regiment"; and Mrs. Ford held out a paper.

Lizzie took it and read: "Lieutenant Ford dangerously wounded in the action of yesterday. You had better come on."

"I should like to go myself," said Lizzie: "I think Jack would like to have me."

"Nonsense! A pretty place for a young girl! I am not going for sentiment; I am going for use."

Lizzie leaned her head back in her chair, and closed her eyes. From the moment they had fallen upon Mrs. Ford, she had felt a certain

46

quiescence. And now it was a relief to have responsibility denied her. Like most weak persons, she was glad to step out of the current of life, now that it had begun to quicken into action. In emergencies, such persons are tacitly counted out; and they as tacitly consent to the arrangement. Even to the sensitive spirit there is a certain meditative rapture in standing on the quiet shore, (beside the ruminating cattle,) and watching the hurrying, eddying flood, which makes up for the loss of dignity. Lizzie's heart resumed its peaceful throbs. She sat, almost dreamily, with her eyes shut.

"I leave in an hour," said Mrs. Ford. "I am going to get ready.— Do you hear?"

The young girl's silence was a deeper consent than her companion supposed.

· *IV* ·

It was a week before Lizzie heard from Mrs. Ford. The letter, when it came, was very brief. Jack still lived. The wounds were three in number, and very serious; he was unconscious; he had not recognized her; but still the chances either way were thought equal. They would be much greater for his recovery nearer home; but it was impossible to move him. "I write from the midst of horrible scenes," said the poor lady. Subjoined was a list of necessary medicines, comforts, and delicacies, to be boxed up and sent.

For a while Lizzie found occupation in writing a letter to Jack, to be read in his first lucid moment, as she told Mrs. Ford. This lady's man-of-business came up from the village to superintend the packing of the boxes. Her directions were strictly followed; and in no point were they found wanting. Mr. Mackenzie bespoke Lizzie's admiration for their friend's wonderful clearness of memory and judgment. "I wish we had that woman at the head of affairs," said he. " 'Gad, I'd apply for a Brigadier-Generalship."—"I'd apply to be sent South," thought Lizzie. When the boxes and letter were despatched, she sat down to await more news. Sat down, say I? Sat down, and rose, and wondered, and sat down again. These were lonely, weary days. Very different are the idleness of love and the idleness of grief. Very different is it to be alone with your hope and alone with your despair. Lizzie failed to rally her musings. I do not mean to say that her sorrow was very poignant, although she fancied it was. Habit was a great

47

force in her simple nature; and her chief trouble now was that habit refused to work. Lizzie had to grapple with the stern tribulation of a decision to make, a problem to solve. She felt that there was some spiritual barrier between herself and repose. So she began in her usual fashion to build up a false repose on the hither side of belief. She might as well have tried to float on the Dead Sea. Peace eluding her, she tried to resign herself to tumult. She drank deep at the well of self-pity, but found its waters brackish. People are apt to think that they may temper the penalties of misconduct by self-commiseration, just as they season the long aftertaste of beneficence by a little spice of self-applause. But the Power of Good is a more grateful master than the Devil. What bliss to gaze into the smooth gurgling wake of a good deed, while the comely bark sails on with floating pennon! What horror to look into the muddy sediment which floats round the piratic keel! Go, sinner, and dissolve it with your tears! And you, scoffing friend, there is the way out! Or would you prefer the window? I'm an honest man forevermore.

One night Lizzie had a dream,—a rather disagreeable one,—which haunted her during many waking hours. It seemed to her that she was walking in a lonely place, with a tall, dark-eyed man who called her wife. Suddenly, in the shadow of a tree, they came upon an un-buried corpse. Lizzie proposed to dig him a grave. They dug a great hole and took hold the corpse to lift him in; when suddenly he opened his eyes. Then they saw that he was covered with wounds. He looked at them intently for some time, turning his eyes from one to the other. At last he solemnly said, "Amen!" and closed his eyes. Then she and her companion placed him in the grave, and shovelled the earth over him, and stamped it down with their feet.

He of the dark eyes and he of the wounds were the two constantly recurring figures of Lizzie's reveries. She could never think of John without thinking of the courteous Leatherborough gentleman, too. These were the *data* of her problem. These two figures stood like opposing knights, (the black and the white,) foremost on the great chess-board of fate. Lizzie was the wearied, puzzled player. She would idly finger the other pieces, and shift them carelessly hither and thither; but it was of no avail: the game lay between the two knights. She would shut her eyes and long for some kind hand to come and tamper with the board; she would open them and see the two knights standing immovable, face to face. It was nothing new. A fancy had come in and offered defiance to a fact; they must fight it out. Lizzie generously inclined to the fancy, the unknown champion, with a reputation to make. Call her *blasée,* if you like, this little girl, whose record told of a couple of dances and a single lover, heartless, old before her time. Perhaps she deserves your scorn. I confess she thought herself ill-used. By whom? by what? wherein? These were questions Miss Crowe was not prepared to answer. Her intellect was unequal to the stern logic of human events. She expected two and two to make five: as why should they not for the nonce? She was like an actor who finds himself on the stage with a half-learned part and without sufficient wit to extemporize. Pray, where is the prompter? Alas, Elizabeth, that you had no mother! Young girls are prone to fancy that when once they have a lover, they have everything they need: a conclusion inconsistent with the belief entertained by many persons, that life begins with love. Lizzie's fortunes became old stories to her before she had half read them through. Jack's wounds and danger were an old story. Do not suppose that she had exhausted the lessons, the suggestions of these awful events, their inspirations, exhortations,— that she had wept as became the horror of the tragedy. No: the curtain had not yet fallen, yet our young lady had begun to yawn. To yawn? Ay, and to long for the afterpiece. Since the tragedy dragged, might she not divert herself with that well-bred man beside her?

Elizabeth was far from owning to herself that she had fallen away from her love. For my own part, I need no better proof of the fact than the dull persistency with which she denied it. What accusing voice broke out of the stillness? Jack's nobleness and magnanimity were the hourly theme of her clogged fancy. Again and again she declared to herself that she was unworthy of them, but that, if he would only recover and come home, she would be his eternal bondslave. So she passed a very miserable month. Let us hope that her childish spirit was being tempered to some useful purpose. Let us hope so.

She roamed about the empty house with her footsteps tracked by an unlaid ghost. She cried aloud and said that she was very unhappy; she groaned and called herself wicked. Then, sometimes, appalled at her moral perplexities, she declared that she was neither wicked nor unhappy; she was contented, patient, and wise. Other girls had lost their lovers: it was the present way of life. Was she weaker than most women? Nay, but Jack was the best of men. If he would only come back directly, without delay, as he was, senseless, dying even, that she might look at him, touch him, speak to him! Then she would say that she could no longer answer for herself, and wonder (or pretend to wonder) whether she were not going mad. Suppose Mrs. Ford should come back and find her in an unswept room, pallid and insane? or suppose she should die of her troubles? What if she should kill herself?—dismiss the servants, and close the house, and lock herself up with a knife? Then she would cut her arm to escape from dismay at what she had already done; and then her courage would ebb away with her blood, and, having so far pledged herself to despair, her life would ebb away with her courage: and then, alone, in darkness, with none to help her, she would vainly scream, and thrust the knife into her temple, and swoon to death. And Jack would come back, and burst into the house, and wander through the empty rooms, calling her name, and for all answer get a deathscent! These imaginings were the more creditable or discreditable to Lizzie, that she had never read "Romeo and Juliet." At any rate, they served to dissipate time,— heavy, weary time,—the more heavy and weary as it bore dark fore-shadowings of some momentous event. If that event would only come, whatever it was, and sever this Gordian knot of doubt!

The days passed slowly: the leaden sands dropped one by one. The roads were too bad for walking; so Lizzie was obliged to confine her restlessness to the narrow bounds of the empty house, or to an occasional journey to the village, where people sickened her by their dull indifference to her spiritual agony. Still they could not fail to remark how poorly Miss Crowe was looking. This was true, and Lizzie knew it. I think she even took a certain comfort in her pallor and in her failing interest in her dress. There was some satisfaction in displaying her white roses amid the apple-cheeked prosperity of Main Street. At last Miss Cooper, the Doctor's sister, spoke to her:—

"How is it, Elizabeth, you look so pale, and thin, and worn out? What you been doing with yourself? Falling in love, eh? It isn't right to be so much alone. Come down and stay with us awhile,—till Mrs. Ford and John come back," added Miss Cooper, who wished to put a cheerful face on the matter.

For Miss Cooper, indeed, any other face would have been difficult.

Lizzie agreed to come. Her hostess was a busy, unbeautiful old maid, sister and housekeeper of the village physician. Her occupation here below was to perform the forgotten tasks of her fellowmen,—to pick up their dropped stitches, as she herself declared. She was never idle, for her general cleverness was commensurate with mortal needs. Her own story was, that she kept moving, so that folks couldn't see how ugly she was. And, in fact, her existence was manifest through her long train of good deeds,—just as the presence of a comet is shown by its tail. It was doubtless on the above principle that her visage was agitated by a perpetual laugh.

Meanwhile more news had been coming from Virginia. "What an absurdly long letter you sent John," wrote Mrs. Ford, in acknowledging the receipt of the boxes. "His first lucid moment would be very short, if he were to take upon himself to read your effusions. Pray keep your long stories till he gets well." For a fortnight the young soldier remained the same,—feverish, conscious only at intervals. Then came a change for the worse, which, for many weary days, however, resulted in nothing decisive. "If he could only be moved to Glenham, home, and old sights," said his mother, "I should have hope. But think of the journey!" By this time Lizzie had stayed out ten days of her visit.

One day Miss Cooper came in from a walk, radiant with tidings. Her face, as I have observed, wore a continual smile, being dimpled and punctured all over with merriment,—so that, when an unusual cheerfulness was super-diffused, it resembled a tempestuous little pool into which a great stone has been cast.

"Guess who's come," said she, going up to the piano, which Lizzie was carelessly fingering, and putting her hands on the young girl's shoulders. "Just guess!"

Lizzie looked up.

"Jack," she half gasped.

"Oh, dear, no, not that! How stupid of me! I mean Mr. Bruce, your Leatherborough admirer."

"Mr. Bruce! Mr. Bruce!" said Lizzie. "Really?"

"True as I live. He's come to bring his sister to the Water-Cure. I met them at the post-office."

Lizzie felt a strange sensation of good news. Her finger-tips were on fire. She was deaf to her companion's rattling chronicle. She broke

51

into the midst of it with a fragment of some triumphant, jubilant melody. The keys rang beneath her flashing hands. And then she suddenly stopped, and Miss Cooper, who was taking off her bonnet at the mirror, saw that her face was covered with a burning flush.

That evening, Mr. Bruce presented himself at Doctor Cooper's, with whom he had a slight acquaintance. To Lizzie he was infinitely courteous and tender. He assured her, in very pretty terms, of his profound sympathy with her in her cousin's danger,—her cousin he still called him,—and it seemed to Lizzie that until that moment no one had begun to be kind. And then he began to rebuke her, playfully and in excellent taste, for her pale cheeks.

"Isn't it dreadful?" said Miss Cooper. "She looks like a ghost. I guess she's in love."

"He must be a good-for-nothing lover to make his mistress look so sad. If I were you, I'd give him up, Miss Crowe."

"I didn't know I looked sad," said Lizzie.

"You don't now," said Miss Cooper. "You're smiling and blushing. A'n't she blushing, Mr. Bruce?"

"I think Miss Crowe has no more than her natural color," said Bruce, dropping his eye-glass. "What have you been doing all this while since we parted?"

"All this while? It's only six weeks. I don't know. Nothing. What have you?"

"I've been doing nothing, too. It's hard work."

"Have you been to any more parties?"

"Not one."

"Any more sleigh-rides?"

"Yes. I took one more dreary drive all alone,—over that same road, you know. And I stopped at the farm-house again, and saw the old woman we had the talk with. She remembered us, and asked me what had become of the young lady who was with me before. I told her you were gone home, but that I hoped soon to go and see you. So she sent you her love"——

"Oh, how nice!" exclaimed Lizzie.

"Wasn't it? And then she made a certain little speech; I won't repeat it, or we shall have Miss Cooper talking about your blushes again."

"I know," cried the lady in question: "she said she was very"——

"Very what?" said Lizzie.

"Very h-a-n-d —— what every one says."

"Very handy?" asked Lizzie. "I'm sure no one ever said that."

"Of course," said Bruce; "and I answered what every one answers."

"Have you seen Mrs. Littlefield lately?"

"Several times. I called on her the day before I left town, to see if she had any message for you."

"Oh, thank you! I hope she's well."

"Oh, she's as jolly as ever. She sent you her love, and hoped you would come back to Leatherborough very soon again. I told her, that, however it might be with the first message, the second should be a joint one from both of us."

"You're very kind. I should like very much to go again.—Do you like Mrs. Littlefield?"

"Like her? Yes. Don't you? She's thought a very pleasing woman."

"Oh, she's very nice.—I don't think she has much conversation."

"Ah, I'm afraid you mean she doesn't backbite. We've always found plenty to talk about."

"That's a very significant tone. What, for instance?"

"Well, we *have* talked about Miss Crowe."

"Oh, you have? Do you call that having plenty to talk about?"

"We *have* talked about Mr. Bruce,—haven't we, Elizabeth?" said Miss Cooper, who had her own notion of being agreeable.

It was not an altogether bad notion, perhaps; but Bruce found her interruptions rather annoying, and insensibly allowed them to shorten his visit. Yet, as it was, he sat till eleven o'clock,—a stay quite unprecedented at Glenham.

When he left the house, he went splashing down the road with a very elastic tread, springing over the starlit puddles, and trolling out some sentimental ditty. He reached the inn, and went up to his sister's sitting-room.

"Why, Robert, where have you been all this while?" said Miss Bruce.

"At Dr. Cooper's."

"Dr. Cooper's? I should think you had! Who's Dr. Cooper?"

"Where Miss Crowe's staying."

"Miss Crowe? Ah, Mrs. Littlefield's friend! Is she as pretty as ever?"

"Prettier,—prettier,—prettier. *Ta-ra-ta! tara-ta!*"

"Oh, Robert, do stop that singing! You'll rouse the whole house."

53

· *V* ·

Late one afternoon, at dusk, about three weeks after Mr. Bruce's arrival, Lizzie was sitting alone by the fire, in Miss Cooper's parlor, musing, as became the place and hour. The Doctor and his sister came in, dressed for a lecture.

"I'm sorry you won't go, my dear," said Miss Cooper. "It's a most interesting subject: 'A Year of the War'. All the battles and things described, you know."

"I'm tired of war," said Lizzie.

"Well, well, if you're tired of the war, we'll leave you in peace. Kiss me good-bye. What's the matter? You look sick. You are home-sick, a'n't you?"

"No, no,—I'm very well."

"Would you like me to stay at home with you?"

"Oh, no! pray, don't!"

"Well, we'll tell you all about it. Will they have programmes, James? I'll bring her a programme.—But you really feel as if you were going to be ill. Feel of her skin, James."

"No, you needn't, Sir," said Lizzie. "How queer of you, Miss Cooper! I'm perfectly well."

And at last her friends departed. Before long the servant came with the lamp, ushering Mr. Mackenzie.

"Good evening, Miss," said he. "Bad news from Mrs. Ford."

"Bad news?"

"Yes, Miss. I've just got a letter stating that Mr. John is growing worse and worse, and that they look for his death from hour to hour.—It's very sad," he added, as Elizabeth was silent.

"Yes, it's very sad," said Lizzie.

"It thought you'd like to hear it."

"Thank you."

"He was a very noble young fellow," pursued Mr. Mackenzie.

Lizzie made no response.

"There's the letter," said Mr. Mackenzie, handing it over to her. Lizzie opened it.

"How long she is reading it!" thought her visitor. "You can't see so far from the light, can you, Miss?"

"Yes," said Lizzie.—"His poor mother! Poor woman!"

"Ay, indeed, Miss,—she's the one to be pitied."

"Yes, she's the one to be pitied," said Lizzie. "Well!" and she gave him back the letter.

"I thought you'd like to see it," said Mackenzie, drawing on his gloves; and then, after a pause,—"I'll call again, Miss, if I hear anything more. Good night!"

Lizzie got up and lowered the light, and then went back to her sofa by the fire.

Half an hour passed; it went slowly; but it passed. Still lying there in the dark room on the sofa, Lizzie heard a ring at the door-bell, a man's voice and a man's tread in the hall. She rose and went to the lamp. As she turned it up, the parlor-door opened. Bruce came in.

"I was sitting in the dark," said Lizzie; "but when I heard you coming, I raised the light."

"Are you afraid of me?" said Bruce.

"Oh, no! I'll put it down again. Sit down."

"I saw your friends going out," pursued Bruce; "so I knew I should find you alone.—What are you doing here in the dark?"

"I've just received very bad news from Mrs. Ford about her son. He's much worse, and will probably not live."

"Is it possible?"

"I was thinking about that."

"Dear me! Well that's a sad subject. I'm told he was a very fine young man."

"He was,—very," said Lizzie.

Bruce was silent awhile. He was a stranger to the young officer, and felt that he had nothing to offer beyond the commonplace expressions of sympathy and surprise. Nor had he exactly the measure of his companion's interest in him.

"If he dies," said Lizzie, "it will be under great injustice."

"Ah! what do you mean?"

"There wasn't a braver man in the army."

"I suppose not."

"And, oh, Mr. Bruce," continued Lizzie, "he was so clever and good and generous! I wish you had known him."

"I wish I had. But what do you mean by injustice? Were these qualities denied him?"

"No indeed! Every one that looked at him could see that he was perfect."

"Where's the injustice, then? It ought to be enough for him that you should think so highly of him."

"Oh, he knew that," said Lizzie.

Bruce was a little puzzled by his companion's manner. He watched her, as she sat with her cheek on her hand, looking at the fire. There was a long pause. Either they were too friendly or too thoughtful for the silence to be embarrassing. Bruce broke it at last.

"Miss Crowe," said he, "on a certain occasion, some time ago, when you first heard of Mr. Ford's wounds, I offered you my company, with the wish to console you as far as I might for what seemed a considerable shock. It was, perhaps, a bold offer for so new a friend; but, nevertheless, in it even then my heart spoke. You turned me off. Will you let me repeat it? Now, with a better right, will you let me speak out all my heart?"

Lizzie heard this speech, which was delivered in a slow and hesitating tone, without looking up or moving her head, except, perhaps, at the words "turned me off". After Bruce had ceased, she still kept her position.

"You'll not turn me off now?" added her companion.

She dropped her hand, raised her head, and looked at him a moment: he thought he saw the glow of tears in her eyes. Then she sank back upon the sofa with her face in the shadow of the mantel-piece.

"I don't understand you, Mr. Bruce," said she.

"Ah, Elizabeth! am I such a poor speaker. How shall I make it plain? When I saw your friends leave home half an hour ago, and reflected that you would probably be alone, I determined to go right in and have a talk with you that I've long been wanting to have. But first I walked half a mile up the road, thinking hard,—thinking how I should say what I had to say. I made up my mind to nothing, but that somehow or other I should say it. I would trust,—I do trust your frankness, kindness, and sympathy, to a feeling corresponding to my own. Do you understand that feeling? Do you know that I love you? I do, I do, I do! You *must* know it. If you don't, I solemnly swear it. I solemnly ask you, Elizabeth, to take me for your husband."

While Bruce said these words, he rose, with their rising passion, and came and stood before Lizzie. Again she was motionless.

"Does it take you so long to think?" said he, trying to read her indistinct features; and he sat down on the sofa beside her and took her hand.

At last Lizzie spoke.

"Are you sure," said she, "that you love me?"

"As sure as that I breathe. Now, Elizabeth, make me as sure that I am loved in return."

"It seems very strange, Mr. Bruce," said Lizzie.

"What seems strange? Why should it? For a month I've been trying, in a hundred dumb ways, to make it plain; and now, when I swear it, it only seems strange!"

"What do you love me for?"

"For? For yourself, Elizabeth."

"Myself? I am nothing."

"I love you for what you are,—for your deep, kind heart,—for being so perfectly a woman."

Lizzie drew away her hand, and her lover rose and stood before her again. But now she looked up into his face, questioning when she should have answered, drinking strength from his entreaties for her replies. There he stood before her, in the glow of the firelight, in all his gentlemanhood, for her to accept or reject. She slowly rose and gave him the hand she had withdrawn.

"Mr. Bruce, I shall be very proud to love you," she said.

And then, as if this effort was beyond her strength, she half staggered back to the sofa again. And still holding her hand, he sat down beside her. And there they were still sitting when they heard the Doctor and his sister come in.

For three days Elizabeth saw nothing of Mr. Mackenzie. At last, on the fourth day, passing his office in the village, she went in and asked for him. He came out of his little back parlor with his mouth full and a beaming face.

"Good-day, Miss Crowe, and good news!"

"*Good* news?" cried Lizzie.

"Capital!" said he, looking hard at her, while he put on his spectacles. "She writes that Mr. John—won't you take a seat?—has taken a sudden and unexpected turn for the better. Now's the moment to save him; it's an equal risk. They were to start for the North the second day after date. The surgeon comes with them. So they'll be home —of course they'll travel slowly—in four or five days. Yes, Miss, it's a remarkable Providence. And that noble young man will be spared to the country, and to those who love him, as I do."

"I had better go back to the house and have it got ready," said Lizzie, for an answer.

"Yes, Miss, I think you had. In fact, Mrs. Ford made that request."

The request was obeyed. That same day Lizzie went home. For two days she found it her interest to overlook, assiduously, a general sweeping, scrubbing, and provisioning. She allowed herself no idle moment until bed-time. Then——But I would rather not be the chamberlain of her agony. It was the easier to work, as Mr. Bruce had gone to Leatherborough on business.

On the fourth evening, at twilight, John Ford was borne up to the door on his stretcher, with his mother stalking beside him in rigid grief, and kind, silent friends pressing about with helping hands.

> "Home they brought her warrior dead,
> She nor swooned nor uttered cry."

It was, indeed, almost a question, whether Jack was not dead. Death is not thinner, paler, stiller. Lizzie moved about like one in a dream. Of course, when there are so many sympathetic friends, a man's family has nothing to do,—except exercise a little self-control. The women huddled Mrs. Ford to bed; rest was imperative; she was killing herself. And it was significant of her weakness that she did not resent this advice. In greeting her, Lizzie felt as if she were embracing the stone image on the top of a sepulchre. She, too, had her cares anticipated. Good Doctor Cooper and his sister stationed themselves at the young man's couch.

The Doctor prophesied wondrous things of the change of climate; he was certain of a recovery. Lizzie found herself very shortly dealt with as an obstacle to this consummation. Access to John was prohibited. "Perfect stillness, you know, my dear," whispered Miss Cooper, opening his chamber-door on a crack, in a pair of very creaking shoes. So for the first evening that her old friend was at home Lizzie caught but a glimpse of his pale, senseless face, as she hovered outside the long train of his attendants. If we may suppose any of these kind people to have had eyes for aught but the sufferer, we may be sure that they saw another visage equally sad and white. The sufferer? It was hardly Jack, after all.

When Lizzie was turned from Jack's door, she took a covering from a heap of draperies that had been hurriedly tossed down in the hall: it was an old army-blanket. She wrapped it round her, and went out on the verandah. It was nine o'clock; but the darkness was filled with light. A great wanton wind—the ghost of the raw blast which travels by day—had arisen, bearing long, soft gusts of inland spring. Scattered clouds were hurrying across the white sky. The bright moon, careering in their midst, seemed to have wandered forth in frantic quest of the hidden stars.

Lizzie nestled her head in the blanket, and sat down on the steps. A strange earthy smell lingered in that faded old rug, and with it a faint perfume of tobacco. Instantly the young girl's senses were transported as they had never been before to those far-off Southern battle-fields. She saw men lying in swamps, puffing their kindly pipes, drawing their blankets closer, canopied with the same luminous dusk that shone down upon her comfortable weakness. Her mind wandered amid these scenes till recalled to the present by the swinging of the garden-gate. She heard a firm, well-known tread crunching the gravel. Mr. Bruce came up the path. As he drew near the steps, Lizzie arose. The blanket fell back from her head, and Bruce started at recognizing her.

"Hullo! You, Elizabeth? What's the matter?"

Lizzie made no answer.

"Are you one of Mr. Ford's watchers?" he continued, coming up the steps; "how is he?"

Still she was silent. Bruce put out his hands to take hers, and bent forward as if to kiss her. She half shook him off, and retreated toward the door.

"Good heavens!" cried Bruce; "what's the matter? Are you moon-struck? Can't you speak?"

"No,—no,—not to-night," said Lizzie, in a choking voice. "Go away, —go away!"

She stood holding the door-handle, and motioning him off. He hesitated a moment, and then advanced. She opened the door rapidly, and went in. He heard her lock it. He stood looking at it stupidly for some time, and then slowly turned round and walked down the steps.

The next morning Lizzie arose with the early dawn, and came down stairs. She went to the room where Jack lay, and gently opened the door. Miss Cooper was dozing in her chair. Lizzie crossed the threshold, and stole up to the bed. Poor Ford lay peacefully sleeping. There was his old face, after all,—his strong, honest features refined, but not weakened, by pain. Lizzie softly drew up a low chair, and sat down beside him. She gazed into his face,—the dear and honored face into which she had so often gazed in health. It was strangely handsomer: body stood for less. It seemed to Lizzie, that, as the fabric of her lover's soul was more clearly revealed,—the veil of the temple rent wellnigh in twain,—she could read the justification of all her old worship. One of Jack's hands lay outside the sheets,—those strong, supple fingers, once so cunning in workmanship, so frank in friendship, now thinner and whiter than her own. After looking at it for some time, Lizzie gently grasped it. Jack slowly opened his eyes. Lizzie's heart began to throb; it was as if the stillness of the sanctuary had given a sign. At first there was no recognition in the young man's gaze. Then the dull pupils began visibly to brighten. There came to his lips the commencement of that strange moribund smile which seems so ineffably satirical of the things of this world. O imposing spectacle of death! O blessed soul, marked for promotion! What earthly favor is like thine? Lizzie sank down on her knees, and, still clasping John's hand, bent closer over him.

"Jack,—dear, dear Jack," she whispered, "do you know me?"

The smile grew more intense. The poor fellow drew out his other hand, and slowly, feebly placed it on Lizzie's head, stroking down her hair with his fingers.

"Yes, yes," she murmured; "you know me, don't you? I am Lizzie, Jack. Don't you remember Lizzie?"

Ford moved his lips inaudibly, and went on patting her head.

"This is home, you know," said Lizzie; "this is Glenham. You haven't forgotten Glenham? You are with your mother and me and your friends. Dear, darling Jack!"

Still he went on, stroking her head; and his feeble lips tried to emit some sound. Lizzie laid her head down on the pillow beside his own, and still his hand lingered caressingly on her hair.

"Yes, you know me," she pursued; "you are with your friends now forever,—with those who will love and take care of you, oh, forever!"

60

"I'm very badly wounded," murmured Jack, close to her ear.

"Yes, yes, my dear boy, but your wounds are healing. I will love you and nurse you forever."

"Yes, Lizzie, our old promise," said Jack: and his hand fell upon her neck, and with its feeble pressure he drew her closer, and she wet his face with her tears.

Then Miss Cooper, awakening, rose and drew Lizzie away.

"I am sure you excite him, my dear. It is best he should have none of his family near him,—persons with whom he has associations, you know."

Here the Doctor was heard gently tapping on the window, and Lizzie went round to the door to admit him.

She did not see Jack again all day. Two or three times she ventured into the room, but she was banished by a frown, or a finger raised to the lips. She waylaid the Doctor frequently. He was blithe and cheerful, certain of Jack's recovery. This good man used to exhibit as much moral elation at the prospect of a cure as an orthodox believer at that of a new convert: it was one more body gained from the Devil. He assured Lizzie that the change of scene and climate had already begun to tell: the fever was lessening, the worst symptoms disappearing. He answered Lizzie's reiterated desire to do something by directions to keep the house quiet and the sick-room empty.

Soon after breakfast, Miss Dawes, a neighbor, came in to relieve Miss Cooper, and this indefatigable lady transferred her attention to Mrs. Ford. Action was forbidden her. Miss Cooper was delighted for once to be able to lay down the law to her vigorous neighbor, of whose fine judgment she had always stood in awe. Having bullied Mrs. Ford into taking her breakfast in the little sitting-room, she closed the doors, and prepared for "a good long talk." Lizzie was careful not to break in upon this interview. She had bidden her patroness good morning, asked after her health, and received one of her temperate osculations. As she passed the invalid's door, Doctor Cooper came out and asked her to go and look for a certain roll of bandages, in Mr. John's trunk, which had been carried into another room. Lizzie hastened to perform this task. In fumbling through the contents of the trunk, she came across a packet of letters in a well-known feminine hand-writing. She pocketed it, and, after disposing of the bandages, went to her own room, locked the door, and sat down to examine the letters. Between

61

reading and thinking and sighing and (in spite of herself) smiling, this process took the whole morning. As she came down to dinner, she encountered Mrs. Ford and Miss Cooper, emerging from the sitting-room, the good long talk being only just concluded.

"How do you feel, Ma'am?" she asked of the elder lady,—"rested?"

For all answer Mrs. Ford gave a look—I had almost said a scowl—so hard, so cold, so reproachful, that Lizzie was transfixed. But suddenly its sickening meaning was revealed to her. She turned to Miss Cooper, who stood pale and fluttering beside the mistress, her ever-lasting smile glazed over with a piteous, deprecating glance; and I fear her eyes flashed out the same message of angry scorn they had just received. These telegraphic operations are very rapid. The ladies hardly halted: the next moment found them seated at the dinner-table with Miss Cooper scrutinizing her napkin-mark and Mrs. Ford saying grace.

Dinner was eaten in silence. When it was over, Lizzie returned to her own room. Miss Cooper went home, and Mrs. Ford went to her son. Lizzie heard the firm low click of the lock as she closed the door. Why did she lock it? There was something fatal in the silence that followed. The plot of her little tragedy thickened. Be it so: she would act her part with the rest. For the second time in her experience, her mind was lightened by the intervention of Mrs. Ford. Before the scorn of her own conscience, (which never came,) before Jack's deepest reproach, she was ready to bow down,—but not before that long-faced Nemesis in black silk. The leaven of resentment began to work. She leaned back in her chair, and folded her arms, brave to await results. But before long she fell asleep. She was aroused by a knock at her chamber-door. The afternoon was far gone. Miss Dawes stood without.

"Elizabeth, Mr. John wants very much to see you, with his love. Come down very gently: his mother is lying down. Will you sit with him while I take my dinner?—Better? Yes, ever so much."

Lizzie betook herself with trembling haste to Jack's bedside.

He was propped up with pillows. His pale cheeks were slightly flushed. His eyes were bright. He raised himself, and, for such feeble arms, gave Lizzie a long, strong embrace.

"I've not seen you all day, Lizzie," said he. "Where have you been?"

"Dear Jack, they wouldn't let me come near you. I begged and

62

prayed. And I wanted so to go to you in the army; but I couldn't. I wish, I wish I had!"

"You wouldn't have liked it, Lizzie. I'm glad you didn't. It's a bad, bad place."

He lay quietly, holding her hands and gazing at her.

"Can I do anything for you, dear?" asked the young girl. "I would work my life out. I'm so glad you're better!"

It was some time before Jack answered,—

"Lizzie," said he, at last, "I sent for you to look at you.—You are more wondrously beautiful than ever. Your hair is brown,—like—like nothing; your eyes are blue; your neck is white. Well, well!"

He lay perfectly motionless, but for his eyes. They wandered over her with a kind of peaceful glee, like sunbeams playing on a statue. Poor Ford lay, indeed, not unlike an old wounded Greek, who at falling dusk has crawled into a temple to die, steeping the last dull interval in idle admiration of sculptured Artemis.

"Ah, Lizzie, this is already heaven!" he murmured.

"It will be heaven when you get well," whispered Lizzie.

He smiled into her eyes:—

"You say more than you mean. There should be perfect truth between us. Dear Lizzie, I am not going to get well. They are all very much mistaken. I am going to die. I've done my work. Death makes up for everything. My great pain is in leaving you. But you, too, will die one of these days; remember that. In all pain and sorrow, remember that."

Lizzie was able to reply only by the tightening grasp of her hands.

"But there is something more," pursued Jack. "Life *is* as good as death. Your heart has found its true keeper; so we shall all three be happy. Tell him I bless him and honor him. Tell him God, too, blesses him. Shake hands with him for me," said Jack, feebly moving his pale fingers. "My mother," he went on,—"be very kind to her. She will have great grief, but she will not die of it. She'll live to great age. Now, Lizzie, I can't talk any more; I wanted to say farewell. You'll keep me farewell,—you'll stay with me awhile,—won't you? I'll look at you till the last. For a little while you'll be mine, holding my hands—so—until death parts us."

Jack kept his promise. His eyes were fixed in a firm gaze long after the sense had left them.

63

In the early dawn of the next day, Elizabeth left her sleepless bed, opened the window, and looked out on the wide prospect, still cool and dim with departing night. It offered freshness and peace to her hot head and restless heart. She dressed herself hastily, crept down stairs, passed the death-chamber, and stole out of the quiet house. She turned away from the still sleeping village and walked towards the open country. She went a long way without knowing it. The sun had risen high when she bethought herself to turn. As she came back along the brightening highway, and drew near home, she saw a tall figure standing beneath the budding trees of the garden, hesitating, apparently, whether to open the gate. Lizzie came upon him almost before he had seen her. Bruce's first movement was to put out his hands, as any lover might; but as Lizzie raised her veil, he dropped them.

"Yes, Mr. Bruce," said Lizzie, "I'll give you my hand once more,—in farewell."

"Elizabeth!" cried Bruce, half stupefied, "in God's name, what do you mean by these crazy speeches?"

"I mean well. I mean kindly and humanely to you. And I mean justice to my old—old love."

She went to him, took his listless hand, without looking into his wild, smitten face, shook it passionately, and then, wrenching her own from his grasp, opened the gate and let it swing behind her.

"No! no! no!" she almost shrieked, turning about in the path. "I forbid you to follow me!"

But for all that, he went in.

MY FRIEND BINGHAM

My Friend Bingham

"My Friend Bingham," Henry James's fourth published tale, appeared in the Atlantic, *March 1867, and is reprinted here for the first time. It is James's first "first person" story.*

*"Poor Richard," his first three-part story (*Atlantic, *June-August 1867) and a second experiment in Civil War fiction, was reprinted in* Stories Revived, Vol. III *(1885). This was followed by a story—first of many in quite another field—never collected by James.*

CONSCIOUS AS I AM OF A DEEP AVERSION TO STORIES OF a painful nature, I have often asked myself whether, in the events here set forth, the element of pain is stronger than that of joy. An affirmative answer to this question would have stood as a veto upon the publication of my story, for it is my opinion that the literature of horrors needs no extension. Such an answer, however, I am unwilling to pronounce; while, on the other hand, I hesitate to assume the responsibility of a decided negative. I have therefore determined to leave the solution to the reader. I may add, that I am very sensible of the superficial manner in which I have handled my facts. I bore no other part in the accomplishment of these facts than that of a cordial observer; and it was impossible that, even with the best will in the world, I should fathom the emotions of the actors. Yet, as the very faintest reflection of human passions, under the pressure of fate, possesses an immortal interest, I am content to appeal to the reader's sympathy, and to assure him of my own fidelity.

Towards the close of summer, in my twenty-eighth year, I went down to the seaside to rest from a long term of work, and to enjoy, after several years of separation, a *tête-à-tête* with an intimate friend. My friend had just arrived from Europe, and we had agreed to spend my vacation together by the side of the sounding sea, and within easy reach of the city. On taking possession of our lodgings, we found that we should have no fellow-idlers, and we hailed joyously the prospect of the great marine solitudes which each of us declared that he found so abundantly peopled by the other. I hasten to impart to the reader the following facts in regard to the man whom I found so good a companion.

George Bingham had been born and bred among people for whom, as he grew to manhood, he learned to entertain a most generous contempt,—people in whom the hereditary possession of a large property— for he assured me that the facts stood in the relation of cause and effect—had extinguished all intelligent purpose and principle. I trust that I do not speak rhetorically when I describe in these terms the combined ignorance and vanity of my friend's progenitors. It was their fortune to make a splendid figure while they lived, and I feel little compunction in hinting at their poverty in certain human essentials. Bingham was no declaimer, and indeed no great talker; and it was only now and then, in an allusion to the past as the field of a wasted youth, that he expressed his profound resentment. I read this for the most part in the severe humility with which he regarded the future, and under cover of which he seemed to salute it as void at least (whatever other ills it might contain) of those domestic embarrassments which had been the bane of his first manhood. I have no doubt that much may be said, within limits, for the graces of that society against which my friend embodied so violent a reaction, and especially for its good-humor,—that home-keeping benevolence which accompanies a sense of material repletion. It is equally probable that to persons of a simple constitution these graces may wear a look of delightful and enduring mystery; but poor Bingham was no simpleton. He was a man of opinions numerous, delicate, and profound. When, with the lapse of his youth, he awoke to a presentiment of these opinions, and cast his first interrogative glance upon the world, he found that in his own little section of it he and his opinions were a piece of melancholy impertinence. Left, at twenty-three years of age, by his father's death, in possession of a handsome property, and absolute master of his

68

actions, he had thrown himself blindly into the world. But, as he afterwards assured me, so superficial was his knowledge of the real world,—the world of labor and inquiry,—that he had found himself quite incapable of intelligent action. In this manner he had wasted a great deal of time. He had travelled much, however; and, being a keen observer of men and women, he had acquired a certain practical knowledge of human nature. Nevertheless, it was not till he was nearly thirty years old that he had begun to live for himself. "By myself," he explained, "I mean something else than this monstrous hereditary faculty for doing nothing and thinking of nothing." And he led me to believe, or I should rather say he allowed me to believe, that at this moment he had made a serious attempt to study. But upon this point he was not very explicit; for if he blushed for the manner in which he had slighted his opportunities, he blushed equally for the manner in which he had used them. It is my belief that he had but a limited capacity for study, and I am certain that to the end of his days there subsisted in his mind a very friendly relation between fancies and facts.

Bingham was *par excellence* a moralist, a man of sentiment. I know —he knew himself—that, in this busy Western world, this character represents no recognized avocation; but in the absence of such avocation, its exercise was nevertheless very dear to him. I protest that it was very dear to me, and that, at the end of a long morning devoted to my office-desk, I have often felt as if I had contributed less to the common cause than I have felt after moralizing—or, if you please, sentimentalizing—half an hour with my friend. He was an idler, assuredly; but his candor, his sagacity, his good taste, and, above all, a certain diffident enthusiasm which followed its objects with the exquisite trepidation of an unconfessed and despairing lover,—these things, and a hundred more, redeemed him from vulgarity. For three years before we came together, as I have intimated, my impressions of my friend had rested on his letters; and yet, from the first hour which we spent together, I felt that they had done him no wrong. We were genuine friends. I don't know that I can offer better proof of this than by saying that, as our old personal relations resumed their force, and the time-shrunken outlines of character filled themselves out, I greeted the reappearance of each familiar foible on Bingham's part quite as warmly as I did that of the less punctual virtue. Compared, indeed, with the comrade of earlier years, my actual companion was a well-seasoned man of the world; but with all his acquired humility and his disciplined *bonhomie*, he had failed to divest himself of a certain fastidiousness of mind, a certain formalism of manner, which are the token and the prerogative of one who has not been obliged to address himself to practical questions. The charm bestowed by these facts upon Bingham's conversation—a charm often vainly invoked in their absence—is explained by his honest indifference to their action, and his indisposition to turn them to account in the interest of the picturesque,—an advantage but too easy of conquest for a young man, rich, accomplished, and endowed with good looks and a good name. I may say, perhaps, that to a critical mind my friend's prime distinction would have been his very positive refusal to drape himself, after the current taste, with those brilliant stuffs which fortune had strewn at his feet.

Of course, a great deal of our talk bore upon Bingham's recent travels, adventures, and sensations. One of these last he handled very frankly, and treated me to a bit of genuine romance. He had been in love, and had been cruelly jilted, but had now grown able to view the matter with much of the impartial spirit of those French critics whose works were his favorite reading. His account of the young lady's character and motives would indeed have done credit to many a clever *feuilleton*. I was the less surprised, however, at his severely dispassionate tone, when, in retracing the process of his opinions, I discerned the traces—the ravages, I may almost say—of a solemn act of renunciation. Bingham had forsworn marriage. I made haste to assure him that I considered him quite too young for so austere a resolve.

"I can't help it," said he; "I feel a foreboding that I shall live and die alone."

"A foreboding?" said I. "What's a foreboding worth?"

"Well, then, rationally considered, my marriage is improbable."

"But it's not to be rationally considered," I objected. "It belongs to the province of sentiment."

"But you deny me sentiment. I fall back upon my foreboding."

"That's not sentiment,—it's superstition," I answered. "Your marrying will depend upon your falling in love; and your falling in love will certainly not depend upon yourself."

"Upon whom, then?"

"Upon some unknown fair one,—Miss A, B, or C."

"Well," said Bingham, submissively, "I wish she would make haste and reveal herself."

These remarks had been exchanged in the hollow of a cliff which sloped seaward, and where we had lazily stretched ourselves at length on the grass. The grass had grown very long and brown; and as we lay with our heads quite on a level with it, the view of the immediate beach and the gentle breakers was so completely obstructed by the rank, coarse herbage, that our prospect was reduced to a long, narrow band of deep blue ocean traversing its black fibres, and to the great vault of the sky. We had strolled out a couple of hours before, bearing each a borrowed shot-gun and accompanied by a friendly water-dog, somewhat languidly disposed towards the slaughter of wild ducks. We were neither of us genuine sportsmen, and it is certain that, on the whole, we meant very kindly to the ducks. It was at all events fated that on that day they should suffer but lightly at our hands. For the half-hour previous to the exchange of the remarks just cited, we had quite forgotten our real business; and, with our pieces lost in the grass beside us, and our dog, weary of inaction, wandering far beyond call, we looked like any straw-picking truants. At last Bingham rose to his feet, with the asseveration that it would never do for us to return empty-handed. "But, behold," he exclaimed, as he looked down across the breadth of the beach, "there is our friend of the cottage, with the sick little boy."

I brought myself into a sitting posture, and glanced over the cliff. Down near the edge of the water sat a young woman, tossing stones into it for the amusement of a child, who stood lustily crowing and clapping his hands. Her title to be called our friend lay in the fact, that on our way to the beach we had observed her issuing from a cottage hard by the hotel, leading by the hand a pale-faced little boy, muffled like an invalid. The hotel, as I have said, was all but deserted, and this young woman had been the first person to engage our idle observation. We had seen that, although plainly dressed, she was young, pretty, and modest; and, in the absence of heavier cares, these facts had sufficed to make her interesting. The question had arisen between us, whether she was a native of the shore, or a visitor like ourselves. Bingham inclined to the former view of the case, and I to the latter. There was, indeed, a certain lowliness in her aspect; but

71

I had contended that it was by no means a rustic lowliness. Her dress was simple, but it was well made and well worn; and I noticed that, as she strolled along, leading her little boy, she cast upon sky and sea the lingering glance of one to whom, in their integrity, these were unfamiliar objects. She was the wife of some small tradesman, I argued, who had brought her child to the seaside by the physician's decree. But Bingham declared that it was utterly illogical to suppose her to be a mother of five years' motherhood; and that, for his part, he saw nothing in her appearance inconsistent with rural influences. The child was her nephew, the son of a married sister, and she a sentimental maiden aunt. Obviously the volume she had in her hand was Tennyson. In the absence on both sides of authentic data, of course the debate was not prolonged; and the subject of it had passed from our memories some time before we again met her on the beach. She soon became aware of our presence, however; and, with a natural sense of intrusion, we immediately resumed our walk. The last that I saw of her, as we rounded a turn in the cliff which concealed the backward prospect, was a sudden grasp of the child's arm, as if to withdraw him from the reach of a hastily advancing wave.

Half an hour's further walk led us to a point which we were not tempted to exceed. We shot between us some half a dozen birds; but as our dog, whose talents had been sadly misrepresented, proved very shy of the deep water, and succeeded in bringing no more than a couple of our victims to shore, we resolved to abstain from further destruction, and to return home quietly along the beach, upon which we had now descended.

"If we meet our young lady," said Bingham, "we can gallantly offer her our booty."

Some five minutes after he had uttered these words, a couple of great sea-gulls came flying landward over our heads, and, after a long gyration in mid-air, boldly settled themselves on the slope of the cliff at some three hundred yards in front of us, a point at which it projected almost into the waves. After a momentary halt, one of them rose again on his long pinions and soared away seaward; the other remained. He sat perched on a jutting boulder some fifteen feet high, sunning his fishy breast.

"I wonder if I could put a shot into him," said Bingham.

72

"Try," I answered; and, as he rapidly charged and levelled his piece, I remember idly repeating, while I looked at the great bird,

> "God save thee, ancient mariner,
> From the fiends that plague thee thus!
> Why look'st thou so? 'With my cross-bow
> I shot the albatross.' "

"He's going to rise," I added.

But Bingham had fired. The creature rose, indeed, half sluggishly, and yet with too hideous celerity. His movement drew from us a cry which was almost simultaneous with the report of Bingham's gun. I cannot express our relation to what followed it better than by saying that it exposed to our sight, beyond the space suddenly left vacant, the happy figure of the child from whom we had parted but an hour before. He stood with his little hands extended, and his face raised toward the retreating bird. Of the sickening sensation which assailed our common vision as we saw him throw back his hands to his head, and reel downwards out of sight, I can give no verbal account, nor of the rapidity with which we crossed the smooth interval of sand, and rounded the bluff.

The child's companion had scrambled up the rocky bank towards the low ledge from which he had fallen, and to which access was of course all too easy. She had sunk down upon the stones, and was wildly clasping the boy's body. I turned from this spectacle to my friend, as to an image of equal woe. Bingham, pale as death, bounded over the stones, and fell on his knees. The woman let him take the child out of her arms, and bent over, with her forehead on a rock, moaning. I have never seen helplessness so vividly embodied as in this momentary group.

"Did it strike his head?" cried Bingham. "What the devil was he doing up there?"

"I told him he'd get hurt," said the young woman, with harrowing simplicity. "To shoot straight at him!—He's killed!"

"Great heavens! Do you mean to say that I saw him?" roared Bingham. "How did I know he was there? Did you see us?"

The young woman shook her head. "Of course I didn't see you. I saw you with your guns before. Oh, he's killed!"

"He's not killed. It was mere duck shot. Don't talk such stuff.—

My own poor little man!" cried George. "Charles, where *were* our eyes?"

"He wanted to catch the bird," moaned our companion. "Baby, my boy! open your eyes. Speak to your mother. For God's sake, get some help!"

She had put out her hands to take the child from Bingham, who had half angrily lifted him out of her reach. The senseless movement with which, as she disengaged him from Bingham's grasp, he sank into her arms, was clearly the senselessness of death. She burst into sobs. I went and examined the child.

"He *may* not be killed," I said, turning to Bingham; "keep your senses. It's not your fault. We *couldn't* see each other."

Bingham rose stupidly to his feet.

"She must be got home," I said.

"We must get a carriage. Will you go or stay?"

I saw that he had seen the truth. He looked about him with an expression of miserable impotence. "Poor little devil!" he said, hoarsely.

"Will you go for a carriage?" I repeated, taking his hand, "or will you stay?"

Our companion's sobs redoubled their violence.

"I'll stay," said he. "Bring some woman."

I started at a hard run. I left the beach behind me, passed the white cottage at whose garden gate two women were gossiping, and reached the hotel stable, where I had the good fortune to find a vehicle at my disposal. I drove straight back to the white cottage. One of the women had disappeared, and the other was lingering among her flowers,—a middle-aged, keen-eyed person. As I descended and hastily addressed her, I read in her rapid glance an anticipation of evil tidings.

"The young woman who stays with you—" I began.

"Yes," she said, "my second-cousin. Well?"

"She's in trouble. She wants you to come to her. Her little boy has hurt himself." I had time to see that I need fear no hysterics.

"Where did you leave her?" asked my companion.

"On the beach."

"What's the matter with the child?"

"He fell from a rock. There's no time to be lost." There was a certain antique rigidity about the woman which was at once irritating and reassuring. I was impelled both to quicken her apprehensions

74

and to confide in her self-control. "For all I know, ma'am," said I, "the child is killed."

She gave me an angry stare. "For all you know!" she exclaimed. "Where were your wits? Were you afraid to look at him?"

"Yes, half afraid."

She glanced over the paling at my vehicle. "Am I to get into that?" she asked.

"If you will be so good."

She turned short about, and re-entered the house, where, as I stood out among the dahlias and the pinks, I heard a rapid opening and shutting of drawers. She shortly reappeared, equipped for driving; and, having locked the house door, and pocketed the key, came and faced me, where I stood ready to help her into the wagon.

"We'll stop for the doctor," she began.

"The doctor," said I, "is of no use."

A few moments of hard driving brought us to my starting-point. The tide had fallen perceptibly in my absence; and I remember receiving a strange impression of the irretrievable nature of the recent event from the sight of poor Bingham, standing down at the low-water-mark, and looking seaward with his hands in his pockets. The mother of his little victim still sat on the heap of stones where she had fallen, pressing her child to her breast. I helped my companion to descend, which she did with great deliberation. It is my belief that, as we drove along the beach, she derived from the expression of Bingham's figure, and from the patient aversion of his face, a suspicion of his relation to the opposite group. It was not till the elder woman had come within a few steps of her, that the younger became aware of her approach. I merely had time to catch the agonized appeal of her upward glance, and the broad compassion of the other's stooping movement, before I turned my back upon their encounter, and walked down towards my friend. The monotonous murmur of the waves had covered the sound of our wagonwheels, and Bingham stood all unconscious of the coming of relief,—distilling I know not what divine relief from the simple beauty of sea and sky. I had laid my hand on his shoulder before he turned about. He looked towards the base of the cliff. I knew that a great effusion of feeling would occur in its natural order; but how should I help him across the interval?

"That's her cousin," I said at random. "She seems a very capable woman."

"The child is quite dead," said Bingham, for all answer. I was struck by the plainness of his statement. In the comparative freedom of my own thoughts I had failed to make allowance for the embarrassed movement of my friend's. It was not, therefore, until afterwards that I acknowledged he had thought to better purpose than I; inasmuch as the very simplicity of his tone implied a positive acceptance (for the moment) of the dreadful fact which he uttered.

"The sooner they get home, the better," I said. It was evident that the elder of our companions had already embraced this conviction. She had lifted the child and placed him in the carriage, and she was now turning towards his mother and inviting her to ascend. Even at the distance at which I stood, the mingled firmness and tenderness of her gestures were clearly apparent. They seemed, moreover, to express a certain indifference to our movements, an independence of our further interference, which—fanciful as the assertion may look—was not untinged with irony. It was plain that, by whatever rapid process she had obtained it, she was already in possession of our story. "Thank God for strongminded women!" I exclaimed;—and yet I could not repress a feeling that it behooved me, on behalf of my friend, to treat as an equal with the vulgar movement of antipathy which he was destined to encounter, and of which, in the irresistible sequence of events, the attitude of this good woman was an index.

We walked towards the carriage together. "I shall not come home directly," said Bingham; "but don't be alarmed about me."

I looked at my watch. "I give you two hours," I said, with all the authority of my affection.

The new-comer had placed herself on the back seat of the vehicle beside the sufferer, who on entering had again possessed herself of her child. As I went about to mount in front, Bingham came and stood by the wheel. I read his purpose in his face,—the desire to obtain from the woman he had wronged some recognition of his *human* character, some confession that she dimly distinguished him from a wild beast or a thunderbolt. One of her hands lay exposed, pressing together on her knee the lifeless little hands of her boy. Bingham removed his hat, and placed his right hand on that of the young woman. I saw

76

that she started at his touch, and that he vehemently tightened his grasp.

"It's too soon to talk of forgiveness," said he, "for it's too soon for me to think intelligently of the wrong I have done you. God has brought us together in a very strange fashion."

The young woman raised her bowed head, and gave my friend, if not just the look he coveted, at least the most liberal glance at her command,—a look which, I fancy, helped him to face the immediate future. But these are matters too delicate to be put into words.

I spent the hours that elapsed before Bingham's return to the inn in gathering information about the occupants of the cottage. Impelled by that lively intuition of calamity which is natural to women, the housekeeper of the hotel, a person of evident kindliness and discretion, lost no time in winning my confidence. I was not unwilling that the tragic incident which had thus arrested our idleness should derive its earliest publicity from my own lips; and I was forcibly struck with the exquisite impartiality with which this homely creature bestowed her pity. Miss Horner, I learned, the mistress of the cottage, was the last representative of a most respectable family, native to the neighboring town. It had been for some years her practice to let lodgings during the summer. At the close of the present season she had invited her kinswoman, Mrs. Hicks, to spend the autumn with her. That this lady was the widow of a Baptist minister; that her husband had died some three years before; that she was very poor; that her child had been sickly, and that the care of his health had so impeded her exertions for a livelihood, that she had been intending to leave him with Miss Horner for the winter, and obtain a "situation" in town;—these facts were the salient points of the housekeeper's somewhat prolix recital.

The early autumn dusk had fallen when Bingham returned. He looked very tired. He had been walking for several hours, and, as I fancied, had grown in some degree familiar with his new responsibilities. He was very hungry, and made a vigorous attack upon his supper. I had been indisposed to eat, but the sight of his healthy appetite restored my own. I had grown weary of my thoughts, and I found something salutary in the apparent simplicity and rectitude of Bingham's state of mind.

"I find myself taking it very quietly," he said, in the course of his

77

repast. "There is something so absolute in the nature of the calamity, that one is compelled to accept it. I don't see how I could endure to have mutilated the poor little mortal. To kill a human being is, after all, the least injury you can do him." He spoke these words deliberately, with his eyes on mine, and with an expression of perfect candor. But as he paused, and in spite of my perfect assent to their meaning, I could not help mentally reverting to the really tragic phase of the affair; and I suppose my features revealed to Bingham's scrutiny the process of my thoughts. His pale face flushed a burning crimson, his lips trembled. "Yes, my boy!" he cried; "that's where it's damnable." He buried his head in his hands, and burst into tears.

We had a long talk. At the end of it, we lit our cigars, and came out upon the deserted piazza. There was a lovely starlight, and, after a few turns in silence, Bingham left my side and strolled off towards a bend in the road, in the direction of the sea. I saw him stand motionless for a long time, and then I heard him call me. When I reached his side, I saw that he had been watching a light in the window of the white cottage. We heard the village bell in the distance striking nine.

"Charles," said Bingham, "suppose you go down there and make some offer of your services. God knows whom the poor creatures have to look to. She has had a couple of men thrust into her life. She must take the good with the bad."

I lingered a moment. "It's a difficult task," I said. "What shall I say?"

Bingham silently puffed his cigar. He stood with his arms folded, and his head thrown back, slowly measuring the starry sky. "I wish she could come out here and look at that sky," he said at last. "It's a sight for bereaved mothers. Somehow, my dear boy," he pursued, "I never felt less depressed in my life. It's none of my doing."

"It would hardly do for me to tell her that," said I.

"I don't know," said Bingham. "This isn't an occasion for the exchange of compliments. I'll tell you what you may tell her. I suppose they will have some funeral services within a day or two. Tell her that I should like very much to be present."

I set off for the cottage. Its mistress in person introduced me into the little parlor.

"Well, sir?" she said, in hard, dry accents.

78

"I've come," I answered, "to ask whether I can be of any assistance to Mrs. Hicks."

Miss Horner shook her head in a manner which deprived her negation of half its dignity. "What assistance is possible?" she asked.

"A man," said I, "may relieve a woman of certain cares—"

"O, men are a blessed set! You had better leave Mrs. Hicks to me."

"But will you at least tell me how she is,—if she has in any degree recovered herself?"

At this moment the door of the adjoining room was opened, and Mrs. Hicks stood on the threshold, bearing a lamp,—a graceful and pathetic figure. I now had occasion to observe that she was a woman of decided beauty. Her fair hair was drawn back into a single knot behind her head, and the lamplight deepened the pallor of her face and the darkness of her eyes. She wore a calico dressing-gown and a shawl.

"What do you wish?" she asked, in a voice clarified, if I may so express it, by long weeping.

"He wants to know whether he can be of any assistance," said the elder lady.

Mrs. Hicks glanced over her shoulder into the room she had left. "Would you like to look at the child?" she asked, in a whisper.

"Lucy!" cried Miss Horner.

I walked straight over to Mrs. Hicks, who turned and led the way to a little bed. My conductress raised her lamp aloft, and let the light fall gently on the little white-draped figure. Even the bandage about the child's head had not dispelled his short-lived prettiness. Heaven knows that to remain silent was easy enough; but Heaven knows, too, that to break the silence—and to break it as I broke it—was equally easy. "He must have been a very pretty child," I said.

"Yes, he was very pretty. He had black eyes. I don't know whether you noticed."

"No, I didn't notice," said I. "When is he to be buried?"

"The day after to-morrow. I am told that I shall be able to avoid an inquest."

"Mr. Bingham has attended to that," I said. And then I paused, revolving his petition.

But Mrs. Hicks anticipated it. "If you would like to be present at the funeral," she said, "you are welcome to come.—And so is your friend."

"Mr. Bingham bade me ask leave. There is a great deal that I should like to say to you for him," I added, "but I won't spoil it by trying. It's his own business."

The young woman looked at me with her deep, dark eyes. "I pity him from my heart," she said, pressing her hands to her breast. "I had rather have my sorrow than his."

"They are pretty much one sorrow," I answered. "I don't see that you can divide it. You are two to bear it. Bingham is a wise, good fellow," I went on. "I have shared a great many joys with him. In Heaven's name," I cried, "don't bear hard on him!"

"How can I bear hard?" she asked, opening her arms and letting them drop. The movement was so deeply expressive of weakness and loneliness, that, feeling all power to reply stifled in a rush of compassion, I silently made my exit.

On the following day, Bingham and I went up to town, and on the third day returned in time for the funeral. Besides the two ladies, there was no one present but ourselves and the village minister, who of course spoke as briefly as decency allowed. He had accompanied the ladies in a carriage to the graveyard, while Bingham and I had come on foot. As we turned away from the grave, I saw my friend approach Mrs. Hicks. They stood talking beside the freshly-turned earth, while the minister and I attended Miss Horner to the carriage. After she had seated herself, I lingered at the door, exchanging sober commonplaces with the reverend gentleman. At last Mrs. Hicks followed us, leaning on Bingham's arm.

"Margaret," she said, "Mr. Bingham and I are going to stay here awhile. Mr. Bingham will walk home with me. I'm *very* much obliged to you, Mr. Bland," she added, turning to the minister and extending her hand.

I bestowed upon my friend a glance which I felt to be half interrogative and half sympathetic. He gave me his hand, and answered the benediction by its pressure, while he answered the inquiry by his words. "If you are still disposed to go back to town this afternoon," he said, "you had better not wait for me. I may not have time to catch the boat."

I of course made no scruple of returning immediately to the city.

Some ten days elapsed before I again saw Bingham; but I found my attention so deeply engrossed with work, that I scarcely measured the interval. At last, one morning, he came into my office.

"I take for granted," I said, "that you have not been all this time at B——."

"No; I've been on my travels. I came to town the day after you came. I found at my rooms a letter from a lawyer in Baltimore, proposing the sale of some of my property there, and I seized upon it as an excuse for making a journey to that city. I felt the need of movement, of action of some kind. But when I reached Baltimore, I didn't even go to see my correspondent. I pushed on to Washington, walked about for thirty-six hours, and came home."

He had placed his arm on my desk, and stood supporting his head on his hand, with a look of great physical exhaustion.

"You look very tired," said I.

"I haven't slept," said he. "I had such a talk with that woman!"

"I'm sorry that you should have felt the worse for it."

"I feel both the worse and the better. She talked about the child."

"It's well for her," said I, "that she was able to do it."

"She wasn't able, strictly speaking. She began calmly enough, but she very soon broke down."

"Did you see her again?"

"I called upon her the next day, to tell her that I was going to town, and to ask if I could be useful to her. But she seems to stand in perfect isolation. She assured me that she was in want of nothing."

"What sort of a woman does she seem to be, taking her in herself?"

"Bless your soul! I can't take her in herself!" cried Bingham, with some vehemence. "And yet, stay," he added; "she's a very pleasing woman."

"She's very pretty."

"Yes; she's very pretty. In years, she's little more than a young girl. In her ideas, she's one of 'the people'."

"It seems to me," said I, "that the frankness of her conduct toward you is very much to her credit."

"It doesn't offend you, then?"

"Offend me? It gratifies me beyond measure."

"I think that, if you had seen her as I have seen her, it would interest you deeply. I'm at a loss to determine whether it's the result of great

81

simplicity or great sagacity. Of course, it's absurd to suppose that, ten days ago, it could have been the result of anything but a beautiful impulse. I think that to-morrow I shall again go down to B——."

I allowed Bingham time to have made his visit and to have brought me an account of his further impressions; but as three days went by without his reappearance, I called at his lodgings. He was still out of town. The fifth day, however, brought him again to my office.

"I've been at B—— constantly," he said, "and I've had several interviews with our friend."

"Well; how fares it?"

"It fares well. I'm forcibly struck with her good sense. In matters of mind—in matters of soul, I may say—she has the touch of an angel, or rather the touch of a woman. That's quite sufficient."

"Does she keep her composure?"

"Perfectly. You can imagine nothing simpler and less sentimental than her manner. She makes me forget myself most divinely. The child's death colors our talk; but it doesn't confine or obstruct it. You see she has her religion: she can afford to be natural."

Weary as my friend looked, and shaken by his sudden subjection to care, it yet seemed to me, as he pronounced these words, that his eye had borrowed a purer light and his voice a fresher tone. In short, where I discerned it, how I detected it, I know not; but I felt that he carried a secret. He sat poking with his walking-stick at a nail in the carpet, with his eyes dropped. I saw about his mouth the faint promise of a distant smile,—a smile which six months would bring to maturity.

"George," said I, "I have a fancy."

He looked up. "What is it?"

"You've lost your heart."

He stared a moment, with a sudden frown. "To whom?" he asked. "To Mrs. Hicks."

With a frown, I say, but a frown that was as a smile to the effect of my rejoinder. He rose to his feet; all his color deserted his face and rushed to his eyes.

"I beg your pardon if I'm wrong," I said.

Bingham had turned again from pale to crimson. "Don't beg *my* pardon," he cried. "You may say what you please. Beg *hers!*" he added, bitterly.

I resented the charge of injustice. "I've done *her* no wrong!" I

82

answered. "I haven't said," I went on with a certain gleeful sense that I was dealing with massive truths,—"I haven't said that she had lost her heart to you!"

"Good God, Charles!" cried Bingham, "what a horrid imagination you have!"

"I am not responsible for my imagination."

"Upon my soul, I hope *I'm* not!" cried Bingham, passionately. "I have enough without that."

"George," I said, after a moment's reflection, "if I thought I had insulted you, I would make amends. But I have said nothing to be ashamed of. I believe that I have hit the truth. Your emotion proves it. I spoke hastily; but you must admit that, having caught a glimpse of the truth, I couldn't stand indifferent to it."

"The truth! the truth! What truth?"

"Aren't you in love with Mrs. Hicks? Admit it like a man."

"Like a man! Like a brute. Haven't I done the woman wrong enough?"

"Quite enough, I hope."

"Haven't I turned her simple joys to bitterness?"

"I grant it."

"And now you want me to insult her by telling her that I love her?"

"I want you to tell her nothing. What you tell her is your own affair. Remember that, George. It's as little mine as it is the rest of the world's."

Bingham stood listening, with a contracted brow and his hand grasping his stick. He walked to the dusty office-window and halted a moment, watching the great human throng in the street. Then he turned and came towards me. Suddenly he stopped short. "God forgive me!" he cried; "I believe I do love her."

The fountains of my soul were stirred. "Combining my own hasty impressions of Mrs. Hicks with yours, George," I said, "the consummation seems to me exquisitely natural."

It was in these simple words that we celebrated the sacred fact. It seemed as if, by tacit agreement, the evolution of this fact was result enough for a single interview.

A few days after this interview, in the evening, I called at Bingham's lodgings. His servant informed me that my friend was out of town, although he was unable to indicate his whereabouts. But as I turned away from the door a hack drew up, and the object of my quest descended, equipped with a travelling-bag. I went down and greeted him under the gas-lamp.

"Shall I go in with you?" I asked; "or shall I go my way?"

"You had better come in," said Bingham. "I have something to say.—I have been down to B——," he resumed, when the servant had left us alone in his sitting-room. His tone bore the least possible tinge of a confession; but of course it was not as a confessor that I listened.

"Well," said I, "how is our friend?"

"Our friend—" answered Bingham. "Will you have a cigar?"

"No, I thank you."

"Our friend— Ah, Charles, it's a long story."

"I sha'n't mind that, if it's an interesting one."

"To a certain extent it's a painful one. It's painful to come into collision with incurable vulgarity of feeling."

I was puzzled. "Has that been your fortune?" I asked.

"It has been my fortune to bring Mrs. Hicks into a great deal of trouble. The case, in three words, is this. Miss Horner has seen fit to resent, in no moderate terms, what she calls the 'extraordinary intimacy' existing between Mrs. Hicks and myself. Mrs. Hicks, as was perfectly natural, has resented her cousin's pretension to regulate her conduct. Her expression of this feeling has led to her expulsion from Miss Horner's house."

"Has she any other friend to turn to?"

"No one, except some relatives of her husband, who are very poor people, and of whom she wishes to ask no favors."

"Where has she placed herself?"

"She is in town. We came up together this afternoon. I went with her to some lodgings which she had formerly occupied, and which were fortunately vacant."

"I suppose it's not to be regretted that she has left B——. She breaks with sad associations."

"Yes; but she renews them too, on coming to town."

"How so?"

"Why, damn it," said Bingham, with a tremor in his voice, "the woman is utterly poor."

"Has she no resources whatever?"

"A hundred dollars a year, I believe,—worse than nothing."

84

"Has she any marketable talents or accomplishments?"

"I believe she is up to some pitiful needle-work or other. Such a woman! O horrible world!"

"Does *she* say so?" I asked.

"She? No indeed. She thinks it's all for the best. I suppose it is. But it seems but a bad best."

"I wonder," said I, after a pause, "whether I might see Mrs. Hicks. Do you think she would receive me?"

Bingham looked at me an instant keenly. "I suppose so," said he. "You can try."

"I shall go, not out of curiosity," I resumed, "but out of—"

"Out of what?"

"Well, in fine, I should like to see her again."

Bingham gave me Mrs. Hicks's address, and in the course of a few evenings I called upon her. I had abstained from bestowing a fine name upon the impulse which dictated this act; but I am nevertheless free to declare that kindliness and courtesy had a large part in it. Mrs. Hicks had taken up her residence in a plain, small house, in a decent by-street, where, upon presenting myself, I was ushered into a homely sitting-room (apparently her own), and left to await her coming. Her greeting was simple and cordial, and not untinged with a certain implication of gratitude. She had taken for granted, on my part, all possible sympathy and good-will; but as she had regarded me besides as a man of many cares, she had thought it improbable that we should meet again. It was no long time before I became conscious of that generous charm which Bingham had rigorously denominated her good-sense. Good-sense assuredly was there, but good-sense mated and prolific. Never had I seen, it seemed to me, as the moments elapsed, so exquisitely modest a use of such charming faculties,—an intelligence so sensible of its obligations and so indifferent to its privileges. It was obvious that she had been a woman of plain associations: her allusions were to homely facts, and her manner direct and unstudied; and yet, in spite of these limitations, it was equally obvious that she was a person to be neither patronized, dazzled, nor deluded. O the satisfaction which, in the course of that quiet dialogue, I took in this sweet infallibility! How it effaced her loneliness and poverty, and added dignity to her youth and beauty! It made her, potentially at least, a woman of the world. It was an anticipation of the self-possession, the wisdom, and perhaps even in some degree of the wit, which comes through the experience of society,—the result, on Mrs. Hicks's part, of I know not what hours of suffering, despondency, and self-dependence. With whatever intentions, therefore, I might have come before her, I should have found it impossible to address her as any other than an equal, and to regard her affliction as anything less than an absolute mystery. In fact, we hardly touched upon it; and it was only covertly that we alluded to Bingham's melancholy position. I will not deny that in a certain sense I regretted Mrs. Hicks's reserve. It is true that I had a very informal claim upon her confidence; but I had gone to her with a half-defined hope that this claim would be liberally interpreted. It was not even recognized; my vague intentions of counsel and assistance had lain undivined; and I departed with the impression that my social horizon had been considerably enlarged, but that my charity had by no means secured a pensioner.

Mrs. Hicks had given me permission to repeat my visit, and after the lapse of a fortnight I determined to do so. I had seen Bingham several times in the interval. He was of course much interested in my impressions of our friend; and I fancied that my admiration gave him even more pleasure than he allowed himself to express. On entering Mrs. Hicks's parlor a second time, I found him in person standing before the fireplace, and talking apparently with some vehemence to Mrs. Hicks, who sat listening on the sofa. Bingham turned impatiently to the door as I crossed the threshold, and Mrs. Hicks rose to welcome me with all due composure. I was nevertheless sensible that my entrance was ill-timed; yet a retreat was impossible. Bingham kept his place on the hearth-rug, and mechanically gave me his hand,—standing irresolute, as I thought, between annoyance and elation. The fact that I had interrupted a somewhat passionate interview was somehow so obvious, that, at the prompting of a very delicate feeling, Mrs. Hicks hastened to anticipate my apologies.

"Mr. Bingham was giving me a lecture," she said; and there was perhaps in her accent a faint suspicion of bitterness. "He will doubtless be glad of another auditor."

"No," said Bingham, "Charles is a better talker than listener. You shall have two lectures instead of one." He uttered this sally without even an attempt to smile.

"What is your subject?" said I. "Until I know that, I shall promise neither to talk nor to listen."

Bingham laid his hand on my arm. "He represents the world," he said, addressing our hostess. "You're afraid of the world. There, make your appeal."

Mrs. Hicks stood silent a moment, with a contracted brow and a look of pain on her face. Then she turned to me with a half-smile. "I don't believe you represent the world," she said; "you are too good."

"She flatters you," said Bingham. "You wish to corrupt him, Mrs. Hicks."

Mrs. Hicks glanced for an instant from my friend to myself. There burned in her eyes a far-searching light, which consecrated the faint irony of the smile which played about her lips. "O you men!" she said,—"you are so wise, so deep!" It was on Bingham that her eyes rested last; but after a pause, extending her hand, she transferred them to me. "Mr. Bingham," she pursued, "seems to wish you to be admitted to our counsels. There is every reason why his friends should be my friends. You will be interested to know that he has asked me to be his wife."

"Have you given him an answer?" I asked.

"He was pressing me for an answer when you came in. He conceives me to have a great fear of the judgments of men, and he was saying very hard things about them. But they have very little, after all, to do with the matter. The world may heed it, that Mr. Bingham should marry Mrs. Hicks, but it will care very little whether or no Mrs. Hicks marries Mr. Bingham. You are the world, for me," she cried with beautiful inconsequence, turning to her suitor; "I know no other." She put out her hands, and he took them.

I am at a loss to express the condensed force of these rapid words,— the amount of passion, of reflection, of experience, which they seemed to embody. They were the simple utterance of a solemn and intelligent choice; and, as such, the whole phalanx of the Best Society assembled in judgment could not have done less than salute them. What honest George Bingham said, what I said, is of little account. The proper conclusion of my story lies in the highly dramatic fact that out of the depths of her bereavement—out of her loneliness and her pity—this richly gifted woman had emerged, responsive to the passion of him who had wronged her all but as deeply as he loved her. The reader will decide, I think, that this catastrophe offers as little occasion for smiles as for tears. My narrative is a piece of genuine prose.

It was not until six months had elapsed that Bingham's marriage took place. It has been a truly happy one. Mrs. Bingham is now, in the fulness of her bloom, with a single exception, the most charming woman I know. I have often assured her—once too often, possibly—that, thanks to that invaluable good-sense of hers, she is also the happiest. She has made a devoted wife; but—and in occasional moments of insight it has seemed to me that this portion of her fate is a delicate tribute to a fantastic principle of equity—she has never again become a mother. In saying that she has made a devoted wife, it may seem that I have written Bingham's own later history. Yet as the friend of his younger days, the comrade of his *belle jeunesse*, the partaker of his dreams, I would fain give him a sentence apart. What shall it be? He is a truly incorruptible soul; he is a confirmed philosopher; he has grown quite stout.

THE STORY OF A MASTERPIECE

The Story of a Masterpiece

In Two Parts

"The Story of a Masterpiece," Henry James's sixth published tale, appeared in two parts in the Galaxy, *January-February 1868, just before his twenty-fifth birthday. It is reprinted here for the first time. The January number carried a frontispiece illustration for the story by Gaston Fay—the artist at work with his model before him. It is the first of a goodly group of tales devoted to the problems of painters and painting and, as the Introduction here points out, foreshadows ideas and material developed in several later stories.*

*It was followed by "The Romance of Certain Old Clothes" (*Atlantic, *February 1868) and "A Most Extraordinary Case" (*Atlantic, *April 1868), reprinted respectively in* A Passionate Pilgrim *(1875) and in* Stories Revived, Vol. III *(1885); then by the fourth of the uncollected tales.*

· I ·

NO LONGER AGO THAN LAST SUMMER, DURING A SIX weeks' stay at Newport, John Lennox became engaged to Miss Marian Everett of New York. Mr. Lennox was a widower, of large estate, and without children. He was thirty-five years old, of a sufficiently distinguished appearance, of excellent manners, of an unusual share of sound information, of irreproachable habits and of a temper which was understood to have suffered a trying and salutary probation during the short term of his wedded life. Miss Everett was, therefore, all things considered, believed to be making a very good match and to be having by no means the worst of the bargain.

And yet Miss Everett, too, was a very marriageable young lady— the pretty Miss Everett, as she was called, to distinguish her from certain plain cousins, with whom, owing to her having no mother and no sisters, she was constrained, for decency's sake, to spend a great deal of her time—rather to her own satisfaction, it may be conjectured, than to that of these excellent young women.

Marian Everett was penniless, indeed; but she was richly endowed with all the gifts which make a woman charming. She was, without dispute, the most charming girl in the circle in which she lived and moved. Even certain of her elders, women of a larger experience, of a heavier calibre, as it were, and, thanks to their being married ladies, of greater freedom of action, were practically not so charming as she. And yet, in her emulation of the social graces of these, her more fully licensed sisters, Miss Everett was quite guiltless of any aberration from the strict line of maidenly dignity. She professed an almost religious devotion to good taste, and she looked with horror upon the boisterous graces of many of her companions. Beside being the most entertaining girl in New York, she was, therefore, also the most irreproachable. Her beauty was, perhaps, contestable, but it was certainly uncontested. She was the least bit below the middle height, and her person was marked by a great fulness and roundness of outline; and yet, in spite of this comely ponderosity, her movements were perfectly light and elastic. In complexion, she was a genuine blonde—a warm blonde; with a midsummer bloom upon her cheek, and the light of a midsummer sun wrought into her auburn hair. Her features were not cast upon a classical model, but their expression was in the highest degree pleasing. Her forehead was low and broad, her nose small, and her mouth—well, by the envious her mouth was called *enormous*. It is certain that it had an immense capacity for smiles, and that when she opened it to sing (which she did with infinite sweetness) it emitted a copious flood of sound. Her face was, perhaps, a trifle too circular, and her shoulders a trifle too high; but, as I say, the general effect left nothing to be desired. I might point out a dozen discords in the character of her face and figure, and yet utterly fail to invalidate the impression they produced. There is something essentially uncivil, and, indeed, unphilosophical, in the attempt to verify or to disprove a woman's beauty in detail, and a man gets no more than he deserves when he finds that, in strictness, the aggregation of the different features fails to make up the total. Stand off, gentlemen, and let *her* make the addition. Beside her beauty, Miss Everett shone by her good nature and her lively perceptions. She neither made harsh speeches nor resented them; and, on the other hand, she keenly enjoyed intellectual cleverness, and even cultivated it. Her great merit was that she made no claims or pretensions. Just as there was nothing artificial in her beauty, so there was nothing pedantic in her acuteness and nothing sentimental in her amiability. The one was all freshness and the others all *bonhomie*.

John Lennox saw her, then loved her and offered her his hand. In accepting it Miss Everett acquired, in the world's eye, the one advantage which she lacked—a complete stability and regularity of position. Her friends took no small satisfaction in contrasting her brilliant and comfortable future with her somewhat precarious past. Lennox, nevertheless, was congratulated on the right hand and on the left; but none too often for his faith. That of Miss Everett was not put to so severe a test, although she was frequently reminded by acquaintances of a moralizing turn that she had reason to be very thankful for Mr. Lennox's choice. To these assurances Marian listened with a look of patient humility, which was extremely becoming. It was as if for *his* sake she could consent even to be bored.

Within a fortnight after their engagement had been made known, both parties returned to New York. Lennox lived in a house of his own, which he now busied himself with repairing and refurnishing; for the wedding had been fixed for the end of October. Miss Everett lived in lodgings with her father, a decayed old gentleman, who rubbed his idle hands from morning till night over the prospect of his daughter's marriage.

John Lennox, habitually a man of numerous resources, fond of reading, fond of music, fond of society and not averse to politics, passed the first weeks of the Autumn in a restless, fidgety manner. When a man approaches middle age he finds it difficult to wear gracefully the distinction of being engaged. He finds it difficult to discharge with becoming alacrity the various *petits soins* incidental to the position. There was a certain pathetic gravity, to those who knew him well, in Lennox's attentions. One-third of his time he spent in foraging in

Broadway, whence he returned half-a-dozen times a week, laden with trinkets and gimcracks, which he always finished by thinking it puerile and brutal to offer his mistress. Another third he passed in Mr. Everett's drawing-room, during which period Marian was denied to visitors. The rest of the time he spent, as he told a friend, God knows how. This was stronger language than his friend expected to hear, for Lennox was neither a man of precipitate utterance, nor, in his friend's belief, of a strongly passionate nature. But it was evident that he was very much in love; or at least very much off his balance.

"When I'm with her it's all very well," he pursued, "but when I'm away from her I feel as if I were thrust out of the ranks of the living."

"Well, you must be patient," said his friend; "you're destined to live hard, yet."

Lennox was silent, and his face remained rather more sombre than the other liked to see it.

"I hope there's no particular difficulty," the latter resumed; hoping to induce him to relieve himself of whatever weighed upon his consciousness.

"I'm afraid sometimes I—afraid sometimes she doesn't really love me."

"Well, a little doubt does no harm. It's better than to be too sure of it, and to sink into fatuity. Only be sure you love her."

"Yes," said Lennox, solemnly, "that's the great point."

One morning, unable to fix his attention on books and papers, he bethought himself of an expedient for passing an hour.

He had made, at Newport, the acquaintance of a young artist named Gilbert, for whose talent and conversation he had conceived a strong relish. The painter, on leaving Newport, was to go to the Adirondacks, and to be back in New York on the first of October, after which time he begged his friend to come and see him.

It occurred to Lennox on the morning I speak of that Gilbert must already have returned to town, and would be looking for his visit. So he forthwith repaired to his studio.

Gilbert's card was on the door, but, on entering the room, Lennox found it occupied by a stranger—a young man in painter's garb, at work before a large panel. He learned from this gentleman that he was a temporary sharer of Mr. Gilbert's studio, and that the latter had stepped out for a few moments. Lennox accordingly prepared to

94

await his return. He entered into conversation with the young man, and, finding him very intelligent, as well as, apparently, a great friend of Gilbert, he looked at him with some interest. He was of something less than thirty, tall and robust, with a strong, joyous, sensitive face, and a thick auburn beard. Lennox was struck with his face, which seemed both to express a great deal of human sagacity and to indicate the essential temperament of a painter.

"A man with that face," he said to himself, "does work at least worth look'ng at."

He accordingly asked his companion if he might come and look at his picture. The latter readily assented, and Lennox placed himself before the canvas.

It bore a representation of a half-length female figure, in a costume and with an expression so ambiguous that Lennox remained uncertain whether it was a portrait or a work of fancy: a fair-haired young woman, clad in a rich mediæval dress, and looking like a countess of the Renaissance. Her figure was relieved against a sombre tapestry, her arms loosely folded, her head erect and her eyes on the spectator, toward whom she seemed to move—"*Dans un flot de velours traînant ses petits pieds.*"

As Lennox inspected her face it seemed to reveal a hidden likeness to a face he well knew—the face of Marian Everett. He was of course anxious to know whether the likeness was accidental or designed.

"I take this to be a portrait," he said to the artist, "a portrait 'in character'."

"No," said the latter, "it's a mere composition: a little from here and a little from there. The picture has been hanging about me for the last two or three years, as a sort of receptacle of waste ideas. It has been the victim of innumerable theories and experiments. But it seems to have survived them all. I suppose it possesses a certain amount of vitality."

"Do you call it anything?"

"I called it originally after something I'd read—Browning's poem, 'My Last Duchess'. Do you know it?"

"Perfectly."

"I am ignorant of whether it's an attempt to embody the poet's impression of a portrait actually existing. But why should I care? This is simply an attempt to embody my own private impression of the poem, which has always had a strong hold on my fancy. I don't know whether it agrees with your own impression and that of most readers. But I don't insist upon the name. The possessor of the picture is free to baptize it afresh."

The longer Lennox looked at the picture the more he liked it, and the deeper seemed to be the correspondence between the lady's expression and that with which he had invested the heroine of Browning's lines. The less accidental, too, seemed that element which Marian's face and the face on the canvas possessed in common. He thought of the great poet's noble lyric and of its exquisite significance, and of the physiognomy of the woman he loved having been chosen as the fittest exponent of that significance.

He turned away his head; his eyes filled with tears. "If I were possessor of the picture," he said, finally, answering the artist's last words, "I should feel tempted to call it by the name of a person of whom it very much reminds me."

"Ah?" said Baxter; and then, after a pause—"a person in New York?"

It had happened, a week before, that, at her lover's request, Miss Everett had gone in his company to a photographer's and had been photographed in a dozen different attitudes. The proofs of these photographs had been sent home for Marian to choose from. She had made a choice of half a dozen—or rather Lennox had made it —and the latter had put them in his pocket, with the intention of stopping at the establishment and giving his orders. He now took out of his pocket-book and showed the painter one of the cards.

"I find a great resemblance," said he, "between your Duchess and that young lady."

The artist looked at the photograph. "If I am not mistaken," he said, after a pause, "the young lady is Miss Everett."

Lennox nodded assent.

His companion remained silent a few moments, examining the photograph with considerable interest; but, as Lennox observed, without comparing it with his picture.

"My Duchess very probably bears a certain resemblance to Miss Everett, but a not exactly intentional one," he said, at last. "The picture was begun before I ever saw Miss Everett. Miss Everett, as you see—or as you know—has a very charming face, and, during

96

the few weeks in which I saw her, I continued to work upon it. You know how a painter works—how artists of all kinds work: they claim their property wherever they find it. What I found to my purpose in Miss Everett's appearance I didn't hesitate to adopt; especially as I had been feeling about in the dark for a type of countenance which her face effectually realized. The Duchess was an Italian, I take it; and I had made up my mind that she was to be a blonde. Now, there is a decidedly southern depth and warmth of tone in Miss Everett's complexion, as well as that breadth and thickness of feature which is common in Italian women. You see the resemblance is much more a matter of type than of expression. Nevertheless, I'm sorry if the copy betrays the original."

"I doubt," said Lennox, "whether it would betray it to any other perception than mine. I have the honor," he added, after a pause, "to be engaged to Miss Everett. You will, therefore, excuse me if I ask whether you mean to sell your picture?"

"It's already sold—to a lady," rejoined the artist, with a smile; "a maiden lady, who is a great admirer of Browning."

At this moment Gilbert returned. The two friends exchanged greetings, and their companion withdrew to a neighboring studio. After they had talked a while of what had happened to each since they parted, Lennox spoke of the painter of the Duchess and of his remarkable talent, expressing surprise that he shouldn't have heard of him before, and that Gilbert should never have spoken of him.

"His name is Baxter—Stephen Baxter," said Gilbert, "and until his return from Europe, a fortnight ago, I knew little more about him than you. He's a case of improvement. I met him in Paris in '62; at that time he was doing absolutely nothing. He has learned what you see in the interval. On arriving in New York he found it impossible to get a studio big enough to hold him. As, with my little sketches, I need only occupy one corner of mine, I offered him the use of the other three, until he should be able to bestow himself to his satisfaction. When he began to unpack his canvases I found I had been entertaining an angel unawares."

Gilbert then proceeded to uncover, for Lennox's inspection, several of Baxter's portraits, both of men and women. Each of these works confirmed Lennox's impression of the painter's power. He returned to the picture on the easel. Marian Everett reappeared at his silent call, and looked out of the eyes with a most penetrating tenderness and melancholy.

"He may say what he pleases," thought Lennox, "the resemblance *is,* in some degree, also a matter of expresion. Gilbert," he added, wishing to measure the force of the likeness, "whom does it remind you of?"

"I know," said Gilbert, "of whom it reminds *you.*"

"And do you see it yourself?"

"They are both handsome, and both have auburn hair. That's all I can see."

Lennox was somewhat relieved. It was not without a feeling of discomfort—a feeling by no means inconsistent with his first moment of pride and satisfaction—that he thought of Marian's peculiar and individual charms having been subjected to the keen appreciation of another than himself. He was glad to be able to conclude that the painter had merely been struck with what was most superficial in her appearance, and that his own imagination supplied the rest. It occurred to him, as he walked home, that it would be a not unbecoming tribute to the young girl's loveliness on his own part, to cause her portrait to be painted by this clever young man. Their engagement had as yet been an affair of pure sentiment, and he had taken an almost fastidious care not to give himself the vulgar appearance of a mere purveyor of luxuries and pleasures. Practically, he had been as yet for his future wife a poor man—or rather a man, pure and simple, and not a millionaire. He had ridden with her, he had sent her flowers, and he had gone with her to the opera. But he had neither sent her sugar-plums, nor made bets with her, nor made her presents of jewelry. Miss Everett's female friends had remarked that he hadn't as yet given her the least little betrothal ring, either of pearls or of diamonds. Marian, however, was quite content. She was, by nature, a great artist in the *mise en scène* of emotions, and she felt instinctively that this classical moderation was but the converse presentment of an immense matrimonial abundance. In his attempt to make it impossible that his relations with Miss Everett should be tinged in any degree with the accidental condition of the fortunes of either party, Lennox had thoroughly understood his own instinct. He knew that he should some day feel a strong and irresistible impulse to offer his mistress some visible and artistic token of his affection, and that his gift would convey a greater satisfaction from being sole of its kind. It seemed to him now that his chance had come. What gift could be more delicate than the gift of an opportunity to contribute by her patience and good-will to her husband's possession of a perfect likeness of her face?

On that same evening Lennox dined with his future father-in-law, as it was his habit to do once a week.

"Marian," he said, in the course of the dinner, "I saw, this morning, an old friend of yours."

"Ah," said Marian, "who was that?"

"Mr. Baxter, the painter."

Marian changed color—ever so little; no more, indeed, than was natural to an honest surprise.

Her surprise, however, could not have been great, inasmuch as she now said that she had seen his return to America mentioned in a newspaper, and as she knew that Lennox frequented the society of artists. "He was well, I hope," she added, "and prosperous."

"Where did you know this gentleman, my dear?" asked Mr. Everett.

"I knew him in Europe two years ago—first in the Summer in Switzerland, and afterward in Paris. He is a sort of cousin of Mrs. Denbigh." Mrs. Denbigh was a lady in whose company Marian had recently spent a year in Europe—a widow, rich, childless, an invalid, and an old friend of her mother. "Is he always painting?"

"Apparently, and extremely well. He has two or three as good portraits there as one may reasonably expect to see. And he has, moreover, a certain picture which reminded me of you."

"His 'Last Duchess'?" asked Marian with some curiosity. "I should like to see it. If you think it's like me, John, you ought to buy it up."

"I wanted to buy it, but it's sold. You know it then?"

"Yes, through Mr. Baxter himself. I saw it in its rudimentary state, when it looked like nothing that I should care to look like. I shocked Mrs. Denbigh very much by telling him I was glad it was his 'last.' The picture, indeed, led to our acquaintance."

"And not *vice versa*," said Mr. Everett, facetiously.

"How *vice versa?*" asked Marian, innocently. "I met Mr. Baxter for the first time at a party in Rome."

"I thought you said you met him in Switzerland," said Lennox.

"No, in Rome. It was only two days before we left. He was introduced to me without knowing I was with Mrs. Denbigh, and indeed without knowing that she had been in the city. He was very shy of

Americans. The first thing he said to me was that I looked very much like a picture he had been painting."

"That you realized his ideal, etc."

"Exactly, but not at all in that sentimental tone. I took him to Mrs. Denbigh; they found they were sixth cousins by marriage; he came to see us the next day, and insisted upon our going to his studio. It was a miserable place. I believe he was very poor. At least Mrs. Denbigh offered him some money, and he frankly accepted it. She attempted to spare his sensibilities by telling him that, if he liked, he could paint her a picture in return. He said he would if he had time. Later, he came up into Switzerland, and the following Winter we met him in Paris."

If Lennox had had any mistrust of Miss Everett's relations with the painter, the manner in which she told her little story would have effectually blighted it. He forthwith proposed that, in consideration not only of the young man's great talent, but of his actual knowledge of her face, he should be invited to paint her portrait.

Marian assented without reluctance and without alacrity, and Lennox laid his proposition before the artist. The latter requested a day or two to consider, and then replied (by note) that he would be happy to undertake the task.

Miss Everett expected that, in view of the projected renewal of their old acquaintance, Stephen Baxter would call upon her, under the auspices of her lover. He called in effect, alone, but Marian was not at home, and he failed to repeat the visit. The day for the first sitting was therefore appointed through Lennox. The artist had not as yet obtained a studio of his own, and the latter cordially offered him the momentary use of a spacious and well-lighted apartment in his house, which had been intended as a billiard room, but was not yet fitted up. Lennox expressed no wishes with regard to the portrait, being content to leave the choice of position and costume to the parties immediately interested. He found the painter perfectly well acquainted with Marian's "points," and he had an implicit confidence in her own good taste.

Miss Everett arrived on the morning appointed, under her father's escort, Mr. Everett, who prided himself largely upon doing things in proper form, having caused himself to be introduced beforehand to the painter. Between the latter and Marian there was a brief exchange of civilities, after which they addressed themselves to business. Miss Everett professed the most cheerful deference to Baxter's wishes and fancies, at the same time that she made no secret of possessing a number of strong convictions as to what should be attempted and what should be avoided.

It was no surprise to the young man to find her convictions sound and her wishes thoroughly sympathetic. He found himself called upon to make no compromise with stubborn and unnatural prejudices, nor to sacrifice his best intentions to a short-sighted vanity.

Whether Miss Everett was vain or not need not here be declared. She had at least the wit to perceive that the interests of an enlightened sagacity would best be served by a painting which should be good from the painter's point of view, inasmuch as these are the painting's chief end. I may add, moreover, to her very great credit, that she thoroughly understood how great an artistic merit should properly attach to a picture executed at the behest of a passion, in order that it should be anything more than a mockery—a parody—of the duration of that passion; and that she knew instinctively that there is nothing so chilling to an artist's heat as the interference of illogical self-interest, either on his own behalf or that of another.

Baxter worked firmly and rapidly, and at the end of a couple of hours he felt that he had begun his picture. Mr. Everett, as he sat by, threatened to be a bore; laboring apparently under the impression that it was his duty to beguile the session with cheap aesthetic small talk. But Marian good-humoredly took the painter's share of the dialogue, and he was not diverted from his work.

The next sitting was fixed for the morrow. Marian wore the dress which she had agreed upon with the painter, and in which, as in her position, the "picturesque" element had been religiously suppressed. She read in Baxter's eyes that she looked supremely beautiful, and she saw that his fingers tingled to attack his subject. But she caused Lennox to be sent for, under the pretense of obtaining his adhesion to her dress. It was black, and he might object to black. He came, and she read in his kindly eyes an augmented edition of the assurance conveyed in Baxter's. He was enthusiastic for the black dress, which, in truth, seemed only to confirm and enrich, like a grave maternal protest, the young girl's look of undiminished youth.

"I expect you," he said to Baxter, "to make a masterpiece."

"Never fear," said the painter, tapping his forehead. "It's made."

On this second occasion, Mr. Everett, exhausted by the intellectual strain of the preceding day, and encouraged by his luxurious chair, sank into a tranquil sleep. His companions remained for some time, listening to his regular breathing; Marian with her eyes patiently fixed on the opposite wall, and the young man with his glance mechanically travelling between his figure and the canvas. At last he fell back several paces to survey his work. Marian moved her eyes, and they met his own.

"Well, Miss Everett," said the painter, in accents which might have been tremulous if he had not exerted a strong effort to make them firm.

"Well, Mr. Baxter," said the young girl.

And the two exchanged a long, firm glance, which at last ended in a smile—a smile which belonged decidedly to the family of the famous laugh of the two angels behind the altar in the temple.

"Well, Miss Everett," said Baxter, going back to his work; "such is life!"

"So it appears," rejoined Marian. And then, after a pause of some moments: "Why didn't you come and see me?" she added.

"I came and you weren't at home."

"Why didn't you come again?"

"What was the use, Miss Everett?"

"It would simply have been more decent. We might have become reconciled."

"We seem to have done that as it is."

"I mean 'in form'."

"That would have been absurd. Don't you see how true an instinct I had? What could have been easier than our meeting? I assure you that I should have found any talk about the past, and mutual assurances or apologies extremely disagreeable."

Miss Everett raised her eyes from the floor and fixed them on her companion with a deep, half-reproachful glance, "Is the past, then," she asked, "so utterly disagreeable?"

Baxter stared, half amazed. "Good heavens!" he cried, "of course it is."

Miss Everett dropped her eyes and remained silent.

102

I may as well take advantage of the moment, rapidly to make plain to the reader the events to which the above conversation refers.

Miss Everett had found it expedient, all things considered, not to tell her intended husband the whole story of her acquaintance with Stephen Baxter; and when I have repaired her omissions, the reader will probably justify her discretion.

She had, as she said, met this young man for the first time at Rome, and there in the course of two interviews had made a deep impression upon his heart. He had felt that he would give a great deal to meet Miss Everett again. Their reunion in Switzerland was therefore not entirely fortuitous; and it had been the more easy for Baxter to make it possible, for the reason that he was able to claim a kind of round-about relationship with Mrs. Denbigh, Marian's companion. With this lady's permission he had attached himself to their party. He had made their route of travel his own, he had stopped when they stopped and been prodigal of attentions and civilities. Before a week was over, Mrs. Denbigh, who was the soul of confiding good nature, exulted in the discovery of an invaluable kinsman. Thanks not only to her naturally unexacting disposition, but to the apathetic and inactive habits induced by constant physical suffering, she proved a very insignificant third in her companions' spending of the hours. How delightfully these hours were spent, it requires no great effort to imagine. A suit conducted in the midst of the most romantic scenery in Europe is already half won. Marian's social graces were largely enhanced by the satisfaction which her innate intelligence of natural beauty enabled her to take in the magnificent scenery of the Alps. She had never appeared to such advantage; she had never known such perfect freedom and frankness and gayety. For the first time in her life she had made a captive without suspecting it. She had surrendered her heart to the mountains and the lakes, the eternal snows and the pastoral valleys, and Baxter, standing by, had intercepted it. He felt his long-projected Swiss tour vastly magnified and beautified by Miss Everett's part in it—by the constant feminine sympathy which gushed within earshot, with the coolness and clearness of a mountain spring. Oh! if only it too had not been fed by the eternal snows! And then her beauty—her indefatigable beauty—was a continual enchantment. Miss Everett looked so thoroughly in her place in a drawing-room that it was almost logical to suppose that she looked well nowhere else. But in fact, as

Baxter learned, she looked quite well enough in the character of what ladies call a "fright"—that is, sunburnt, travel-stained, overheated, exhilarated and hungry—to elude all invidious comparisons.

At the end of three weeks, one morning as they stood together on the edge of a falling torrent, high above the green concavities of the hills, Baxter felt himself irresistibly urged to make a declaration. The thunderous noise of the cataract covered all vocal utterance; so, taking out his sketch-book, he wrote three short words on a blank leaf. He handed her the book. She read his message with a beautiful change of color and a single rapid glance at his face. She then tore out the leaf.

"Don't tear it up!" cried the young man.

She understood him by the movement of his lips and shook her head with a smile. But she stooped, picked up a little stone, and wrapping it in the bit of paper, prepared to toss it into the torrent.

Baxter, uncertain, put out his hand to take it from her. She passed it into the other hand and gave him the one he had attempted to take.

She threw away the paper, but she let him keep her hand.

Baxter had still a week at his disposal, and Marian made it a very happy one. Mrs. Denbigh was tired; they had come to a halt, and there was no interruption to their being together. They talked a great deal of the long future, which, on getting beyond the sound of the cataract, they had expeditiously agreed to pursue in common.

It was their misfortune both to be poor. They determined, in view of this circumstance, to say nothing of their engagement until Baxter, by dint of hard work, should have at least quadrupled his income. This was cruel, but it was imperative, and Marian made no complaint. Her residence in Europe had enlarged her conception of the material needs of a pretty woman, and it was quite natural that she should not, close upon the heels of this experience, desire to rush into marriage with a poor artist. At the end of some days Baxter started for Germany and Holland, portions of which he wished to visit for purposes of study. Mrs. Denbigh and her young friend repaired to Paris for the Winter. Here, in the middle of February, they were rejoined by Baxter, who had achieved his German tour. He had received, while absent, five little letters from Marian, full of affection. The number was small, but the young man detected in the very temperance of his mistress a certain delicious flavor of implicit constancy. She received

104

him with all the frankness and sweetness that he had a right to expect, and listened with great interest to his account of the improvement in his prospects. He had sold three of his Italian pictures and had made an invaluable collection of sketches. He was on the high road to wealth and fame, and there was no reason their engagement should not be announced. But to this latter proposition Marian demurred—demurred so strongly, and yet on grounds so arbitrary, that a somewhat painful scene ensued. Stephen left her, irritated and perplexed. The next day, when he called, she was unwell and unable to see him; and the next—and the next. On the evening of the day that he had made his third fruitless call at Mrs. Denbigh's, he overheard Marian's name mentioned at a large party. The interlocutors were two elderly women. On giving his attention to their talk, which they were taking no pains to keep private, he found that his mistress was under accusal of having trifled with the affections of an unhappy young man, the only son of one of the ladies. There was apparently no lack of evidence or of facts which might be construed as evidence. Baxter went home, *la mort dans l'âme,* and on the following day called again on Mrs. Denbigh. Marian was still in her room, but the former lady received him. Stephen was in great trouble, but his mind was lucid, and he addressed himself to the task of interrogating his hostess. Mrs. Denbigh, with her habitual indolence, had remained unsuspicious of the terms on which the young people stood.

"I'm sorry to say," Baxter began, "that I heard Miss Everett accused last evening of very sad conduct."

"Ah, for heaven's sake, Stephen," returned his kinswoman, "don't go back to that. I've done nothing all Winter but defend and palliate her conduct. It's hard work. Don't make me do it for you. You know her as well as I do. She was indiscreet, but I know she is penitent, and for that matter she's well out of it. He was by no means a desirable young man."

"The lady whom I heard talking about the matter," said Stephen, "spoke of him in the highest terms. To be sure, as it turned out, she was his mother."

"His mother? You're mistaken. His mother died ten years ago."

Baxter folded his arms with a feeling that he needed to sit firm. "*Allons,*" said he, "of whom do you speak?"

"Of young Mr. King."

105

"Good heavens," cried Stephen. "So there are two of them?"

"Pray, of whom do *you* speak?"

"Of a certain Mr. Young. The mother is a handsome old woman with white curls."

"You don't mean to say there has been anything between Marian and Frederic Young?"

"*Voilà!* I only repeat what I hear. It seems to me, my dear Mrs. Denbigh, that you ought to know."

Mrs. Denbigh shook her head with a melancholy movement. "I'm sure I don't," she said. "I give it up. I don't pretend to judge. The manners of young people to each other are very different from what they were in my day. One doesn't know whether they mean nothing or everything."

"You know, at least, whether Mr. Young has been in your drawing-room?"

"Oh, yes, frequently. I'm very sorry that Marian is talked about. It's very unpleasant for me. But what can a sick woman do?"

"Well," said Stephen, "so much for Mr. Young. And now for Mr. King."

"Mr. King is gone home. It's a pity he ever came away."

"In what sense?"

"Oh, he's a silly fellow. He doesn't understand young girls."

"Upon my word," said Stephen, 'with expression', as the music sheets say, "he might be very wise and not do that."

"Not but that Marian was injudicious. She meant only to be amiable, but she went too far. She became adorable. The first thing she knew he was holding her to an account."

"Is he good-looking?"

"Well enough."

"And rich?"

"Very rich, I believe."

"And the other?"

"What other—Marian?"

"No, no; your friend Young."

"Yes, he's quite handsome."

"And rich, too?"

"Yes, I believe he's also rich."

106

Baxter was silent a moment. "And there's no doubt," he resumed, "that they were both far gone?"

"I can only answer for Mr. King."

"Well, I'll answer for Mr. Young. His mother wouldn't have talked as she did unless she'd seen her son suffer. After all, then, it's perhaps not so much to Marian's discredit. Here are two handsome young millionaires, madly smitten. She refuses them both. She doesn't care for good looks and money."

"I don't say that," said Mrs. Denbigh, sagaciously. "She doesn't care for those things alone. She wants talent, and all the rest of it. Now, if you were only rich, Stephen—" added the good lady, innocently.

Baxter took up his hat. "When you wish to marry Miss Everett," he said, "you must take good care not to say too much about Mr. King and Mr. Young."

Two days after this interview, he had a conversation with the young girl in person. The reader may like him the less for his easily-shaken confidence, but it is a fact that he had been unable to make light of these lightly-made revelations. For him his love had been a passion; for *her*, he was compelled to believe, it had been a vulgar pastime. He was a man of a violent temper; he went straight to the point.

"Marian," he said, "you've been deceiving me."

Marian knew very well what he meant; she knew very well that she had grown weary of her engagement and that, however little of a fault her conduct had been to Messrs. Young and King, it had been an act of grave disloyalty to Baxter. She felt that the blow was struck and that their engagement was clean broken. She knew that Stephen would be satisfied with no half-excuses or half-denials; and she had none others to give. A hundred such would not make a perfect confession. Making no attempt, therefore, to save her "prospects," for which she had ceased to care, she merely attempted to save her dignity. Her dignity for the moment was well enough secured by her natural half-cynical coolness of temper. But this same vulgar placidity left in Stephen's memory an impression of heartlessness and shallowness, which in that particular quarter, at least, was destined to be forever fatal to her claims to real weight and worth. She denied the young man's right to call her to account and to interfere with her conduct; and she almost anticipated his proposal that they should consider their engagement at an end. She even declined the use of the simple logic of tears. Under these circumstances, of course, the interview was not of long duration.

"I regard you," said Baxter, as he stood on the threshold, "as the most superficial, most heartless of women."

He immediately left Paris and went down into Spain, where he remained till the opening of the Summer. In the month of May Mrs. Denbigh and her *protégé* went to England, where the former, through her husband, possessed a number of connections, and where Marian's thoroughly un-English beauty was vastly admired. In September they sailed for America. About a year and a half, therefore, had elapsed between Baxter's separation from Miss Everett and their meeting in New York.

During this interval the young man's wounds had had time to heal. His sorrow, although violent, had been short-lived, and when he finally recovered his habitual equanimity, he was very glad to have purchased exemption at the price of a simple heart-ache. Reviewing his impressions of Miss Everett in a calmer mood, he made up his mind that she was very far from being the woman of his desire, and that she had not really been the woman of his choice. "Thank God," he said to himself, "it's over. She's irreclaimably light. She's hollow, trivial, vulgar." There had been in his addresses something hasty and feverish, something factitious and unreal in his fancied passion. Half of it had been the work of the scenery, of the weather, of mere juxtaposition, and, above all, of the young girl's picturesque beauty; to say nothing of the almost suggestive tolerance and indolence of poor Mrs. Denbigh. And finding himself very much interested in Velasquez, at Madrid, he dismissed Miss Everett from his thoughts. I do not mean to offer his judgment of Miss Everett as final; but it was at least conscientious. The ample justice, moreover, which, under the illusion of sentiment, he had rendered to her charms and graces, gave him a right, when free from that illusion, to register his estimate of the arid spaces of her nature. Miss Everett might easily have accused him of injustice and brutality; but this fact would still stand to plead in his favor, that he cared with all his strength for truth. Marian, on the contrary, was quite indifferent to it. Stephen's angry sentence on her conduct had awakened no echo in her contracted soul.

The reader has now an adequate conception of the feelings with which these two old friends found themselves face to face. It is needful to add, however, that the lapse of time had very much diminished the force of those feelings. A woman, it seems to me, ought to desire no easier company, none less embarrassed or embarrassing; than a disenchanted lover; premising, of course, that the process of disenchantment is thoroughly complete, and that some time has elapsed since its completion.

Marian herself was perfectly at her ease. She had not retained her equanimity—her philosophy, one might almost call it—during that painful last interview, to go and lose it now. She had no ill feeling toward her old lover. His last words had been—like all words in Marian's estimation—a mere *façon de parler*. Miss Everett was in so perfect a good humor during these last days of her maidenhood that there was nothing in the past that she could not have forgiven.

She blushed a little at the emphasis of her companion's remark; but she was not discountenanced. She summoned up her good humor. "The truth is, Mr. Baxter," she said, "I feel at the present moment on perfect good terms with the world; I see everything *en rose*; the past as well as the future."

"I, too, am on very good terms with the world," said Mr. Baxter, "and my heart is quite reconciled to what you call the past. But, nevertheless, it's very disagreeable to me to think about it."

"Ah then," said Miss Everett, with great sweetness, "I'm afraid you're not reconciled."

Baxter laughed—so loud that Miss Everett looked about at her father. But Mr. Everett still slept the sleep of gentility. "I've no doubt," said the painter, "that I'm far from being so good a Christian as you. But I assure you I'm very glad to see you again."

"You've but to say the word and we're friends," said Marian.

"We were very foolish to have attempted to be anything else."

" 'Foolish', yes. But it was a pretty folly."

"Ah no, Miss Everett. I'm an artist, and I claim a right of property in the word 'pretty'. You mustn't stick it in there. Nothing could be pretty which had such an ugly termination. It was all false."

"Well—as you will. What have you been doing since we parted?"

"Travelling and working. I've made great progress in my trade. Shortly before I came home I became engaged."

"Engaged?—*à la bonne heure*. Is she good?—is she pretty?"

"She's not nearly so pretty as you."

"In other words, she's infinitely more good. I'm sure I hope she is. But why did you leave her behind you?"

"She's with a sister, a sad invalid, who is drinking mineral waters on the Rhine. They wished to remain there to the cold weather. They're to be home in a couple of weeks, and we are straightway to be married."

"I congratulate you, with all my heart," said Marian.

"Allow me to do as much, sir," said Mr. Everett, waking up; which he did by instinct whenever the conversation took a ceremonious turn.

Miss Everett gave her companion but three more sittings, a large part of his work being executed with the assistance of photographs. At these interviews also, Mr. Everett was present, and still delicately sensitive to the soporific influences of his position. But both parties had the good taste to abstain from further reference to their old relations, and to confine their talk to less personal themes.

· *II* ·

One afternoon, when the picture was nearly finished, John Lennox went into the empty painting-room to ascertain the degree of its progress. Both Baxter and Marian had expressed a wish that he should not see it in its early stages, and this, accordingly, was his first view. Half an hour after he had entered the room, Baxter came in, unannounced, and found him sitting before the canvas, deep in thought. Baxter had been furnished with a house-key, so that he might have immediate and easy access to his work whenever the humor came upon him.

"I was passing," he said, "and I couldn't resist the impulse to come in and correct an error which I made this morning, now that a sense of its enormity is fresh in my mind." He sat down to work, and the other stood watching him.

"Well," said the painter, finally, "how does it satisfy you?"

"Not altogether."

"Pray develop your objections. It's in your power materially to assist me."

"I hardly know how to formulate my objections. Let me, at all events,

110

in the first place, say that I admire your work immensely. I'm sure it's the best picture you've painted."

"I honestly believe it is. Some parts of it," said Baxter, frankly, "are excellent."

"It's obvious. But either those very parts or others are singularly disagreeable. That word isn't criticism, I know; but I pay you for the right to be arbitrary. They are too hard, too strong, of too frank a reality. In a word, your picture frightens me, and if I were Marian I should feel as if you'd done me a certain violence."

"I'm sorry for what's disagreeable; but I meant it all to be real. I go in for reality; you must have seen that."

"I approve you; I can't too much admire the broad and firm methods you've taken for reaching this same reality. But you can be real without being brutal—without attempting, as one may say, to be *actual*."

"I deny that I'm brutal. I'm afraid, Mr. Lennox, I haven't taken quite the right road to please you. I've taken the picture too much *au sérieux*. I've striven too much for completeness. But if it doesn't please you it will please others."

"I've no doubt of it. But that isn't the question. The picture is good enough to be a thousand times better."

"That the picture leaves room for infinite improvement, I, of course, don't deny; and, in several particulars, I see my way to make it better. But, substantially, the portrait is there. I'll tell you what you miss. My work isn't 'classical'; in fine, I'm not a man of genius."

"No; I rather suspect you are. But, as you say, your work isn't classical. I adhere to my term *brutal*. Shall I tell you? It's too much of a study. You've given poor Miss Everett the look of a professional model."

"If that's the case I've done very wrong. There never was an easier, a less conscious sitter. It's delightful to look at her."

"Confound it, you've given all her ease, too. Well, I don't know what's the matter. I give up."

"I think," said Baxter, "you had better hold your verdict in abeyance until the picture is finished. The classical element is there, I'm sure; but I've not brought it out. Wait a few days, and it will rise to the surface."

Lennox left the artist alone; and the latter took up his brushes and painted hard till nightfall. He laid them down only when it was too dark to see. As he was going out, Lennox met him in the hall.

"*Exegi monumentum,*" said Baxter; "it's finished. Go and look at your ease. I'll come to-morrow and hear your impressions."

The master of the house, when the other had gone, lit half a dozen lights and returned to the study of the picture. It had grown prodigiously under the painter's recent handling, and whether it was that, as Baxter had said, the classical element had disengaged itself, or that Lennox was in a more sympathetic mood, it now impressed him as an original and powerful work, a genuine portrait, the deliberate image of a human face and figure. It was Marian, in very truth, and Marian most patiently measured and observed. Her beauty was there, her sweetness, and her young loveliness and her aerial grace, imprisoned forever, made inviolable and perpetual. Nothing could be more simple than the conception and composition of the picture. The figure sat peacefully, looking slightly to the right, with the head erect and the hands—the virginal hands, without rings or bracelets—lying idle on its knees. The blonde hair was gathered into a little knot of braids on the top of the head (in the fashion of the moment), and left free the almost childish contour of the ears and cheeks. The eyes were full of color, contentment and light; the lips were faintly parted. Of color in the picture, there was, in strictness, very little; but the dark draperies told of reflected sunshine, and the flesh-spaces of human blushes and pallors, of throbbing life and health. The work was strong and simple, the figure was thoroughly void of affectation and stiffness, and yet supremely elegant.

"That's what it is to be an artist," thought Lennox. "All this has been done in the past two hours."

It was his Marian, assuredly, with all that had charmed him—with all that still charmed him when he saw her: her appealing confidence, her exquisite lightness, her feminine enchantments. And yet, as he looked, an expression of pain came into his eyes, and lingered there, and grew into a mortal heaviness.

Lennox had been as truly a lover as a man may be; but he loved with the discretion of fifteen years' experience of human affairs. He had a penetrating glance, and he liked to use it. Many a time when Marian, with eloquent lips and eyes, had poured out the treasures of her nature into his bosom, and he had taken them in his hands and covered them with kisses and passionate vows, he had dropped them all with a sudden shudder and cried out in silence, "But ah! where is the heart?" One day he had said to her (irrelevantly enough, doubtless), "Marian, where *is* your heart?"

"*Where*—what do you mean?" Miss Everett had said.

"I think of you from morning till night. I put you together and take you apart, as people do in that game where they make words out of a parcel of given letters. But there's always one letter wanting. I can't put my hand on your heart."

"My heart, John," said Marian, ingeniously, "is the whole word. My heart's everywhere."

This may have been true enough. Miss Everett had distributed her heart impartially throughout her whole organism, so that, as a natural consequence, its native seat was somewhat scantily occupied. As Lennox sat and looked at Baxter's consummate handiwork, the same question rose again to his lips; and if Marian's portrait suggested it, Marian's portrait failed to answer it. It took Marian to do that. It seemed to Lennox that some strangely potent agency had won from his mistress the confession of her inmost soul, and had written it there upon the canvas in firm yet passionate lines. Marian's person was lightness— her charm was lightness; could it be that her soul was levity too? Was she a creature without faith and without conscience? What else was the meaning of that horrible blankness and deadness that quenched the light in her eyes and stole away the smile from her lips? These things were the less to be eluded because in so many respects the painter had been profoundly just. He had been as loyal and sympathetic as he had been intelligent. Not a point in the young girl's appearance had been slighted; not a feature but had been forcibly and delicately rendered. Had Baxter been a man of marvellous insight— an unparalleled observer; or had he been a mere patient and unflinching painter, building infinitely better than he knew? Would not a mere painter have been content to paint Miss Everett in the strong, rich, objective manner of which the work was so good an example, and to do nothing more? For it was evident that Baxter had done more. He had painted with something more than knowledge—with imagination, with feeling. He had almost *composed;* and his composition had embraced the truth. Lennox was unable to satisfy his doubts. He would have been glad to believe that there was no imagination in the picture but what his own mind supplied; and that the unsubstantial sweetness on the eyes and lips of the image was but the smile of youth and innocence. He was in a muddle—he was absurdly suspicious and capricious; he put out the lights and left the portrait in kindly darkness. Then, half as a reparation to his mistress, and half as a satisfaction to himself, he went up to spend an hour with Marian. She, at least, as he found, had no scruples. She thought the portrait altogether a success, and she was very willing to be handed down in that form to posterity. Nevertheless, when Lennox came in, he went back into the painting-room to take another glance. This time he lit but a single light. Faugh! it was worse than with a dozen. He hastily turned out the gas.

Baxter came the next day, as he had promised. Meanwhile poor Lennox had had twelve hours of uninterrupted reflection, and the expression of distress in his eyes had acquired an intensity which, the painter saw, proved it to be of far other import than a mere tribute to his power.

"Can the man be jealous?" thought Baxter. Stephen had been so innocent of any other design than that of painting a good portrait, that his conscience failed to reveal to him the source of his companion's trouble. Nevertheless he began to pity him. He had felt tempted, indeed, to pity him from the first. He had liked him and esteemed him; he had taken him for a man of sense and of feeling, and he had thought it a matter of regret that such a man—a creature of strong spiritual needs—should link his destiny with that of Marian Everett. But he had very soon made up his mind that Lennox knew very well what he was about, and that he needed no enlightenment. He was marrying with his eyes open, and had weighed the risks against the profits. Every one had his particular taste, and at thirty-five years of age John Lennox had no need to be told that Miss Everett was not quite all that she might be. Baxter had thus taken for granted that his friend had designedly selected as his second wife a mere pretty woman—a woman with a genius for receiving company, and who would make a picturesque use of his money. He knew nothing of the serious character of the poor man's passion, nor of the extent to which his happiness was bound up in what the painter would have called his delusion. His only concern had been to do his work well; and he had done it the better because of his old interest in Marian's bewitching face. It is

114

very certain that he had actually infused into his picture that force of characterization and that depth of reality which had arrested his friend's attention; but he had done so wholly without effort and without malice. The artistic half of Baxter's nature exerted a lusty dominion over the human half—fed upon its disappointments and grew fat upon its joys and tribulations. This, indeed, is simply saying that the young man was a true artist. Deep, then, in the unfathomed recesses of his strong and sensitive nature, his genius had held communion with his heart and had transferred to canvas the burden of its disenchantment and its resignation. Since his little affair with Marian, Baxter had made the acquaintance of a young girl whom he felt that he could love and trust forever; and, sobered and strengthened by this new emotion, he had been able to resume with more distinctness the shortcomings of his earlier love. He had, therefore, painted with feeling. Miss Everett could not have expected him to do otherwise. He had done his honest best, and conviction had come in unbidden and made it better.

Lennox had begun to feel very curious about the history of his companion's acquaintance with his destined bride; but he was far from feeling jealous. Somehow he felt that he could never again be jealous. But in ascertaining the terms of their former intercourse, it was of importance that he should not allow the young man to suspect that he discovered in the portrait any radical defect.

"Your old acquaintance with Miss Everett," he said, frankly, "has evidently been of great use to you."

"I suppose it has," said Baxter. "Indeed, as soon as I began to paint, I found her face coming back to me like a half-remembered tune. She was wonderfully pretty at that time."

"She was two years younger."

"Yes, and I was two years younger. Decidedly, you are right. I *have* made use of my old impressions."

Baxter was willing to confess to so much; but he was resolved not to betray anything that Marian had herself kept secret. He was not surprised that she had not told her lover of her former engagement; he expected as much. But he would have held it inexcusable to attempt to repair her omission.

Lennox's faculties were acutely sharpened by pain and suspicion,

115

and he could not help detecting in his companion's eyes an intention of reticence. He resolved to baffle it.

"I am curious to know," he said, "whether you were ever in love with Miss Everett?"

"I have no hesitation in saying Yes," rejoined Baxter; fancying that a general confession would help him more than a particular denial. "I'm one of a thousand, I fancy. Or one, perhaps, of only a hundred. For you see I've got over it. I'm engaged to be married."

Lennox's countenance brightened. "That's it," said he. "Now I know what I didn't like in your picture—the point of view. I'm not jealous," he added. "I should like the picture better if I were. You evidently care nothing for the poor girl. You have got over your love rather too well. You loved her, she was indifferent to you, and now you take your revenge." Distracted with grief, Lennox was taking refuge in irrational anger.

Baxter was puzzled. "You'll admit," said he, with a smile, "that it's a very handsome revenge." And all his professional self-esteem rose to his assistance. "I've painted for Miss Everett the best portrait that has yet been painted in America. She herself is quite satisfied."

"Ah!" said Lennox, with magnificent dissimulation; "Marian is generous."

"Come, then," said Baxter; "what do you complain of? You accuse me of scandalous conduct, and I'm bound to hold you to an account." Baxter's own temper was rising, and with it his sense of his picture's merits. "How have I perverted Miss Everett's expression? How have I misrepresented her? What does the portrait lack? Is it ill-drawn? Is it vulgar? Is it ambiguous? Is it immodest?" Baxter's patience gave out as he recited these various charges. "Fiddlesticks!" he cried; "you know as well as I do that the picture is excellent."

"I don't pretend to deny it. Only I wonder that Marian was willing to come to you."

It is very much to Baxter's credit that he still adhered to his resolution not to betray the young girl, and that rather than do so he was willing to let Lennox suppose that he had been a rejected adorer.

"Ah, as you say," he exclaimed, "Miss Everett is so generous!"

Lennox was foolish enough to take this as an admission. "When I say, Mr. Baxter," he said, "that you have taken your revenge, I don't mean that you've done so wantonly or consciously. My dear fellow,

116

how could you help it? The disappointment was proportionate to the loss and the reaction to the disappointment."

"Yes, that's all very well; but, meanwhile, I wait in vain to learn wherein I've done wrong."

Lennox looked from Baxter to the picture, and from the picture back to Baxter.

"I defy you to tell me," said Baxter. "I've simply kept Miss Everett as charming as she is in life."

"Oh, damn her charms!" cried Lennox.

"If you were not the gentleman, Mr. Lennox," continued the young man, "which, in spite of your high temper, I believe you to be, I should believe you—"

"Well, you should believe me?"

"I should believe you simply bent on cheapening the portrait."

Lennox made a gesture of vehement impatience. The other burst out laughing and the discussion closed. Baxter instinctively took up his brushes and approached his canvas with a vague desire to detect latent errors, while Lennox prepared to take his departure.

"Stay!" said the painter, as he was leaving the room; "if the picture really offends you, I'll rub it out. Say the word," and he took up a heavy brush, covered with black paint.

But Lennox shook his head with decision and went out. The next moment, however, he reappeared. "You *may* rub it out," he said. "The picture is, of course, already mine."

But now Baxter shook his head. "Ah! now it's too late," he answered. "Your chance is gone."

Lennox repaired directly to Mr. Everett's apartments. Marian was in the drawing-room with some morning callers, and her lover sat by until she had got rid of them. When they were alone together, Marian began to laugh at her visitors and to parody certain of their affectations, which she did with infinite grace and spirit. But Lennox cut her short and returned to the portrait. He had thought better of his objections of the preceding evening; he liked it.

"But I wonder, Marian," he said, "that you were willing to go to Mr. Baxter."

"Why so?" asked Marian, on her guard. She saw that her lover knew something, and she intended not to commit herself until she knew how much he knew.

117

"An old lover is always dangerous."

"An old lover?" and Marian blushed a good honest blush. But she rapidly recovered herself. "Pray where did you get that charming news?"

"Oh, it slipped out," said Lennox.

Marian hesitated a moment. Then with a smile: "Well, I was brave," she said. "I went."

"How came it," pursued Lennox, "that you didn't tell me?"

"Tell you what, my dear John?"

"Why, about Baxter's little passion. Come, don't be modest."

Modest! Marian breathed freely. "What do you mean, my dear, by telling your wife not to be modest? Pray don't ask me about Mr. Baxter's passions. What do I know about them?"

"Did you know nothing of this one?"

"Ah, my dear, I know a great deal too much for my comfort. But he's got bravely over it. He's engaged."

"Engaged, but not quite disengaged. He's an honest fellow, but he remembers his *penchant*. It was as much as he could do to keep his picture from turning to the sentimental. He saw you as he fancied you —as he wished you; and he has given you a little look of what he imagines moral loveliness, which comes within an ace of spoiling the picture. Baxter's imagination isn't very strong, and this same look expresses, in point of fact, nothing but inanity. Fortunately he's a man of extraordinary talent, and a real painter, and he has made a good portrait in spite of himself."

To such arguments as these was John Lennox reduced, to stifle the evidence of his senses. But when once a lover begins to doubt, he cannot cease at will. In spite of his earnest efforts to believe in Marian as before, to accept her without scruple and without second thought, he was quite unable to repress an impulse of constant mistrust and aversion. The charm was broken, and there is no mending a charm. Lennox stood half-aloof, watching the poor girl's countenance, weighing her words, analyzing her thoughts, guessing at her motives.

Marian's conduct under this trying ordeal was truly heroic. She felt that some subtle change had taken place in her future husband's feelings, a change which, although she was powerless to discover its cause, yet obviously imperilled her prospects. Something had snapped between them; she had lost half of her power. She was horribly dis-

118

tressed, and the more so because that superior depth of character which she had all along gladly conceded to Lennox, might now, as she conjectured, cover some bold and portentous design. Could he meditate a direct rupture? Could it be his intention to dash from her lips the sweet, the spiced and odorous cup of being the wife of a good-natured millionaire? Marian turned a tremulous glance upon her past, and wondered if he had discovered any dark spot. Indeed, for that matter, might she not defy him to do so? She had done nothing really amiss. There was no visible blot in her history. It was faintly discolored, indeed, by a certain vague moral dinginess; but it compared well enough with that of other girls. She had cared for nothing but pleasure; but to what else were girls brought up? On the whole, might she not feel at ease? She assured herself that she might; but she nevertheless felt that if John wished to break off his engagement, he would do it on high abstract grounds, and not because she had committed a naughtiness the more or the less. It would be simply because he had ceased to love her. It would avail her but little to assure him that she would kindly overlook this circumstance and remit the obligations of the heart. But, in spite of her hideous apprehensions, she continued to smile and smile.

The days passed by, and John consented to be still engaged. Their marriage was only a week off—six days, five days, four. Miss Everett's smile became less mechanical. John had apparently been passing through a crisis—a moral and intellectual crisis, inevitable in a man of his constitution, and with which she had nothing to do. On the eve of marriage he had questioned his heart; he had found that it was no longer young and capable of the vagaries of passion, and he had made up his mind to call things by their proper names, and to admit to himself that he was marrying not for love, but for friendship, and a little, perhaps, for prudence. It was only out of regard for what he supposed Marian's own more exalted theory of the matter, that he abstained from revealing to her this common-sense view of it. Such was Marian's hypothesis.

Lennox had fixed his wedding-day for the last Thursday in October. On the preceding Friday, as he was passing up Broadway, he stopped at Goupil's to see if his order for the framing of the portrait had been fulfilled. The picture had been transferred to the shop, and, when duly framed, had been, at Baxter's request and with Lennox's consent, placed

119

for a few days in the exhibition room. Lennox went up to look at it.

The portrait stood on an easel at the end of the hall, with three spectators before it—a gentleman and two ladies. The room was otherwise empty. As Lennox went toward the picture, the gentleman turned out to be Baxter. He proceeded to introduce his friend to his two companions, the younger of whom Lennox recognized as the artist's betrothed. The other, her sister, was a plain, pale woman, with the look of ill health, who had been provided with a seat and made no attempt to talk. Baxter explained that these ladies had arrived from Europe but the day before, and that his first care had been to show them his masterpiece.

"Sarah," said he, "has been praising the model very much to the prejudice of the copy."

Sarah was a tall, black-haired girl of twenty, with irregular features, a pair of luminous dark eyes, and a smile radiant of white teeth—evidently an excellent person. She turned to Lennox with a look of frank sympathy, and said in a deep, rich voice:

"She must be very beautiful."

"Yes, she's very beautiful," said Lennox, with his eyes lingering on her own pleasant face. "You must know her—she must know you."

"I'm sure I should like very much to see her," said Sarah.

"This is very nearly as good," said Lennox. "Mr. Baxter is a great genius."

"I know Mr. Baxter is a genius. But what is a picture, at the best? I've seen nothing but pictures for the last two years, and I haven't seen a single pretty girl."

The young girl stood looking at the portrait in very evident admiration, and, while Baxter talked to the elder lady, Lennox bestowed a long, covert glance upon his *fiancée*. She had brought her head into almost immediate juxtaposition with that of Marian's image, and, for a moment, the freshness and the strong animation which bloomed upon her features seemed to obliterate the lines and colors on the canvas. But the next moment, as Lennox looked, the roseate circle of Marian's face blazed into remorseless distinctness, and her careless blue eyes looked with cynical familiarity into his own.

He bade an abrupt good morning to his companions, and went toward the door. But beside it he stopped. Suspended on the wall was Baxter's picture, *My Last Duchess*. He stood amazed. Was *this* the face and figure that, a month ago, had reminded him of his mistress? Where was the likeness now? It was as utterly absent as if it had never existed. The picture, moreover, was a very inferior work to the new portrait. He looked back at Baxter, half tempted to demand an explanation, or at least to express his perplexity. But Baxter and his sweetheart had stooped down to examine a minute sketch near the floor, with their heads in delicious contiguity.

How the week elapsed, it were hard to say. There were moments when Lennox felt as if death were preferable to the heartless union which now stared him in the face, and as if the only possible course was to transfer his property to Marian and to put an end to his existence. There were others, again, when he was fairly reconciled to his fate. He had but to gather his old dreams and fancies into a faggot and break them across his knee, and the thing were done. Could he not collect in their stead a comely cluster of moderate and rational expectations, and bind them about with a wedding favor? His love was dead, his youth was dead; that was all. There was no need of making a tragedy of it. His love's vitality had been but small, and since it was to be short-lived it was better that it should expire before marriage than after. As for marriage, that should stand, for that was not of necessity a matter of love. He lacked the brutal consistency necessary for taking away Marian's future. If he had mistaken her and overrated her, the fault was his own, and it was a hard thing that she should pay the penalty. Whatever were her failings, they were profoundly involuntary, and it was plain that with regard to himself her intentions were good. She would be no companion, but she would be at least a faithful wife.

With the help of this grim logic, Lennox reached the eve of his wedding day. His manner toward Miss Everett during the preceding week had been inveterately tender and kind. He felt that in losing his love she had lost a heavy treasure, and he offered her instead the most unfailing devotion. Marian had questioned him about his lassitude and his preoccupied air, and he had replied that he was not very well. On the Wednesday afternoon, he mounted his horse and took a long ride. He came home toward sunset, and was met in the hall by his old housekeeper.

"Miss Everett's portrait, sir," she said, "has just been sent home, in the most beautiful frame. You gave no directions, and I took the liberty of having it carried into the library. I thought," and the old woman smiled deferentially, "you'd like best to have it in your own room."

Lennox went into the library. The picture was standing on the floor, back to back with a high arm-chair, and catching, through the window, the last horizontal rays of the sun. He stood before it a moment, gazing at it with a haggard face.

"Come!" said he, at last, "Marian may be what God has made her; but *this* detestable creature I can neither love nor respect!"

He looked about him with an angry despair, and his eye fell on a long, keen poinard, given him by a friend who had bought it in the East, and which lay as an ornament on his mantel-shelf. He seized it and thrust it, with barbarous glee, straight into the lovely face of the image. He dragged it downward, and made a long fissure in the living canvas. Then, with half a dozen strokes, he wantonly hacked it across. The act afforded him an immense relief.

I need hardly add that on the following day Lenox was married. He had locked the library door on coming out the evening before, and he had the key in his waistcoat pocket as he stood at the altar. As he left town, therefore, immediately after the ceremony, it was not until his return, a fortnight later, that the fate of the picture became known. It is not necessary to relate how he explained his exploit to Marian and how he disclosed it to Baxter. He at least put on a brave face. There is a rumor current of his having paid the painter an enormous sum of money. The amount is probably exaggerated, but there can be no doubt that the sum was very large. How he has fared—how he is destined to fare—in matrimony, it is rather too early to determine. He has been married scarcely three months.

A PROBLEM

A Problem

"A Problem," Henry James's ninth published tale, appeared in the Galaxy, June 1868, with an illustration by W. J. Hennessy. It is reprinted here for the first time. James not infrequently paints into American scenery some figure of its pre-European inhabitants, but Magawisca here is, so far as the record reads, the single American Indian with a "speaking part" in his long repertory of characters.

Two other of the uncollected tales immediately followed in the next month. "De Grey: A Romance" (Atlantic, July 1868), tenth of the published and fifth of the uncollected tales (so numbered solely by virtue of the Atlantic's alphabetical rank) is in Mordell's Travelling Companions; the other is in this collection.

SEPTEMBER WAS DRAWING TO AN END, AND WITH IT THE honeymoon of two young persons in whom I shall be glad to interest the reader. They had stretched it out in sovereign contempt of the balance of the calendar. That September hath thirty days is a truth known to the simplest child; but our young lovers had given it at least forty. Nevertheless, they were on the whole not sorry to have the overture play itself out, and to see the curtain rise on the drama in which they had undertaken the leading parts. Emma thought very often of the charming little house which was awaiting her in town, and of the servants whom her dear mother had promised to engage; and, indeed, for that matter, the young wife let her imagination hover about the choice groceries with which she expected to find her cupboards stocked through the same kind agency. Moreover, she had left her wedding-gown at home—thinking it silly to carry her finery into the country—and she felt a great longing to refresh her memory as to the particular shade of a certain lavendar silk, and the exact length of a certain train. The reader will see that Emma was a simple, unsophisticated person, and that her married life was likely to be made up of small joys and vexations. She was simple and gentle and pretty and young; she adored her husband. He, too, had begun to feel that it was time they were married in earnest. His thoughts wandered back to his counting-room and his vacant desk, and to the possible contents of the letters which he had requested his fellow-clerk to open in his absence. For David, too, was a simple, natural fellow, and although he thought his wife the sweetest of human creatures—or, indeed, for that very reason—he was unable to forget that life is full of bitter inhuman necessities and perils which muster in force about you when you stand idle. He was happy, in short, and he felt it unfair that he should any longer have his happiness for nothing.

The two, therefore, had made up their trunks again, and ordered the vehicle in time for the morrow's train. Twilight had come on, and Emma sat at the window empty-handed, taking a silent farewell of the landscape, which she felt that they had let into the secret of their young love. They had sat in the shade of every tree, and watched the sunset from the top of every rock.

David had gone to settle his account with the landlord, and to bid good-by to the doctor, who had been of such service when Emma had caught cold by sitting for three hours on the grass after a day's rain.

Sitting alone was dull work. Emma crossed the threshold of the long window, and went to the garden gate to look for her husband. The doctor's house was a mile away, close to the village. Seeing nothing of David, she strolled along the road, bareheaded, in her shawl. It was a lovely evening. As there was no one to say so to, Emma said so with some fervor, to herself; and to this she added a dozen more remarks, equally original and eloquent—and equally sincere. That David was, ah! so good, and that she ought to be so happy. That she would have a great many cares, but that she would be orderly, and saving, and vigilant, and that her house should be a sanctuary of modest elegance and good taste; and, then, that she might be a mother.

When Emma reached this point, she ceased to meditate and to whisper virtuous nothings to her conscience. She rejoiced; she walked

ı̣ore slowly, and looked about at the dark hills, rising in soft undula-
ions against the luminous west, and listened to the long pulsations of
ound mounting from woods and hedges and the margins of pools.
Ier ears rang, and her eyes filled with tears.

Meanwhile she had walked a half-mile, and as yet David was not in
ight. Her attention, however, was at this moment diverted from her
uest. To her right, on a level with the road, stretched a broad, circular
oace, half meadow, half common, enclosed in the rear by a wood. At
ome distance, close to the wood, stood a couple of tents, such as are
sed by the vagrant Indians who sell baskets and articles of bark. In
ront, close to the road, on a fallen log, sat a young Indian woman,
eaving a basket, with two children beside her. Emma looked at her
uriously as she drew near.

"Good evening," said the woman, returning her glance with hard,
right black eyes. "Don't you want to buy something?"

"What have you got to sell?" asked Emma, stopping.

"All sorts of things. Baskets, and pincushions, and fans."

"I should like a basket well enough—a little one—if they're pretty."

"Oh, yes, they're pretty, you'll see." And she said something to one
f the children, in her own dialect. He went off, in compliance, to the
ents.

While he was gone, Emma looked at the other child, and pronounced
very handsome; but without touching it, for the little savage was
ı the last degree unclean. The woman doggedly continued her work,
xamining Emma's person from head to foot, and staring at her dress,
er hands, and her rings.

In a few moments the child came back with a number of baskets
rung together, followed by an old woman, apparently the mother of
ıe first. Emma looked over the baskets, selected a pretty one, and
ook out her purse to pay for it. The price was a dollar, but Emma
ad nothing smaller than a two-dollar note, and the woman professed
erself unable to give change.

"Give her the money," said the old woman, "and, for the difference,
'll tell your fortune."

Emma looked at her, hesitating. She was a repulsive old squaw, with
ıllen, black eyes, and her swarthy face hatched across with a myriad
rinkles.

The younger woman saw that Emma looked a little frightened, and

127

said something in her barbarous native gutturals to her companion. The latter retorted, and the other burst out into a laugh.

"Give me your hand," said the old woman, "and I'll tell your fortune." And, before Emma found time to resist, she came and took hold of her left hand. She held it awhile, with the back upwards, looking at its fair surface, and at the diamonds on her third finger. Then turning up the palm, she began to mutter and grumble. Just as she was about to speak, Emma saw her look half-defiantly at some one apparently behind her. Turning about, she saw that her husband had come up unperceived. She felt relieved. The woman had a horrible vicious look, and she exhaled, moreover, a strong odor of whiskey. Of this David immediately became sensible.

"What is she doing?" he asked of his wife.

"Don't you see. She's telling my fortune."

"What has she told you."

"Nothing yet. She seems to be waiting for it to come to her."

The squaw looked at David cunningly, and David returned her gaze with ill-concealed disgust. "She'll have to wait a long time," he said to his wife. "She has been drinking."

He had lowered his voice, but the woman heard him. The other began to laugh, and said something in her own tongue to her mother. The latter still kept Emma's hand and remained silent.

"This your husband?" she said, at last, nodding at David.

Emma nodded assent. The woman again examined her hand. "Within the year," she said, "you'll be a mother."

"That's wonderful news," said David. "Is it to be a boy or a girl?"

The woman looked hard at David. "A girl," she said. And then she transferred her eyes to Emma's palm.

"Well, is that all?" said Emma.

"She'll be sick."

"Very likely," said David. "And we'll send for the doctor."

"The doctor'll do no good."

"Then we shall send for another," said Emma, laughing—but not without an effort.

"He'll do no good. She'll die."

The young squaw began to laugh again. Emma drew her hand away, and looked at her husband. He was a little pale, and Emma put her hand into his arm.

"We're very much obliged to you for the information," said David. "At what age is our little girl to die?"

"Oh, very young."

"How young?"

"Oh, very young." The old woman seemed indisposed to commit herself further, and David led his wife away.

"Well," said Emma, "she gave us a good dollar's worth."

"I think," said David, "she had been giving herself a good dollar's worth. She was full of liquor."

From this assurance Emma drew for twenty-four hours to come a good deal of comfort. As for David, in the course of an hour he had quite forgotten the prophecy.

The next day they went back to town. Emma found her house all that she had desired, and her lavender silk not a shade too pale, nor her train an inch too short. The winter came and went, and she was still a very happy woman. The spring arrived, the summer drew near, and her happiness increased. She became the mother of a little girl.

For some time after the child was born Emma was confined to her room. She used to sit with the infant on her lap, nursing her, counting her breathings, wondering whether she would be pretty. David was at his place of business, with his head full of figures. A dozen times Emma recurred to the old woman's prophecy, sometimes with a tremor, sometimes with indifference, sometimes almost with defiance. Then, she declared that it was silly to remember it. A tipsy old squaw—a likely providence for her precious child. She was, perhaps, dead herself by this time. Nevertheless, her prophecy was odd; she seemed so positive. And the other woman laughed so disagreeably. Emma had not forgotten that laugh. She might well laugh, with her own lusty little savages beside her.

The first day that Emma left her room, one evening, at dinner, she couldn't help asking her husband whether he remembered the Indian woman's prediction. David was taking a glass of wine. He nodded.

"You see it's half come true," said Emma. "A little girl."

"My dear," said David, "one would think you believed it."

"Of course she'll be sick," said Emma. "We must expect that."

"Do you think, my dear," pursued David, "that it's a little girl because that venerable person said so?"

129

"Why no, of course not. It's only a coincidence."

"Well, then, if it's merely a coincidence, we may let it rest. If the old woman's *dictum* was a real prediction, we may also let it rest. That it has half come true lessens the chances for the other half."

The reader may detect a flaw in David's logic; but it was quite good enough for Emma. She lived upon it for a year, at the end of which it was in a manner put to the test.

It were certainly incorrect to say that Emma guarded and cherished her little girl any the more carefully by reason of the old woman's assurance; her natural affection was by itself a guaranty of perfect vigilance. But perfect vigilance is not infallible. When the child was a twelvemonth old it fell grievously sick, and for a week its little life hung by a thread. During this time I am inclined to think that Emma quite forgot the sad prediction suspended over the infant's head; it is certain, at least, that she never spoke of it to her husband, and that he made no attempt to remind her of it. Finally, after a hard struggle, the little girl came out of the cruel embrace of disease, panting and exhausted, but uninjured. Emma felt as if her child was immortal, and as if, henceforth, life would have no trials for her. It was not till then that she thought once more of the prophecy of the swarthy sybil.

She was sitting on the sofa in her chamber, with the child lying asleep in her lap, watching the faint glow of returning life in its poor little wasted cheeks. David came in from his day's labor and sat down beside her.

"I wonder," said Emma, "what our friend Magawisca—or whatever her name is—would say to that."

"She would feel desperately snubbed," said David. "Wouldn't she little transcendent convalescent?" And he gently tickled the tip of his little girl's nose with the end of his moustache. The baby softly opened her eyes, and, vaguely conscious of her father, lifted her hand and languidly clutched his nose. "Upon my soul," said David, "she's positively boisterous. There's life in the old dog yet."

"Oh, David, how can you?" said Emma. But she sat watching her husband and child with a placid, gleeful smile. Gradually, her smile grew the least bit serious, and then vanished, though she still looked like the happy woman that she was. The nurse came up from supper and took possession of the baby. Emma let it go, and remained sitting on the sofa. When the nurse had gone into the adjoining room, she laid a hand in one of her husband's.

"David," she said, "I have a little secret."

"I've no doubt," said David, "that you have a dozen. You're the most secretive, clandestine, shady sort of woman I ever came across."

It is needless to say that this was merely David's exuberant humor; for Emma was the most communicative, sympathetic soul in the world. She practised, in a quiet way, a passionate devotion to her husband, and it was a part of her religion to make him her confidant. She had, of course, in strictness, very little to confide to him. But she confided to him her little, in the hope that he would one day confide to her what she was pleased to believe his abundance.

"It's not exactly a secret," Emma pursued; "only I've kept it so long that it almost seems like one. You'll think me very silly, David. I couldn't bear to mention it so long as there was any chance of truth in the talk of that horrible old squaw. But now, that it's disproved, it seems absurd to keep it on my mind; not that I really ever felt it there, but if I said nothing about it, it was for your sake. I'm sure you'll not mind it; and if you don't, David, I'm sure I needn't."

"My dear girl, what on earth is coming?" said David. " 'If you don't, I'm sure I needn't!'—you make a man's flesh crawl."

"Why, it's another prophecy," said Emma.

"Another prophecy? Let's have it, then, by all means."

"But you don't mean, David, that you're going to believe it?"

"That depends. If it's to my advantage, of course I shall."

"To your advantage! Oh, David!"

"My dear Emma, prophecies are not to be sneered at. Look at this one about the baby."

"Look at the baby, I should say."

"Exactly. Isn't she a girl? hasn't she been at death's door?"

"Yes; but the old woman made her go through."

"Nay; you've no imagination. Of course, they pull off short of the catastrophe; but they give you a good deal, by the way."

"Well, my dear, since you're so determined to believe in them, I should be sorry to prevent you. I make you a present of this one."

"Was it a squaw, this time?"

"No, it was an old Italian—a woman who used to come on Saturday mornings at school and sell us sugar-plums and trinkets. You see it

131

was ten years ago. Our teachers used to dislike her; but we let her into the garden by a back-gate. She used to carry a little tray, like a pedler. She had candy and cakes, and kid-gloves. One day, she offered to tell our fortunes with cards. She spread out her cards on the top of her tray, and half a dozen of us went through the ceremony. The rest were afraid. I believe I was second. She told me a long rigmarole that I have forgotten, but said nothing about lovers or husbands. That, of course, was all we wanted to hear; and, though I was disappointed, I was ashamed to ask any questions. To the girls who came after me, she promised successively the most splendid marriages. I wondered whether I was to be an old maid. The thought was horrible, and I determined to try and conjure such a fate. 'But I?' I said, as she was going to put up her cards; 'am I never to be married?' She looked at me, and then looked over her cards again. I suppose she wished to make up for her neglect. 'Ah, you, Miss,' she said—'you are better off than any of them. You are to marry twice!' Now, my dear," Emma added, "make the most of that." And she leaned her head on her husband's shoulder and looked in his face, smiling.

But David smiled not at all. On the contrary, he looked grave. Hereupon, Emma put by her smile, and looked grave, too. In fact, she looked pained. She thought it positively unkind of David to take her little story in such stiff fashion.

"It's very strange," said David.

"It's very silly," said Emma. "I'm sorry I told you, David."

"I'm very glad. It's extremely curious. Listen, and you'll see—I, too, have a secret, Emma."

"Nay, I don't want to hear it," said Emma.

"You shall hear it," said the young man. "I never mentioned it before, simply because I had forgotten it—utterly forgotten it. But your story calls it back to my memory. I, too, once had my fortune told. It was neither a squaw nor a gypsy. It was a young lady, in company. I forget her name. I was less than twenty. It was at a party, and she was telling people's fortunes. She had cards; she pretended to have a gift. I don't know what I had been saying. I suppose that, as boys of that age are fond of doing, I had been showing off my wit at the expense of married life. I remember a young lady introducing me to this person, and saying that here was a young man who declared he never would marry. Was it true? She looked at her cards, and said that it was completely false, and that I should marry twice. The company began to laugh. I was mortified. 'Why don't you say three times?' I said. 'Because,' answered the young lady, 'my cards say only twice.'" David had got up from the sofa, and stood before his wife. "Don't you think it's curious?" he said.

"Curious enough. One would say you thought it something more."

"You know," continued David, "we can't both marry twice."

"'You know'," cried Emma. "Bravo, my dear. 'You know' is delightful. Perhaps you would like me to withdraw and give you a chance."

David looked at his wife, half surprised at the bitterness of her words. He was apparently on the point of making some conciliatory speech; but he seemed forcibly struck, afresh, with the singular agreement of the two predictions. "Upon my soul!" he said, "it's preternaturally odd!" He burst into a fit of laughter.

Emma put her hands to her face and sat silent. Then, after a few moments: "For my part," she said, "I think it's extremely disagreeable!" Overcome by the effort to speak, she burst into tears.

Her husband again placed himself at her side. He still took the humorous view of the case—on the whole, perhaps, indiscreetly. "Come, Emma," he said, "dry your tears, and consult your memory. Are you sure you've never been married before?"

Emma shook off his caresses and got up. Then, suddenly turning around, she said, with vehemence, "And you, sir?"

For an answer David laughed afresh; and then, looking at his wife a moment, he rose and followed her. *"Où diable la jalousie va-t-elle se nicher?"* he cried. He put his arm about her, she yielded, and he kissed her. At this moment a little wail went up from the baby in the neighboring room. Emma hastened away.

Where, indeed, as David had asked, will jealousy stow herself away? In what odd, unlikely corners will she turn up? She made herself a nest in poor Emma's innocent heart, and, at her leisure, she lined and feathered it. The little scene I have just described left neither party, indeed, as it found them. David had kissed his wife and shown the folly of her tears, but he had not taken back his story. For ten years he hadn't thought of it; but, now that he had been reminded of it, he was quite unable to dismiss it from his thoughts. It besieged him, and harassed and distracted him; it thrust itself into his mind at the most inopportune moments; it buzzed in his ears and danced among the columns of figures in his great folio account books. Sometimes the young lady's prediction conjoined itself with a prodigious array of numerals, and roamed away from its modest place among the units into the hundreds of thousands. David read himself a million times a husband. But, after all, as he reflected, the oddity was not in his having been predestined, according to the young lady, to marry twice; but in poor Emma having drawn exactly the same lot. It was a conflict of oracles. It would be an interesting inquiry, although now, of course, quite impracticable, to ascertain which of the two was more to be trusted. For how under the sun could both have revealed the truth? The utmost ingenuity was powerless to reconcile their mutual incompatibility. Could either of the soothsayers have made her statement in a figurative sense? It seemed to David that this was to fancy them a grain too wise. The simplest solution—except not to think of the matter at all, which he couldn't bring himself to accomplish—was to fancy that each of the prophecies nullified the other, and that when he became Emma's husband, their counterfeit destinies had been put to confusion.

Emma found it quite impossible to take the matter so easily. She pondered it night and day for a month. She admitted that the prospect of a second marriage was, of necessity, unreal for one of them; but her heart ached to discover for which of them it was real. She had laughed at the folly of the Indian's threat; but she found it impossible to laugh at the extraordinary coincidence of David's promised fate with her own. That it was absurd and illogical made it only the more painful. It filled her life with a horrible uncertainty. It seemed to indicate that whether or no the silly gossip of a couple of jugglers was, on either side, strictly fulfilled; yet there was some dark cloud hanging over their marriage. Why should an honest young couple have such strange things said of them? Why should they be called upon to reach such an illegible riddle? Emma repented bitterly of having told her secret. And yet, too, she rejoiced; for it was a dreadful thought that David, unprompted to reveal his own adventure should have kept such a dreadful occurrence locked up in his breast, shedding, Heaven knows what baleful influence, on her life and fortunes. Now she could live it down; she could combat it, laugh at it. And David, too, could do as much for the mysterious prognostic of his own extinction.

Never had Emma's fancy been so active. She placed the two faces of her destiny in every conceivable light. At one moment, she imagined that David might succumb to the pressure of his fancied destiny, and leave her a widow, free to marry again; and at another that he would grow enamored of the thought of obeying his own oracle, and crush her to death by the masculine vigor of his will. Then, again, she felt as if her own will were strong, and as if she bore on her head the protecting hand of fate. Love was much, assuredly, but fate was more. And here, indeed, what was fate but love? As she had loved David, so she would love another. She racked her poor little brain to conjure up this future master of her life. But, to do her justice, it was quite in vain. She could not forget David. Nevertheless, she felt guilty. And then she thought of David, and wondered whether he was guilty, too— whether he was dreaming of another woman.

In this way it was that Emma became jealous. That she was a very silly girl I don't pretend to deny. I have expressly said that she was a person of a very simple make; and in proportion to the force of her old straightforward confidence in her husband, was that of her present suspicion and vagaries.

From the moment that Emma became jealous, the household angel of peace shook its stainless wings and took a melancholy flight. Emma immediately betrayed herself. She accused her husband of indifference, and of preferring the society of other women. Once she told him that he might, if he pleased. It was à propos of an evening party, to which they had both been asked. During the afternoon, while David was still at his business, the baby had been taken sick, and Emma had written a note to say that they should not be able to come. When David returned, she told him of her note, and he laughed and said that he wondered whether their intended hostess would fancy that it was his practice to hold the baby. For his part, he declared that he meant to go; and at nine o'clock he appeared, dressed. Emma looked at him, pale and indignant.

"After all," she said, "you're right. Make the most of your time."

These were horrible words, and, as was natural, they made a vast breach between the husband and wife.

Once in awhile Emma felt an impulse to take her revenge, and look for happiness in society, and in the sympathy and attention of agreeable men. But she never went very far. Such happiness seemed but a troubled repose, and the world at large had no reason to suspect that she was not on the best of terms with her husband.

David, on his side, went much further. He was gradually transformed from a quiet, home-keeping, affectionate fellow, into a nervous, restless, querulous man of pleasure, a diner-out and a haunter of clubs and theatres. From the moment that he detected their influence on his life, he had been unable to make light of the two prophecies. Then one, now the other, dominated his imagination, and, in either event, it was impossible to live as he would have lived in ignorance. Sometimes, at the thought of an early death, he was seized with a passionate attachment to the world, and an irresistible desire to plunge into worldly joys. At other moments, thinking of his wife's possible death, and of her place being taken by another woman, he felt a fierce and unnatural impatience of all further delay in the evolution of events. He wished to annihilate the present. To live in expectation so acute and so feverish was not to live. Poor David was occasionally tempted by desperate expedients to kill time. Gradually the perpetual oscillation from one phase of his destiny to the other, and the constant change from passionate exaltation to equally morbid depression, induced a state of chronic excitement, not far removed from insanity.

At about this moment he made the acquaintance of a young unmarried woman whom I may call Julia—a very charming, superior person, of a character to exert a healing, soothing influence upon his troubled spirit. In the course of time, he told her the story of his domestic revolution. At first, she was very much amused; she laughed at him, and called him superstitious, fantastic, and puerile. But he took her levity so ill, that she changed her tactics, and humored his delusion.

It seemed to her, however, that his case was serious, and that, if some attempt were not made to arrest his growing alienation from his wife, the happiness of both parties might depart forever. She believed that the flimsy ghost of their mysterious future could be effectually laid only by means of a reconciliation. She doubted that their love was dead and gone. It was only dormant. If she might once awaken it, she would retire with a light heart, and leave it lord of the house.

So, without informing David of her intention, Julia ventured to call upon Emma, with whom she had no personal acquaintance. She hardly knew what she should say; she would trust to the inspiration of the moment; she merely wished to kindle a ray of light in the young wife's darkened household. Emma, she fancied, was a simple, sensitive person; she would be quickly moved by proffered kindness.

But, although she was unacquainted with Emma, the young wife had considerable knowledge of Julia. She had had her pointed out to her in public. Julia was handsome. Emma hated her. She thought of her as her husband's temptress and evil genius. She assured herself that they were longing for her death, so that they might marry. Perhaps he was already her lover. Doubtless they would be glad to kill her. In this way it was that, instead of finding a gentle, saddened, sensitive person, Julia found a bitter, scornful woman, infuriated by a sense of insult and injury. Julia's visit seemed to Emma the climax of insolence. She refused to listen to her. Her courtesy, her gentleness, her attempt at conciliation, struck her as a mockery and a snare. Finally, losing all self-control, she called her a very hard name.

Then Julia, who had a high temper of her own, plucked up a spirit, and struck a blow for her dignity—a blow, however, which unfortunately rebounded on David. "I had steadily refused, Madam," she said, "to believe that you are a fool. But you quite persuade me."

With these words she withdrew. But it mattered little to Emma whether she remained or departed. She was conscious only of one thing, that David had called her a fool to another woman. "A fool?" she cried. "Truly I have been. But I shall be no longer."

She immediately made her preparations for leaving her husband's house, and when David came home he found her with her child and a servant on the point of departure. She told him in a few words that she was going to her mother's, that in his absence he had employed persons to insult her in her own house, it was necessary that she should seek protection in her family. David offered no resistance. He made no attempt to resent her accusation. He was prepared for anything. It was fate.

Emma accordingly went to her mother's. She was supported in this extraordinary step, and in the long months of seclusion which followed it, by an exalted sense of her own comparative integrity and virtue. She, at least, had been a faithful wife. She had endured, she had been patient. Whatever her destiny might be, she had made no indecent attempt to anticipate it. More than ever she devoted herself to her little girl. The comparative repose and freedom of her life gave her almost a feeling of happiness. She felt that deep satisfaction which comes upon the spirit when it has purchased contentment at the expense of reputation. There was now, at least, no falsehood in her life. She neither valued her marriage nor pretended to value it.

As for David, he saw little of any one but Julia. Julia, I have said, was a woman of great merit and of perfect generosity. She very soon ceased to resent the check she had received from Emma, and not despairing, still, of seeing peace once more established in the young man's household, she made it a matter of conscience to keep David by her influence in as sane and unperverted a state of mind as circumstances would allow. "She may hate me," thought Julia, "but I'll keep him for her." Julia's, you see, in all this business was the only wise head.

David took his own view of their relations. "I shall certainly see you as often as I wish," he declared. "I shall take consolation where I find it. She has her child—her mother. Does she begrudge me a friend? She may thank her stars I don't take to drink or to play."

For six months David saw nothing of his wife. Finally, one evening, when he was at Julia's house, he received this note:

"Your daughter died this morning, after several hours' suffering. She will be buried to-morrow morning."   E."

David handed the note to Julia. "After all," he said, "she was right."

"Who was right, my poor friend?" asked Julia.

"The old squaw. We cried out too soon."

The next morning he went to the house of his mother-in-law. The servant, recognizing him, ushered him into the room in which the remains of his poor little girl lay, ready for burial. Near the darkened window stood his mother-in-law, in conversation with a gentleman —a certain Mr. Clark—whom David recognized as a favorite clergyman of his wife, and whom he had never liked. The lady, on his entrance, made him a very grand curtsy—if, indeed, that curtsy may be said to come within the regulations which govern salutations of this sort, in which the head is tossed up in proportion as the body is depressed— and swept out of the room. David bowed to the clergyman, and went and looked at the little remnant of mortality which had once been his daughter. After a decent interval, Mr. Clark ventured to approach him.

"You have met with a great trial, sir," said the clergyman.

David assented in silence.

"I suppose," continued Mr. Clark, "it is sent, like all trials, to remind us of our feeble and dependent condition—to purge us of pride and stubbornness—to make us search our hearts and see whether we have not by chance allowed the noisome weeds of folly to overwhelm and suffocate the modest flower of wisdom."

That Mr. Clark had deliberately prepared this speech, with a view to the occasion, I should hesitate to affirm. Gentlemen of his profession have these little parcels of sentiment ready to their hands. But he was, of course, acquainted with Emma's estrangement from her husband (although not with its original motives), and, like a man of genuine feeling, he imagined that under the softening action of a common sorrow, their two hardened hearts might be made to melt and again to flow into one. "The more we lose, my friend," he pursued, "the more we should cherish and value what is left."

"You speak to very good purpose, sir," said David; "but I, unfortunately, have nothing left."

At this moment the door opened, and Emma came in—pale, and clad in black. She stopped, apparently unprepared to see her husband. But, on David's turning toward her, she came forward.

David felt as if Heaven had sent an angel to give the lie to his last words. His face flushed—first with shame, and then with joy. He put out his arms. Emma halted an instant, struggling with her pride, and looked at the clergyman. He raised his hand, with a pious sacramental gesture, and she fell on her husband's neck.

The clergyman took hold of David's hand and pressed it; and, although, as I have said, the young man had never been particularly fond of Mr. Clark, he devoutly returned the pressure.

"Well," said Julia, a fortnight later—for in the interval Emma had been brought to consent to her husband's maintaining his acquaintance with this lady, and even herself to think her a very good sort of person—"well, I don't see but that the terrible problem is at last solved, and that you have each been married twice."

139

OSBORNE'S REVENGE

Osborne's Revenge

"Osborne's Revenge," Henry James's eleventh published tale, appeared in the Galaxy, *July 1868, with a frontispiece illustration by W. J. Hennessy. It is reprinted here for the first time. This tale and the two preceding ones—all of the* Galaxy *group of 1868—were the first and for a long time the last of James's stories to be "illustrated."*

*This story was followed by "A Light Man" (*Galaxy, *July 1869), reprinted in* Stories Revived, *Vol. I (1885). In this same month the first part of "Gabrielle de Bergerac" appeared.*

· *I* ·

PHILIP OSBORNE AND ROBERT GRAHAM WERE INTIMATE friends. The latter had been spending the summer at certain medicinal springs in New York, the use of which had been recommended by his physician. Osborne, on the other hand—a lawyer by profession, and with a rapidly increasing practice—had been confined to the city, and had suffered June and July to pass, not unheeded, heaven knows, but utterly unhonored. Toward the middle of July he began to feel uneasy at not hearing from his friend, habitually the best of correspondents. Graham had a charming literary talent, and plenty of leisure, being without a family, and without business. Osborne wrote to him, asking the reason of his silence, and demanding an immediate reply. He received in the course of a few days the following letter:

Dear Philip: I am, as you conjectured, not well. These infernal waters have done me no good. On the contrary—they have poisoned me. They have poisoned my life, and I wish to God I had never come to them. Do you remember the *White Lady* in *The Monastery,* who used to appear to the hero at the spring? There is such a one here, at this spring—which you know tastes of sulphur. Judge of the quality of the young woman. She has charmed me, and I can't get away. But I mean to try again. Don't think I'm cracked, but expect me next week. Yours always,

R.G.

The day after he received this letter, Osborne met, at the house of a female friend detained in town by the illness of one of her children, a lady who had just come from the region in which Graham had fixed himself. This lady, Mrs. Dodd by name, and a widow, had seen a great deal of the young man, and she drew a very long face and threw great expression into her eyes as she spoke of him. Seeing that she was inclined to be confidential, Osborne made it possible that she should converse with him privately. She assured him, behind her fan, that his friend was dying of a broken heart. Something should be done. The story was briefly this. Graham had made the acquaintance, in the early part of the summer, of a young lady, a certain Miss Congreve, who was living in the neighborhood with a married sister. She was not pretty, but she was clever, graceful, and pleasing, and Graham had immediately fallen in love with her. She had encouraged his addresses, to the knowledge of all their friends, and at the end of a month—heart-histories are very rapid at the smaller watering places—their engagement, although not announced, was hourly expected. But at this moment a stranger had effected an entrance into the little society of which Miss Congreve was one of the most brilliant ornaments —a Mr. Holland, out of the West—a man of Graham's age, but better favored in person. Heedless of the circumstance that her affections were notoriously preoccupied, he had immediately begun to be attentive to the young girl. Equally reckless of the same circumstance, Henrietta Congreve had been all smiles—all seduction. In the course of a week, in fact, she had deliberately transferred her favors from the old love to the new. Graham had been turned out into the cold; she had ceased to look at him, to speak to him, to think of him. He nevertheless remained at the springs, as if he found a sort of fascination in the sense of his injury, and in seeing Miss Congreve and Holland together. Besides, he doubtless wished people to fancy that, for good reasons, he had withdrawn his suit, and it was therefore not for him to hide himself. He was proud, reserved, and silent, but his friends had no difficulty in seeing that his pain was intense, and that his wound was almost mortal. Mrs. Dodd declared that unless he was diverted from his sorrow, and removed from contact with the various scenes and objects which reminded him of his unhappy passion—and above all, deprived of the daily chance of meeting Miss Congreve—she would not answer for his sanity.

Osborne made all possible allowances for exaggeration. A woman, he reflected, likes so to round off her story—especially if it is a dismal one. Nevertheless he felt very anxious, and he forthwith wrote his friend a long letter, asking him to what extent Mrs. Dodd's little romance was true, and urging him to come immediately to town, where, if it was substantially true, he might look for diversion. Graham answered by arriving in person. At first, Osborne was decidedly relieved. His friend looked better and stronger than he had looked for months. But on coming to talk with him, he found him morally, at least, a sad invalid. He was listless, abstracted, and utterly inactive in mind. Osborne observed with regret that he made no response to his attempts at interrogation and to his proffered sympathy. Osborne had by nature no great respect for sentimental woes. He was not a man to lighten his tread because his neighbor below stairs was laid up with a broken heart. But he saw that it would never do to poke fun at poor Graham, and that he was quite proof against the contagion of gayety. Graham begged him not to think him morbid or indifferent to his kindness, and to allow him not to speak of his trouble until it was over. He had resolved to forget it. When he had forgotten it—as one forgets such things—when he had contrived to push the further end of it at least into the past—then he would tell him all about it. For the present he must occupy his thoughts with something else. It was hard to decide what to do. It was hard to travel without an aim. Yet the intolerable heat made it impossible that he should stay in New York. He might go to Newport.

"A moment," said Osborne. "Has Miss Congreve gone to Newport?"

"Not that I know of."

"Does she intend to go?"

Graham was silent. "Good heavens!" he cried, at last, "forbid it then! All I want is to have it forbidden. *I* can't forbid it. Did you ever see a human being so degraded?" he added, with a ghastly smile. "Where *shall* I go?"

Philip went to his table and began to overhaul a mass of papers fastened with red tape. He selected several of these documents and placed them apart. Then, turning to his friend, "You're to go out to Minnesota," he said, looking him in the eyes. The proposal was a grave one, and gravely as it was meant, Osborne would have been glad to have Graham offer some resistance. But he sat looking at him with a solemn stare which (in the light of subsequent events) cast a lugubrious shade over the whole transaction. "The deuce!" thought Osborne. "Has it made him stupid?—What you need," he said aloud, "is to have something else to think about. An idle man can't expect to get over such troubles. I have some business to be done at St. Paul, and I know that if you'll give your attention to it, you're as well able to do it as any man. It's a simple matter, but it needs a trustworthy person. So I shall depend upon you."

Graham came and took up the papers and looked over them mechanically.

"Never mind them now," said Osborne; "it's past midnight; you must go to bed. To-morrow morning I'll put you *au fait,* and the day after, if you like, you can start."

The next morning Graham seemed to have recovered a considerable portion of his old cheerfulness. He talked about indifferent matters, laughed, and seemed for a couple of hours to have forgotten Miss Congreve. Osborne began to doubt that the journey was necessary, and he was glad to be able to think, afterwards, that he had expressed his doubts, and that his friend had strongly combatted them and insisted upon having the affair explained to him. He mastered it, to Osborne's satisfaction, and started across the continent.

During the ensuing week Philip was so pressed with business that he had very little time to think of the success of Graham's mission. Within the fortnight he received the following letter:

Dear Philip: Here I am, safe, but anything but sound. I don't know what to think of it, but I have completely forgotten the terms of my embassy. I can't for my life remember what I'm to do or say, and neither the papers nor your notes assist me a whit. 12th.—I wrote so much yesterday and then went out to take a walk and collect my thoughts. I *have* collected them, once for all. Do you understand, dearest Philip? Don't call me insane, or impious, or anything that merely expresses your own impatience and intolerance, without throwing a ray of light on the state of my own mind. He can only understand it who has felt it, and he who has felt it can do but as I do. Life has lost, I don't say its charm—that I could willingly dispense with—but its meaning. I shall live in your memory and your love, which is a vast deal better than living in my own self-contempt. Farewell.

R.G.

Osborne learned the circumstances of his friend's death three days later, through his correspondent at St. Paul—the person to whom Graham had been addressed. The unhappy young man had shot himself through the head in his room at the hotel. He had left money, and written directions for the disposal of his remains—directions which were, of course, observed. As Graham possessed no near relative, the effect of his death was confined to a narrow circle; to the circle, I may say, of Philip Osborne's capacious personality. The two young men had been united by an almost passionate friendship. Now that Graham had ceased to be, Osborne became sensible of the strength of this bond; he felt that he cared more for it than for any human tie. They had known each other ten years, and their intimacy had grown with their growth during the most active period of their lives. It had been strengthened within and without by the common enjoyment of so many pleasures, the experience of so many hazards, the exchange of so much advice, so much confidence, and so many pledges of mutual interest, that each had grown to regard it as the single absolute certainty in life, the one fixed fact in a shifting world. As constantly happens with intimate friends, the two were perfectly diverse in character, tastes and appearance. Graham was three years the elder, slight, undersized, feeble in health, sensitive, indolent, whimsical, generous, and in reality of a far finer clay than his friend, as the latter, moreover, perfectly well knew. Their intimacy was often a puzzle to observers. Disinterested parties were at a loss to discover how Osborne had come to set his heart upon an insignificant, lounging invalid, who, in general company, talked in monosyllables, in a weak voice, and gave himself the airs of one whom nature had endowed with the right to be fastidious, without ever having done a stroke of work. Graham's partisans, on the other hand, who were chiefly women (which, by the

147

way, effectually relieves him from the accusation occasionally brought against him of being "effeminate") were quite unable to penetrate the motives of his interest in a commonplace, hard-working lawyer, who addressed a charming woman as if he were exhorting a jury of grocers and undertakers, and viewed the universe as one vast "case." This account of Osborne's mind and manners would have been too satirical to be wholly just, and yet it would have been excusable as an attempt to depict a figure in striking contrast with poor Graham. Osborne was in all respects a large fellow. He was six feet two in height, with a chest like a boxing-master, and a clear, brown complexion, which successfully resisted the deleterious action of a sedentary life. He was, in fact, without a particle of vanity, a particularly handsome man. His character corresponded to his person, or, as one may say, continued and completed it, and his mind kept the promise of his character. He was all of one piece—all health and breadth, capacity and energy. Graham had once told his friend somewhat brutally—for in his little, weak voice Graham said things far more brutal than Osborne, just as he said things far more fine—he had told him that he worked like a horse and loved like a dog.

Theoretically, Osborne's remedy for mental trouble was work. He redoubled his attention to his professional affairs, and strove to reconcile himself, once for all, to his loss. But he found his grief far stronger than his will, and felt that it obstinately refused to be pacified without some act of sacrifice or devotion. Osborne had an essentially kind heart and plenty of pity and charity for deserving objects; but at the bottom of his soul there lay a well of bitterness and resentment which, when his nature was strongly shaken by a sense of wrong, was sure to ferment and raise its level, and at last to swamp his conscience. These bitter waters had been stirred, and he felt that they were rising fast. His thoughts travelled back with stubborn iteration from Graham's death to the young girl who figured in the prologue to the tragedy. He felt in his breast a savage need of hating her. Osborne's friends observed in these days that he looked by no means pleasant; and if he had not been such an excellent fellow he might easily have passed for an intolerable brute. He was not softened and mellowed by suffering; he was exasperated. It seemed to him that justice cried aloud that Henrietta Congreve should be confronted with the results of her folly, and made to carry forever in her thoughts, in all the hideousness of suicide, the image of her miserable victim. Osborne was, perhaps, in error, but he was assuredly sincere; and it is strong evidence of the energy of genuine affection that this lusty intellect should have been brought, in the interest of another, to favor a scheme which it would have deemed wholly, ludicrously impotent to assuage the injured dignity of its own possessor. Osborne must have been very fond of his friend not to have pronounced him a drivelling fool. It is true that he had always pitied him as much as he loved him, although Graham's incontestable gifts and virtues had kept this feeling in the background. Now that he was gone, pity came uppermost, and bade fair to drive him to a merciless disallowance of all claims to extenuation on the part of the accused. It was unlikely that, for a long time at least, he would listen to anything but that Graham had been foully wronged, and that the light of his life had been wantonly quenched. He found it impossible to sit down in resignation. The best that he could do, indeed, would not call Graham back to life; but he might at least discharge his gall, and have the comfort of feeling that Miss Congreve was the worse for it. He was quite unable to work. He roamed about for three days in a disconsolate, angry fashion. On the third, he called upon Mrs. Dodd, from whom he learned that Miss Congreve had gone to Newport, to stay with a second married sister. He went home and packed up a valise, and—without knowing why, feeling only that to do so was to do something, and to put himself in the way of doing more—drove down to the Newport boat.

· *II* ·

His first inquiry on his arrival, after he had looked up several of his friends and encountered a number of acquaintances, was about Miss Congreve's whereabouts and habits. He found that she was very little known. She lived with her sister, Mrs. Wilkes, and as yet had made but a single appearance in company. Mrs. Wilkes, moreover, he learned, was an invalid and led a very quiet life. He ascertained the situation of her house and gave himself the satisfaction of walking past it. It was a pretty place, on a secluded by-road, marked by various tokens of wealth and comfort. He heard, as he passed, through the closed shutters of the drawing-room window, the sound of a high, melodious voice, warbling and trilling to the accompaniment of a piano. Osborne had no soul for music, but he stopped and listened, and as he did so, he remembered Graham's passion for the charming art and fancied that these were the very accents that had lured him to his sorrow. Poor Graham! here too, as in all things, he had showed his taste. The singer discharged a magnificent volley of roulades and flourishes and became silent. Osborne, fancying he heard a movement of the lattice of the shutters, slowly walked away. A couple of days later he found himself strolling, alone and disconsolate, upon the long avenue which runs parallel to the Newport cliffs, which, as all the world knows, may be reached by five minutes' walk from any part of it. He had been on the field, now, for nearly a week, and he was no nearer his revenge. His unsatisfied desire haunted his steps and hovered in a ghostly fashion about thoughts which perpetual contact with old friends and new, and the entertaining spectacle of a heterogeneous throng of pleasure seekers and pleasure venders, might have made free and happy. Osborne was very fond of the world, and while he still clung to his resentment, he yet tacitly felt that it lurked as a skeleton at his banquet. He was fond of nature, too, and betwixt these two predilections, he grew at moments ashamed of his rancor. At all events, he felt a grateful sense of relief when as he pursued his course along this sacred way of fashion, he caught a glimpse of the deep blue expanse of the ocean, shining at the end of a cross road. He forthwith took his way down to the cliffs. At the point where the road ceased, he found an open barouche, whose occupants appeared to have wandered out of sight. Passing this carriage, he reached a spot where the surface of the cliff communicates with the beach, by means of an abrupt footpath. This path he descended and found himself on a level with the broad expanse of sand and the rapidly rising tide. The wind was blowing fresh from the sea and the little breakers tumbling in with their multitudinous liquid clamor. In a very few moments Osborne felt a sensible exhilaration of spirits. He had not advanced many steps under the influence of this joyous feeling, when, on turning a slight projection in the cliff, he descried a sight which caused him to hasten forward. On a broad flat rock, at about a dozen yards from the shore, stood a child of some five years—a handsome boy, fair-haired and well dressed—stamping his feet and wringing his hands in an apparent agony of terror. It was easy to understand the situation. The child had ventured out on the rock while the water was still low, and had become so much absorbed in paddling with his little wooden spade among the rich marine deposits on its surface, that he had failed to observe the advance of the waves, which had now completely covered the intermediate fragments of rock and were foaming and weltering betwixt him and the shore. The poor little fellow stood screaming to the winds and waters, and quite unable to answer Osborne's shouts of interrogation and comfort. Meanwhile, the latter prepared to fetch him ashore. He saw with some disgust that the channel was too wide to warrant a leap, and yet, as the child's companions might at any moment appear, in the shape of distracted importunate women, he judged it imprudent to divest himself of any part of his apparel. He accordingly plunged in without further ado, waded forward, seized the child and finally restored him to *terra firma*. He felt him trembling in his arms like a frightened bird. He set him on his feet, soothed him, and asked him what had become of his guardians.

The boy pointed toward a rock, lying at a certain distance, close under the cliff, and Osborne, following his gesture, distinguished what seemed to be the hat and feather of a lady sitting on the further side of it.

"That's Aunt Henrietta," said the child.

"Aunt Henrietta deserves a scolding," said Osborne. "Come, we'll go and give it to her." And he took the boy's hand and led him toward his culpable relative. They walked along the beach until they came abreast of the rock, and approached the lady in front. At the sound of their feet on the stones, she raised her head. She was a young woman, seated on a boulder, with an album in her lap, apparently absorbed in the act of sketching. Seeing at a glance that something was amiss, she rose to her feet and thrust the album into her pocket. Osborne's wet trousers and the bespattered garments and discomposed physiognomy of the child revealed the nature of the calamity. She held out her arms to her little nephew. He dropped Philip's hand, and ran and threw himself on his aunt's neck. She raised him up and kissed him, and looked interrogatively at Osborne.

"I couldn't help seeing him safely in your hands," said the latter, removing his hat. "He has had a terrific adventure."

"What is it, darling?" cried the young lady, again kissing the little fellow's bloodless face.

"He came into the water after me," cried the boy. "Why did you leave me there?"

"What has happened, sir?" asked the young girl, in a somewhat preemptory tone.

"You had apparently left him on that rock, madame, with a channel betwixt him and the shore deep enough to drown him. I took the liberty of displacing him. But he's more frightened than hurt."

The young girl had a pale face and dark eyes. There was no beauty in her features; but Osborne had already perceived that they were extremely expressive and intelligent. Her face flushed a little, and her eyes flashed; the former, it seemed to Philip, with mortification at her own neglect, and the latter with irritation at the reproach conveyed in his accents. But he may have been wrong. She sat down on the rock, with the child on her knees, kissing him repeatedly and holding him with a sort of convulsive pressure. When she looked up, the flashes in her eyes had melted into a couple of tears. Seeing that Philip was a gentleman, she offered a few words of self-justification. She had kept the boy constantly within sight, and only within a few minutes had allowed her attention to be drawn away. Her apology was interrupted by the arrival of a second young woman—apparently a nursery-maid—who emerged from the concealment of the neighboring rocks, leading a little girl by the hand. Instinctively, her eyes fell upon the child's wet clothes.

"Ah, Miss Congreve," she cried, in true nursery-maid style, "what'll Mrs. Wilkes say to that?"

"She will say that she is very thankful to this gentleman," said Miss Congreve, with decision.

Philip had been looking at the young girl as she spoke, forcibly struck by her face and manner. He detected in her appearance a peculiar union of modesty and frankness, of youthful freshness and elegant mannerism, which suggested vague possibilities of further acquaintance. He had already found it pleasant to observe her. He had been for ten days in search of a wicked girl, and it was a momentary relief to find himself suddenly face to face with a charming one. The nursery-maid's apostrophe was like an electric shock.

It is, nevertheless, to be supposed that he concealed his surprise, inasmuch as Miss Congreve gave no sign of having perceived that he was startled. She had come to a tardy sense of his personal discomfort.

She besought him to make use of her carriage, which he would find on the cliff, and quickly return home. He thanked her and declined her offer, declaring that it was better policy to walk. He put out his hand to his little friend and bade him good-by. Miss Congreve liberated the child and he came and put his hand in Philip's.

"One of these days," said Osborne, "you'll have long legs, too, and then you'll not mind the water." He spoke to the boy, but he looked hard at Miss Congreve, who, perhaps, thought he was asking for some formal expression of gratitude.

"His mother," she said, "will give herself the pleasure of thanking you."

"The trouble," said Osborne, "the very unnecessary trouble. Your best plan," he added, with a smile (for, wonderful to tell, he actually smiled) "is to say nothing about it."

"If I consulted my own interests alone," said the young girl, with a gracious light in her dark eyes, "I should certainly hold my tongue. But I hope my little victim is not so ungrateful as to promise silence."

Osborne stiffened himself up; for this was more or less of a compliment. He made his bow in silence and started for home at a rapid pace. On the following day he received this note by post:

Mrs. Wilkes begs to thank Mr. Osborne most warmly for the prompt and generous relief afforded to her little boy. She regrets that Mr. Osborne's walk should have been interrupted, and hopes that his exertions have been attended with no bad effects.

Enclosed in the note was a pocket-handkerchief, bearing Philip's name, which he remembered to have made the child take, to wipe his tears. His answer was, of course, brief.

Mr. Osborne begs to assure Mrs. Wilkes that she exaggerates the importance of the service rendered to her son, and that he has no cause to regret his very trifling efforts. He takes the liberty of presenting his compliments to Master Wilkes, and of hoping that he has recovered from his painful sensations.

The correspondence naturally went no further, and for some days no additional light was thrown upon Miss Congreve. Now that Philip had met her, face to face, and found her a commonplace young girl— a clever girl, doubtless, for she looked it, and an agreeable one—but still a mere young lady, mindful of the proprieties, with a face innocent enough, and even a trifle sad, and a couple of pretty children who called her "aunt," and whom, indeed, in a moment of enthusiastic devotion to nature and art, she left to the mercy of the waves, but whom she finally kissed and comforted and handled with all due tenderness—now that he had met Miss Congreve under these circumstances, he felt his mission sitting more lightly on his conscience. Ideally she had been repulsive; actually, she was a person whom, if he had not been committed to detest her, he would find it very pleasant to like. She had been humanized, to his view, by the mere accidents of her flesh and blood. Philip was by no means prepared to give up his resentment. Poor Graham's ghost sat grim and upright in his memory, and fed the flickering flame. But it was something of a problem to reconcile the heroine of his vengeful longings, with the heroine of the little scene on the beach, and to accommodate this inoffensive figure, in turn, to the color of his retribution. A dozen matters conspired to keep him from coming to the point, and to put him in a comparatively good humor. He was invited to the right and the left; he lounged and bathed, and talked, and smoked, and rode, and dined out, and saw an endless succession of new faces, and in short, reduced the vestments of his outward mood to a suit of very cheerful half-mourning. And all this, moreover, without any sense of being faithless to his friend. Oddly enough, Graham had never seemed so living as now that he was dead. In the flesh, he had possessed but a half-vitality. His spirit had been exquisitely willing, but his flesh had been fatally weak. He was at best a baffled, disappointed man. It was his spirit, his affections, his sympathies and perceptions, that were warm and active, and Osborne knew that he had fallen sole heir to these. He felt his bosom swell with a wholesome sense of the magnitude of the heritage, and he was conscious with each successive day, of less desire to invoke poor Graham in dark corners, and mourn him in lonely places. By a single solemn, irrevocable aspiration, he had placed his own tough organism and his energetic will at the service of his friend's virtues. So as he found his excursion turning into a holiday, he stretched his long limbs and with the least bit of a yawn whispered *Amen.*

Within a week after his encounter with Miss Congreve, he went with a friend to witness some private theatricals, given in the house of a lady of great social repute. The entertainment consisted of two plays, the first of which was so flat and poor that when the curtain fell Philip prepared to make his escape, thinking he might easily bring the day to some less impotent conclusion. As he passed along the narrow alley between the seats and the wall of the drawing-room, he brushed a printed program out of a lady's hand. Stooping to pick it up, his eye fell upon the name of Miss Congreve among the performers in the second piece. He immediately retraced his steps. The overture began, the curtain rose again, and several persons appeared on the stage, arrayed in the powder and patches of the last century. Finally, amid loud acclamations, walked on Miss Congreve, as the heroine, powdered and patched in perfection. She represented a young countess —a widow in the most interesting predicament—and for all good histrionic purposes, she was irresistibly beautiful. She was dressed, painted, and equipped with great skill and in the very best taste. She looked as if she had stepped out of the frame of one of those charming full-length pastel portraits of fine ladies in Louis XV's time, which they show you in French palaces. But she was not alone all grace and elegance and *finesse;* she had dignity; she was serious at moments, and severe; she frowned and commanded; and, at the proper time, she wept the most natural tears. It was plain that Miss Congreve was a true artist. Osborne had never seen better acting—never, indeed, any so good; for here was an actress who was at once a perfect young lady and a consummate mistress of dramatic effect. The audience was roused to the highest pitch of enthusiasm, and Miss Congreve's fellow-players were left quite in the lurch. The beautiful Miss Latimer, celebrated in polite society for her face and figure, who had undertaken the second female part, was compelled for the nonce to have neither figure nor face. The play had been marked in the bills as adapted from the French "especially for this occasion;" and when the curtain fell for the last time, the audience, in great good humor, clamored for the adapter. Some time elapsed before any notice was taken of their call, which they took as a provocation of their curiosity. Finally, a gentleman made his way before the curtain, and proclaimed that the version of the piece which his associates had had the honor of performing was from the accomplished pen of the young lady who had won their applause in the character of the heroine. At this announcement, a dozen enthusiasts lifted their voices and demanded that Miss Congreve should be caused to re-appear; but the gentleman cut short their appeal by saying that she had already left the house. This was not true, as Osborne subsequently learned. Henrietta was sitting on a sofa behind the scenes, waiting for her carriage, fingering an immense bouquet, and listening with a tired smile to compliments—hard by Miss Latimer, who sat eating an ice beside her mother, the latter lady looking in a very grim fashion at that very plain, dreadfully thin Miss Congreve.

Osborne walked home thrilled and excited, but decidedly bewildered. He felt that he had reckoned without his host, and that Graham's fickle mistress was not a person to be snubbed and done for. He was utterly at loss as to what to think of her. She broke men's hearts and turned their heads; whatever she put her hand to she marked with her genius. She was a coquette, a musician, an artist, an actress, an author—a prodigy. Of what stuff was she made? What had she done with her heart and her conscience? She painted her face, and frolicked among lamps and flowers to the clapping of a thousand hands, while poor Graham lay imprisoned in eternal silence. Osborne was put on his mettle. To draw a penitent tear from those deep and charming eyes was assuredly a task for a clever man.

The plays had been acted on a Wednesday. On the following Saturday Philip was invited to take part in a picnic, organized by Mrs. Carpenter, the lady who had conducted the plays, and who had a mania for making up parties. The persons whom she had now enlisted were to proceed by water to a certain pastoral spot consecrated by nature to picnics, and there to have lunch upon the grass, to dance and play nursery-games. They were carried over in two large sailing boats, and during the transit Philip talked a while with Mrs. Carpenter, whom he found a very amiable, loquacious person. At the further end of the boat in which, with his hostess, he had taken his place, he observed a young girl in a white dress, with a thick, blue veil drawn over her face. Through the veil, directed toward his own person, he perceived the steady glance of two fine, dark eyes. For a moment he was at a loss to recognize their possessor; but his uncertainty was rapidly dispelled.

"I see you have Miss Congreve," he said to Mrs. Carpenter—"the actress of the other evening."

"Yes," said Mrs. Carpenter, "I persuaded her to come. She's all the fashion since Wednesday."

"Was she unwilling to come?" asked Philip.

"Yes, at first. You see, she's a good, quiet girl; she hates to have a noise made about her."

"She had enough noise the other night. She has wonderful talent."

"Wonderful, wonderful. And heaven knows where she gets it. Do you know her family? The most matter-of-fact, least dramatic, least imaginative people in the world—people who are shy of the theatre on moral grounds."

"I see. They won't go to the theatre; the theatre comes to them."

"Exactly. It serves them right. Mrs. Wilkes, Henrietta's sister, was in a dreadful state about her attempting to act. But now, since Henrietta's success, she's talking about it to all the world."

When the boat came to shore, a plank was stretched from the prow to an adjacent rock for the accommodation of the ladies. Philip stood at the head of the plank, offering his hand for their assistance. Mrs. Carpenter came last, with Miss Congreve, who declined Osborne's aid but gave him a little bow, through her veil. Half an hour later Philip again found himself at the side of his hostess, and again spoke of Miss Congreve. Mrs. Carpenter warned him that she was standing close at hand, in a group of young girls.

"Have you heard," he asked, lowering his voice, "of her being engaged to be married—or of her having been?"

"No," said Mrs. Carpenter, "I've heard nothing. To whom?—stay. I've heard vaguely of something this summer at Sharon. She had a sort of flirtation with some man, whose name I forget."

"Was it Holland?"

"I think not. He left her for that very silly little Mrs. Dodd—who hasn't been a widow six months. I think the name was Graham."

Osborne broke into a peal of laughter so loud and harsh that his companion turned upon him in surprise. "Excuse me," said he. "It's false."

"You ask questions, Mr. Osborne," said Mrs. Carpenter, "but you seem to know more about Miss Congreve than I do."

"Very likely. You see, I knew Robert Graham." Philip's words were uttered with such emphasis and resonance that two or three of the young girls in the adjoining group turned about and looked at him.

"She heard you," said Mrs. Carpenter.

"She didn't turn round," said Philip.

"That proves what I say. I meant to introduce you, and now I can't."

"Thank you," said Philip. "I shall introduce myself." Osborne felt in his bosom all the heat of his old resentment. This perverse and heartless girl, then, his soul cried out, not content with driving poor Graham to impious self-destruction, had caused it to be believed that he had killed himself from remorse at his own misconduct. He resolved to strike while the iron was hot. But although he was an avenger, he was still a gentleman, and he approached the young girl with a very civil face.

"If I am not mistaken," he said, removing his hat, "you have already done me the honor of recognising me."

Miss Congreve's bow, as she left the boat, had been so obviously a sign of recognition, that Philip was amazed at the vacant smile with which she received his greeting. Something had happened in the interval to make her change her mind. Philip could think of no other motive than her having overheard his mention of Graham's name.

"I have an impression," she said, "of having met you before; but I confess that I'm unable to place you."

Osborne looked at her a moment. "I can't deny myself," he said, "the pleasure of asking about little Mr. Wilkes."

"I remember you now," said Miss Congreve, simply. "You carried my nephew out of the water."

"I hope he has got over his fright."

"He denies, I believe, that he was frightened. Of course, for my credit, I don't contradict him."

Miss Congreve's words were followed by a long pause, by which she seemed in no degree embarrassed. Philip was confounded by her apparent self-possession—to call it by no worse name. Considering that she had Graham's death on her conscience, and that, hearing his name on Osborne's lips, she must have perceived the latter to be identical with that dear friend of whom Graham must often have spoken, she was certainly showing a very brave face. But had she indeed heard of Graham's death? For a moment Osborne gave her the benefit of the doubt. He felt that he would take a grim satisfaction in being bearer of the tidings. In order to confer due honor on the disclosure, he saw that it was needful to detach the young girl from her companions. As, therefore, the latter at this moment began to disperse in clusters and

couples along the shore, he proposed that they should stroll further
a-field. Miss Congreve looked about at the other young girls as if to
call one of them to her side, but none of them seemed available. So
she slowly moved forward under Philip's guidance, with a half-sup-
pressed look of reluctance. Philip began by paying her a very substantial compliment upon her acting. It was a most inconsequential speech,
in the actual state of his feelings, but he couldn't help it. She was
perhaps as wicked a girl as you shall easily meet, but her acting was
perfect. Having paid this little tribute to equity, he broke ground for
Graham.

"I don't feel, Miss Congreve," he said, "as if you were a new acquaintance. I have heard you a great deal talked about." This was
not literally true, the reader will remember. All Philip's information
had been acquired in his half hour with Mrs. Dodd.

"By whom, pray?" asked Henrietta.

"By Robert Graham."

"Ah yes. I was half prepared to hear you speak of him. I remember
hearing him speak of a person of your name."

Philip was puzzled. Did she know, or not? "I believe you knew
him quite well yourself," he said, somewhat preemptorily.

"As well as he would let me—I doubt if any one knew him well."

"So you've heard of his death," said Philip.

"Yes, from himself."

"How, from himself?"

"He wrote me a letter, in his last hours, leaving his approaching end
to be inferred, rather than positively announcing it. I wrote an answer,
with the request that if my letter was not immediately called for, it
should be returned by the post office. It was returned within a week.—
And now, Mr. Osborne," the young girl added, "let me make a
request."

Philip bowed.

"I shall feel particularly obliged if you will say no more about Mr.
Graham."

This was a stroke for which Osborne was not prepared. It had at
least the merit of directness. Osborne looked at his companion. There
was a faint flush in her cheeks, and a serious light in her eyes. There
was plainly no want of energy in her wish. He felt that he must sus-
pend operations and make his approach from another quarter. But

159

it was some moments before he could bring himself to accede to her request. She looked at him, expecting an answer, and he felt her dark eyes on his face.

"Just as you please," he said, at last, mechanically.

They walked along for some moments in silence. Then, suddenly coming upon a young married woman, whom Mrs. Carpenter had pressed into her service as a lieutenant, Miss Congreve took leave of Philip, on a slight pretext, and entered into talk with this lady. Philip strolled away and walked about for an hour alone. He had met with a check, but he was resolved that, though he had fallen back, it would be only to leap the further. During the half-hour that Philip sauntered along by the water, the dark cloud suspended above poor Miss Congreve's head doubled its portentous volume. And, indeed, from Philip's point of view, could anything well be more shameless and more heartless than the young girl's request?

At last Osborne remembered that he was neglecting the duties laid upon him by Mrs. Carpenter. He retraced his steps and made his way back to the spot devoted to the banquet. Mrs. Carpenter called him to her, said that she had been looking for him for an hour, and, when she learned how he had been spending his time, slapped him with her parasol, called him a horrid creature, and declared that she would never again invite him to anything of hers. She then introduced him to her niece, a somewhat undeveloped young lady, with whom he went and sat down over the water. They found very little to talk about. Osborne was thinking of Miss Congreve, and Mrs. Carpenter's niece, who was very timid and fluttering, having but one foot yet, as one may say, in society, was abashed and unnerved at finding herself alone with so very tall and mature and handsome a gentleman as Philip. He gave her a little confidence in the course of time, however, by making little stones skip over the surface of the water for her amusement. But he still kept thinking of Henrietta Congreve, and he at last bethought himself of asking his companion whether she knew her. Yes, she knew her slightly; but she threw no light on the subject. She was evidently not of an analytical turn of mind, and she was too innocent to gossip. She contented herself with saying that she believed Henrietta was wonderfully clever, and that she read Latin and Greek.

"Clever, clever," said Philip, "I hear nothing else. I shall begin to think she's a demon."

"No, Henrietta Congreve is very good," said his companion. "She's very religious. She visits the poor and reads sermons. You know the other night she acted for the poor. She's anything but a demon. I think she's so nice."

Before long the party was summoned to lunch. Straggling couples came wandering into sight, gentlemen assisting young girls out of rocky retreats into which no one would have supposed them capable of penetrating, and to which—more wonderful still—no one had observed them to direct their steps.

The table was laid in the shade, on the grass, and the feasters sat about on rugs and shawls. As Osborne took his place along with Mrs. Carpenter's niece, he noticed that Miss Congreve had not yet re-appeared. He called his companion's attention to the circumstance, and she mentioned it to her aunt, who said that the young girl had last been seen in company with Mr. Stone—a person unknown to Osborne—and that she would, doubtless, soon turn up.

"I suppose she's quite safe," said Philip's neighbor—innocently or wittily, he hardly knew which; "she's with a clergyman."

In a few moments the missing couple appeared on the crest of an adjacent hill. Osborne watched them as they came down. Mr. Stone was a comely-faced young man, in a clerical necktie and garments of an exaggerated sacerdotal cut—a divine, evidently of strong "ritualistic" tendencies. Miss Congreve drew near, pale, graceful, and grave, and Philip, with his eyes fixed on her in the interval, lost not a movement of her person, nor a glance of her eyes. She wore a white muslin dress, short, in the prevailing fashion, with trimmings of yellow ribbon inserted in the skirt; and round her shoulders a shawl of heavy black lace, crossed over her bosom and tied in a big knot behind. In her hand she carried a great bunch of wild flowers, with which, as Philip's neighbor whispered to him, she had "ruined" her gloves. Osborne wondered whether there was any meaning in her having taken up with a clergyman. Had she suddenly felt the tardy pangs of remorse, and been moved to seek spiritual advice? Neither on the countenance of her ecclesiastical gallant, nor on her own, were there any visible traces of pious discourse. On the contrary, poor Mr. Stone looked sadly demoralized; their conversation had been wholly of profane things. His white cravat had lost its conservative rigidity, and his hat its unimpassioned equipoise. Worse than all, a little blue

161

forget-me-not had found its way into his button-hole. As for Henrietta, her face wore that look of half-severe serenity which was its wonted expression, but there was no sign of her having seen her lover's ghost.

Osborne went mechanically through the movements of being attentive to the insipid little person at his side. But his thoughts were occupied with Miss Congreve and his eyes constantly turning to her face. From time to time, they met her own. A fierce disgust muttered in his bosom. What Henrietta Congreve needed, he said to himself, was to be used as she used others, as she was evidently now using this poor little parson. He was already over his ears in love—vainly feeling for bottom in midstream, while she sat dry-shod on the brink. She needed a lesson; but who should give it? She knew more than all her teachers. Men approached her only to be dazzled and charmed. If she could only find her equal or her master! one with as clear a head, as lively a fancy, as relentless a will as her own; one who would turn the tables, anticipate her, fascinate her, and then suddenly look at his watch and bid her good morning. Then, perhaps, Graham might settle to sleep in his grave. Then she would feel what it was to play with hearts, for then her own would have been as glass against bronze. Osborne looked about the table, but none of Mrs. Carpenter's male guests bore the least resemblance to the hero of his vision—a man with a heart of bronze and a head of crystal. They were, indeed, very proper swains for the young ladies at their sides, but Henrietta Congreve was not one of these. She was not a mere twaddling ball-room flirt. There was in her coquetry something serious and exalted. It was an intellectual joy. She drained honest men's hearts to the last drop, and bloomed white upon the monstrous diet. As Philip glanced around the circle, his eye fell upon a young girl who seemed for a moment to have forgotten her neighbors, her sandwiches and her champagne, and was very innocently contemplating his own person. As soon as she perceived that he had observed her, she of course dropped her eyes on her plate. But Philip had read the meaning of her glance. It seemed to say— this lingering virginal eyebeam—in language easily translated, Thou art the man! It said, in other words, in less transcendental fashion, My dear Mr. Osborne, you are a very good looking fellow. Philip felt his pulse quicken; he had received his baptism. Not that good looks were a sufficient outfit for breaking Miss Congreve's heart; but they were the outward signs of his mission.

The feasting at last came to an end. A fiddler, who had been brought along, began to tune his instrument, and Mrs. Carpenter proceeded to organize a dance. The *débris* of the collation was cleared away, and the level space thus uncovered converted into a dancing floor. Osborne, not being a dancing man, sat at a distance, with two or three other spectators, among whom was the Rev. Mr. Stone. Each of these gentlemen watched with close attention the movements of Henrietta Congreve. Osborne, however, occasionally glanced at his companion, who, on his side, was quite too absorbed in looking at Miss Congreve to think of anything else.

"They look very charming, those young ladies," said Philip, addressing the young clergyman, to whom he had just been introduced. "Some of them dance particularly well."

"Oh, yes!" said Mr. Stone, with fervor. And then, as if he feared that he had committed himself to an invidious distinction unbecoming his cloth: "I think they all dance well."

But Philip, as a lawyer, naturally took a different view of the matter from Mr. Stone, as a clergyman. "Some of them very much better than others, it seems to me. I had no idea that there could be such a difference. Look at Miss Congreve, for instance."

Mr. Stone, whose eyes were fixed on Miss Congreve, obeyed this injunction by moving them away for a moment, and directing them to a very substantial and somewhat heavy-footed young lady, who was figuring beside her. "Oh, yes, she's very graceful," he said, with unction. "So light, so free, so quiet!"

Philip smiled. "You, too, most excellent simpleton," he said to himself—"you, too, shall be avenged." And then—"Miss Congreve is a very remarkable person," he added, aloud.

"Oh, very!"

"She has extraordinary versatility."

"Most extraordinary."

"Have you seen her act?"

"Yes—yes; I infringed upon my usage in regard to entertainments of that nature, and went the other evening. It was a most brilliant performance."

"And you know she wrote the play."

"Ah, not exactly," said Mr. Stone, with a little protesting gesture; "she translated it."

163

"Yes; but she had to write it quite over. Do you know it in French?"
—and Philip mentioned the original title.

Mr. Stone signified that he was unacquainted with the work.

"It would never have done, you know," said Philip, "to play it as it stands. I saw it in Paris. Miss Congreve eliminated the little difficulties with uncommon skill."

Mr. Stone was silent. The violin uttered a long-drawn note, and the ladies curtsied low to their gentlemen. Miss Congreve's partner stood with his back to our two friends, and her own obeisance was, therefore, executed directly in front of them. If Mr. Stone's enthusiasm had been damped by Philip's irreverent freedom, it was rekindled by this glance. "I suppose you've heard her sing," he said, after a pause.

"Yes, indeed," said Philip, without hesitation.

"She sings sacred music with the most beautiful fervor."

"Yes, so I'm told. And I'm told, moreover, that she's very learned—that she has a passion for books."

"I think it very likely. In fact, she's quite an accomplished theologian. We had this morning a very lively discussion."

"You differed, then?" said Philip.

"Oh," said Mr. Stone, with charming *naïveté*, "*I* didn't differ. It was she!"

"Isn't she a little—the least bit—" and Philip paused, to select his word.

"The least bit?" asked Mr. Stone, in a benevolent tone. And then, as Philip still hesitated—"The least bit heterodox?"

"The least bit of a coquette?"

"Oh, Mr. Osborne!" cried the young divine—"that's the last thing I should call Miss Congreve."

At this moment, Mrs. Carpenter drew nigh. "What is the last thing you should call Miss Congreve?" she asked, overhearing the clergyman's words.

"A coquette."

"It seems to me," said the lady, "that it's the first thing I should call her. You have to come to it, I fancy. You always do, you know. I should get it off my mind at once, and then I should sing her charms."

"Oh, Mrs. Carpenter!" said Mr. Stone.

"Yes, my dear young man. She's quiet but she's deep—I see Mr. Osborne knows," and Mrs. Carpenter passed on.

"She's deep—that's what I say," said Mr. Stone, with mild firmness. —"What do you know, Mr. Osborne?"

Philip fancied that the poor fellow had turned pale; he certainly looked grave.

"Oh, I know nothing," said Philip. "I affirmed nothing. I merely inquired."

"Well then, my dear sir"—and the young man's candid visage flushed a little with the intensity of his feelings—"I give you my word for it, that I believe Miss Congreve to be not only the most accomplished, but the most noble-minded, the most truthful, the most truly christian young lady—in this whole assembly."

"I'm sure, I'm much obliged to you for the assurance," said Philip. "I shall value it and remember it."

It would not have been hard for Philip to set down Mr. Stone as a mere soft-hearted, philandering parson—a type ready made to his hand. Mrs. Carpenter, on the other hand, was a shrewd sagacious woman. But somehow he was impressed by the minister's words, and quite untouched by those of the lady. At last those of the dancers who were tired of the sport, left the circle and wandered back to the shore. The afternoon was drawing to a close, the western sky was beginning to blush crimson and the shadows to grow long on the grass. Only half an hour remained before the moment fixed for the return to Newport. Philip resolved to turn it to account. He followed Miss Congreve to a certain rocky platform, overlooking the water, whither, with a couple of elderly ladies, she had gone to watch the sunset. He found no difficulty in persuading her to wander aside from her companions. There was no mistrust in her keen and delicate face. It was incredible that she should have meant defiance; but her very repose and placidity had a strangely irritating action upon Philip. They affected him as the climax of insolence. He drew from his breast-pocket a small portfolio, containing a dozen letters, among which was the last one he had received from Graham.

"I shall take the liberty, for once, Miss Congreve," he said, "of violating the injunction which you laid upon me this morning with regard to Robert Graham. I have here a letter which I should like you to see."

"From Mr. Graham himself?"

"From Graham himself—written just before his death." He held it out, but Henrietta made no movement to take it.

"I have no desire to see it," she said. "I had rather not. You know he wrote also to me at that moment."

"I'm sure," said Philip, "I should not refuse to see your letter."

"I can't offer to show it to you. I immediately destroyed it."

"Well, you see I've kept mine.—It's not long," Osborne pursued.

Miss Congreve, as if with a strong effort, put out her hand and took the document. She looked at the direction for some moments, in silence, and then raised her eyes toward Osborne. "Do you value it?" she asked. "Does it contain anything you wish to keep?"

"No; I give it to you, for that matter."

"Well then!" said Henrietta. And she tore the letter twice across, and threw the scraps into the sea.

"Ah!" cried Osborne, "what the devil have you done?"

"Don't be violent, Mr. Osborne," said the young girl. "I hadn't the slightest intention of reading it. You are properly punished for having disobeyed me."

Philip swallowed his rage at a gulp, and followed her as she turned away.

· *III* ·

In the middle of September Mrs. Dodd came to Newport, to stay with a friend—somewhat out of humor at having been invited at the fag end of the season, but on the whole very much the same Mrs. Dodd as before; or rather not quite the same, for, in her way, she had taken Graham's death very much to heart. A couple of days after her arrival, she met Philip in the street, and stopped him, "I'm glad to find *some* one still here," she said; for she was with her friend, and having introduced Philip to this lady, she begged him to come and see her. On the next day but one, accordingly, Philip presented himself, and saw Mrs. Dodd alone. She began to talk about Graham; she became very much affected, and with a little more encouragement from Osborne, she would certainly have shed tears. But, somehow, Philip was loth to countenance her grief; he made short responses. Mrs. Dodd struck him as weak and silly and morbidly sentimental. He wondered whether there could have been any truth in the rumor that Graham had cared for her. Not certainly if there was any truth in the story

166

of his passion for Henrietta Congreve. It was impossible that he should have cared for both. Philip made this reflection, but he stopped short of adding that Mrs. Dodd failed signally to please him, because during the past three weeks he had constantly enjoyed Henrietta's society.

For Mrs. Dodd, of course, the transition was easy from Graham to Miss Congreve. "I'm told Miss Congreve is still here," she said. "Have you made her acquaintance?"

"Perfectly," said Philip.

"You seem to take it very easily. I hope you have brought her to a sense of her iniquities. There's a task, Mr. Osborne. You ought to convert her."

"I've not attempted to convert her. I've taken her as she is."

"Does she wear mourning for Mr. Graham? It's the least she can do."

"Wear mourning?" said Philip. "Why, she has been going to a party every other night."

"Of course I don't suppose she has put on a black dress. But does she mourn *here*?" And Mrs. Dodd laid her hand on her heart.

"You mean in her heart? Well, you know, it's problematical that she has one."

"I suppose she disapproves of suicide," said Mrs. Dodd, with a little acrid smile. "Bless my soul, so do I."

"So do I, Mrs. Dodd," said Philip. And he remained for a moment thoughtful. "I wish to heaven," he cried, "that Graham were here! It seems to me at moments that he and Miss Congreve might have come to an understanding again."

Mrs. Dodd threw out her hands in horror. "Why, has she given up her last lover?"

"Her last lover? Whom do you mean?"

"Why, the man I told you of—Mr. Holland."

Philip appeared quite to have forgotten this point in Mrs. Dodd's recital. He broke into a loud, nervous laugh. "I'll be hanged," he cried, "if I know! One thing is certain," he pursued, with emphasis, recovering himself; "Mr. Holland—whoever he is—has for the past three weeks seen nothing of Miss Congreve."

Mrs. Dodd sat silent, with her eyes lowered. At last, looking up,

"You, on the other hand, I infer," she said, "have seen a great deal of her."

"Yes, I've seen her constantly."

Mrs. Dodd raised her eyebrows and distended her lips in a smile which was emphatically not a smile. "Well, you'll think it an odd question, Mr. Osborne," she said, "but how do you reconcile your intimacy with Miss Congreve with your devotion to Mr. Graham?"

Philip frowned—quite too severely for good manners. Decidedly, Mrs. Dodd was extremely silly. "Oh," he rejoined, "I reconcile the two things perfectly. Moreover, my dear Mrs. Dodd, allow me to say that it's my own business. At all events," he added, more gently, "perhaps, one of these days, you'll read the enigma."

"Oh, if it's an enigma," cried the lady, "perhaps I can guess it."

Philip had risen to his feet to take his leave, and Mrs. Dodd threw herself back on the sofa, clasped her hands in her lap, and looked up at him with a penetrating smile. She shook her finger at him reproachfully. Philip saw that she had an idea; perhaps it was the right one. At all events, he blushed. Upon this Mrs. Dodd cried out.

"I've guessed it," she said. "Oh, Mr. Osborne!"

"What have you guessed?" asked Philip, not knowing why in the world he should blush.

"If I've guessed right," said Mrs. Dodd, "it's a charming idea. It does you credit. It's quite romantic. It would do in a novel."

"I doubt," said Philip, "whether I know what you're talking about."

"Oh, yes, you do. I wish you good luck. To another man I should say it was a dangerous game. But to you!"—and with an insinuating movement of her head, Mrs. Dodd measured with a glance the length and breadth of Philip's fine person.

Osborne was inexpressibly disgusted, and without further delay he took his leave.

The reader will be at a loss to understand why Philip should have been disgusted with the mere foreshadowing on the part of another, of a scheme which, three weeks before, he had thought a very happy invention. For we may as well say outright, that although Mrs. Dodd was silly, she was not so silly but that she had divined his original intentions with regard to Henrietta. The fact is that in three weeks Philip's humor had undergone a great change. The reader has gathered for himself that Henrietta Congreve was no ordinary girl, that she was, on the contrary, a person of distinguished gifts and remarkable character. Until within a very few months she had seen very little of the world, and her mind and talents had been gradually formed in seclusion, study, and it is not too much to say, meditation. Thanks to her circumscribed life and her long contemplative leisures, she had reached a pitch of rare intellectual perfection. She was educated, one may say, in a sense in which the term may be used of very few young girls, however richly endowed by nature. When at a later period than most girls, owing to domestic circumstances which it is needless to unfold, she made her entrance into society and learned what it was to be in the world and of the world, to talk and listen, to please and be pleased, to be admired, flattered and interested, her admirable faculties and beautiful intellect, ripened in studious solitude, burst into luxuriant bloom and bore the fairest fruit. Miss Congreve was accordingly a person for whom a man of taste and of feeling could not help entertaining a serious regard. Philip Osborne was emphatically such a man; the manner in which he was affected by his friend's death proves, I think, that he had feeling; and it is ample evidence of his taste that he had chosen such a friend. He had no sooner begun to act in obedience to the impulse mystically bestowed, as it were, at the close of Mrs. Carpenter's feast—he had no sooner obtained an introduction at Mrs. Wilkes's, and, with excellent tact and discretion, made good his footing there, than he began to feel in his inmost heart that in staking his life upon Miss Congreve's favor, poor Graham had indeed revealed the depths of his exquisite sensibility. For a week at least—a week during which, with unprecedented good fortune and a degree of assurance worthy of a better cause, Philip contrived in one way and another to talk with his fair victim no less than a dozen times—he was under the empire of a feverish excitement which kept him from seeing the young girl in all her beautiful integrity. He was pre-occupied with his own intentions and the effect of his own manoeuvres. But gradually he quite forgot himself while he was in her presence, and only remembered that he had a sacred part to play, after he had left the house. Then it was that he conceived the intensity of Graham's despair, and then it was that he began to be sadly, wofully puzzled by the idea that a woman could unite so much loveliness with so much treachery, so much light with so much darkness. He was as certain of the bright surface of her nature as of its cold and dark reverse, and he was utterly unable to discover a link of connection between the two. At moments he wondered how in the world he had become saddled with this metaphysical burden: *que diable venait-il faire dans cette galère?* But nevertheless he was afloat; he must row his boat over the current to where the restless spirit of his friend paced the opposite shore.

Henrietta Congreve, after a first movement of apparent aversion, was very well pleased to accept Osborne as a friend and as an *habitué* of her sister's house. Osborne fancied that he might believe without fatuity—for whatever the reader may think, it is needless to say that Philip was very far from supposing his whole course to be a piece of infatuated coxcombry—that she preferred him to most of the young men of her circle. Philip had a just estimate of his own endowments, and he knew that for the finer social purposes, if not for strictly sentimental ones, he contained the stuff of an important personage. He had no taste for trivialities, but trivialities played but a small part in Mrs. Wilkes's drawing-room. Mrs. Wilkes was a simple woman, but she was neither silly nor frivolous; and Miss Congreve was exempt from these foibles for even better reasons. "Women really care only for men who can tell them something," Osborne remembered once to have heard Graham say, not without bitterness. "They are always famished for news." Philip now reflected with satisfaction that he could give Miss Congreve more news than most of her constituted gossips. He had an admirable memory and a very lively observation. In these respects Henrietta was herself equally well endowed; but Philip's experience of the world had of course been tenfold more extensive, and he was able continually to complete her partial inductions and to rectify her false conjectures. Sometimes they seemed to him wonderfully shrewd, and sometimes delightfully innocent. He nevertheless frequently found himself in a position to make her acquainted with facts possessing the charm of absolute novelty. He had travelled and seen a great variety of men and women, and of course he had read a number of books which a woman is not expected to read. Philip was keenly sensible of these advantages; but it nevertheless seemed to him that if the exhibition of his mental treasures furnished Miss Congreve with a great deal of entertainment, her attention, on the other hand, had a most refreshing effect upon his mind.

At the end of three weeks Philip might, perhaps not unreasonably, have supposed himself in a position to strike his blow. It is true that, for a woman of sense, there is a long step between thinking a man an excellent friend and a charming talker, and surrendering her heart to him. Philip had every reason to believe that Henrietta thought these good things of himself; but if he had hereupon turned about to make his exit, with the conviction that when he had closed the parlor-door behind him he should, by lending an attentive ear, hear her fall in a swoon on the carpet, he might have been sadly snubbed and disappointed. He longed for an opportunity to test the quality of his empire. If he could only pretend for a week to be charmed by another woman, Miss Congreve might perhaps commit herself. Philip flattered himself that he could read very small signs. But what other woman could decently serve as the object of a passion thus extemporized? The only woman Philip could think of was Mrs. Dodd; and to think of Mrs. Dodd was to give it up. For a man who was intimate with Miss Congreve to pretend to care for any other woman (except a very old friend) was to act in flagrant contempt of all verisimilitude. Philip had, therefore, to content himself with playing off his own assumed want of heart against Henrietta's cordial regard. But at this rate the game moved very slowly. Work was accumulating at a prodigious rate at his office, and he couldn't dangle about Miss Congreve forever. He bethought himself of a harmless artifice for drawing her out. It seemed to him that his move was not altogether unsuccessful, and that, at a pinch, Henrietta might become jealous of a rival in his affections. Nevertheless, he was strongly tempted to take up his hand and leave the game. It was too confoundedly exciting.

The incident of which I speak happened within a few days after Osborne's visit to Mrs. Dodd. Finding it impossible to establish an imaginary passion for an actual, visible young lady, Philip resolved to invent not only the passion, but the young lady, too. One morning, as he was passing the show-case of one of the several photographers who came to Newport for the season, he was struck by the portrait of a very pretty young girl. She was fair in color, graceful, well dressed, well placed, her face was charming, she was plainly a lady. Philip went in and asked who she was. The photographer had destroyed the negative and had kept no register of her name. He remembered her, however, distinctly. The portrait had not been taken during the summer; it had been taken during the preceding winter, in Boston, the photographer's headquarters. "I kept it," he said, "because I thought it so very perfect a picture. And such a charming sitter! We haven't many like that." He added, however, that it was too good to please the masses, and that Philip was the first gentleman who had had the taste to observe it.

"So much the better," thought Philip, and forthwith proposed to the man to part with it. The latter, of course, had conscientious scruples; it was against his principles to dispose of the portraits of ladies who came to him in confidence. To do him justice, he adhered to his principles, and Philip was unable to persuade him to sell it. He consented, however, to give it to Mr. Osborne, *gratis*. Mr. Osborne deserved it, and he had another for himself. By this time Philip had grown absolutely fond of the picture; at this latter intelligence he looked grave, and suggested that if the artist would not sell one, perhaps he would sell two. The photographer declined, reiterated his offer, and Philip finally accepted. By way of compensation, however, he proceeded to sit for his own portrait. In the course of half an hour the photographer gave him a dozen reflections of his head and shoulders, distinguished by as many different attitudes and expressions.

"You sit first-rate, sir," said the artist. "You take beautifully. You're quite a match for my young lady."

Philip went off with his dozen prints, promising to examine them at his leisure, select and give a liberal order.

In the evening he went to Mrs. Wilkes's. He found this lady on her verandah, drinking tea in the open air with a guest, whom in the darkness he failed to recognize. As Mrs. Wilkes proceeded to introduce him, her companion graciously revealed herself as Mrs. Dodd. "How on earth," thought Philip, "did she get here?" To find Mrs. Dodd instead of Miss Congreve was, of course, a gross discomforture. Philip sat down, however, with a good grace, to all appearance, hoping that Henrietta would turn up. Finally, moving his chair to a line with the drawing-room window, he saw the young girl within, reading by the lamp. She was alone and intent upon her book. She wore a dress of white grenadine, covered with ornaments and arabesques of crimson silk, which gave her a somewhat fantastical air. For the rest, her expression was grave enough, and her brows contracted, as if she were completely absorbed in her book. Her right elbow rested on the table, and with her hand she mechanically twisted the long curl depending from her *chignon*. Watching his opportunity, Osborne escaped from the ladies on the verandah and made his way into the drawing-room. Miss Congreve received him as an old friend, without rising from her chair.

Philip began by pretending to scold her for shirking the society of Mrs. Dodd.

"Shirking!" said Henrietta. "You are very polite to Mrs. Dodd."

"It seems to me," rejoined Osborne, "that I'm quite as polite as you."

"Well, perhaps you are. To tell the truth, I'm not very polite. At all events, she don't care to see me. She must have come to see my sister."

"I didn't know she knew Mrs. Wilkes."

"It's an acquaintance of a couple of hours' standing. I met her, you know, at Sharon in July. She was once very impertinent to me, and I fancied she had quite given me up. But this afternoon, during our drive, as my sister and I got out of the carriage, on the rocks, who should I see but Mrs. Dodd, wandering about alone, with a bunch of sea-weed as big as her head. She rushed up to me; I introduced her to Anna, and finding that she had walked quite a distance, Anna made her get into the carriage. It appears that she's staying with a friend, who has no carriage, and she's very miserable. We drove her about for an hour. Mrs. Dodd was fascinating, she threw away her sea-weed, and Anna asked her to come home to tea. After tea, having endured her for two mortal hours, I took refuge here."

"If she was fascinating," said Philip, "why do you call it enduring her?"

"It's all the more reason, I assure you."

"I see, you have not forgiven her impertinence."

"No, I confess I have not. The woman was positively revolting."

"She appears, nevertheless, to have forgiven you."

"She has nothing to forgive."

In a few moments Philip took his photographs out of his pocket, handed them to Henrietta, and asked her advice as to which he should choose. Miss Congreve inspected them attentively, and selected but one. "This one is excellent," she said. "All the others are worthless in comparison."

"You advise me then to order that alone?"

"Why, you'll do as you please. I advise you to order that, at any rate. If you do, I shall ask you for one; but I shall care nothing for the rest."

Philip protested that he saw very little difference between this favored picture and the others, and Miss Congreve declared that there was all the difference in the world. As Philip replaced the specimens in his pocket-book, he dropped on the carpet the portrait of the young lady of Boston.

"Ah," said Henrietta, "a young lady. I suppose I may see it."

"On one condition," said Philip, picking it up. "You'll please not to look at the back of the card."

I am very much ashamed to have to tell such things of poor Philip; for in point of fact, the back of the card was a most innocent blank. If Miss Congreve had ventured to disobey him, he would have made a very foolish figure. But there was so little that was boisterous in Henrietta's demeanor, that Osborne felt that he ran no risk.

"Who is she?" asked Henrietta, looking at the portrait. "She's charming."

"She's a Miss Thompson, of Philadelphia."

"Dear me, not Dora Thompson, assuredly."

"No, indeed," said Philip, a little nervously. "Her name's not Dora —nor anything like it."

"You needn't resent the insinuation, sir. Dora's a very pretty name."

"Yes, but her own is prettier."

"I'm very curious to hear it."

Philip suddenly found himself in deep waters. He struck out blindly and answered at random, "Angelica."

Miss Congreve smiled—somewhat ironically, it seemed to Philip. "Well," she said, "I like her face better than her name."

"Dear me, if you come to that, so do I," cried Philip, with a laugh.

"Tell me about her, Mr. Osborne," pursued Henrietta. "She must be, with that face and figure, just the nicest girl in the world."

"Well, well, well," said Philip, leaning back in his chair, and looking at the ceiling—"perhaps she is—or at least, you'll excuse me if I say *I* think she is."

"I should think it inexcusable if you didn't say so," said Henrietta, giving him the card. "I'm sure I've seen her somewhere."

"Very likely. She comes to New York," said Philip. And he thought it prudent, on the whole, to divert the conversation to another topic. Miss Congreve remained silent and he fancied pensive. Was she jealous of Angelica Thompson? It seemed to Philip that, without fatuity, he might infer that she was, and that she was too proud to ask questions.

Mrs. Wilkes had enabled Mrs. Dodd to send tidings to her hostess of her whereabouts, and had promised to furnish her with an escort on her return. When Mrs. Dodd prepared to take her leave, Philip, finding himself also ready to depart, offered to walk home with her.

"Well, sir," said the lady, when they had left the house, "your little game seems to be getting on."

Philip said nothing.

"Ah, Mr. Osborne," said Mrs. Dodd, with ill-concealed impatience, "I'm afraid you're too good for it."

"Well, I'm afraid I am."

"If you hadn't been in such a hurry to agree with me," said Mrs. Dodd, "I should have said that I meant, in other words, that you're too stupid."

"Oh, I agree to that, too," said Philip.

The next day he received a letter from his partner in business, telling him of a great pressure of work, and urging him to return at his earliest convenience. "We are told," added this gentleman, "of a certain Miss ——, I forget the name. If she's essential to your comfort, bring her along; but, at any rate, come yourself. In your absence the office is at a stand-still—a fearful case of repletion without digestion."

This appeal came home to Philip's mind, to use a very old metaphor, like the sound of the brazen trumpet to an old cavalry charger. He felt himself overwhelmed with a sudden shame at the thought of the precious hours he had wasted and the long mornings he had consigned to perdition. He had been burning incense to a shadow, and the fumes had effaced it. In the afternoon he walked down toward the cliffs, feeling wofully perplexed, and exasperated in mind, and longing only to take a farewell look at the sea. He was not prepared to admit that he had played with fire and burned his fingers; but it was certain that he had gained nothing at the game. How the deuce had Henrietta Congreve come to thrust herself into his life—to steal away his time and his energies and to put him into a savage humor with himself? He would have given a great deal to be able to banish her from his thoughts; but she remained, and, while she remained, he hated her.

After all, he had not been wholly cheated of his revenge. He had begun by hating her and he hated her still. On his way to the cliffs he met Mrs. Wilkes, driving alone. Henrietta's place, vacant beside her, seemed to admonish him that she was at home, and almost, indeed, that she expected him. At all events, instead of going to bid farewell to the sea, he went to bid farewell to Miss Congreve. He felt that his farewell might easily be cold and formal, and indeed bitter.

He was admitted, he passed through the drawing-room to the veran-dah, and found Henrietta sitting on the grass, in the garden, holding her little nephew on her knee and reading him a fairy tale. She made room for him on the garden bench beside her, but kept the child. Philip felt himself seriously discomposed by this spectacle. In a few moments he took the boy upon his own knees. He then told Miss Con-greve briefly that he intended that evening to leave Newport. "And you," he said, "when are you coming?"

"My sister," said Henrietta, "means to stay till Christmas. I hope to be able to remain as long."

Poor Philip bowed his head and heard his illusions tumbling most unmusically about his ears. His blow had smitten but the senseless air. He waited to see her color fade, or to hear her voice tremble. But he waited in vain. When he looked up and his eyes met Henrietta's, she was startled by the expression of his face.

"Tom," she said to the child, "go and ask Jane for my fan."

The child walked off, and Philip rose to his feet. Henrietta, hesi-tating a moment, also rose. "Must you go?" she asked.

Philip made no answer, but stood looking at her with blood-shot eyes, and with an intensity which puzzled and frightened the young girl.

"Miss Congreve," he said, abruptly, "I'm a miserable man!"

"Oh, no!" said Henrietta, gently.

"I love a woman who doesn't care a straw for me."

"Are you sure?" said Henrietta, innocently.

"Sure! I adore her!"

"Are you sure she doesn't care for you?"

"Ah, Miss Congreve!" cried Philip. "If I could imagine, if I could hope—" and he put out his hand, as if to take her own.

Henrietta drew back, pale and frowning, carrying her hand to her heart. "Hope for nothing!" she said.

176

At this moment, little Tom Wilkes re-appeared, issuing from the drawing-room window. "Aunt Henrietta," he cried, "here's a new gentleman!"

Miss Congreve and Philip turned about, and saw a young man step out upon the verandah from the drawing-room. Henrietta, with a little cry, hastened to meet him. Philip stood in his place. Miss Congreve exchanged a cordial greeting with the stranger, and led him down to the lawn. As she came toward him, Philip saw that Henrietta's pallor had made way for a rosy flush. She was beautiful.

"Mr. Osborne," she said, "Mr. Holland."

Mr. Holland bowed graciously; but Philip bowed not at all. "Goodby, then," he said, to the young girl.

She bowed, without speaking.

"Who's your friend, Henrietta?" asked her companion, when they were alone.

"He's a Mr. Osborne, of New York," said Miss Congreve; "a friend of poor Mr. Graham."

"By the way, I suppose you've heard of poor Graham's death."

"Oh, yes; Mr. Osborne told me. And indeed—what do you think? Mr. Graham wrote to me that he expected to die."

"Expected? Is that what he said?"

"I don't remember his words. I destroyed the letter."

"I must say, I think it would have been in better taste not to write."

"Taste! He had long since parted company with taste."

"I don't know. There was a method in his madness; and, as a rule, when a man kills himself, he shouldn't send out circulars."

"Kills himself? Good heavens, George! what do you mean?" Miss Congreve had turned pale, and stood looking at her companion with eyes dilated with horror.

"Why, my dear Henrietta," said the young man, "excuse my abruptness. Didn't you know it?"

"How strange—how fearful!" said Henrietta, slowly. "I wish I had kept his letter."

"I'm glad you didn't," said Holland. "It's a horrible business. Forget it."

"Horrible—horrible," murmured the young girl, in a tremulous tone. Her voice was shaken with irrepressible tears. Poor girl! in the space of five minutes she had been three times surprised. She gave way to her emotion and burst into sobs. George Holland drew her against him, and pressed his arm about her, and kissed her, and whispered comfort in her ear.

In the evening, Philip started for New York. On the steamer he found Mrs. Dodd, who had come to an end of her visit. She was accompanied by a certain Major Dodd, of the Army, a brother of her deceased husband, and in addition, as it happened, her cousin. He was an unmarried man, a good-natured man, and a very kind friend to his sister-in-law, who had no family of her own, and who was in a position to be grateful for the services of a gentleman. In spite of a general impression to the contrary, I may affirm that the Major had no desire to make his little services a matter of course. "I'm related to Maria twice over already," he had been known to say, in a moment of expansion. "If I ever marry, I shall prefer to do it not quite so much in the family." He had come to Newport to conduct his sister home, who forthwith introduced him to Philip.

It was a clear, mild night, and, when the steamer had got under way, Mrs. Dodd and the two gentlemen betook themselves to the upper deck, and sat down in the starlight. Philip, it may be readily imagined, was in no humor for conversation; but he felt that he could not wholly neglect Mrs. Dodd. Under the influence of the beautiful evening, the darkly-shining sea, the glittering constellations, this lady became rabidly sentimental. She talked of friendship, and love, and death, and immortality. Philip saw what was coming. Before many moments, she had the bad taste (considering the Major's presence, as it seemed to Philip) to take poor Graham as a text for a rhapsody. Osborne lost patience, and interrupted her by asking if she would mind his lighting a cigar. She was scandalized, and immediately announced that she would go below. Philip had no wish to be uncivil. He attempted to restore himself to her favor by offering to see her down to the cabin. She accepted his escort, and he went with her to the door of her state-room, where she gave him her hand for goodnight.

"Well," she said—"and Miss Congreve?"

Philip positively scowled. "Miss Congreve," he said, "is engaged to be married."

"To Mr. ——?"

"To Mr. Holland."

178

"Ah!" cried Mrs. Dodd, dropping his hand, "why didn't you break the engagement!"

"My dear Mrs. Dodd," said Philip, "you don't know what you're talking about."

Mrs. Dodd smiled a pitiful smile, shrugged her shoulders, and turned away. "Poor Graham!" she said.

Her words came to Philip like a blow in the face. "Graham!" he cried. "Graham was a fool!" He had struck back; he couldn't help it.

He made his way up stairs again, and came out on the deck, still trembling with the violence of his retort. He walked to the edge of the boat and leaned over the railing, looking down into the black gulfs of water which foamed and swirled in the wake of the vessel. He knocked off the end of his cigar, and watched the red particles fly downward and go out in the darkness. He was a disappointed, saddened man. There in the surging, furious darkness, yawned instant death. Did it tempt him, too? He drew back with a shudder, and returned to his place by Major Dodd.

The Major preserved for some moments a meditative silence. Then, at last, with a half apologetic laugh, "Mrs. Dodd," he said, "labors under a singular illusion."

"Ah?" said Philip.

"But you knew Mr. Graham yourself?" pursued the Major.

"Oh, yes; I knew him."

"It was a very melancholy case," said Major Dodd.

"A very melancholy case;" and Philip repeated his words.

"I don't know how it is that Mrs. Dodd was beguiled into such fanaticism on the subject. I believe she went so far as once to blow out at the young lady."

"The young lady?" said Philip.

"Miss Congreve, you know, the object of his persecutions."

"Oh, yes," said Philip, painfully mystified.

"The fact is," said the Major, leaning over, and lowering his voice confidentially, "Mrs. Dodd was in love with him—as far, that is, as a woman can be in love with a man in that state."

"Is it possible?" said Philip, disgusted and revolted at he knew not what; for his companion's allusions were an enigma.

"Oh, I was at Sharon for three weeks," the Major continued; "I went up for my sister-in-law; I saw it all. I wanted to bring poor Graham away, but he wouldn't listen to me—not that he wasn't very quiet. He made no talk, and opened himself only to Mrs. Dodd and me—we lived in the same house, you know. Of course I very soon saw through it, and I felt very sorry for poor Miss Congreve. She bore it very well, but it must have been very annoying."

Philip started up from his chair. "For heaven's sake, Major Dodd," he cried, "what are you talking about?"

The Major stared a moment, and then burst into a peal of laughter. "You agree, then, with Mrs. Dodd?" he said, recovering himself.

"I understand Mrs. Dodd no better than I do you."

"Why, my dear sir," said the Major, rising to his feet and extending his hand, "I beg a hundred pardons. But you must excuse me if I adhere to my opinion."

"First, please, be so good as to inform me of your opinion."

"Why, sir, the whole story is simply bosh."

"Good heavens," cried Philip, "that's no opinion!"

"Well, then, sir, if you will have it: the man was as mad as a March hare."

"Oh!" cried Philip. His exclamation said a great many things, but the Major took it as a protest.

"He was a monomaniac."

Philip said nothing.

"The idea is not new to you?"

"Well," said Philip, "to tell the truth, it is."

"Well," said the Major, with a courteous flourish, "there you have it—for nothing."

Philip drew a long breath. "Ah, no!" he said, gravely, "not for nothing." He stood silent for some time, with his eyes fixed on the deck. Major Dodd puffed his cigar and eyed him askance. At last Philip looked up. "And Henrietta Congreve?"

"Henrietta Congreve," said the Major, with military freedom and gallantry, "is the sweetest girl in the world. Don't talk to me! I know her."

"She never became engaged to Graham?"

"Engaged? She never looked at him."

"But he was in love with her."

180

"Ah, that was his own business. He worried her to death. She tried gentleness and kindness—it made him worse. Then, when she declined to see him, the poor fellow swore that she had jilted him. It was a fixed idea. He got Mrs. Dodd to believe it."

Philip's silent reflections—the hushed eloquence of his amazed unburdened heart—we have no space to interpret. But as the Major lightened the load with one hand, he added to it with the other. Philip had never pitied his friend till now. "I knew him well," he said, aloud. "He was the best of men. She might very well have cared for him."

"Good heavens! my dear sir, how could the woman love a madman?"

"You use strong language. When I parted with him in June, he was sane as you or I."

"Well, then, apparently, he lost his mind in the interval. He was in wretched health."

"But a man doesn't lose his mind without a cause."

"Let us admit, then," said the Major, "that Miss Congreve was the cause. I insist that she was the innocent cause. How should she have trifled with him? She was engaged to another man. The ways of the Lord are inscrutable. Fortunately," continued the Major, "she doesn't know the worst."

"How, the worst?"

"Why, you know he shot himself."

"Bless your soul, Miss Congreve knows it."

"I think you're mistaken. She didn't know it this morning."

Philip was sickened and bewildered by the tissue of horrors in which he found himself entangled. "Oh," he said, bitterly, "she has forgotten it then. She knew it a month ago."

"No, no, no," rejoined the Major, with decision. "I took the liberty, this morning, of calling upon her, and as we had had some conversation upon Mr. Graham at Sharon, I touched upon his death. I saw she had heard of it, and I said nothing more—"

"Well then?" said Philip.

"Well, then, my dear sir, she thinks he died in his bed. May she never think otherwise!"

In the course of that night—he sat out on the deck till two o'clock, alone—Philip, revolving many things, fervently echoed this last wish of Major Dodd.

Aux grands maux les grands remèdes. Philip is now a married man; and curious to narrate, his wife bears a striking likeness to the young lady whose photograph he purchased for the price of six dozen of his own. And yet her name is not Angelica Thompson—nor even Dora.

GABRIELLE DE BERGERAC

Gabrielle de Bergerac

"Gabrielle de Bergerac," Henry James's thirteenth published tale, appeared in the Atlantic, July-September, 1869. A long three-part story, it had its first reprint in a single volume in 1918.

Allusion was made in the Introduction to an extraordinary conjunction of names in this tale. Bergerac is a name of old Gascony. Savien Cyrano de Bergerac was born in the early seventeenth century at the Chateau de Bergerac in the Périgord. Add to this name the tutor's, Pierre Coquelin. Recall C.-B. Coquelin, James's schoolmate at Boulogne in 1859, who in that same year entered the Conservatoire at Paris and five years later was a sociétaire of the Comédie Française. Be reminded of James's early interest in the Théâtre Français and its playwrights and actors, interest too keen to have missed Coquelin's quick rise to fame. Read in his "Coquelin" (Century, January, 1887) of his first night at the Théâtre Français—in late January, 1870—which was his first sight also of Coquelin as actor. Read his query in "Edmond Rostand" (Critic, November, 1901): " . . . was the author's original vision [of Cyrano de Bergerac], the first flush of the idea, suggested to him across the footlights by a present personality? Did the happy thought of the character, in other words, glimmer into life as the happy consciousness of M. Coquelin's countenance and genius?" With all this in mind we may counter James's query with another: Was James's original vision of Coquelin as actor, sight yet unseen, his own earlier matching, by virtue of his own critical nose, of the physiognomy of the Cyrano de Bergerac of literary anecdote with his quondam schoolmate's "countenance and genius?" If so, it is reason enough, after he and Coquelin met again, for never reprinting the tale. If not *so, the conjunction of these two names here is one of the most interesting coincidences in literary annals.*

Of the fifteen tales published through 1870-1876 only seven were reprinted by James (for their titles and dates see the Chronological List at the end of this volume). Six of the remaining eight stories are in Mordell's Travelling Companions. *The other two were the total short story output of 1876.*

· *I* ·

MY GOOD OLD FRIEND, IN HIS WHITE FLANNEL DRESSING-gown, with his wig "removed," as they say of the dinner-service, by a crimson nightcap, sat for some moments gazing into the fire. At last he looked up. I knew what was coming. "Apropos, that little debt of mine—"

Not that the debt was really very little. But M. de Bergerac was a man of honor, and I knew I should receive my dues. He told me frankly that he saw no way, either in the present or the future, to reimburse me in cash. His only treasures were his paintings; would I choose one of them? Now I had not spent an hour in M. de Bergerac's little parlor twice a week for three winters, without learning that the Baron's paintings were, with a single exception, of very indifferent merit. On the other hand, I had taken a great fancy to the picture thus excepted. Yet, as I knew it was a family portrait, I hesitated to claim it. I refused to make a choice. M. de Bergerac, however, insisted, and I finally laid my finger on the charming image of my friend's aunt. I of course insisted, on my side, that M. de Bergerac should retain it during the remainder of his life, and so it was only after his decease that I came into possession of it. It hangs above my table as I write, and I have only to glance up at the face of my heroine to feel how vain it is to attempt to describe it. The portrait represents, in dimensions several degrees below those of nature, the head and shoulders of a young girl of two-and-twenty. The execution of the work is not especially strong, but it is thoroughly respectable, and one may easily see that the painter deeply appreciated the character of the face. The countenance is interesting rather than beautiful,—the forehead broad and

186

open, the eyes slightly prominent, all the features full and firm and yet replete with gentleness. The head is slightly thrown back, as if in movement, and the lips are parted in a half-smile. And yet, in spite of this tender smile, I always fancy that the eyes are sad. The hair, dressed without powder, is rolled back over a high cushion (as I suppose), and adorned just above the left ear with a single white rose; while, on the other side, a heavy tress from behind hangs upon the neck with a sort of pastoral freedom. The neck is long and full, and the shoulders rather broad. The whole face has a look of mingled softness and decision, and seems to reveal a nature inclined to revery, affection, and repose, but capable of action and even of heroism. Mlle. de Bergerac died under the axe of the Terrorists. Now that I had acquired a certain property in this sole memento of her life, I felt a natural curiosity as to her character and history. Had M. de Bergerac known his aunt? Did he remember her? Would it be a tax on his good-nature to suggest that he should favor me with a few reminiscences? The old man fixed his eyes on the fire, and laid his hand on mine, as if his memory were fain to draw from both sources— from the ruddy glow and from my fresh young blood—a certain vital, quickening warmth. A mild, rich smile ran to his lips, and he pressed my hand. Somehow,—I hardly know why,—I felt touched almost to tears. Mlle. de Bergerac had been a familiar figure in her nephew's boyhood, and an important event in her life had formed a sort of episode in his younger days. It was a simple enough story; but such as it was, then and there, settling back into his chair, with the fingers of the clock wandering on to the small hours of the night, he told it with a tender, lingering garrulity. Such as it is, I repeat it. I shall give, as far as possible, my friend's words, or the English of them; but the reader will have to do without his inimitable accents. For them there is no English.

My father's household at Bergerac (said the Baron) consisted, exclusive of the servants, of five persons,—himself, my mother, my aunt (Mlle. de Bergerac), M. Coquelin (my preceptor), and M. Coquelin's pupil, the heir of the house. Perhaps, indeed, I should have numbered M. Coquelin among the servants. It is certain that my mother did. Poor little woman! she was a great stickler for the rights of birth. Her own birth was all she had, for she was without health, beauty, or fortune. My father, on his side, had very little of the last; his property of Bergerac yielded only enough to keep us without discredit. We gave no entertainments, and passed the whole year in the country; and as my mother was resolved that her weak health should do her a kindness as well as an injury, it was put forward as an apology for everything. We led at best a simple, somnolent sort of life. There was a terrible amount of leisure for rural gentlefolks in those good old days. We slept a great deal; we slept, you will say, on a volcano. It was a very different world from this patent new world of yours, and I may say that I was born on a different planet. Yes, in 1789, there came a great convulsion; the earth cracked and opened and broke, and this poor old *pays de France* went whirling through space. When I look back at my childhood, I look over a gulf. Three years ago, I spent a week at a country house in the neighborhood of Bergerac, and my hostess drove me over to the site of the château. The house has disappeared, and there's a homœopathic—hydropathic— what do you call it?—establishment erected in its place. But the little town is there, and the bridge on the river, and the church where I was christened, and the double row of lime-trees on the market-place, and the fountain in the middle. There's only one striking difference: the sky is changed. I was born under the old sky. It was black enough, of course, if we had only had eyes to see it; but to me, I confess, it looked divinely blue. And in fact it was very bright,—the little patch under which I cast my juvenile shadow. An odd enough little shadow you would have thought it. I was promiscuously cuddled and fondled. I was M. le Chevalier, and prospective master of Bergerac; and when I walked to church on Sunday, I had a dozen yards of lace on my coat and a little sword at my side. My poor mother did her best to make me good for nothing. She had her maid to curl my hair with the tongs, and she used with her own fingers to stick little black patches on my face. And yet I was a good deal neglected too, and I would go for days with black patches of another sort. I'm afraid I should have got very little education if a kind Providence hadn't given me poor M. Coquelin. A kind Providence, that is, and my father; for with my mother my tutor was no favorite. She thought him—and, indeed, she called him—a bumpkin, a clown. There was a very pretty abbé among her friends, M. Tiblaud by name, whom she wished to install at the château as my intellectual, and her spiritual, adviser; but my father, who, without being anything of an *esprit fort,* had an incurable aversion to a priest out of church, very soon routed his pious scheme. My poor father was an odd figure of a man. He belonged to a type as completely obsolete as the biggest of those big-boned, pre-historic monsters discovered by M. Cuvier. He was not overburdened with opinions or principles. The only truth that was absolute to his perception was that the house of Bergerac was *de bonne noblesse.* His tastes were not delicate. He was fond of the open air, of long rides, of the smell of the game-stocked woods in autumn, of playing at bowls, of a drinking-cup, of a dirty pack of cards, and a free-spoken tavern Hebe. I have nothing of him but his name. I strike you as an old fossil, a relic, a mummy. Good heavens! you should have seen him,—his good, his bad manners, his arrogance, his *bonhomie,* his stupidity and pluck.

My early years had promised ill for my health; I was listless and languid, and my father had been content to leave me to the women, who, on the whole, as I have said, left me a good deal to myself. But one morning he seemed suddenly to remember that he had a little son and heir running wild. It was, I remember, in my ninth year, a morning early in June, after breakfast, at eleven o'clock. He took me by the hand and led me out on the terrace, and sat down and made me stand between his knees. I was engaged upon a great piece of bread and butter, which I had brought away from the table. He put his hand into my hair, and, for the first time that I could remember, looked me straight in the face. I had seen him take the forelock of a young colt in the same way, when he wished to lóok at its teeth. What did he want? Was he going to send me for sale? His eyes seemed prodigiously black and his eyebrows terribly thick. They were very much the eyebrows of that portrait. My father passed his other hand over the muscles of my arms and the sinews of my poor little legs.

"Chevalier," said he, "you're dreadfully puny. What's one to do with you?"

I dropped my eyes and said nothing. Heaven knows I felt puny.

"It's time you knew how to read and write. What are you blushing at?"

"I *do* know how to read," said I.

My father stared. "Pray, who taught you?"

"I learned in a book."

"What book?"

I looked up at my father before I answered. His eyes were bright, and there was a little flush in his face,—I hardly knew whether of pleasure or anger. I disengaged myself and went into the drawing-room, where I took from a cupboard in the wall an odd volume of Scarron's *Roman comique*. As I had to go through the house, I was absent some minutes. When I came back I found a stranger on the terrace. A young man in poor clothes, with a walking-stick, had come up from the avenue, and stood before my father, with his hat in his hand. At the farther end of the terrace was my aunt. She was sitting on the parapet, playing with a great black crow, which we kept in a cage in the dining-room window. I betook myself to my father's side with my book, and stood staring at our visitor. He was a dark-eyed, sunburnt young man, of about twenty-eight, of middle height, broad in the shoulders and short in the neck, with a slight lameness in one of his legs. He looked travel-stained and weary and pale. I remember there was something prepossessing in his being pale. I didn't know that the paleness came simply from his being horribly hungry.

"In view of these facts," he said, as I came up, "I have ventured to presume upon the good-will of M. le Baron."

My father sat back in his chair, with his legs apart and a hand on each knee and his waistcoat unbuttoned, as was usual after a meal. "Upon my word," he said, "I don't know what I can do for you. There's no place for you in my own household."

The young man was silent a moment. "Has M. le Baron any children?" he asked, after a pause.

"I have my son whom you see here."

"May I inquire if M. le Chevalier is supplied with a preceptor?"

My father glanced down at me. "Indeed, he seems to be," he cried. "What have you got there?" And he took my book. "The little rascal has M. Scarron for a teacher. This is his preceptor!"

I blushed very hard, and the young man smiled. "Is that your only teacher?" he asked.

"My aunt taught me to read," I said, looking round at her.

"And did your aunt recommend this book?" asked my father.

"My aunt gave me M. Plutarque," I said.

My father burst out laughing, and the young man put his hat up to his mouth. But I could see that above it his eyes had a very good-natured look. My aunt, seeing that her name had been mentioned, walked slowly over to where we stood, still holding her crow on her hand. You have her there before you; judge how she looked. I remember that she frequently dressed in blue, my poor aunt, and I know that she must have dressed simply. Fancy her in a light stuff gown, covered with big blue flowers, with a blue ribbon in her dark hair, and the points of her high-heeled blue slippers peeping out under her stiff white petticoat. Imagine her strolling along the terrace of the château with a villainous black crow perched on her wrist. You'll admit it's a picture.

"Is all this true, sister?" said my father. "Is the Chevalier such a scholar?"

"He's a clever boy," said my aunt, putting her hand on my head.

"It seems to me that at a pinch he could do without a preceptor," said my father. "He has such a learned aunt."

"I've taught him all I know. He had begun to ask me questions that I was quite unable to answer."

"I should think he might," cried my father, with a broad laugh, "when once he had got into M. Scarron!"

"Questions out of Plutarch," said Mlle. de Bergerac, "which you must know Latin to answer."

"Would you like to know Latin, M. le Chevalier?" said the young man, looking at me with a smile.

"Do you know Latin,—you?" I asked.

"Perfectly," said the young man, with the same smile.

"Do you want to learn Latin, Chevalier?" said my aunt.

"Every gentleman learns Latin," said the young man.

I looked at the poor fellow, his dusty shoes and his rusty clothes. 'But you're not a gentleman," said I.

He blushed up to his eyes. "Ah, I only teach it," he said.

In this way it was that Pierre Coquelin came to be my governor. My father, who had a mortal dislike to all kinds of cogitation and inquiry, engaged him on the simple testimony of his face and of his own account of his talents. His history, as he told it, was in three words as follows: He was of our province, and neither more nor less than the son of a village tailor. He is my hero: *tirez-vous de là*. Showing a lively taste for books, instead of being promoted to the paternal bench, he had been put to study with the Jesuits. After a residence of some

three years with these gentlemen, he had incurred their displeasur
by a foolish breach of discipline, and had been turned out into th
world. Here he had endeavored to make capital out of his excellen
education, and had gone up to Paris with the hope of earning h
bread as a scribbler. But in Paris he scribbled himself hungry an
nothing more, and was in fact in a fair way to die of starvation. A
last he encountered an agent of the Marquis de Rochambeau, who wa
collecting young men for the little army which the latter was prepare
to conduct to the aid of the American insurgents. He had engage
himself among Rochambeau's troops, taken part in several battles, an
finally received a wound in his leg of which the effect was still pe
ceptible. At the end of three years he had returned to France, an
repaired on foot, with what speed he might, to his native town; but on
to find that in his absence his father had died, after a tedious illnes
in which he had vainly lavished his small earnings upon the physician
and that his mother had married again, very little to his taste. Poo
Coquelin was friendless, penniless, and homeless. But once back on h
native soil, he found himself possessed again by his old passion fo
letters, and, like all starving members of his craft, he had turned h
face to Paris. He longed to make up for his three years in the wilde
ness. He trudged along, lonely, hungry, and weary, till he came t
the gates of Bergerac. Here, sitting down to rest on a stone, he sa
us come out on the terrace to digest our breakfast in the sun. Poo
Coquelin! he had the stomach of a gentleman. He was filled with a
irresistible longing to rest awhile from his struggle with destiny, an
it seemed to him that for a mess of smoking pottage he would glad
exchange his vague and dubious future. In obedience to this simp
impulse,—an impulse touching in its humility, when you knew th
man,—he made his way up the avenue. We looked affable enough,—
an honest country gentleman, a young girl playing with a crow, an
a little boy eating bread and butter; and it turned out, we were a
kindly as we looked.

For me, I soon grew extremely fond of him, and I was glad to thin
in later days that he had found me a thoroughly docile child. In thos
days, you know, thanks to Jean Jacques Rousseau, there was a va
stir in men's notions of education, and a hundred theories afloat abou
the perfect teacher and the perfect pupil. Coquelin was a firm devote
of Jean Jacques, and very possibly applied some of his precepts to m

own little person. But of his own nature Coquelin was incapable of anything that was not wise and gentle, and he had no need to learn humanity in books. He was, nevertheless, a great reader, and when he had not a volume in his hand he was sure to have two in his pockets. He had half a dozen little copies of the Greek and Latin poets, bound in yellow parchment, which, as he said, with a second shirt and a pair of white stockings, constituted his whole library. He had carried these books to America, and read them in the wilderness, and by the light of camp-fires, and in crowded, steaming barracks in winter-quarters. He had a passion for Virgil. M. Scarron was very soon dismissed to the cupboard, among the dice-boxes and the old packs of cards, and I was confined for the time to Virgil and Ovid and Plutarch, all of which, with the stimulus of Coquelin's own delight, I found very good reading. But better than any of the stories I read were those stories of his wanderings, and his odd companions and encounters, and charming tales of pure fantasy, which, with the best grace in the world, he would recite by the hour. We took long walks, and he told me the names of the flowers and the various styles of the stars, and I remember that I often had no small trouble to keep them distinct. He wrote a very bad hand, but he made very pretty drawings of the subjects then in vogue,—nymphs and heroes and shepherds and pastoral scenes. I used to fancy that his knowledge and skill were inexhaustible, and I pestered him so for entertainment that I certainly proved that there were no limits to his patience.

When he first came to us he looked haggard and thin and weary; but before the month was out, he had acquired a comfortable rotundity of person, and something of the sleek and polished look which befits the governor of a gentleman's son. And yet he never lost a certain gravity and reserve of demeanor which was nearly akin to a mild melancholy. With me, half the time, he was of course intolerably bored, and he must have had hard work to keep from yawning in my face,—which, as he knew I knew, would have been an unwarrantable liberty. At table, with my parents, he seemed to be constantly observing himself and inwardly regulating his words and gestures. The simple truth, I take it, was that he had never sat at a gentleman's table, and although he must have known himself incapable of a real breach of civility,—essentially delicate as he was in his feelings,—he was too proud to run the risk of violating etiquette. My poor mother was a

great stickler for ceremony, and she would have had her majordom
to lift the covers, even if she had had nothing to put into the dishes
I remember a cruel rebuke she bestowed upon Coquelin, shortly afte
his arrival. She could never be brought to forget that he had bee:
picked up, as she said, on the roads. At dinner one day, in the absenc
of Mlle. de Bergerac, who was indisposed, he inadvertently occupie
her seat, taking me as a *vis-à-vis* instead of a neighbor. Shortly afte
wards, coming to offer wine to my mother, he received for all respons
a stare so blank, cold, and insolent as to leave no doubt of her estimat
of his presumption. In my mother's simple philosophy, Mlle. de Be
gerac's seat could be decently occupied only by herself, and in defaul
of her presence should remain conspicuously and sacredly vacan
Dinner at Bergerac was at best, indeed, a cold and dismal ceremony
I see it now,—the great dining-room, with its high windows and thei
faded curtains, and the tiles upon the floor, and the immense wainscots
and the great white marble chimney-piece, reaching to the ceiling,—
triumph of delicate carving,—and the panels above the doors, wit]
their *galant* mythological paintings. All this had been the work of m
grandfather, during the Regency, who had undertaken to renovate an
beautify the château; but his funds had suddenly given out, and w
could boast but a desultory elegance. Such talk as passed at table wa
between my mother and the Baron, and consisted for the most part o
a series of insidious attempts on my mother's part to extort informatio:
which the latter had no desire, or at least no faculty, to impart. M
father was constitutionally taciturn and apathetic, and he invariabl
made an end of my mother's interrogation by proclaiming that h
hated gossip. He liked to take his pleasure and have done with it
or at best, to ruminate his substantial joys within the conservativ
recesses of his capacious breast. The Baronne's inquisitive tongu
was like a lambent flame, flickering over the sides of a rock. She ha
a passion for the world, and seclusion had only sharpened the edg
of her curiosity. She lived on old memories—shabby, tarnished bit
of intellectual finery—and vagrant humors, anecdotes, and scandals
    Once in a while, however, her curiosity held high revel; for once
week we had the Vicomte de Treuil to dine with us. This gentlema:
was, although several years my father's junior, his most intimat
friend and the only constant visitor at Bergerac. He brought with hir
a sort of intoxicating perfume of the great world, which I myself wa

not too young to feel. He had a marvellous fluency of talk; he was polite and elegant; and he was constantly getting letters from Paris, books, newspapers, and prints, and copies of the new songs. When he dined at Bergerac, my mother used to rustle away from table, kissing her hand to him, and actually light-headed from her deep potations of gossip. His conversation was a constant popping of corks. My father and the Vicomte, as I have said, were firm friends,—the firmer for the great diversity of their characters. M. de Bergerac was dark, grave, and taciturn, with a deep, sonorous voice. He had in his nature a touch of melancholy, and, in default of piety, a broad vein of superstition. The foundations of his soul, moreover, I am satisfied, in spite of the somewhat ponderous superstructure, were laid in a soil of rich tenderness and pity. Gaston de Treuil was of a wholly different temper. He was short and slight, without any color, and with eyes as blue and lustrous as sapphires. He was so careless and gracious and mirthful, that to an unenlightened fancy he seemed the model of a joyous, reckless, gallant, impenitent *veneur*. But it sometimes struck me that, as he revolved an idea in his mind, it produced a certain flinty ring, which suggested that his nature was built, as it were, on rock, and that the bottom of his heart was hard. Young as he was, besides, he had a tired, jaded, exhausted look, which told of his having played high at the game of life, and, very possibly, lost. In fact, it was notorious that M. de Treuil had run through his property, and that his actual business in our neighborhood was to repair the breach in his fortunes by constant attendance on a wealthy kinsman, who occupied an adjacent château, and who was dying of age and his infirmities. But while I thus hint at the existence in his composition of these few base particles, I should be sorry to represent him as substantially less fair and clear and lustrous than he appeared to be. He possessed an irresistible charm, and that of itself is a virtue. I feel sure, moreover, that my father would never have reconciled himself to a real scantiness of masculine worth. The Vicomte enjoyed, I fancy, the generous energy of my father's good-fellowship, and the Baron's healthy senses were flattered by the exquisite perfume of the other's infallible *savoir-vivre*. I offer a hundred apologies, at any rate, to the Vicomte's luminous shade, that I should have ventured to cast a dingy slur upon his name. History has commemorated it. He perished on the scaffold, and showed that he knew how to die as well as to live.

He was the last relic of the lily-handed youth of the *bon temps;* and as he looks at me out of the poignant sadness of the past, with a reproachful glitter in his cold blue eyes, and a scornful smile on his fine lips, I feel that, elegant and silent as he is, he has the last word in our dispute. I shall think of him henceforth as he appeared one night, or rather one morning, when he came home from a ball with my father, who had brought him to Bergerac to sleep. I had my bed in a closet out of my mother's room, where I lay in a most unwholesome fashion among her old gowns and hoops and cosmetics. My mother slept little; she passed the night in her dressing-gown, bolstered up in her bed, reading novels. The two gentlemen came in at four o'clock in the morning and made their way up to the Baronne's little sitting-room, next to her chamber. I suppose they were highly exhilarated, for they made a great noise of talking and laughing, and my father began to knock at the chamber door. He called out that he had M. de Treuil, and that they were cold and hungry. The Baronne said that she had a fire and they might come in. She was glad enough, poor lady, to get news of the ball, and to catch their impressions before they had been dulled by sleep. So they came in and sat by the fire, and M. de Treuil looked for some wine and some little cakes where my mother told him. I was wide awake and heard it all. I heard my mother protesting and crying out, and the Vicomte laughing, when he looked into the wrong place; and I am afraid that in my mother's room there were a great many wrong places. Before long, in my little stuffy, dark closet, I began to feel hungry too; whereupon I got out of bed and ventured forth into the room. I remember the whole picture, as one remembers isolated scenes of childhood: my mother's bed, with its great curtains half drawn back at the side, and her little eager face and dark eyes peeping out of the recess; then the two men at the fire,—my father with his hat on, sitting and looking drowsily into the flames, and the Vicomte standing before the hearth, talking, laughing, and gesticulating, with the candlestick in one hand and a glass of wine in the other,—dropping the wax on one side and the wine on the other. He was dressed from head to foot in white velvet and white silk, with embroideries of silver, and an immense *jabot*. He was very pale, and he looked lighter and slighter and wittier and more elegant than ever. He had a weak voice, and when he laughed, after one feeble little spasm, it went off into nothing, and you only knew he

196

was laughing by his nodding his head and lifting his eyebrows and showing his handsome teeth. My father was in crimson velvet, with tarnished gold facings. My mother bade me get back into bed, but my father took me on his knees and held out my bare feet to the fire. In a little while, from the influence of the heat, he fell asleep in his chair, and I sat in my place and watched M. de Treuil as he stood in the firelight drinking his wine and telling stories to my mother, until at last I too relapsed into the innocence of slumber. They were very good friends, the Vicomte and my mother. He admired the turn of her mind. I remember his telling me several years later, at the time of her death, when I was old enough to understand him, that she was a very brave, keen little woman, and that in her musty solitude of Bergerac she said a great many more good things than the world ever heard of.

During the winter which preceded Coquelin's arrival, M. de Treuil used to show himself at Bergerac in a friendly manner; but about a month before this event, his visits became more frequent and assumed a special import and motive. In a word, my father and his friend between them had conceived it to be a fine thing that the latter should marry Mlle. de Bergerac. Neither from his own nor from his friend's point of view was Gaston de Treuil a marrying man or a desirable *parti*. He was too fond of pleasure to conciliate a rich wife, and too poor to support a penniless one. But I fancy that my father was of the opinion that if the Vicomte came into his kinsman's property, the best way to insure the preservation of it, and to attach him to his duties and responsibilities, would be to unite him to an amiable girl, who might remind him of the beauty of a domestic life and lend him courage to mend his ways. As far as the Vicomte was concerned, this was assuredly a benevolent scheme, but it seems to me that it made small account of the young girl's own happiness. M. de Treuil was supposed, in the matter of women, to have known everything that can be known, and to be as *blasé* with regard to their charms as he was proof against their influence. And, in fact, his manner of dealing with women, and of discussing them, indicated a profound disenchantment, —no bravado of contempt, no affectation of cynicism, but a cold, civil, absolute lassitude. A simply charming woman, therefore, would never have served the purpose of my father's theory. A very sound and liberal instinct led him to direct his thoughts to his sister. There were, of course, various auxiliary reasons for such disposal of Mlle. de Bergerac's hand. She was now a woman grown, and she had as yet received no decent proposals. She had no marriage portion of her own, and my father had no means to endow her. Her beauty, moreover, could hardly be called a dowry. It was without those vulgar allurements which, for many a poor girl, replace the glitter of cash. If within a very few years more she had not succeeded in establishing herself creditably in the world, nothing would be left for her but to withdraw from it, and to pledge her virgin faith to the chilly sanctity of a cloister. I was destined in the course of time to assume the lordship and the slender revenues of Bergerac, and it was not to be expected that I should be burdened on the very threshold of life with the maintenance of a dowerless maiden aunt. A marriage with M. de Treuil would be in all senses a creditable match, and, in the event of his becoming his kinsman's legatee, a thoroughly comfortable one.

It was some time before the color of my father's intentions, and the milder hue of the Vicomte's acquiesence, began to show in our common daylight. It is not the custom, as you know, in our excellent France, to admit a lover on probation. He is expected to make up his mind on a view of the young lady's endowments, and to content himself before marriage with the bare cognition of her face. It is not thought decent (and there is certainly reason in it) that he should dally with his draught, and hold it to the light, and let the sun play through it, before carrying it to his lips. It was only on the ground of my father's warm good-will to Gaston de Treuil, and the latter's affectionate respect for the Baron, that the Vicomte was allowed to appear as a lover, before making his proposals in form. M. de Treuil, in fact, proceeded gradually, and made his approaches from a great distance. It was not for several weeks, therefore, that Mlle. de Bergerac became aware of them. And now, as this dear young girl steps into my story, where, I ask you, shall I find words to describe the broad loveliness of her person, to hint at the perfect beauty of her mind, to suggest the sweet mystery of her first suspicion of being sought, from afar, in marriage? Not in my fancy, surely; for there I should disinter the flimsy elements and tarnished properties of a superannuated comic opera. My taste, my son, was formed once for all fifty years ago. But if I wish to call up Mlle. de Bergerac, I must turn to my earliest memories, and delve in the sweet-smelling virgin soil of my heart. For Mlle. de Bergerac is no misty sylphid nor romantic moonlit nymph. She rises before me now, glowing with life, with the sound of her voice just dying in the air,—the more living for the mark of her crimson death-stain.

There was every good reason why her dawning consciousness of M. de Treuil's attentions—although these were little more than projected as yet—should have produced a serious tremor in her heart. It was not that she was aught of a coquette; I honestly believe that there was no latent coquetry in her nature. At all events, whatever she might have become after knowing M. de Treuil, she was no coquette to speak of in her ignorance. Her ignorance of men, in truth, was great. For the Vicomte himself, she had as yet known him only distantly, formally, as a gentleman of rank and fashion; and for others of his quality, she had seen but a small number, and not seen them intimately. These few words suffice to indicate that my aunt led a life of unbroken monotony. Once a year she spent six weeks with certain ladies of the Visitation, in whose convent she had received her education, and of whom she continued to be very fond. Half a dozen times in the twelve-month she went to a ball, under convoy of some haply ungrudging *châtelaine*. Two or three times a month, she received a visit at Bergerac. The rest of the time she paced, with the grace of an angel and the patience of a woman, the dreary corridors and unclipt garden walks of Bergerac. The discovery, then, that the brilliant Vicomte de Treuil was likely to make a proposal for her hand was an event of no small importance. With precisely what feelings she awaited its coming, I am unable to tell; but I have no hesitation in saying that even at this moment (that is, in less than a month after my tutor's arrival) her feelings were strongly modified by her acquaintance with Pierre Coquelin.

The word "acquaintance" perhaps exaggerates Mlle. de Bergerac's relation to this excellent young man. Twice a day she sat facing him at table, and half a dozen times a week she met him on the staircase, in the saloon, or in the park. Coquelin had been accommodated with an apartment in a small untenanted pavilion, within the enclosure of our domain, and except at meals, and when his presence was especially requested at the château, he confined himself to his own precinct. It was there, morning and evening, that I took my lesson. It was impossible, therefore, that an intimacy should have arisen between these two young persons, equally separated as they were by material and conventional barriers. Nevertheless, as the sequel proved, Coquelin must, by his mere presence, have begun very soon to exert a subtle action on Mlle. de Bergerac's thoughts. As for the young girl's influence on Coquelin, it is my belief that he fell in love with her the very first moment he beheld her,—that morning when he trudged wearily up our avenue. I need certainly make no apology for the poor fellow's audacity. You tell me that you fell in love at first sight with my aunt's portrait; you will readily excuse the poor youth for having been smitten with the original. It is less logical perhaps, but it is certainly no less natural, that Mlle. de Bergerac should have ventured to think of my governor as a decidedly interesting fellow. She saw so few men that one the more or the less made a very great difference. Coquelin's importance, moreover, was increased rather than diminished by the fact that, as I may say, he was a son of the soil. Marked as he was, in aspect and utterance, with the genuine plebeian stamp, he opened a way for the girl's fancy into a vague, unknown world. He stirred her imagination, I conceive, in very much the same way as such a man as Gaston de Treuil would have stirred—actually had stirred, of course —the grosser sensibilities of many a little *bourgeoise*. Mlle. de Bergerac was so thoroughly at peace with the consequences of her social position, so little inclined to derogate in act or in thought from the perfect dignity of her birth, that with the best conscience in the world, she entertained, as they came, the feelings provoked by Coquelin's manly virtues and graces. She had been educated in the faith that *noblesse oblige*, and she had seen none but gentlefolks and peasants. I think that she felt a vague, unavowed curiosity to see what sort of a figure you might make when you were under no obligations to nobleness. I think, finally, that unconsciously and in the interest simply of her unsubstantial dreams, (for in those long summer days at Bergerac, without finery, without visits, music, or books, or anything that a well-to-do grocer's daughter enjoys at the present day, she must, unless she was a far greater simpleton than I wish you to suppose, have spun a thousand airy, idle visions,) she contrasted Pierre Coquelin with the Vicomte de Treuil. I protest that I don't see how Coquelin bore the contrast. I frankly admit that, in her place, I would have given all my admiration to the Vicomte. At all events, the chief result of any such comparison must have been to show how, in spite of real trials and troubles, Coquelin had retained a certain masculine freshness and elasticity, and how, without any sorrows but those of his own wanton making, the Vicomte had utterly rubbed off this primal bloom of manhood. There was that about Gaston de Treuil that reminded you of an actor by daylight. His little row of foot-lights had burned itself out. But this is assuredly a more pedantic view of the case than any that Mlle. de Bergerac was capable of taking. The Vicomte had but to learn his part and declaim it, and the illusion was complete.

Mlle. de Bergerac may really have been a great simpleton, and my theory of her feelings—vague and imperfect as it is—may be put together quite after the fact. But I see you protest; you glance at the picture; you frown. *C'est bon;* give me your hand. She received the Vicomte's gallantries, then, with a modest, conscious dignity, and courtesied to exactly the proper depth when he made her one of his inimitable bows.

One evening—it was, I think, about ten days after Coquelin's arrival —she was sitting reading to my mother, who was ill in bed. The Vicomte had been dining with us, and after dinner we had gone into the drawing-room. At the drawing-room door Coquelin had made his bow to my father, and carried me off to his own apartment. Mlle. de Bergerac and the two gentlemen had gone into the drawing-room together. At dusk I had come back to the château, and, going up to my mother, had found her in company with her sister-in-law. In a few moments my father came in, looking stern and black.

"Sister," he cried, "why did you leave us alone in the drawing-room? Didn't you see I wanted you to stay?"

Mlle. de Bergerac laid down her book and looked at her brother before answering. "I had to come to my sister," she said: "I couldn't leave her alone."

My mother, I'm sorry to say, was not always just to my aunt. She used to lose patience with her sister's want of coquetry, of ambition, of desire to make much of herself. She divined wherein my aunt had offended. "You're very devoted to your sister, suddenly," she said. "There are duties and duties, mademoiselle. I'm very much obliged to you for reading to me. You can put down the book."

"The Vicomte swore very hard when you went out," my father went on.

Mlle. de Bergerac laid aside her book. "Dear me!" she said, "if he was going to swear, it's very well I went."

"Are you afraid of the Vicomte?" said my mother. "You're twenty-two years old. You're not a little girl."

"Is she twenty-two?" cried my father. "I told him she was twenty-one."

"Frankly, brother," said Mlle. de Bergerac, "what does he want? Does he want to marry me?"

My father stared a moment. *"Pardieu!"* he cried.

"She looks as if she didn't believe it," said my mother. "Pray, did you ever ask him?"

"No, madam; did you? You are very kind." Mlle. de Bergerac was excited; her cheek flushed.

"In the course of time," said my father, gravely, "the Vicomte proposes to demand your hand."

"What is he waiting for?" asked Mlle. de Bergerac, simply.

"Fi donc, mademoiselle!" cried my mother.

"He is waiting for M. de Sorbières to die," said I, who had got this bit of news from my mother's waiting-woman.

My father stared at me, half angrily; and then,—"He expects to inherit," he said, boldly. "It's a very fine property."

"He would have done better, it seems to me," rejoined Mlle. de Bergerac, after a pause, "to wait till he had actually come into possession of it."

"M. de Sorbières," cried my father, "has given him his word a dozen times over. Besides, the Vicomte loves you."

Mlle. de Bergerac blushed, with a little smile, and as she did so her eyes fell on mine. I was standing gazing at her as a child gazes at a familiar friend who is presented to him in a new light. She put out her hand and drew me towards her. "The truth comes out of the mouths of children," she said. "Chevalier, does he love me?"

"Stuff!" cried the Baronne; "one doesn't speak to children of such things. A young girl should believe what she's told. I believed my mother when she told me that your brother loved me. He didn't, but I believed it, and as far as I know I'm none the worse for it."

For ten days after this I heard nothing more of Mlle. de Bergerac's marriage, and I suppose that, childlike, I ceased to think of what I had already heard. One evening, about midsummer, M. de Treuil came over to supper, and announced that he was about to set out in company with poor M. de Sorbières for some mineral springs in the South, by the use of which the latter hoped to prolong his life.

I remember that, while we sat at table, Coquelin was appealed to as an authority upon some topic broached by the Vicomte, on which he found himself at variance with my father. It was the first time, I fancy, that he had been so honored and that his opinions had been deemed worth hearing. The point under discussion must have related to the history of the American War, for Coquelin spoke with the firmness and fulness warranted by personal knowledge. I fancy that he was a little frightened by the sound of his own voice, but he acquitted himself with perfect good grace and success. We all sat attentive; my mother even staring a little, surprised to find in a beggarly pedagogue a perfect *beau diseur*. My father, as became so great a gentleman, knew by a certain rough instinct when a man had something amusing to say. He leaned back, with his hands in his pockets, listening and paying the poor fellow the tribute of a half-puzzled frown. The Vicomte, like a man of taste, was charmed. He told stories himself, he was a good judge.

After supper we went out on the terrace. It was a perfect summer night, neither too warm nor too cool. There was no moon, but the stars flung down their languid light, and the earth, with its great dark masses of vegetation and the gently swaying tree-tops, seemed to answer back in a thousand vague perfumes. Somewhere, close at hand, out of an enchanted tree, a nightingale raved and carolled in delirious music. We had the good taste to listen in silence. My mother sat down on a bench against the house, and put out her hand and made my father sit beside her. Mlle. de Bergerac strolled to the edge of the terrace, and leaned against the balustrade, whither M. de Treuil soon followed her. She stood motionless, with her head raised, intent upon the music. The Vicomte seated himself upon the parapet, with his face towards her and his arms folded. He may perhaps have been talking, under cover of the nightingale. Coquelin seated himself near the other end of the terrace, and drew me between his knees. At last the nightingale ceased. Coquelin got up, and bade good night to the company, and made his way across the park to his lodge. I went over to my aunt and the Vicomte.

"M. Coquelin is a clever man," said the Vicomte, as he disappeared down the avenue. "He spoke very well this evening."

"He never spoke so much before," said I. "He's very shy."

"I think," said my aunt, "he's a little proud."

"I don't understand," said the Vicomte, "how a man with any pride can put up with the place of a tutor. I had rather dig in the fields."

"The Chevalier is much obliged to you," said my aunt, laughing. "In fact, M. Coquelin has to dig a little, hasn't he, Chevalier?"

"Not at all," said I. "But he keeps some plants in pots."

At this my aunt and the Vicomte began to laugh. "He keeps one precious plant," cried my aunt, tapping my face with her fan.

At this moment my mother called me away. "He makes them laugh," I heard her say to my father, as I went to her.

"She had better laugh about it than cry," said my father.

Before long, Mlle. de Bergerac and her companion came back toward the house.

"M. le Vicomte, brother," said my aunt, "invites me to go down and walk in the park. May I accept?"

"By all means," said my father. "You may go with the Vicomte as you would go with me."

"Ah!" said the Vicomte.

"Come then, Chevalier," said my aunt. "In my turn, I invite you."

"My son," said the Baronne, "I forbid you."

"But my brother says," rejoined Mlle. de Bergerac, "that I may go with M. de Treuil as I would go with himself. He would not object to my taking my nephew." And she put out her hand.

"One would think," said my mother, "that you were setting out for Siberia."

"For Siberia!" cried the Vicomte, laughing; "O no!"

I paused, undecided. But my father gave me a push. "After all," he said, "it's better."

When I overtook my aunt and her lover, the latter, losing no time, appeared to have come quite to the point.

"Your brother tells me, mademoiselle," he had begun, "that he has spoken to you."

The young girl was silent.

"You may be indifferent," pursued the Vicomte, "but I can't believe you're ignorant."

204

"My brother has spoken to me," said Mlle. de Bergerac at last, with an apparent effort,—"my brother has spoken to me of his project."

"I'm very glad he seemed to you to have espoused my cause so warmly that you call it his own. I did my best to convince him that I possess what a person of your merit is entitled to exact of the man who asks her hand. In doing so, I almost convinced myself. The point is now to convince you."

"I listen."

"You admit, then, that your mind is not made up in advance against me."

"*Mon Dieu!*" cried my aunt, with some emphasis, "a poor girl like me doesn't make up her mind. You frighten me, Vicomte. This is a serious question. I have the misfortune to have no mother. I can only pray God. But prayer helps me not to choose, but only to be resigned."

"Pray often, then, mademoiselle. I'm not an arrogant lover, and since I have known you a little better, I have lost all my vanity. I'm not a good man nor a wise one. I have no doubt you think me very light and foolish, but you can't begin to know how light and foolish I am. Marry me and you'll never know. If you don't marry me, I'm afraid you'll never marry."

"You're very frank, Vicomte. If you think I'm afraid of never marrying, you're mistaken. One can be very happy as an old maid. I spend six weeks every year with the ladies of the Visitation. Several of them are excellent women, charming women. They read, they educate young girls, they visit the poor—"

The Vicomte broke into a laugh. "They get up at five o'clock in the morning; they breakfast on boiled cabbage; they make flannel waistcoats, and very good sweetmeats! Why do you talk so, mademoiselle? Why do you say that you would like to lead such a life? One might almost believe it is coquetry. *Tenez,* I believe it's ignorance,—ignorance of your own feelings, your own nature, and your own needs." M. de Treuil paused a moment, and, although I had a very imperfect notion of the meaning of his words, I remember being struck with the vehement look of his pale face, which seemed fairly to glow in the darkness. Plainly, he was in love. "You are not made for solitude," he went on; "you are not made to be buried in a dingy old château, in the depths of a ridiculous province. You are made for the world, for the court, for pleasure, to be loved, admired, and envied. No, you don't know yourself, nor does Bergerac know you, nor his wife! I, at least, appreciate you. I know that you are supremely beautiful—"

"Vicomte," said Mlle. de Bergerac, "you forget—the child."

"Hang the child! Why did you bring him along? *You* are no child. You can understand me. You are a woman, full of intelligence and goodness and beauty. They don't know you here, they think you a little demoiselle in pinafores. Before Heaven, mademoiselle, there is that about you,—I see it, I feel it here at your side, in this rustling darkness,—there is that about you that a man would gladly die for."

Mlle. de Bergerac interrupted him with energy. "You talk extravagantly. I don't understand you; you frighten me."

"I talk as I feel. I frighten you? So much the better. I wish to stir your heart and get some answer to the passion of my own."

Mlle. de Bergerac was silent a moment, as if collecting her thoughts. "If I talk with you on this subject, I must do it with my wits about me," she said at last. "I must know exactly what we each mean."

"It's plain then that I can't hope to inspire you with any degree of affection."

"One doesn't promise to love, Vicomte; I can only answer for the present. My heart is so full of good wishes toward you that it costs me comparatively little to say I don't love you."

"And anything I may say of my own feelings will make no difference to you?"

"You have said you love me. Let it rest there."

"But you look as if you doubted my word."

"You can't see how I look; Vicomte, I believe you."

"Well then, there is one point gained. Let us pass to the others. I'm thirty years old. I have a very good name and a very bad reputation. I honestly believe that, though I've fallen below my birth, I've kept above my fame. I believe that I have no vices of temper; I'm neither brutal, nor jealous, nor miserly. As for my fortune, I'm obliged to admit that it consists chiefly in my expectations. My actual property is about equal to your brother's and you know how your sister-in-law is obliged to live. My expectations are thought particularly good. My great-uncle, M. de Sorbières, possesses, chiefly in landed estates, a fortune of some three millions of livres. I have no important competitors, either in blood or devotion. He is eighty-seven years old and paralytic, and within the past year I have been laying siege to his favor with such constancy that his surrender, like his extinction, is only a question of time. I received yesterday a summons to go with him to the Pyrenees, to drink certain medicinal waters. The least he can do, on my return, is to make me a handsome allowance, which with my own revenues will make—*en attendant* better things—a sufficient income for a reasonable couple."

There was a pause of some moments, during which we slowly walked along in the obstructed starlight, the silence broken only by the train of my aunt's dress brushing against the twigs and pebbles.

"What a pity," she said, at last, "that you are not able to speak of all this good fortune as in the present rather than in the future."

"There it is! Until I came to know you, I had no thoughts of marriage. What did I want of wealth? If five years ago I had foreseen this moment, I should stand here with something better than promises."

"Well, Vicomte," pursued the young girl, with singular composure, "you do me the honor to think very well of me: I hope you will not be vexed to find that prudence is one of my virtues. If I marry, I wish to marry well. It's not only the husband, but the marriage that counts. In accepting you as you stand, I should make neither a sentimental match nor a brilliant one."

"Excellent. I love you, prudence and all. Say, then, that I present myself here three months hence with the titles and tokens of property amounting to a million and a half of livres, will you consider that I am a *parti* sufficiently brilliant to make you forget that you don't love me?"

"I should never forget that."

"Well, nor I either. It makes a sort of sorrowful harmony! If three months hence, I repeat, I offer you a fortune instead of this poor empty hand, will you accept the one for the sake of the other?"

My aunt stopped short in the path. "I hope, Vicomte," she said, with much apparent simplicity, "that you are going to do nothing indelicate."

"God forbid, mademoiselle! It shall be a clean hand and a clean fortune."

"If you ask then a promise, a pledge—"

"You'll not give it. I ask then only for a little hope. Give it in what form you will."

We walked a few steps farther and came out from among the

shadows, beneath the open sky. The voice of M. de Treuil, as he uttered these words, was low and deep and tender and full of entreaty. Mlle. de Bergerac cannot but have been deeply moved. I think she was somewhat awe-struck at having called up such a force of devotion in a nature deemed cold and inconstant. She put out her hand. "I wish success to any honorable efforts. In any case you will be happier for your wealth. In one case it will get you a wife, and in the other it will console you."

"Console me! I shall hate it, despise it, and throw it into the sea!"

Mlle. de Bergerac had no intention, of course, of leaving her companion under an illusion. "Ah, but understand, Vicomte," she said, "I make no promise. My brother claims the right to bestow my hand. If he wishes our marriage now, of course he will wish it three months hence. I have never gainsaid him."

"From now to three months a great deal may happen."

"To you, perhaps, but not to me."

"Are you going to your friends of the Visitation?"

"No, indeed. I have no wish to spend the summer in a cloister. I prefer the green fields."

"Well, then, *va* for the green fields! They're the next best thing. I recommend you to the Chevalier's protection."

We had made half the circuit of the park, and turned into an alley which stretched away towards the house, and about midway in its course separated into two paths, one leading to the main avenue, and the other to the little pavilion inhabited by Coquelin. At the point where the alley was divided stood an enormous oak of great circumference, with a circular bench surrounding its trunk. It occupied, I believe, the central point of the whole domain. As we reached the oak, I looked down along the footpath towards the pavilion, and saw Coquelin's light shining in one of the windows. I immediately proposed that we should pay him a visit. My aunt objected, on the ground that he was doubtless busy and would not thank us for interrupting him. And then, when I insisted, she said it was not proper.

"How not proper?"

"It's not proper for me. A lady doesn't visit young men in their own apartments."

At this the Vicomte cried out. He was partly amused, I think, at my aunt's attaching any compromising power to poor little Coquelin, and partly annoyed at her not considering his own company, in view of his pretensions, a sufficient guaranty.

"I should think," he said, "that with the Chevalier and me you might venture—"

"As you please, then," said my aunt. And I accordingly led the way to my governor's abode.

It was a small edifice of a single floor, standing prettily enough among the trees, and still habitable, although very much in disrepair. It had been built by that same ancestor to whom Bergerac was indebted, in the absence of several of the necessities of life, for many of its elegant superfluities, and had been designed, I suppose, as a scene of pleasure,—such pleasure as he preferred to celebrate elsewhere than beneath the roof of his domicile. Whether it had ever been used I know not; but it certainly had very little of the look of a pleasure-house. Such furniture as it had once possessed had long since been transferred to the needy saloons of the château, and it now looked dark and bare and cold. In front, the shrubbery had been left to grow thick and wild and almost totally to exclude the light from the windows; but behind, outside of the two rooms which he occupied, and which had been provided from the château with the articles necessary for comfort, Coquelin had obtained my father's permission to effect a great clearance in the foliage, and he now enjoyed plenty of sunlight and a charming view of the neighboring country. It was in the larger of these two rooms, arranged as a sort of study, that we found him.

He seemed surprised and somewhat confused by our visit, but he very soon recovered himself sufficiently to do the honors of his little establishment.

"It was an idea of my nephew," said Mlle. de Bergerac. "We were walking in the park, and he saw your light. Now that we are here, Chevalier, what would you have us do?"

"M. Coquelin has some very pretty things to show you," said I.

Coquelin turned very red. "Pretty things, Chevalier? Pray, what do you mean? I have some of your nephew's copy-books," he said, turning to my aunt.

"Nay, you have some of your own," I cried. "He has books full of drawings, made by himself."

"Ah, you draw?" said the Vicomte.

"M. le Chevalier does me the honor to think so. My drawings are meant for no critics but children."

"In the way of criticism," said my aunt, gently, "we too are children." Her beautiful eyes, as she uttered these words, must have been quite as gentle as her voice. Coquelin looked at her, thinking very modestly of his little pictures, but loth to refuse the first request she had ever made him.

"Show them, at any rate," said the Vicomte, in a somewhat peremptory tone. In those days, you see, a man occupying Coquelin's place was expected to hold all his faculties and talents at the disposal of his patron, and it was thought an unwarrantable piece of assumption that he should cultivate any of the arts for his own peculiar delectation. In withholding his drawings, therefore, it may have seemed to the Vicomte that Coquelin was unfaithful to the service to which he was held,—that, namely, of instructing, diverting, and edifying the household of Bergerac. Coquelin went to a little cupboard in the wall, and took out three small albums and a couple of portfolios. Mlle. de Bergerac sat down at the table, and Coquelin drew up the lamp and placed his drawings before her. He turned them over, and gave such explanations as seemed necessary. I have only my childish impressions of the character of these sketches, which, in my eyes, of course, seemed prodigiously clever. What the judgment of my companions was worth I know not, but they appeared very well pleased. The Vicomte probably knew a good sketch from a poor one, and he very good-naturedly pronounced my tutor an extremely knowing fellow. Coquelin had drawn anything and everything,—peasants and dumb brutes, landscapes and Parisian types and figures, taken indifferently from high and low life. But the best pieces in the collection were a series of illustrations and reminiscences of his adventures with the American army, and of the figures and episodes he had observed in the Colonies. They were for the most part rudely enough executed, owing to his want of time and materials, but they were full of *finesse* and character. M. de Treuil was very much amused at the rude equipments of your ancestors. There were sketches of the enemy too, whom Coquelin had apparently not been afraid to look in the face. While he was turning over these designs for Mlle. de Bergerac, the Vicomte took up one of his portfolios, and, after a short inspection, drew from it, with a cry of surprise, a large portrait in pen and ink.

210

GABRIELLE DE BERGERAC

"Tiens!" said I; "it's my aunt!"

Coquelin turned pale. Mlle. de Bergerac looked at him, and turned the least bit red. As for the Vicomte, he never changed color. There was no eluding the fact that it was a likeness, and Coquelin had to pay the penalty of his skill.

"I didn't know," he said, at random, "that it was in that portfolio. Do you recognize it, mademoiselle?"

"Ah," said the Vicomte, dryly, "M. Coquelin meant to hide it."

"It's too pretty to hide," said my aunt; "and yet it's too pretty to show. It's flattered."

"Why should I have flattered you, mademoiselle?" asked Coquelin. "You were never to see it."

"That's what it is, mademoiselle," said the Vicomte, "to have such dazzling beauty. It penetrates the world. Who knows where you'll find it reflected next?"

However pretty a compliment this may have been to Mlle. de Bergerac, it was decidedly a back-handed blow to Coquelin. The young girl perceived that he felt it.

She rose to her feet. "My beauty," she said, with a slight tremor in her voice, "would be a small thing without M. Coquelin's talent. We are much obliged to you. I hope that you'll bring your pictures to the château, so that we may look at the rest."

"Are you going to leave him this?" asked M. de Treuil, holding up the portrait.

"If M. Coquelin will give it to me, I shall be very glad to have it."

"One doesn't keep one's own portrait," said the Vicomte. "It ought to belong to me." In those days, before the invention of our sublime machinery for the reproduction of the human face, a young fellow was very glad to have his mistress's likeness in pen and ink.

But Coquelin had no idea of contributing to the Vicomte's gallery. "Excuse me," he said, gently, but looking the nobleman in the face. "The picture isn't good enough for Mlle. de Bergerac, but it's too good for any one else"; and he drew it out of the other's hands, tore it across, and applied it to the flame of the lamp.

We went back to the château in silence. The drawing-room was empty; but as we went in, the Vicomte took a lighted candle from a table and raised it to the young girl's face. *"Parbleu!"* he exclaimed, "the vagabond had looked at you to good purpose!"

211

Mlle. de Bergerac gave a half-confused laugh. "At any rate," she said, "he didn't hold a candle to me as if I were my old smoke-stained grandame, yonder!" and she blew out the light. "I'll call my brother," she said, preparing to retire.

"A moment," said her lover; "I shall not see you for some weeks. I shall start to-morrow with my uncle. I shall think of you by day, and dream of you by night. And meanwhile I shall very much doubt whether you think of me."

Mlle. de Bergerac smiled. "Doubt, doubt. It will help you to pass the time. With faith alone it would hang very heavy."

"It seems hard," pursued M. de Treuil, "that I should give you so many pledges, and that you should give me none."

"I give all I ask."

"Then, for Heaven's sake, ask for something!"

"Your kind words are all I want."

"Then give me some kind word yourself."

"What shall I say, Vicomte?"

"Say,—say that you'll wait for me."

They were standing in the centre of the great saloon, their figures reflected by the light of a couple of candles in the shining inlaid floor. Mlle. de Bergerac walked away a few steps with a look of agitation. Then turning about, "Vicomte," she asked, in a deep, full voice, "do you truly love me?"

"Ah, Gabrielle!" cried the young man.

I take it that no woman can hear her baptismal name uttered for the first time as that of Mlle. de Bergerac then came from her suitor's lips without being thrilled with joy and pride.

"Well, M. de Treuil," she said, "I will wait for you."

· II ·

I remember distinctly the incidents of that summer at Bergerac; or at least its general character, its tone. It was a hot, dry season; we lived with doors and windows open. M. Coquelin suffered very much from the heat, and sometimes, for days together, my lessons were suspended. We put our books away and rambled out for a long day in the fields. My tutor was perfectly faithful; he never allowed me to wander beyond call. I was very fond of fishing, and I used to sit for hours, like a little old man, with my legs dangling over the bank of our slender river, patiently awaiting the bite that so seldom came. Near at hand, in the shade, stretched at his length on the grass, Coquelin read and re-read one of his half dozen Greek and Latin poets. If we had walked far from home, we used to go and ask for some dinner at the hut of a neighboring peasant. For a very small coin we got enough bread and cheese and small fruit to keep us over till supper. The peasants, stupid and squalid as they were, always received us civilly enough, though on Coquelin's account quite as much as on my own. He addressed them with an easy familiarity, which made them feel, I suppose, that he was, if not quite one of themselves, at least by birth and sympathies much nearer to them than to the future Baron de Bergerac. He gave me in the course of these walks a great deal of good advice; and without perverting my signorial morals or instilling any notions that were treason to my rank and position, he kindled in my childish breast a little democratic flame which has never quite become extinct. He taught me the beauty of humanity, justice, and tolerance; and whenever he detected me in a precocious attempt to assert my baronial rights over the wretched little *manants* who crossed my path, he gave me morally a very hard drubbing. He had none of the base complaisance and cynical nonchalance of the traditional tutor of our old novels and comedies. Later in life I might have found him too rigorous a moralist; but in those days I liked him all the better for letting me sometimes feel the curb. It gave me a highly agreeable sense of importance and maturity. It was a tribute to half-divined possibilities of naughtiness. In the afternoon, when I was tired of fishing, he would lie with his thumb in his book and his eyes half closed and tell me fairy-tales till the eyes of both of us closed together. Do the instructors of youth nowadays condescend to the fairy-tale pure and simple? Coquelin's stories belonged to the old, old world: no political economy, no physics, no application to anything in life. Do you remember in Doré's illustrations to Perrault's tales, the picture of the enchanted castle of the Sleeping Beauty? Back in the distance, in the bosom of an ancient park and surrounded by thick baronial woods which blacken all the gloomy horizon, on the farther side of a great abysmal hollow of tangled forest verdure, rise the long façade, the moss-grown terraces, the towers, the purple roofs, of a château of the time of Henry IV. Its massive foundations plunge far down into the wild chasm of the woodland, and its cold pinnacles of slate tower upwards, close to the rolling autumn clouds. The afternoon is closing in and a chill October wind is beginning to set the forest a-howling. In the foreground, on an elevation beneath a mighty oak, stand a couple of old woodcutters pointing across into the enchanted distance and answering the questions of the young prince. They are the bent and blackened woodcutters of old France, of La Fontaine's Fables and the *Médecin malgré lui*. What does the castle contain? What secret is locked in its stately walls? What revel is enacted in its long saloons? What strange figures stand aloof from its vacant windows? You ask the question, and the answer is a long revery. I never look at the picture without thinking of those summer afternoons in the woods and of Coquelin's long stories. His fairies were the fairies of the *Grand Siècle*, and his princes and shepherds the godsons of Perrault and Madame d'Aulnay. They lived in such palaces and they hunted in such woods.

Mlle. de Bergerac, to all appearance, was not likely to break her promise to M. de Treuil,—for lack of the opportunity, quite as much as of the will. Those bright summer days must have seemed very long to her, and I can't for my life imagine what she did with her time. But she, too, as she had told the Vicomte, was very fond of the green fields; and although she never wandered very far from the house, she spent many an hour in the open air. Neither here nor within doors was she likely to encounter the happy man of whom the Vicomte might be jealous. Mlle. de Bergerac had a friend, a single intimate friend, who came sometimes to pass the day with her, and whose visits she occasionally returned. Marie de Chalais, the granddaughter of the Marquis de Chalais, who lived some ten miles away, was in all respects the exact counterpart and foil of my aunt. She was extremely plain, but with that sprightly, highly seasoned ugliness which is often so agreeable to men. Short, spare, swarthy, light, with an immense mouth, a most impertinent little nose, an imperceptible foot, a charming hand, and a delightful voice, she was, in spite of her great name and her fine clothes, the very ideal of the old stage *soubrette*. Frequently, indeed, in her dress and manner, she used to provoke a comparison with this incomparable type. A cap, an apron, and a short petticoat were all sufficient; with these and her bold, dark eyes she could impersonate the very genius of impertinence and intrigue.

She was a thoroughly light creature, and later in life, after her marriage, she became famous for her ugliness, her witticisms, and her adventures; but that she had a good heart is shown by her real attachment to my aunt. They were forever at cross-purposes, and yet they were excellent friends. When my aunt wished to walk, Mlle. de Chalais wished to sit still; when Mlle. de Chalais wished to laugh, my aunt wished to meditate; when my aunt wished to talk piety, Mlle. de Chalais wished to talk scandal. Mlle. de Bergerac, however, usually carried the day and set the tune. There was nothing on earth that Marie de Chalais so despised as the green fields; and yet you might have seen her a dozen times that summer wandering over the domain of Bergerac, in a short muslin dress and a straw hat, with her arm entwined about the waist of her more stately friend. We used often to meet them, and as we drew near Mlle. de Chalais would always stop and offer to kiss the Chevalier. By this pretty trick Coquelin was subjected for a few moments to the influence of her innocent *agaceries;* for rather than have no man at all to prick with the little darts of her coquetry, the poor girl would have gone off and made eyes at the scare-crow in the wheat-field. Coquelin was not at all abashed by her harmless advances; for although, in addressing my aunt, he was apt to lose his voice or his countenance, he often showed a very pretty wit in answering Mlle. de Chalais.

On one occasion she spent several days at Bergerac, and during her stay she proffered an urgent entreaty that my aunt should go back with her to her grandfather's house, where, having no parents, she lived with her governess. Mlle. de Bergerac declined, on the ground of having no gowns fit to visit in; whereupon Mlle. de Chalais went to my mother, begged the gift of an old blue silk dress, and with her own cunning little hands made it over for my aunt's figure. That evening Mlle. de Bergerac appeared at supper in this renovated garment,—the first silk gown she had ever worn. Mlle. de Chalais had also dressed her hair, and decked her out with a number of trinkets and furbelows; and when the two came into the room together, they reminded me of the beautiful Duchess in Don Quixote, followed by a little dark-visaged Spanish waiting-maid. The next morning Coquelin and I rambled off as usual in search of adventures, and the day after that they were to leave the château. Whether we met with any adventures or not I forget; but we found ourselves at dinner-time at some distance from home, very hungry after a long tramp. We directed our steps to a little road-side hovel, where we had already purchased hospitality, and made our way in unannounced. We were somewhat surprised at the scene that met our eyes.

On a wretched bed at the farther end of the hut lay the master of the household, a young peasant whom we had seen a fortnight before in full health and vigor. At the head of the bed stood his wife, moaning, crying, and wringing her hands. Hanging about her, clinging to her skirts, and adding their piping cries to her own lamentations, were four little children, unwashed, unfed, and half clad. At the foot, facing the dying man, knelt his old mother—a horrible hag, so bent and brown and wrinkled with labor and age that there was nothing womanly left of her but her coarse, rude dress and cap, nothing of maternity but her sobs. Beside the pillow stood the priest, who had apparently just discharged the last offices of the Church. On the other side, on her knees, with the poor fellow's hand in her own, knelt Mlle. de Bergerac, like a consoling angel. On a stool near the door, looking on from a distance, sat Mlle. de Chalais, holding a little bleating kid in her arms. When she saw us, she started up. "Ah, M. Coquelin!" she cried, "do persuade Mlle. de Bergerac to leave this horrible place."

I saw Mlle. de Bergerac look at the curé and shake her head, as if to say that it was all over. She rose from her knees and went round to the wife, telling the same tale with her face. The poor, squalid *paysanne* gave a sort of savage, stupid cry, and threw herself and her rags on the young girl's neck. Mlle. de Bergerac caressed her, and whispered heaven knows what divinely simple words of comfort. Then, for the first time, she saw Coquelin and me, and beckoned us to approach.

"Chevalier," she said, still holding the woman on her breast, "have you got any money?"

At these words the woman raised her head. I signified that I was penniless.

My aunt frowned impatiently. "M. Coquelin, have you?"

Coquelin drew forth a single small piece, all that he possessed; for it was the end of his month. Mlle. de Bergerac took it, and pursued her inquiry.

"Curé, have you any money?"

"Not a sou," said the curé, smiling sweetly.

216

"Bah!" said Mlle. de Bergerac, with a sort of tragic petulence. "What can I do with twelve sous?"

"Give it all the same," said the woman, doggedly, putting out her hand.

"They want money," said Mlle. de Bergerac, lowering her voice to Coquelin. "They have had this great sorrow, but a *louis d'or* would dull the wound. But we're penniless. O for the sight of a little gold!"

"I have a *louis* at home," said I; and I felt Coquelin lay his hand on my head.

"What was the matter with the husband?" he asked.

"*Mon Dieu!*" said my aunt, glancing round at the bed. "I don't know."

Coquelin looked at her, half amazed, half worshipping.

"Who are they, these people? What are they?" she asked.

"Mademoiselle," said Coquelin, fervently, "you're an angel!"

"I wish I were," said Mlle. de Bergerac, simply; and she turned to the old mother.

We walked home together,—the curé with Mlle. de Chalais and me, and Mlle. de Bergerac in front with Coquelin. Asking how the two young girls had found their way to the deathbed we had just left, I learned from Mlle. de Chalais that they had set out for a stroll together, and, striking into a footpath across the fields, had gone farther than they supposed, and lost their way. While they were trying to recover it, they came upon the wretched hut where we had found them, and were struck by the sight of two children, standing crying at the door. Mlle. de Bergerac had stopped and questioned them to acertain the cause of their sorrow, which with some difficulty she found to be that their father was dying of a fever. Whereupon, in spite of her companion's lively opposition, she had entered the miserable abode, and taken her place at the wretched couch, in the position in which we had discovered her. All this, doubtless, implied no extraordinary merit on Mlle. de Bergerac's part; but it placed her in a gracious, pleasing light.

The next morning the young girls went off in the great coach of M. de Chalais, which had been sent for them overnight, my father riding along as an escort. My aunt was absent a week, and I think I may say we keenly missed her. When I say we, I mean Coquelin and I, and when I say Coquelin and I, I mean Coquelin in particular; for it had come to this, that my tutor was roundly in love with my aunt. I didn't know it then, of course; but looking back, I see that he must already have been stirred to his soul's depths. Young as I was, moreover, I believe that I even then suspected his passion, and, loving him as I did, watched it with a vague, childish awe and sympathy. My aunt was to me, of course, a very old story, and I am sure she neither charmed nor dazzled my boyish fancy. I was quite too young to apprehend the meaning or the consequences of Coquelin's feelings; but I knew that he had a secret, and I wished him joy of it. He kept so jealous a guard on it that I would have defied my elders to discover the least reason for accusing him; but with a simple child of ten, thinking himself alone and uninterpreted, he showed himself plainly a lover. He was absent, restless, preoccupied; now steeped in languid revery, now pacing up and down with the exaltation of something akin to hope. Hope itself he could never have felt; for it must have seemed to him that his passion was so audacious as almost to be criminal. Mlle. de Bergerac's absence showed him, I imagine, that to know her had been the event of his life; to see her across the table, to hear her voice, her tread, to pass her, to meet her eye, a deep, consoling, healing joy. It revealed to him the force with which she had grasped his heart, and I think he was half frightened at the energy of his passion.

One evening, while Mlle. de Bergerac was still away, I sat in his window, committing my lesson for the morrow by the waning light. He was walking up and down among the shadows. "Chevalier," said he, suddenly, "what should you do if I were to leave you?"

My poor little heart stood still. "Leave me?" I cried, aghast; "why should you leave me?"

"Why, you know I didn't come to stay forever."

"But you came to stay till I'm a man grown. Don't you like your place?"

"Perfectly."

"Don't you like my father?"

"Your father is excellent."

"And my mother?"

"Your mother is perfect."

"And me, Coquelin?"

"You, Chevalier, are a little goose."

218

And then, from a sort of unreasoned instinct that Mlle. de Bergerac was somehow connected with his idea of going away, "And my aunt?" I added.

"How, your aunt?"

"Don't you like her?"

Coquelin had stopped in his walk, and stood near me and above me. He looked at me some moments without answering, and then sat down beside me in the window-seat, and laid his hand on my head.

"Chevalier," he said, "I will tell you something."

"Well?" said I, after I had waited some time.

"One of these days you will be a man grown, and I shall have left you long before that. You'll learn a great many things that you don't know now. You'll learn what a strange, vast world it is, and what strange creatures men are—and women; how strong, how weak, how happy, how unhappy. You'll learn how many feelings and passions they have, and what a power of joy and of suffering. You'll be Baron de Bergerac and master of the château and of this little house. You'll sometimes be very proud of your title, and you'll sometimes feel very sad that it's so little more than a bare title. But neither your pride nor your grief will come to anything beside this, that one day, in the prime of your youth and strength and good looks, you'll see a woman whom you will love more than all these things,—more than your name, your lands, your youth, and strength, and beauty. It happens to all men, especially the good ones, and you'll be a good one. But the woman you love will be far out of your reach. She'll be a princess, perhaps she'll be the Queen. How can a poor little Baron de Bergerac expect her to look at him? You will give up your life for a touch of her hand; but what will she care for your life or your death? You'll curse your love, and yet you'll bless it, and perhaps—not having your living to get—you'll come up here and shut yourself up with your dreams and regrets. You'll come perhaps into this pavilion, and sit here alone in the twilight. And then, my child, you'll remember this evening; that I foretold it all and gave you my blessing in advance and—kissed you." He bent over, and I felt his burning lips on my forehead.

I understood hardly a word of what he said; but whether it was that I was terrified by his picture of the possible insignificance of a Baron de Bergerac, or that I was vaguely overawed by his deep, solemn tones,

I know not; but my eyes very quietly began to emit a flood of tears. The effect of my grief was to induce him to assure me that he had no present intention of leaving me. It was not, of course, till later in life, that, thinking over the situation, I understood his impulse to arrest his hopeless passion for Mlle. de Bergerac by immediate departure. He was not brave in time.

At the end of a week she returned one evening as we were at supper. She came in with M. de Chalais, an amiable old man, who had been so kind as to accompany her. She greeted us severally, and nodded to Coquelin. She talked, I remember, with great volubility, relating what she had seen and done in her absence, and laughing with extraordinary freedom. As we left the table, she took my hand, and I put out the other and took Coquelin's.

"Has the Chevalier been a good boy?" she asked.

"Perfect," said Coquelin; "but he has wanted his aunt sadly."

"Not at all," said I, resenting the imputation as derogatory to my independence.

"You have had a pleasant week, mademoiselle?" said Coquelin.

"A charming week. And you?"

"M. Coquelin has been very unhappy," said I. "He thought of going away."

"Ah?" said my aunt.

Coquelin was silent.

"You think of going away?"

"I merely spoke of it, mademoiselle. I must go away some time, you know. The Chevalier looks upon me as something eternal."

"What's eternal?" asked the Chevalier.

"There is nothing eternal, my child," said Mlle. de Bergerac. "Nothing lasts more than a moment."

"O," said Coquelin, "I don't agree with you!"

"You don't believe that in this world everything is vain and fleeting and transitory?"

"By no means; I believe in the permanence of many things."

"Of what, for instance?"

"Well, of sentiments and passions."

"Very likely. But not of the hearts that hold them. 'Lovers die, but love survives.' I heard a gentleman say that at Chalais."

"It's better, at least, than if he had put it the other way. But lovers last too. They survive; they outlive the things that would fain destroy them,—indifference, denial, and despair."

"But meanwhile the loved object disappears. When it isn't one, it's the other."

"O, I admit that it's a shifting world. But I have a philosophy for that."

"I'm curious to know your philosophy."

"It's a very old one. It's simply to make the most of life while it lasts. I'm very fond of life," said Coquelin, laughing.

"I should say that as yet, from what I know of your history, you have had no great reason to be."

"Nay, it's like a cruel mistress," said Coquelin. "When once you love her, she's absolute. Her hard usage doesn't affect you. And certainly I have nothing to complain of now."

"You're happy here then?"

"Profoundly, mademoiselle, in spite of the Chevalier."

"I should suppose that with your tastes you would prefer something more active, more ardent."

"*Mon Dieu,* my tastes are very simple. And then—happiness, *cela ne se raisonne pas.* You don't find it when you go in quest of it. It's like fortune; it comes to you in your sleep."

"I imagine," said Mlle. de Bergerac, "that I was never happy."

"That's a sad story," said Coquelin.

The young girl began to laugh. "And never unhappy."

"Dear me, that's still worse. Never fear, it will come."

"What will come?"

"That which is both bliss and misery at once."

Mlle. de Bergerac hesitated a moment. "And what is this strange thing?" she asked.

On his side Coquelin was silent. "When it comes to you," he said, at last, "you'll tell me what you call it."

About a week after this, at breakfast, in pursuance of an urgent request of mine, Coquelin proposed to my father to allow him to take me to visit the ruins of an ancient feudal castle some four leagues distant, which he had observed and explored while he trudged across the country on his way to Bergerac, and which, indeed, although the taste for ruins was at that time by no means so general as since the Revolution (when one may say it was in a measure created), enjoyed a certain notoriety throughout the province. My father good-naturedly consented; and as the distance was too great to be achieved on foot, he placed his two old coach-horses at our service. You know that although I affected, in boyish sort, to have been indifferent to my aunt's absence, I was really very fond of her, and it occurred to me that our excursion would be more solemn and splendid for her taking part in it. So I appealed to my father and asked if Mlle. de Bergerac might be allowed to go with us. What the Baron would have decided had he been left to himself I know not; but happily for our cause my mother cried out that, to her mind, it was highly improper that her sister-in-law should travel twenty miles alone with two young men.

"One of your young men is a child," said my father, "and her nephew into the bargain; and the other,"—and he laughed, coarsely but not ill-humoredly,—"the other is—Coquelin!"

"Coquelin is not a child nor is mademoiselle either," said my mother.

"All the more reason for their going. Gabrielle, will you go?" My father, I fear, was not remarkable in general for his tenderness or his *prévenance* for the poor girl whom fortune had given him to protect; but from time to time he would wake up to a downright sense of kinship and duty, kindled by the pardonable aggressions of my mother, between whom and her sister-in-law there existed a singular antagonism of temper.

Mlle. de Bergerac looked at my father intently and with a little blush. "Yes, brother, I'll go. The Chevalier can take me *en croupe.*"

So we started, Coquelin on one horse, and I on the other, with my aunt mounted behind me. Our sport for the first part of the journey consisted chiefly in my urging my beast into a somewhat ponderous gallop, so as to terrify my aunt, who was not very sure of her seat, and who, at moments, between pleading and laughing, had hard work to preserve her balance. At these times Coquelin would ride close alongside of us, at the same cumbersome pace, declaring himself ready to catch the young girl if she fell. In this way we jolted along, in a cloud of dust, with shouts and laughter.

"Madame the Baronne was wrong," said Coquelin, "in denying that we are children."

"O, this is nothing yet," cried my aunt.

The castle of Fossy lifted its dark and crumbling towers with a decided air of feudal arrogance from the summit of a gentle eminence in the recess of a shallow gorge among the hills. Exactly when it had flourished and when it had decayed I knew not, but in the year of grace of our pilgrimage it was a truly venerable, almost a formidable, ruin. Two great towers were standing,—one of them diminished by half its upper elevation, and the other sadly scathed and shattered, but still exposing its hoary head to the weather, and offering the sullen hospitality of its empty skull to a colony of swallows. I shall never forget that day at Fossy; it was one of those long raptures of childhood which seem to imprint upon the mind an ineffaceable stain of light. The novelty and mystery of the dilapidated fortress,—its antiquity, its intricacy, its sounding vaults and corridors, its inaccessible heights and impenetrable depths, the broad sunny glare of its grass-grown courts and yards, the twilight of its passages and midnight of its dungeons, and along with all this my freedom to rove and scramble, my perpetual curiosity, my lusty absorption of the sun-warmed air, and the contagion of my companions' careless and sensuous mirth,—all these things combined to make our excursion one of the memorable events of my youth. My two companions accepted the situation and drank in the beauty of the day and the richness of the spot with all my own reckless freedom. Coquelin was half mad with the joy of spending a whole unbroken summer's day with the woman whom he secretly loved. He was all motion and humor and resonant laughter; and yet intermingled with his random gayety there lurked a solemn sweetness and reticence, a feverish concentration of thought, which to a woman with a woman's senses must have fairly betrayed his passion. Mlle. de Bergerac, without quite putting aside her natural dignity and gravity of mien, lent herself with a charming girlish energy to the undisciplined spirit of the hour.

Our first thoughts, after Coquelin had turned the horses to pasture in one of the grassy courts of the castle, were naturally bestowed upon our little basket of provisions; and our first act was to sit down on a heap of fallen masonry and divide its contents. After that we wandered. We climbed the still practicable staircases, and wedged ourselves into the turrets and strolled through the chambers and halls; we started from their long repose every echo and bat and owl within the innumerable walls.

Finally, after we had rambled a couple of hours, Mlle. de Bergerac betrayed signs of fatigue. Coquelin went with her in search of a place of rest, and I was left to my own devices. For an hour I found plenty of diversion, at the end of which I returned to my friends. I had some difficulty in finding them. They had mounted by an imperfect and somewhat perilous ascent to one of the upper platforms of the castle. Mlle. de Bergerac was sitting in a listless posture on a block of stone, against the wall, in the shadow of the still surviving tower; opposite, in the light, half leaning, half sitting on the parapet of the terrace, was her companion.

"For the last half-hour, mademoiselle," said Coquelin, as I came up, "you've not spoken a word."

"All the morning," said Mlle. de Bergerac, "I've been scrambling and chattering and laughing. Now, by reaction, I'm *triste*."

"I protest, so am I," said Coquelin. "The truth is, this old feudal fortress is a decidedly melancholy spot. It's haunted with the ghost of the past. It smells of tragedies, sorrows, and cruelties." He uttered these words with singular emphasis. "It's a horrible place," he pursued, with a shudder.

Mlle. de Bergerac began to laugh. "It's odd that we should only just now have discovered it!"

"No, it's like the history of that abominable past of which it's a relic. At the first glance we see nothing but the great proportions, the show, and the splendor; but when we come to explore, we detect a vast underground world of iniquity and suffering. Only half this castle is above the soil; the rest is dungeons and vaults and *oubliettes*."

"Nevertheless," said the young girl, "I should have liked to live in those old days. Shouldn't you?"

"Verily, no, mademoiselle!" And then after a pause, with a certain irrepressible bitterness: "Life is hard enough now."

Mlle. de Bergerac stared but said nothing.

"In those good old days," Coquelin resumed, "I should have been a brutal, senseless peasant, yoked down like an ox, with my forehead in the soil. Or else I should have been a trembling, groaning, fasting monk, moaning my soul away in the ecstacies of faith."

Mlle. de Bergerac rose and came to the edge of the platform. "Was no other career open in those days?"

"To such a one as me,—no. As I say, mademoiselle, life is hard now, but it was a mere dead weight then. It know it was. I feel in my bones and pulses that awful burden of despair under which my wretched ancestors struggled. *Tenez*, I'm the great man of the race. My father came next; he was one of four brothers, who all thought it a prodigious rise in the world when he became a village tailor. If we had lived five hundred years ago, in the shadow of these great towers, we should never have risen at all. We should have stuck with our feet in the clay. As I'm not a fighting man, I suppose I should have gone into the Church. If I hadn't died from an overdose of inanition, very likely I might have lived to be a cardinal."

Mlle. de Bergerac leaned against the parapet, and with a meditative droop of the head looked down the little glen toward the plain and the highway. "For myself," she said, "I can imagine very charming things of life in this castle of Fossy."

"For yourself, very likely."

"Fancy the great moat below filled with water and sheeted with lilies, and the drawbridge lowered, and a company of knights riding into the gates. Within, in one of those vaulted, quaintly timbered rooms, the châtelaine stands ready to receive them, with her women, her chaplain, her physician, and her little page. They come clanking up the staircase, with ringing swords, sweeping the ground with their plumes. They are all brave and splendid and fierce, but one of them far more than the rest. They each bend a knee to the lady—"

"But he bends two," cried Coquelin. "They wander apart into one of those deep embrasures and spin the threads of perfect love. Ah, I could fancy a sweet life, in those days, mademoiselle, if I could only fancy myself a knight!"

"And you can't," said the young girl, gravely, looking at him.

"It's an idle game; it's not worth trying."

"Apparently then, you're a cynic; you have an equally small opinion of the past and the present."

"No; you do me injustice."

"But you say that life is hard."

"I speak not for myself, but for others; for my brothers and sisters and kinsmen in all degrees; for the great mass of *petits gens* of my own class."

"Dear me, M. Coquelin, while you're about it, you can speak for others still; for poor portionless girls, for instance."

"Are they very much to be pitied?"

225

Mlle. de Bergerac was silent. "After all," she resumed, "they oughtn't to complain."

"Not when they have a great name and beauty," said Coquelin.

"O heaven!" said the young girl, impatiently, and turned away. Coquelin stood watching her, his brow contracted, his lips parted. Presently, she came back. "Perhaps you think," she said, "that I care for my name,—my great name, as you call it."

"Assuredly, I do."

She stood looking at him, blushing a little and frowning. As he said these words, she gave an impatient toss of the head and turned away again. In her hand she carried an ornamented fan, an antiquated and sadly dilapidated instrument. She suddenly raised it above her head, swung it a moment, and threw it far across the parapet. "There goes the name of Bergerac!" she said; and sweeping round, made the young man a very low courtesy.

There was in the whole action a certain passionate freedom which set poor Coquelin's heart a-throbbing. "To have a good name, mademoiselle," he said, "and to be indifferent to it, is the sign of a noble mind." (In parenthesis, I may say that I think he was quite wrong.)

"It's quite as noble, monsieur," returned my aunt, "to have a small name and not to blush for it."

With these words I fancy they felt as if they had said enough; the conversation was growing rather too pointed.

"I think," said my aunt, "that we had better prepare to go." And she cast a farewell glance at the broad expanse of country which lay stretched out beneath us, striped with the long afternoon shadows.

Coquelin followed the direction of her eyes. "I wish very much," he said, "that before we go we might be able to make our way up into the summit of the great tower. It would be worth the attempt. The view from here, charming as it is, must be only a fragment of what you see from that topmost platform."

"It's not likely," said my aunt, "that the staircase is still in a state to be used."

"Possibly not; but we can see."

"Nay," insisted my aunt, "I'm afraid to trust the Chevalier. There are great breaches in the sides of the ascent, which are so many open doors to destruction."

I strongly opposed this view of the case; but Coquelin, after scan-

226

ning the elevation of the tower and such of the fissures as were visible from our standpoint, declared that my aunt was right and that it was my duty to comply. "And you, too, mademoiselle," he said, "had better not try it, unless you pride yourself on your strong head."

"No, indeed, I have a particularly weak one. And you?"

"I confess I'm very curious to see the view. I always want to read to the end of a book, to walk to the turn of a road, and to climb to the top of a building."

"Good," said Mlle. de Bergerac. "We'll wait for you."

Although in a straight line from the spot which we occupied, the distance through the air to the rugged sides of the great cylinder of masonry which frowned above us was not more than thirty yards, Coquelin was obliged, in order to strike at the nearest accessible point the winding staircase which clung to its massive ribs, to retrace his steps through the interior of the castle and make a *détour* of some five minutes' duration. In ten minutes more he showed himself at an aperture in the wall, facing our terrace.

"How do you prosper?" cried my aunt, raising her voice.

"I've mounted eighty steps," he shouted; "I've a hundred more." Presently he appeared again at another opening. "The steps have stopped," he cried.

"You've only to stop too," rejoined Mlle. de Bergerac. Again he was lost to sight and we supposed he was returning. A quarter of an hour elapsed, and we began to wonder at his not having overtaken us, when we heard a loud call high above our heads. There he stood, on the summit of the edifice, waving his hat. At this point he was so far above us that it was difficult to communicate by sounds, in spite of our curiosity to know how, in the absence of a staircase, he had effected the rest of the ascent. He began to represent, by gestures of pretended rapture, the immensity and beauty of the prospect. Finally Mlle. de Bergerac beckoned to him to descend, and pointed to the declining sun, informing him at the same time that we would go down and meet him in the lower part of the castle. We left the terrace accordingly, and, making the best of our way through the intricate passages of the edifice, at last, not without a feeling of relief, found ourselves on the level earth. We waited quite half an hour without seeing anything of our companion. My aunt, I could see, had become anxious, although she endeavored to appear at her ease. As the time elapsed, however, it became so evident that Coquelin had encountered some serious obstacle to his descent, that Mlle. de Bergerac proposed we should, in so far as was possible, betake ourselves to his assistance. The point was to approach him within speaking distance.

We entered the body of the castle again, climbed to one of the upper levels, and reached a spot where an extensive destruction of the external wall partially exposed the great tower. As we approached this crumbling breach, Mlle. de Bergerac drew back from its brink with a loud cry of horror. It was not long before I discerned the cause of her movement. The side of the tower visible from where we stood presented a vast yawning fissure, which explained the interruption of the staircase, the latter having fallen for want of support. The central column, to which the steps had been fastened, seemed, nevertheless, still to be erect, and to have formed, with the agglomeration of fallen fragments and various occasional projections of masonry, the means by which Coquelin, with extraordinary courage and skill, had reached the topmost platform. The ascent, then, had been possible; the descent, curiously enough, he seemed to have found another matter; and after striving in vain to retrace his footsteps, had been obliged to commit himself to the dangerous experiment of passing from the tower to the external surface of the main fortress. He had accomplished half his journey and now stood directly over against us in a posture which caused my young limbs to stiffen with dismay. The point to which he had directed himself was apparently the breach at which we stood; meanwhile he had paused, clinging in mid-air to heaven knows what narrow ledge or flimsy iron clump in the stone-work, and straining his nerves to an agonized tension in the effort not to fall, while his eyes vaguely wandered in quest of another footing. The wall of the castle was so immensely thick, that wherever he could embrace its entire section, progress was comparatively easy; the more especially as, above our heads, this same wall had been demolished in such a way as to maintain a rapid upward inclination to the point where it communicated with the tower.

I stood staring at Coquelin with my heart in my throat, forgetting (or rather too young to reflect) that the sudden shock of seeing me where I was might prove fatal to his equipoise. He perceived me, however, and tried to smile. "Don't be afraid," he cried, "I'll be with you in a moment." My aunt, who had fallen back, returned to the aperture, and gazed at him with pale cheeks and clasped hands. He made a long step forward, successfully, and, as he recovered himself, caught sight of her face and looked at her with fearful intentness. Then seeing, I suppose, that she was sickened by his insecurity, he disengaged one hand and motioned her back. She retreated, paced in a single moment the length of the enclosure in which we stood, returned and stopped just short of the point at which she would have seen him again. She buried her face in her hands, like one muttering a rapid prayer, and then advanced once more within range of her friend's vision. As she looked at him, clinging in midair and planting step after step on the jagged and treacherous edge of the immense perpendicular chasm, she repressed another loud cry only by thrusting her handkerchief into her mouth. He caught her eyes again, gazed into them with piercing keenness, as if to drink in coolness and confidence, and then, as she closed them again in horror, motioned me with his head to lead her away. She returned to the farther end of the apartment and leaned her head against the wall. I remained staring at poor Coquelin, fascinated by the spectacle of his mingled danger and courage. Inch by inch, yard by yard, I saw him lessen the interval which threatened his life. It was a horrible, beautiful sight. Some five minutes elapsed; they seemed like fifty. The last few yards he accomplished with a rush; he reached the window which was the goal of his efforts, swung himself in and let himself down by a prodigious leap to the level on which we stood. Here he stopped, pale, lacerated, and drenched with perspiration. He put out his hand to Mlle. de Bergerac, who, at the sound of his steps, had turned herself about. On seeing him she made a few steps forward and burst into tears. I took his extended hand. He bent over me and kissed me, and then giving me a push, "Go and kiss your poor aunt," he said. Mlle. de Bergerac clasped me to her breast with a most convulsive pressure. From that moment till we reached home, there was very little said. Both my companions had matter for silent reflection,—Mlle. de Bergerac in the deep significance of that offered hand, and Coquelin in the rich avowal of her tears.

· *III* ·

A week after this memorable visit to Fossy, in emulation of my good preceptor, I treated my friends, or myself at least, to a five minutes' fright. Wandering beside the river one day when Coquelin had been detained within doors to overlook some accounts for my father, I amused myself, where the bank projected slightly over the stream, with kicking the earth away in fragments, and watching it borne down the current. The result may be anticipated: I came very near going the way of those same fragments. I lost my foothold and fell into the stream, which, however, was so shallow as to offer no great obstacle to self-preservation. I scrambled ashore, wet to the bone, and, feeling rather ashamed of my misadventure, skulked about in the fields for a couple of hours, in my dripping clothes. Finally, there being no sun and my garments remaining inexorably damp, my teeth began to chatter and my limbs to ache. I went home and surrendered myself. Here again the result may be foreseen: the next day I was laid up with a high fever.

Mlle. de Bergerac, as I afterwards learned, immediately appointed herself my nurse, removed me from my little sleeping-closet to her own room, and watched me with the most tender care. My illness lasted some ten days, my convalescence a week. When I began to mend, my bed was transferred to an unoccupied room adjoining my aunt's. Here, late one afternoon, I lay languidly singing to myself and watching the western sunbeams shimmering on the opposite wall. If you were ever ill as a child, you will remember such moments. You look by the hour at your thin, white hands; you listen to the sounds in the house, the opening of doors and the tread of feet; you murmur strange odds and ends of talk; and you watch the fading of the day and the dark flowering of the night. Presently my aunt came in, introducing Coquelin, whom she left by my bedside. He sat with me a long time, talking in the old, kind way, and gradually lulled me to sleep with the gentle murmur of his voice. When I awoke again it was night. The sun was quenched on the opposite wall, but through a window on the same side came a broad ray of moonlight. In the window sat Coquelin, who had apparently not left the room. Near him was Mlle. de Bergerac.

Some time elapsed between my becoming conscious of their presence and my distinguishing the sense of the words that were passing between

230

them. When I did so, if I had reached the age when one ponders and interprets what one hears, I should readily have perceived that since those last thrilling moments at Fossy their friendship had taken a very long step, and that the secret of each heart had changed place with its mate. But even now there was little that was careless and joyous in their young love; the first words of Mlle. de Bergerac that I distinguished betrayed the sombre tinge of their passion.

"I don't care what happens now," she said. "It will always be something to have lived through these days."

"You're stronger than I, then," said Coquelin. "I haven't the courage to defy the future. I'm afraid to think of it. Ah, why can't we make a future of our own?"

"It would be a greater happiness than we have a right to. Who are you, Pierre Coquelin, that you should claim the right to marry the girl you love, when she's a demoiselle de Bergerac to begin with? And who am I, that I should expect to have deserved a greater blessing than that one look of your eyes, which I shall never, never forget? It is more than enough to watch you and pray for you and worship you in silence."

"What am I? what are you? We are two honest mortals, who have a perfect right to repudiate the blessings of God. If ever a passion deserved its reward, mademoiselle, it's the absolute love I bear you. It's not a spasm, a miracle, or a delusion; it's the most natural emotion of my nature."

"We don't live in a natural world, Coquelin. If we did, there would be no need of concealing this divine affection. Great heavens! who's natural? Is it my sister-in-law? Is it M. de Treuil? Is it my brother? My brother is sometimes so natural that he's brutal. Is it I myself? There are moments when I'm afraid of my nature."

It was too dark for me to distinguish my companions' faces in the course of this singular dialogue; but it's not hard to imagine how, as my aunt uttered these words, with a burst of sombre *naïveté*, her lover must have turned upon her face the puzzled brightness of his eyes.

"What do you mean?" he asked.

"*Mon Dieu!* think how I have lived! What a senseless, thoughtless, passionless life! What solitude, ignorance, and languor! What trivial duties and petty joys! I have fancied myself happy at times, for it was God's mercy that I didn't know what I lacked. But now that my soul begins to stir and throb and live, it shakes me with its mighty pulsations. I feel as if in the mere wantonness of strength and joy it might drive me to some extravagance. I seem to feel myself making a great rush, with my eyes closed and my heart in my throat. And then the earth sinks away from under my feet, and in my ears is the sound of a dreadful tumult."

"Evidently we have very different ways of feeling. For you our love is action, passion; for me it's rest. For you it's romance; for me it's reality. For me it's a necessity; for you (how shall I say it?) it's a luxury. In point of fact, mademoiselle, how should it be otherwise? When a demoiselle de Bergerac bestows her heart upon an obscure adventurer, a man born in poverty and servitude, it's a matter of charity, of noble generosity."

Mlle. de Bergerac received this speech in silence, and for some moments nothing was said. At last she resumed: "After all that has passed between us, Coquelin, it seems to me a matter neither of generosity nor of charity to allude again to that miserable fact of my birth."

"I was only trying to carry out your own idea, and to get at the truth with regard to our situation. If our love is worth a straw, we needn't be afraid of that. Isn't it true—blessedly true, perhaps, for all I know—that you shrink a little from taking me as I am? Except for my character, I'm so little! It's impossible to be less of a *personage*. You can't quite reconcile it to your dignity to love a nobody, so you fling over your weakness a veil of mystery and romance and exaltation. You regard your passion, perhaps, as more of an escapade, an adventure, than it needs to be."

"My 'nobody,'" said Mlle. de Bergerac, gently, "is a very wise man, and a great philosopher. I don't understand a word you say."

"Ah, so much the better!" said Coquelin with a little laugh.

"Will you promise me," pursued the young girl, "never again by word or deed to allude to the difference of our birth? If you refuse, I shall consider you an excellent pedagogue, but no lover."

"Will you in return promise me—"

"Promise you what?"

Coquelin was standing before her, looking at her, with folded arms. "Promise me likewise to forget it!"

Mlle. de Bergerac stared a moment, and also rose to her feet. "Forget it! Is this generous?" she cried. "Is it delicate? I had pretty well forgot it, I think, on that dreadful day at Fossy!" Her voice trembled and swelled; she burst into tears. Coquelin attempted to remonstrate, but she motioned him aside, and swept out of the room.

It must have been a very genuine passion between these two, you'll observe, to allow this handling without gloves. Only a plant of hardy growth could have endured this chilling blast of discord and disputation. Ultimately, indeed, its effect seemed to have been to fortify and consecrate their love. This was apparent several days later; but I know not what manner of communication they had had in the interval. I was much better, but I was still weak and languid. Mlle. de Bergerac brought me my breakfast in bed, and then, having helped me to rise and dress, led me out into the garden, where she had caused a chair to be placed in the shade. While I sat watching the bees and butterflies, and pulling the flowers to pieces, she strolled up and down the alley close at hand, taking slow stitches in a piece of embroidery. We had been so occupied about ten minutes, when Coquelin came towards us from his lodge,—by appointment, evidently, for this was a roundabout way to the house. Mlle. de Bergerac met him at the end of the path, where I could not hear what they said, but only see their gestures. As they came along together, she raised both hands to her ears, and shook her head with vehemence, as if to refuse to listen to what he was urging. When they drew near my resting-place, she had interrupted him.

"No, no, no!" she cried, "I will never forget it to my dying day. How should I? How can I look at you without remembering it? It's in your face, your figure, your movements, the tones of your voice. It's you,—it's what I love in you! It was that which went through my heart that day at Fossy. It was the look, the tone, with which you called the place horrible; it was your bitter plebeian hate. When you spoke of the misery and baseness of your race, I could have cried out in an anguish of love! When I contradicted you, and pretended that I prized and honored all these tokens of your servitude,—just heaven! you know now what my words were worth!"

Coquelin walked beside her with his hands clasped behind him, and his eyes fixed on the ground with a look of repressed sensibility. He passed his poor little convalescent pupil without heeding him. When they came down the path again, the young girl was still talking with the same feverish volubility.

"But most of all, the first day, the first hour, when you came up the avenue to my brother! I had never seen any one like you. I had seen others, but you had something that went to my soul. I devoured you with my eyes,—your dusty clothes, your uncombed hair, your pale face, the way you held yourself not to seem tired. I went down on my knees, then; I haven't been up since."

The poor girl, you see, was completely possessed by her passion, and yet she was in a very strait place. For her life she wouldn't recede; and yet how was she to advance? There must have been an odd sort of simplicity in her way of bestowing her love; or perhaps you'll think it an odd sort of subtlety. It seems plain to me now, as I tell the story, that Coquelin, with his perfect good sense, was right, and that there was, at this moment, a large element of romance in the composition of her feelings. She seemed to feel no desire to realize her passion. Her hand was already bestowed; fate was inexorable. She wished simply to compress a world of bliss into her few remaining hours of freedom.

The day after this interview in the garden I came down to dinner; on the next I sat up to supper, and for some time afterwards, thanks to my aunt's preoccupation of mind. On rising from the table, my father left the château; my mother, who was ailing, returned to her room. Coquelin disappeared, under pretence of going to his own apartments; but, Mlle. de Bergerac having taken me into the drawing-room and detained me there some minutes, he shortly rejoined us.

"Great heaven, mademoiselle, this must end!" he cried, as he came into the room. "I can stand it no longer."

"Nor can I," said my aunt. "But I have given my word."

"Take back your word, then! Write him a letter—go to him—send me to him—anything! I can't stay here on the footing of a thief and impostor. I'll do anything," he continued, as she was silent. "I'll go to him in person; I'll go to your brother; I'll go to your sister even. I'll proclaim it to the world. Or, if you don't like that, I'll keep it a mortal secret. I'll leave the château with you without an hour's delay. I'll defy pursuit and discovery. We'll go to America,—anywhere you wish, if it's only action. Only spare me the agony of seeing you drift along into that man's arms."

Mlle. de Bergerac made no reply for some moments. At last, "I will never marry M. de Treuil," she said.

To this declaration Coquelin made no response; but after a pause, "Well, well, well?" he cried.

"Ah, you're pitiless!" said the young girl.

"No, mademoiselle, from the bottom of my heart I pity you."

"Well, then, think of all you ask! Think of the inexpiable criminality of my love. Think of me standing here,—here before my mother's portrait,—murmuring out my shame, scorched by my sister's scorn, buffeted by my brother's curses! Gracious heaven, Coquelin, suppose after all I were a bad, hard girl!"

"I'll suppose nothing; this is no time for hair-splitting." And then, after a pause, as if with a violent effort, in a voice hoarse and yet soft: "Gabrielle, passion is blind. Reason alone is worth a straw. I'll not counsel you in passion, let us wait till reason comes to us." He put out his hand; she gave him her own; he pressed it to his lips and departed.

On the following day, as I still professed myself too weak to resume my books, Coquelin left the château alone, after breakfast, for a long walk. He was going, I suppose, into the woods and meadows in quest of Reason. She was hard to find, apparently, for he failed to return to dinner. He reappeared, however, at supper, but now my father was absent. My mother, as she left the table, expressed the wish that Mlle. de Bergerac should attend her to her own room. Coquelin, meanwhile, went with me into the great saloon, and for half an hour talked to me gravely and kindly about my studies, and questioned me on what we had learned before my illness. At the end of this time Mlle. de Bergerac returned.

"I got this letter to-day from M. de Treuil," she said, and offered him a missive which had apparently been handed to her since dinner.

"I don't care to read it," he said.

She tore it across and held the pieces to the flame of the candle. "He is to be here to-morrow," she added finally.

"Well?" asked Coquelin gravely.

"You know my answer."

"Your answer to him, perfectly. But what is your answer to me?"

She looked at him in silence. They stood for a minute, their eyes locked together. And then, in the same posture,—her arms loose at her sides, her head slightly thrown back,—"To you," she said, "my answer is—farewell."

The word was little more than whispered; but, though he heard it, he neither started nor spoke. He stood unmoved, all his soul trembling under his brows and filling the space between his mistress and himself with a sort of sacred stillness. Then, gradually, his head sank on his breast, and his eyes dropped on the ground.

"It's reason," the young girl began. "Reason has come to me. She tells me that if I marry in my brother's despite, and in opposition to all the traditions that have been kept sacred in my family, I shall neither find happiness nor give it. I must choose the simplest course. The other is a gulf; I can't leap it. It's harder than you think. Something in the air forbids it,—something in the very look of these old walls, within which I was born and I've lived. I shall never marry; I shall go into religion. I tried to fling away my name; it was sowing dragons' teeth. I don't ask you to forgive me. It's small enough comfort that you should have the right to think of me as a poor, weak heart. Keep repeating that: it will console you. I shall not have the compensation of doubting the perfection of what I love."

Coquelin turned away in silence. Mlle. de Bergerac sprang after him. "In Heaven's name," she cried, "say something! Rave, storm, swear, but don't let me think I've broken your heart."

"My heart's sound," said Coquelin, almost with a smile. "I regret nothing that has happened. O, how I love you!"

The young girl buried her face in her hands.

"This end," he went on, "is doubtless the only possible one. It's thinking very lightly of life to expect any other. After all, what call had I to interrupt your life,—to burden you with a trouble, a choice, a decision? As much as anything that I have ever known in you I admire your beautiful delicacy of conscience."

"Ah," said the young girl, with a moan, "don't kill me with fine names!"

And then came the farewell. "I feel," said poor Coquelin, "that I can't see you again. We must not meet. I will leave Bergerac immediately,—to-night,—under pretext of having been summoned home by my mother's illness. In a few days I will write to your brother that circumstances forbid me to return."

My own part in this painful interview I shall not describe at length.

When it began to dawn upon my mind that my friend was actually going to disappear, I was seized with a convulsion of rage and grief. "Ah," cried Mlle. de Bergerac bitterly, "that was all that was wanting!" What means were taken to restore me to composure, what promises were made me, what pious deception was practised, I forget; but, when at last I came to my senses, Coquelin had made his exit.

My aunt took me by the hand and prepared to lead me up to bed, fearing naturally that my ruffled aspect and swollen visage would arouse suspicion. At this moment I heard the clatter of hoofs in the court, mingled with the sound of voices. From the window, I saw M. de Treuil and my father alighting from horseback. Mlle. de Bergerac, apparently, made the same observation; she dropped my hand and sank down in a chair. She was not left long in suspense. Perceiving a light in the saloon, the two gentlemen immediately made their way to this apartment. They came in together, arm in arm, the Vicomte dressed in mourning. Just within the threshold they stopped; my father disengaged his arm, took his companion by the hand and led him to Mlle. de Bergerac. She rose to her feet as you may imagine a sitting statue to rise. The Vicomte bent his knee.

"At last, mademoiselle," said he,—"sooner than I had hoped,—my long probation is finished."

The young girl spoke, but no one would have recognized her voice. "I fear, M. le Vicomte," she said, "that it has only begun."

The Vicomte broke into a harsh, nervous laugh.

"Fol de rol, mademoiselle," cried my father, "your pleasantry is in very bad taste."

But the Vicomte had recovered himself. "Mademoiselle is quite right," he declared; "she means that I must now begin to deserve my happiness." This little speech showed a very brave fancy. It was in flagrant discord with the expression of the poor girl's figure, as she stood twisting her hands together and rolling her eyes,—an image of sombre desperation.

My father felt there was a storm in the air. "M. le Vicomte is in mourning for M. de Sorbières," he said. "M. le Vicomte is his sole legatee. He comes to exact the fulfilment of your promise."

"I made no promise," said Mlle. de Bergerac.

"Excuse me, mademoiselle; you gave your word that you'd wait for me."

"Gracious heaven!" cried the young girl; "haven't I waited for you!"

"*Ma toute belle*," said the Baron, trying to keep his angry voice within the compass of an undertone, and reducing it in the effort to a very ugly whisper, "if I had supposed you were going to make us a scene, *nom de Dieu!* I would have taken my precautions beforehand! You know what you're to expect. Vicomte, keep her to her word. I'll give you half an hour. Come, Chevalier." And he took me by the hand.

We had crossed the threshold and reached the hall, when I heard the Vicomte give a long moan, half plaintive, half indignant. My father turned, and answered with a fierce, inarticulate cry, which I can best describe as a roar. He straightway retraced his steps, I, of course, following. Exactly what, in the brief interval, had passed between our companions I am unable to say; but it was plain that Mlle. de Bergerac, by some cruelly unerring word or act, had discharged the bolt of her refusal. Her gallant lover had sunk into a chair, burying his face in his hands, and stamping his feet on the floor in a frenzy of disappointment. She stood regarding him in a sort of helpless, distant pity. My father had been going to break out into a storm of imprecations; but he suppressed them, and folded his arms.

"And now, mademoiselle," he said, "will you be so good as to inform me of your intentions?"

Beneath my father's gaze the softness passed out of my aunt's face and gave place to an angry defiance, which he must have recognized as cousin-german, at least, to the passion in his own breast. "My intentions had been," she said, "to let M. le Vicomte know that I couldn't marry him, with as little offence as possible. But you seem determined, my brother, to thrust in a world of offence somewhere."

You must not blame Mlle. de Bergerac for the sting of her retort. She foresaw a hard fight; she had only sprung to her arms.

My father looked at the wretched Vicomte, as he sat sobbing and stamping like a child. His bosom was wrung with pity for his friend. "Look at that dear Gaston, that charming man, and blush for your audacity."

"I know a great deal more about my audacity than you, brother. I might tell you things that would surprise you."

"Gabrielle, you are mad!" the Baron broke out.

"Perhaps I am," said the young girl. And then, turning to M. de Treuil, in a tone of exquisite reproach, "M. le Vicomte, you suffer less well than I had hoped."

My father could endure no more. He seized his sister by her two wrists, so that beneath the pressure her eyes filled with tears. "Heartless fool!" he cried, "do you know what I can do to you?"

"I can imagine, from this specimen," said the poor creature.

The Baron was beside himself with passion. "Down, down on your knees," he went on, "and beg our pardon all round for your senseless, shameless perversity!" As he spoke, he increased the pressure of his grasp to that degree that, after a vain struggle to free herself, she uttered a scream of pain. The Vicomte sprang to his feet. "In heaven's name, Gabrielle," he cried,—and it was the only real *naïveté* that he had ever uttered,—"isn't it all a horrible jest?"

Mlle. de Bergerac shook her head. "It seems hard, Vicomte," she said, "that I should be answerable for your happiness."

"You hold it there in your hand. Think of what I suffer. To have lived for weeks in the hope of this hour, and to find it what you would fain make it! To have dreamed of rapturous bliss, and to wake to find it hideous misery! Think of it once again!"

"She shall have a chance to think of it," the Baron declared; "she shall think of it quite at her ease. Go to your room, mademoiselle, and remain there till further notice."

Gabrielle prepared to go, but, as she moved away, "I used to fear you, brother," she said with homely scorn, "but I don't fear you now. Judge whether it's because I love you more!"

"Gabrielle," the Vicomte cried out, "I haven't given you up."

"Your feelings are your own, M. le Vicomte. I would have given more than I can say rather than have caused you to suffer. Your asking my hand has been the great honor of my life; my withholding it has been the great trial." And she walked out of the room with the step of unacted tragedy. My father, with an oath, despatched me to bed in her train. Heavy-headed with the recent spectacle of so much half-apprehended emotion, I speedily fell asleep.

I was aroused by the sound of voices, and the grasp of a heavy hand on my shoulder. My father stood before me, holding a candle, with M. de Treuil beside him. "Chevalier," he said, "open your eyes like a man, and come to your senses."

Thus exhorted, I sat up and stared. The Baron sat down on the edge of the bed. "This evening," he began, "before the Vicomte and I came in, were you alone with your aunt?"—My dear friend, you see the scene from here. I answered with the cruel directness of my years. Even if I had had the wit to dissemble, I should have lacked the courage. Of course I had no story to tell. I had drawn no inferences; I didn't say that my tutor was my aunt's lover. I simply said that he had been with us after supper, and that he wanted my aunt to go away with him. Such was my part in the play. I see the whole picture again,—my father brandishing the candlestick, and devouring my words with his great flaming eyes; and the Vicomte behind, portentously silent, with his black clothes and his pale face.

They had not been three minutes out of the room when the door leading to my aunt's chamber opened and Mlle. de Bergerac appeared. She had heard sounds in my apartment, and suspected the visit of the gentlemen and its motive. She immediately won from me the recital of what I had been forced to avow. "Poor Chevalier," she cried, for all commentary. And then, after a pause, "What made them suspect that M. Coquelin had been with us?"

"They saw him, or some one, leave the château as they came in."

"And where have they gone now?"

"To supper. My father said to M. de Treuil that first of all they must sup."

Mlle. de Bergerac stood a moment in meditation. Then suddenly, "Get up, Chevalier," she said, "I want you to go with me."

"Where are you going?"

"To M. Coquelin's."

I needed no second admonition. I hustled on my clothes; Mlle. de Bergerac left the room and immediately returned, clad in a light mantle. We made our way undiscovered to one of the private entrances of the château, hurried across the park and found a light in the window of Coquelin's lodge. It was about half past nine. Mlle. de Bergerac gave a loud knock at the door, and we entered her lover's apartment.

Coquelin was seated at his table writing. He sprang to his feet with a cry of amazement. Mlle. de Bergerac stood panting, with one hand pressed to her heart, while rapidly moving the other as if to enjoin calmness.

"They are come back," she began,—"M. de Treuil and my brother!"

"I thought he was to come to-morrow. Was it a deception?"

"Ah, no! not from him,—an accident. Pierre Coquelin, I've had such a scene! But it's not your fault."

"What made the scene?"

"My refusal, of course."

"You turned off the Vicomte?"

"Holy Virgin! You ask me?"

"Unhappy girl!" cried Coquelin.

"No, I was a happy girl to have had a chance to act as my heart bade me. I had faltered enough. But it was hard!"

"It's all hard."

"The hardest is to come," said my aunt. She put out her hand; he sprang to her and seized it, and she pressed his own with vehemence. "They have discovered our secret,—don't ask how. It was Heaven's will. From this moment, of course—"

"From this moment, of course," cried Coquelin, "I stay where I am!"

With an impetuous movement she raised his hand to her lips and kissed it. "You stay where you are. We have nothing to conceal, but we have nothing to avow. We have no confessions to make. Before God we have done our duty. You may expect them, I fancy, to-night; perhaps, too, they will honor me with a visit. They are supping between two battles. They will attack us with fury, I know; but let them dash themselves against our silence as against a wall of stone. I have taken my stand. My love, my errors, my longings, are my own affair. My reputation is a sealed book. Woe to him who would force it open!"

The poor girl had said once, you know, that she was afraid of her nature. Assuredly it had now sprung erect in its strength; it came hurrying into action on the wings of her indignation. "Remember, Coquelin," she went on, "you are still and always my friend. You are the guardian of my weakness, the support of my strength."

"Say it all, Gabrielle!" he cried. "I'm for ever and ever your lover!"

Suddenly, above the music of his voice, there came a great rattling

241

knock at the door. Coquelin sprang forward; it opened in his face and disclosed my father and M. de Treuil. I have no words in my dictionary, no images in my rhetoric, to represent the sudden horror that leaped into my father's face as his eye fell upon his sister. He staggered back a step and then stood glaring, until his feelings found utterance in a single word: *"Coureuse!"* I have never been able to look upon the word as trivial since that moment.

The Vicomte came striding past him into the room, like a bolt of lightning from a rumbling cloud, quivering with baffled desire, and looking taller by the head for his passion. "And it was for this, mademoiselle," he cried, "and for *that!*" and he flung out a scornful hand toward Coquelin. "For a beggarly, boorish, ignorant pedagogue!"

Coquelin folded his arms. "Address me directly, M. le Vicomte," he said; "don't fling mud at me over mademoiselle's head."

"You? Who are you?" hissed the nobleman. "A man doesn't address you; he sends his lackeys to flog you!"

"Well, M. le Vicomte, you're complete," said Coquelin, eyeing him from head to foot.

"Complete?" and M. de Treuil broke into an almost hysterical laugh. "I only lack having married your mistress!"

"Ah!" cried Mlle. de Bergerac.

"O, you poor, insensate fool!" said Coquelin.

"Heaven help me," the young man went on, "I'm ready to marry her still."

While these words were rapidly exchanged, my father stood choking with the confusion of amazement and rage. He was stupefied at his sister's audacity,—at the dauntless spirit which ventured to flaunt its shameful passion in the very face of honor and authority. Yet that simple interjection which I have quoted from my aunt's lips stirred a secret tremor in his heart; it was like the striking of some magic silver bell, portending monstrous things. His passion faltered, and, as his eyes glanced upon my innocent head (which, it must be confessed, was sadly out of place in that pernicious scene), alighted on this smaller wrong. "The next time you go on your adventures, mademoiselle," he cried, "I'd thank you not to pollute my son by dragging him at your skirts."

"I'm not sorry to have my family present," said the young girl, who had had time to collect her thoughts. "I should be glad even if my sister were here. I wish simply to bid you farewell."

Coquelin, at these words, made a step towards her. She passed her hand through his arm. "Things have taken place—and chiefly within the last moment—which change the face of the future. You've done the business, brother," and she fixed her glittering eyes on the Baron; "you've driven me back on myself. I spared you, but you never spared me. I cared for my name; you loaded it with dishonor. I chose between happiness and duty,—duty as you would have laid it down: I preferred duty. But now that happiness has become one with simple safety from violence and insult, I go back to happiness. I give you back your name; though I have kept it more jealously than you. I have another ready for me. O Messieurs!" she cried, with a burst of rapturous exaltation, "for what you have done to me I thank you."

My father began to groan and tremble. He had clasped my hand in his own, which was clammy with perspiration. "For the love of God, Gabrielle," he implored, "or the fear of the Devil, speak so that a sickened, maddened Christian can understand you! For what purpose did you come here to-night?"

"*Mon Dieu*, it's a long story. You made short work with it. I might in justice do as much. I came here, brother, to guard my reputation, and not to lose it."

All this while my father had neither looked at Coquelin nor spoken to him, either because he thought him not worth his words, or because he had kept some transcendent insult in reserve. Here my governor broke in. "It seems to me time, M. le Baron, that I should inquire the purpose of your own visit."

My father stared a moment. "I came, M. Coquelin, to take you by the shoulders and eject you through that door, with the further impulsion, if necessary, of a vigorous kick."

"Good! And M. le Vicomte?"

"M. le Vicomte came to see it done."

"Perfect! A little more and you had come too late. I was on the point of leaving Bergerac. I can put the story into three words. I have been so happy as to secure the affections of Mlle. de Bergerac. She asked herself, devoutly, what course of action was possible under the circumstances. She decided that the only course was that we should immediately separate. I had no hesitation in bringing my residence with M. le Chevalier to a sudden close. I was to have quitted the château early to-morrow morning, leaving mademoiselle at absolute liberty. With her refusal of M. de Treuil I have nothing to do. Her action in this matter seems to have been strangely precipitated, and my own departure anticipated in consequence. It was at her adjuration that I was preparing to depart. She came here this evening to command me to stay. In our relations there was nothing that the world had a right to lay a finger upon. From the moment that they were suspected it was of the first importance to the security and sanctity of Mlle. de Bergerac's position that there should be no appearance on my part of elusion or flight. The relations I speak of had ceased to exist; there was, therefore, every reason why for the present I should retain my place. Mlle. de Bergerac had been here some three minutes, and had just made known her wishes, when you arrived with the honorable intentions which you avow, and under that illusion the perfect stupidity of which is its least reproach. In my own turn, Messieurs, I thank you!"

"Gabrielle," said my father, as Coquelin ceased speaking, "the long and short of it appears to be that after all you needn't marry this man. Am I to understand that you intend to?"

"Brother, I mean to marry M. Coquelin."

My father stood looking from the young girl to her lover. The Vicomte walked to the window, as if he were in want of air. The night was cool and the window closed. He tried the sash, but for some reason it resisted. Whereupon he raised his sword-hilt and with a violent blow shivered a pane into fragments. The Baron went on: "On what do you propose to live?"

"It's for me to propose," said Coquelin. "My wife shall not suffer."

"Whither do you mean to go?"

"Since you're so good as to ask,—to Paris."

My father had got back his fire. "Well, then," he cried, "my bitterest unforgiveness go with you, and turn your unholy pride to abject woe! My sister may marry a base-born vagrant if she wants, but I shall not give her away. I hope you'll enjoy the mud in which you've planted yourself. I hope your marriage will be blessed in the good old fashion, and that you'll regard philosophically the sight of a half-dozen starving children. I hope you'll enjoy the company of

244

chandlers and cobblers and scribblers!" The Baron could go no further. "Ah, my sister!" he half exclaimed. His voice broke; he gave a great convulsive sob, and fell into a chair.

"Coquelin," said my aunt, "take me back to the château."

As she walked to the door, her hand in the young man's arm, the Vicomte turned short about from the window, and stood with his drawn sword, grimacing horribly.

"Not if I can help it!" he cried through his teeth, and with a sweep of his weapon he made a savage thrust at the young girl's breast. Coquelin, with equal speed, sprang before her, threw out his arm, and took the blow just below the elbow.

"Thank you, M. le Vicomte," he said, "for the chance of calling you a coward! There was something I wanted."

Mlle. de Bergerac spent the night at the château, but by early dawn she had disappeared. Whither Coquelin betook himself with his gratitude and his wound, I know not. He lay, I suppose, at some neighboring farmer's. My father and the Vicomte kept for an hour a silent, sullen vigil in my preceptor's vacant apartment,—for an hour and perhaps longer, for at the end of this time I fell asleep, and when I came to my senses, the next morning, I was in my own bed.

M. de Bergerac had finished his tale.

"But the marriage," I asked, after a pause,—"was it happy?"

"Reasonably so, I fancy. There is no doubt that Coquelin was an excellent fellow. They had three children, and lost them all. They managed to live. He painted portraits and did literary work."

"And his wife?"

"Her history, I take it, is that of all good wives: she loved her husband. When the Revolution came, they went into politics; but here, in spite of his base birth, Coquelin acted with that superior temperance which I always associate with his memory. He was no *sans-culotte*. They both went to the scaffold among the Girondists."

CRAWFORD'S CONSISTENCY

Crawford's Consistency

"Crawford's Consistency," twenty-seventh of Henry James's published tales, appeared in Scribner's Monthly, *August 1876, and is reprinted here for the first time. Its highly interesting background and genesis as set forth by its author some forty years later, and its foreshadowings of later work and technique are given in the Introduction.*

"The Ghostly Rental," last published tale never collected by James, followed in the next month.

WE WERE GREAT FRIENDS, AND IT WAS NATURAL THAT he should have let me know with all the promptness of his ardor that his happiness was complete. Ardor is here, perhaps, a misleading word, for Crawford's passion burned with a still and hidden flame; if he had written sonnets to his mistress's eyebrow, he had never declaimed them in public. But he was deeply in love; he had been full of tremulous hopes and fears, and his happiness, for several weeks, had hung by a hair—the extremely fine line that appeared to divide the yea and nay of the young lady's parents. The scale descended at last with their heavily-weighted consent in it, and Crawford gave himself up to tranquil bliss. He came to see me at my office—my name, on the little tin placard beneath my window, was garnished with an M. D., as vivid as new gilding could make it—long before that period of the morning at which my irrepressible buoyancy had succumbed to the teachings of experience (as it usually did about twelve o'clock), and resigned itself to believe that that particular day was not to be distinguished by the advent of the female form that haunted my dreams—the confiding old lady, namely, with a large account at the bank, and a mild, but expensive chronic malady. On that day I quite forgot the paucity of my patients and the vanity of my hopes in my enjoyment of Crawford's contagious felicity. If we had been less united in friendship, I might have envied him; but as it was, with my extreme admiration and affection for him, I felt for half an hour as if I were going to marry the lovely Elizabeth myself. I reflected after he had left me that I was very glad I was not, for lovely as Miss Ingram was, she had always inspired me with a vague mistrust. There was no harm in her, certainly; but there was nothing else either. I don't know to what I compared her—to a blushing rose that had no odor, to a blooming peach that had no taste. All that nature had asked of her was to be the prettiest girl of her time, and this request she obeyed to the letter. But when, of a morning, she had opened wide her beautiful, candid eyes, and half parted her clear, pink lips, and gathered up her splendid golden tresses, her day, as far as her own opportunity was concerned, was at an end; she had put her house in order, and she could fold her arms. She did so invariably, and it was in this attitude that Crawford saw her and fell in love with her. I could heartily congratulate him, for the fact that a blooming statue would make no wife for me, did not in the least discredit his own choice. I was human and erratic; I had an uneven temper and a prosaic soul. I wished to get as much as I gave—to be the planet, in short, and not the satellite. But Crawford had really virtue enough for two—enough of vital fire, of intelligence and devotion. He could afford to marry an inanimate beauty, for he had the wisdom which would supply her shortcomings, and the generosity which would forgive them.

Crawford was a tall man, and not particularly well made. He had, however, what is called a gentlemanly figure, and he had a very fine head—the head of a man of books, a student, a philosopher, such as he really was. He had a dark coloring, thin, fine black hair, a very clear, lucid, dark gray eye, and features of a sort of softly-vigorous outline. It was as if his face had been cast first in a rather rugged and irregular mold, and the image had then been lightly retouched, here and there, by some gentler, more feminine hand. His expression was singular; it was a look which I can best describe as a sort of intelligent innocence—the look of an absent-minded seraph. He knew, if you insisted upon it, about the corruptions of this base world; but, left to himself, he never thought of them. What he did think of, I can hardly tell you: of a great many things, often, in which I was not needed. Of this, long and well as I had known him, I was perfectly conscious. I had never got behind him, as it were; I had never walked all round him. He was reserved, as I am inclined to think that all first rate men are; not capriciously or consciously reserved, but reserved in spite of, and in the midst of, an extreme frankness. For most people he was a clear-visaged, scrupulously polite young man, who, in giving up business so suddenly, had done a thing which required a good deal of charitable explanation, and who was not expected to express any sentiments more personal than a literary opinion re-inforced by the name of some authority, as to whose titles and attributes much vagueness of knowledge was excusable. For me, his literary opinions were the lightest of his sentiments; his good manners, too, I am sure, cost him nothing. Bad manners are the result of irritability, and as Crawford was not irritable he found civility very easy. But if his urbanity was not victory over a morose disposition, it was at least the expression of a very agreeable character. He talked a great deal, though not volubly, stammering a little, and casting about him for his words. When you suggested one, he always accepted it thankfully,—though he sometimes brought in a little later the expression he had been looking for and which had since occurred to him. He had a great deal of gayety, and made jokes and enjoyed them—laughing constantly, with a laugh that was not so much audible as visible. He was extremely deferential to old people, and among the fairer sex, his completest conquests, perhaps, were the ladies of sixty-five and seventy. He had also a great kindness for shabby people, if they were only shabby enough, and I remember seeing him, one summer afternoon, carrying a baby across a crowded part of Broadway, accompanied by its mother, —a bewildered pauper, lately arrived from Europe. Crawford's father had left him a very good property; his income, in New York, in those days, passed for a very easy one. Mr. Crawford was a cotton-broker, and on his son's leaving college, he took him into his business. But shortly after his father's death he sold out his interest in the firm— very quietly, and without asking any one's advice, because, as he told me, he hated buying and selling. There were other things, of course, in the world that he hated too, but this is the only thing of which I remember to have heard him say it. He had a large house, quite to

251

himself (he had lost his mother early, and his brothers were dispersed);
he filled it with books and scientific instruments, and passed most of
his time in reading and in making awkward experiments. He had the
tastes of a scholar, and he consumed a vast number of octavos; but in
the way of the natural sciences, his curiosity was greater than his
dexterity. I used to laugh at his experiments and, as a thrifty neophyte
in medicine, to deprecate his lavish expenditure of precious drugs.
Unburdened, independent, master of an all-sufficient fortune, and of the
best education that the country could afford, good-looking, gallant,
amiable, urbane—Crawford at seven and twenty might fairly be believed to have drawn the highest prizes in life. And, indeed, except
that it was a pity he had not stuck to business, no man heard a word
of disparagement either of his merit or of his felicity. On the other
hand, too, he was not envied—envied at any rate with any degree of
bitterness. We are told that though the world worships success, it
hates successful people. Certainly it never hated Crawford. Perhaps
he was not regarded in the light of a success, but rather of an ornament, of an agreeable gift to society. The world likes to be pleased,
and there was something pleasing in Crawford's general physiognomy
and position. They rested the eyes; they were a gratifying change.
Perhaps we were even a little proud of having among us so harmonious
an embodiment of the amenities of life.

In spite of his bookish tastes and habits, Crawford was not a recluse.
I remember his once saying to me that there were some sacrifices that
only a man of genius was justified in making to science, and he knew
very well that he was not a man of genius. He was not, thank heaven;
if he had been, he would have been a much more difficult companion.
It was never apparent, indeed, that he was destined to make any great
use of his acquisitions. Every one supposed, of course, that he would
"write something;" but he never put pen to paper. He liked to bury
his nose in books for the hour's pleasure; he had no dangerous *arrière
pensée,* and he was simply a very perfect specimen of a class which
has fortunately always been numerous—the class of men who contribute
to the advancement of learning by zealously opening their ears and
religiously closing their lips. He was fond of society, and went out,
as the phrase is, a great deal,—the mammas in especial, making him
extremely welcome. What the daughters, in general, thought of him,
I hardly know; I suspect that the younger ones often preferred worse

men. Crawford's merits were rather thrown away upon little girls. To a considerable number of wise virgins, however, he must have been an object of high admiration, and if a good observer had been asked to pick out in the whole town, the most propitious victim to matrimony, he would certainly have designated my friend. There was nothing to be said against him—there was not a shadow in the picture. He himself, indeed, pretended to be in no hurry to marry, and I heard him more than once declare, that he did not know what he should do with a wife, or what a wife would do with him. Of course we often talked of this matter, and I—upon whom the burden of bachelorhood sat heavy—used to say, that in his place, with money to keep a wife, I would change my condition on the morrow. Crawford gave a great many opposing reasons; of course the real one was that he was very happy as he was, and that the most circumspect marriage is always a risk.

"A man should only marry in self-defense," he said, "as Luther became Protestant. He should wait till he is driven to the wall."

Some time passed and our Luther stood firm. I began to despair of ever seeing a pretty Mrs. Crawford offer me a white hand from my friend's fireside, and I had to console myself with the reflection, that some of the finest persons of whom history makes mention, had been celibates, and that a desire to lead a single life is not necessarily a proof of a morose disposition.

"Oh, I give you up," I said at last. "I hoped that if you did not marry for your own sake, you would at least marry for mine. It would make your house so much pleasanter for me. But you have no heart! To avenge myself, I shall myself take a wife on the first opportunity. She shall be as pretty as a picture, and you shall never enter my doors."

"No man should be accounted single till he is dead," said Crawford. "I have been reading Stendhal lately, and learning the philosophy of the *coup de foudre*. It is not impossible that there is a *coup de foudre* waiting for me. All I can say is that it will be lightning from a clear sky."

The lightning fell, in fact, a short time afterward. Crawford saw Miss Ingram, admired her, observed her, and loved her. The impression she produced upon him was indeed a sort of summing up of the impression she produced upon society at large. The circumstances of her education and those under which she made her first appearance in the world, were such as to place her beauty in extraordinary relief. She had been brought up more in the manner of an Italian princess of the middle ages—sequestered from conflicting claims of ward-ship—than as the daughter of a plain American citizen. Up to her eighteenth year, it may be said, mortal eye had scarcely beheld her; she lived behind high walls and triple locks, through which an occasional rumor of her beauty made its way into the world. Mrs. Ingram was a second or third cousin of my mother, but the two ladies, between whom there reigned a scanty sympathy, had never made much of the kinship; I had inherited no claim to intimacy with the family, and Elizabeth was a perfect stranger to me. Her parents had, for economy, gone to live in the country—at Orange—and it was there, in a high-hedged old garden, that her childhood and youth were spent. The first definite mention of her loveliness came to me from old Dr. Beadle, who had been called to attend her in a slight illness. (The Ingrams were poor, but their daughter was their golden goose, and to secure the most expensive medical skill was but an act of common prudence.) Dr. Beadle had a high appreciation of a pretty patient; he, of course, kept it within bounds on the field of action, but he enjoyed expressing it afterward with the freedom of a profound anatomist, to a younger colleague. Elizabeth Ingram, according to this report, was perfect in every particular, and she was being kept in cotton in preparation for her *début* in New York. He talked about her for a quarter of an hour, and concluded with an eloquent pinch of snuff; whereupon I remembered that she was, after a fashion, my cousin, and that pretty cousins are a source of felicity, in this hard world, which no man can afford to neglect. I took a holiday, jumped into the train, and arrived at Orange. There, in a pretty cottage, in a shaded parlor, I found a small, spare woman with a high forehead and a pointed chin, whom I immediately felt to be that Sabrina Ingram, in her occasional allusions to whom my poor mother had expended the very small supply of acerbity with which nature had intrusted her.

"I am told my cousin is extremely beautiful," I said. "I should like so much to see her."

The interview was not prolonged. Mrs. Ingram was frigidly polite; she answered that she was highly honored by my curiosity, but that her daughter had gone to spend the day with a friend ten miles away. On my departure, as I turned to latch the garden gate behind me, I saw dimly through an upper window, the gleam of a golden head, and the orbits of two gazing eyes. I kissed my hand to the apparition, and agreed with Dr. Beadle that my cousin was a beauty. But if her image had been dim, that of her mother had been distinct.

They came up to New York the next winter, took a house, gave a great party, and presented the young girl to an astonished world. I succeeded in making little of our cousinship, for Mrs. Ingram did not approve of me, and she gave Elizabeth instructions in consequence. Elizabeth obeyed them, gave me the tips of her fingers, and answered me in monosyllables. Indifference was never more neatly expressed, and I wondered whether this was mere passive compliance, or whether the girl had put a grain of her own intelligence into it. She appeared to have no more intelligence than a snowy-fleeced lamb, but I fancied that she was, by instinct, a shrewd little politician. Nevertheless, I forgave her, for my last feeling about her was one of compassion. She might be as soft as swan's-down, I said; it could not be a pleasant thing to be her mother's daughter, all the same. Mrs. Ingram had black bands of hair, without a white thread, which descended only to the tops of her ears, and were there spread out very wide, and polished like metallic plates. She had small, conscious eyes, and the tall white forehead I have mentioned, which resembled a high gable beneath a steep roof. Her chin looked like her forehead reversed, and her lips were perpetually graced with a thin, false smile. I had seen how little it cost them to tell a categorical fib. Poor Mr. Ingram was a helpless colossus; an immense man with a small plump face, a huge back to his neck, and a pair of sloping shoulders. In talking to you, he generally looked across at his wife, and it was easy to see that he was mortally afraid of her.

For this lady's hesitation to bestow her daughter's hand upon Crawford, there was a sufficiently good reason. He had money, but he had not money enough. It was a very comfortable match, but it was not a splendid one, and Mrs. Ingram, in putting the young girl forward, had primed herself with the highest expectations. The marriage was so good that it was a vast pity it was not a little better. If Crawford's income had only been twice as large again, Mrs. Ingram would have pushed Elizabeth into his arms, relaxed in some degree the consuming eagerness with which she viewed the social field, and settled down, possibly, to contentment and veracity. That was a bad year in the matrimonial market, for higher offers were not freely made. Elizabeth was greatly admired, but the ideal suitor did not present himself. I suspect that Mrs. Ingram's charms as a mother-in-law had been accurately gauged. Crawford pushed his suit, with low-toned devotion, and he was at last accepted with a good grace. There had been, I think, a certain amount of general indignation at his being kept waiting, and Mrs. Ingram was accused here and there, of not knowing a first-rate man when she saw one. "I never said she was honest," a trenchant critic was heard to observe, "but at least I supposed she was clever." Crawford was not afraid of her; he told me so distinctly. "I defy her to quarrel with me," he said, "and I don't despair of making her like me."

"Like you!" I answered. "That's easily done. The difficulty will be in your liking her."

"Oh, I do better—I admire her," he said. "She knows so perfectly what she wants. It's a rare quality. I shall have a very fine woman for my mother-in-law."

Elizabeth's own preference bore down the scale in Crawford's favor a little, I think; how much I hardly know. She liked him, and thought her mother took little account of her likes (and the young girl was too well-behaved to expect it). Mrs. Ingram reflected probably that her pink and white complexion would last longer if she were married to a man she fancied. At any rate, as I have said, the engagement was at last announced, and Crawford came in person to tell me of it. I had never seen a happier-looking man; and his image, as I beheld it that morning, has lived in my memory all these years, as an embodiment of youthful confidence and deep security. He had said that the art of knowing what one wants was rare, but he apparently possessed it. He had got what he wanted, and the sense of possession was exquisite to him. I see again my shabby little consulting-room, with an oil-cloth on the floor, and a paper, representing seven hundred and forty times (I once counted them) a young woman with a pitcher on her head, on the walls; and in the midst of it I see Crawford standing upright, with his thumbs in the arm-holes of his waistcoat, his head thrown back, and his eyes as radiant as two planets.

"You are too odiously happy," I said. "I should like to give you a dose of something to tone you down."

"If you could give me a sleeping potion," he answered, "I should

256

be greatly obliged to you. Being engaged is all very well, but I want to be married. I should like to sleep through my engagement—to wake up and find myself a husband."

"Is your wedding-day fixed?" I asked.

"The twenty-eighth of April—three months hence. I declined to leave the house last night before it was settled. I offered three weeks, but Elizabeth laughed me to scorn. She says it will take a month to make her wedding-dress. Mrs. Ingram has a list of reasons as long as your arm, and every one of them is excellent; that is the abomination of it. She has a genius for the practical. I mean to profit by it; I shall make her turn my mill-wheel for me. But meanwhile it's an eternity!"

"Don't complain of good things lasting long," said I. "Such eternities are always too short. I have always heard that the three months before marriage are the happiest time of life. I advise you to make the most of these."

"Oh, I am happy, I don't deny it," cried Crawford. "But I propose to be happier yet." And he marched away with the step of a sun-god beginning his daily circuit.

He was happier yet, in the sense that with each succeeding week he became more convinced of the charms of Elizabeth Ingram, and more profoundly attuned to the harmonies of prospective matrimony. I, of course, saw little of him, for he was always in attendance upon his betrothed, at the dwelling of whose parents I was a rare visitor. Whenever I did see him, he seemed to have sunk another six inches further into the mystic depths. He formally swallowed his words when I recalled to him his former brave speeches about the single life.

"All I can say is," he answered, "that I was an immeasurable donkey. Every argument that I formerly used in favor of not marrying, now seems to me to have an exactly opposite application. Every reason that used to seem to me so good for not taking a wife, now seems to me the best reason in the world for taking one. I not to marry, of all men on earth! Why, I am made on purpose for it, and if the thing did not exist, I should have invented it. In fact, I think I *have* invented some little improvements in the institution—of an extremely conservative kind—and when I put them into practice, you shall tell me what you think of them."

This lasted several weeks. The day after Crawford told me of his engagement, I had gone to pay my respects to the two ladies, but they were not at home, and I wrote my compliments on a card. I did not repeat my visit until the engagement had become an old story—some three weeks before the date appointed for the marriage—I had then not seen Crawford in several days. I called in the evening, and was ushered into a small parlor reserved by Mrs. Ingram for familiar visitors. Here I found Crawford's mother-in-law that was to be, seated, with an air of great dignity, on a low chair, with her hands folded rigidly in her lap, and her chin making an acuter angle than ever. Before the fire stood Peter Ingram, with his hands under his coat-tails; as soon as I came in, he fixed his eyes upon his wife. "She has either just been telling, or she is just about to tell, some particularly big fib," I said to myself. Then I expressed my regret at not having found my cousin at home upon my former visit, and hoped it was not too late to offer my felicitations upon Elizabeth's marriage.

For some moments, Mr. Ingram and his wife were silent; after which, Mrs. Ingram said with a little cough, "It *is* too late."

"Really?" said I. "What has happened?"

"Had we better tell him, my dear?" asked Mr. Ingram.

"I didn't mean to receive any one," said Mrs. Ingram. "It was a mistake your coming in."

"I don't offer to go," I answered, "because I suspect that you have some sorrow. I couldn't think of leaving you at such a moment."

Mr. Ingram looked at me with huge amazement. I don't think he detected my irony, but he had a vague impression that I was measuring my wits with his wife. His ponderous attention acted upon me as an incentive, and I continued,

"Crawford has been behaving badly, I suspect?—Oh, the shabby fellow!"

"Oh, not exactly behaving," said Mr. Ingram; "not exactly badly. We can't say that, my dear, eh?"

"It is proper the world should know it," said Mrs. Ingram, addressing herself to me; "and as I suspect you are a great gossip, the best way to diffuse the information will be to intrust it to you."

"Pray tell me," I said bravely, "and you may depend upon it the world shall have an account of it." By this time I knew what was coming. "Perhaps you hardly need tell me," I went on. "I have guessed your news; it is indeed most shocking. Crawford has broken his engagement!"

Mrs. Ingram started up, surprised into self-betrayal. "Oh, really?" she cried, with a momentary flash of elation. But in an instant she perceived that I had spoken fantastically, and her elation flickered down into keen annoyance. But she faced the situation with characteristic firmness. "We have broken the engagement," she said. "Elizabeth has broken it with our consent."

"You have turned Crawford away?" I cried.

"We have requested him to consider everything at an end."

"Poor Crawford!" I exclaimed with ardor.

At this moment the door was thrown open, and Crawford in person stood on the threshold. He paused an instant, like a falcon hovering; then he darted forward at Mr. Ingram.

"In heaven's name," he cried, "what is the meaning of your letter?"

Mr. Ingram looked frightened and backed majestically away. "Really, sir," he said; "I must beg you to desist from your threats."

Crawford turned to Mrs. Ingram; he was intensely pale and profoundly agitated. "Please tell me," he said, stepping toward her with clasped hands. "I don't understand—I can't take it this way. It's a thunderbolt!"

"We were in hopes you would have the kindness not to make a scene," said Mrs. Ingram. "It is very painful for us, too, but we cannot discuss the matter. I was afraid you would come."

"Afraid I would come!" cried Crawford. "Could you have believed I would not come? Where is Elizabeth?"

"You cannot see her!"

"I cannot see her?"

"It is impossible. It is her wish," said Mrs. Ingram.

Crawford stood staring, his eyes distended with grief, and rage, and helpless wonder. I have never seen a man so thoroughly agitated, but I have also never seen a man exert such an effort at self-control. He sat down; and then, after a moment—"What have I done?" he asked.

Mr. Ingram walked away to the window, and stood closely examining the texture of the drawn curtains. "You have done nothing, my dear Mr. Crawford," said Mrs. Ingram. "We accuse you of nothing. We are very reasonable; I'm sure you can't deny that, whatever you may say. Mr. Ingram explained everything in the letter. We have simply thought better of it. We have decided that we can't part with our child for the present. She is all we have, and she is so very young. We

259

ought never to have consented. But you urged us so, and we were so good-natured. We must keep her with us."

"Is that all you have to say?" asked Crawford.

"It seems to me it is quite enough," said Mrs. Ingram.

Crawford leaned his head on his hands. "I must have done something without knowing it," he said at last. "In heaven's name tell me what it is, and I will do penance and make reparation to the uttermost limit."

Mr. Ingram turned round, rolling his expressionless eyes in quest of virtuous inspiration. "We can't say that you have done anything; that would be going too far. But if you had, we would have forgiven you."

"Where is Elizabeth?" Crawford again demanded.

"In her own apartment," said Mrs. Ingram majestically.

"Will you please to send for her?"

"Really, sir, we must decline to expose our child to this painful scene."

"Your tenderness should have begun farther back. Do you expect me to go away without seeing her?"

"We request that you will."

Crawford turned to me. "Was such a request ever made before?" he asked, in a trembling voice.

"For your own sake," said Mrs. Ingram, "go away without seeing her."

"For my own sake? What do you mean?"

Mrs. Ingram, very pale, and with her thin lips looking like the blades of a pair of scissors, turned to her husband. "Mr. Ingram," she said, "rescue me from this violence. Speak out—do your duty."

Mr. Ingram advanced with the air and visage of the stage manager of a theater, when he steps forward to announce that the favorite of the public will not be able to play. "Since you drive us so hard, sir, we must tell the painful truth. My poor child would rather have had nothing said about it. The truth is that she has mistaken the character of her affection for you. She has a high esteem for you, but she does not love you."

Crawford stood silent, looking with formidable eyes from the father to the mother. "I must insist upon seeing Elizabeth," he said at last.

Mrs. Ingram gave a toss of her head. "Remember it was your own demand!" she cried, and rustled stiffly out of the room.

We remained silent; Mr. Ingram sat slowly rubbing his knees, and Crawford, pacing up and down, eyed him askance with an intensely troubled frown, as one might eye a person just ascertained to be liable to some repulsive form of dementia. At the end of five minutes, Mrs. Ingram returned, clutching the arm of her daughter, whom she pushed into the room. Then followed the most extraordinary scene of which I have ever been witness.

Crawford strode toward the young girl, and seized her by both hands; she let him take them, and stood looking at him. "Is this horrible news true?" he cried. "What infernal machination is at the bottom of it?"

Elizabeth Ingram appeared neither more nor less composed than on most occasions; the pink and white of her cheeks was as pure as usual, her golden tresses were as artistically braided, and her eyes showed no traces of weeping. Her face was never expressive, and at this moment it indicated neither mortification nor defiance. She met her lover's eyes with the exquisite blue of her own pupils, and she looked as beautiful as an angel. "I am very sorry that we must separate," she said. "But I have mistaken the nature of my affection for you. I have the highest esteem for you, but I do not love you."

I listened to this, and the clear, just faintly trembling, child-like tone in which it was uttered, with absorbing wonder. Was the girl the most consummate of actresses, or had she, literally, no more sensibility than an expensive wax doll? I never discovered, and she has remained to this day, one of the unsolved mysteries of my experience. I incline to believe that she was, morally, absolutely nothing but the hollow reed through which her mother spoke, and that she was really no more cruel now than she had been kind before. But there was something monstrous in her quiet, flute-like utterance of Crawford's damnation.

"Do you say this from your own heart, or have you been instructed to say it? You use the same words your father has just used."

"What can the poor child do better in her trouble than use her father's words?" cried Mrs. Ingram.

"Elizabeth," cried Crawford, "you don't love me?"

"No, Mr. Crawford."

"Why did you ever say so?"

"I never said so."

He stared at her in amazement, and then, after a little—"It is very true," he exclaimed. "You never said so. It was only I who said so."

"Good-bye!" said Elizabeth; and turning away, she glided out of the room.

"I hope you are satisfied, sir," said Mrs. Ingram. "The poor child is before all things sincere."

In calling this scene the most extraordinary that I ever beheld, I had particularly in mind the remarkable attitude of Crawford at this juncture. He effected a change of base, as it were, under the eyes of the enemy—he descended to the depths and rose to the surface again. Horrified, bewildered, outraged, fatally wounded at heart, he took the full measure of his loss, gauged its irreparableness, and, by an amazing effort of the will, while one could count fifty, superficially accepted the situation.

"I have understood nothing!" he said. "Good-night."

He went away, and of course I went with him. Outside the house, in the darkness, he paused and looked around at me.

"What were you doing there?" he asked.

"I had come—rather late in the day—to pay a visit of congratulation. I rather missed it."

"Do you understand—can you imagine?" He had taken his hat off, and he was pressing his hand to his head.

"They have backed out, simply!" I said. "The marriage had never satisfied their ambition—you were not rich enough. Perhaps they have heard of something better."

He stood gazing, lost in thought. "They," I had said; but he, of course, was thinking only of *her;* thinking with inexpressible bitterness. He made no allusion to her, and I never afterward heard him make one. I felt a great compassion for him, but knew not how to help him, nor hardly, even, what to say. It would have done me good to launch some objurgation against the precious little puppet, within doors, but this delicacy forbade. I felt that Crawford's silence covered a fathomless sense of injury; but the injury was terribly real, and I could think of no healing words. He was injured in his love and his pride, his hopes and his honor, his sense of justice and of decency.

"To treat *me* so!" he said at last, in a low tone. "Me! me!—are they blind—are they imbecile? Haven't they seen what I have been to them —what I was going to be?"

"Yes, they are blind brutes!" I cried. "Forget them—don't think of them again. They are not worth it."

He turned away and, in the dark empty street, he leaned his arm on the iron railing that guarded a flight of steps, and dropped his head upon it. I left him standing so a few moments—I could just hear his sobs. Then I passed my arm into his own and walked home with him. Before I left him, he had recovered his outward composure.

After this, so far as one could see, he kept it uninterruptedly. I saw him the next day, and for several days afterward. He looked like a man who had had a heavy blow, and who had yet not been absolutely stunned. He neither raved nor lamented, nor descanted upon his wrong. He seemed to be trying to shuffle it away, to resume his old occupations, and to appeal to the good offices of the arch-healer, Time. He looked very ill—pale, preoccupied, heavy-eyed, but this was an inevitable tribute to his deep disappointment. He gave me no particular opportunity to make consoling speeches, and not being eloquent, I was more inclined to take one by force. Moral and sentimental platitudes always seemed to me particularly flat upon my own lips, and, addressed to Crawford, they would have been fatally so. Nevertheless, I once told him with some warmth, that he was giving signal proof of being a philosopher. He knew that people always end by getting over things, and he was showing himself able to traverse with a stride a great moral waste. He made no rejoinder at the moment, but an hour later, as we were separating, he told me, with some formalism, that he could not take credit for virtues he had not.

"I am not a philosopher," he said; "on the contrary. And I am not getting over it."

His misfortune excited great compassion among all his friends, and I imagine that this sentiment was expressed, in some cases, with well-meaning but injudicious frankness. The Ingrams were universally denounced, and whenever they appeared in public, at this time, were greeted with significant frigidity. Nothing could have better proved the friendly feeling, the really quite tender regard and admiration that were felt for Crawford, than the manner in which every one took up his cause. He knew it, and I heard him exclaim more than once with intense bitterness that he was that abject thing, an "object of sympathy." Some people flattered themselves that they had made the town, socially speaking, too hot to hold Miss Elizabeth and her parents. The Ingrams anticipated by several weeks their projected departure for Newport—they had given out that they were to spend the summer there —and, quitting New York, quite left, like the gentleman in "The School for Scandal," their reputations behind them.

I continued to observe Crawford with interest, and, although I did full justice to his wisdom and self-control, when the summer arrived I was ill at ease about him. He led exactly the life he had led before his engagement, and mingled with society neither more nor less. If he disliked to feel that pitying heads were being shaken over him, or voices lowered in tribute to his misadventure, he made at least no visible effort to ignore these manifestations, and he paid to the full the penalty of being "interesting." But, on the other hand, he showed no disposition to drown his sorrow in violent pleasure, to deafen himself to its echoes. He never alluded to his disappointment, he discharged all the duties of politeness, and questioned people about their own tribulations or satisfactions as deferentially as if he had had no weight upon his heart. Nevertheless, I knew that his wound was rankling—that he had received a dent, and that he would keep it. From this point onward, however, I do not pretend to understand his conduct. I only was witness of it, and I relate what I saw. I do not pretend to speak of his motives.

I had the prospect of leaving town for a couple of months—a friend and fellow-physician in the country having offered me his practice while he took a vacation. Before I went, I made a point of urging Crawford to seek a change of scene—to go abroad, to travel and distract himself.

"To distract myself from what?" he asked, with his usual clear smile.

"From the memory of the vile trick those people played you."

"Do I look, do I behave as if I remembered it?" he demanded with sudden gravity.

"You behave very well, but I suspect that it is at the cost of a greater effort than it is wholesome for a man—quite unassisted—to make."

"I shall stay where I am," said Crawford, "and I shall behave as I have behaved—to the end. I find the effort, so far as there is an effort, extremely wholesome."

"Well, then," said I, "I shall take great satisfaction in hearing that you have fallen in love again. I should be delighted to know that you were well married."

He was silent a while, and then—"It is not impossible," he said. But, before I left him, he laid his hand on my arm, and, after looking at me with great gravity for some time, declared that it would please him extremely that I should never again allude to his late engagement.

The night before I left town, I went to spend half an hour with him. It was the end of June, the weather was hot, and I proposed that instead of sitting indoors, we should take a stroll. In those days, there stood, in the center of the city, a concert-garden, of a somewhat primitive structure, into which a few of the more adventurous representatives of the best society were occasionally seen—under stress of hot weather —to penetrate. It had trees and arbors, and little fountains and small tables, at which ice-creams and juleps were, after hope deferred, dispensed. Its musical attractions fell much below the modern standard, and consisted of three old fiddlers playing stale waltzes, or an itinerant ballad-singer, vocalizing in a language perceived to be foreign, but not further identified, and accompanied by a young woman who performed upon the triangle, and collected tribute at the tables. Most of the frequenters of this establishment were people who wore their gentility lightly, or had none at all to wear; but in compensation (in the latter case), they were generally provided with a substantial sweetheart. We sat down among the rest, and had each a drink with a straw in it, while we listened to a cracked Italian tenor in a velvet jacket and ear-rings. At the end of half an hour, Crawford proposed we should withdraw, whereupon I busied myself with paying for our juleps. There was some delay in making change, during which, my attention wandered; it was some ten minutes before the waiter returned. When at last he restored me my dues, I said to Crawford that I was ready to depart. He was looking another way and did not hear me; I repeated my observation, and then he started a little, looked round, and said that he would like to remain longer. In a moment I perceived the apparent cause of his changing mind. I checked myself just in time from making a joke about it, and yet—as I did so—I said to myself that it was surely not a thing one could take seriously.

Two persons had within a few moments come to occupy a table near our own. One was a weak-eyed young man with a hat poised into artful crookedness upon a great deal of stiffly brushed and much-anointed

265

straw-colored hair, and a harmless scowl of defiance at the world in general from under certain bare[ly] visible eyebrows. The defiance was probably prompted by the consciousness of the attractions of the person who accompanied him. This was a woman, still young, and to a certain extent pretty, dressed in a manner which showed that she regarded a visit to a concert-garden as a thing to be taken seriously. Her beauty was of the robust order, her coloring high, her glance unshrinking, and her hands large and red. These last were encased in black lace mittens. She had a small dark eye, of a peculiarly piercing quality, set in her head as flatly as a button-hole in a piece of cotton cloth, and a lower lip which protruded beyond the upper one. She carried her head like a person who pretended to have something in it, and she from time to time surveyed the ample expanse of her corsage with a complacent sense of there being something in that too. She was a large woman, and, when standing upright, must have been much taller than her companion. She had a certain conscious dignity of demeanor, turned out her little finger as she ate her pink ice-cream, and said very little to the young man, who was evidently only her opportunity, and not her ideal. She looked about her, while she consumed her refreshment, with a hard, flat, idle stare, which was not that of an adventuress, but that of a person pretentiously and vulgarly respectable. Crawford, I saw, was observing her narrowly, but his observation was earnestly exercised, and she was not—at first, at least,—aware of it. I wondered, nevertheless, why he was observing her. It was not his habit to stare at strange women, and the charms of this florid damsel were not such as to appeal to his fastidious taste.

"I see you are struck by our lovely neighbor," I said. "Have you ever seen her before?"

"Yes!" he presently answered. "In imagination!"

"One's imagination," I answered, "would seem to be the last place in which to look for such a figure as that. She belongs to the most sordid reality."

"She is very fine in her way," said Crawford. "My image of her was vague; she is far more perfect. It is always interesting to see a supreme representation of any type, whether or no the type be one that we admire. That is the merit of our neighbor. She resumes a certain civilization; she is the last word—the flower."

"The last word of coarseness, and the flower of commonness," I interrupted. "Yes, she certainly has the merit of being unsurpassable, in her own line."

"She is a very powerful specimen," he went on. "She is complete."

"What do you take her to be?"

Crawford did not answer for some time, and I suppose he was not heeding me. But at last he spoke. "She is the daughter of a woman who keeps a third-rate boarding-house in Lexington Avenue. She sits at the foot of the table and pours out bad coffee. She is considered a beauty, in the boarding-house. She makes out the bills—'for three weeks' board,' with *week* spelled *weak*. She has been engaged several times. That young man is one of the boarders, inclined to gallantry. He has invited her to come down here and have ice-cream, and she has consented, though she despises him. Her name is Matilda Jane. The height of her ambition is to be 'fashionable.'"

"Where the deuce did you learn all this?" I asked. "I shouldn't wonder if it were true."

"You may depend upon it that it is very near the truth. The boarding-house may be in the Eighth avenue, and the lady's name may be Araminta; but the general outline that I have given is correct."

We sat awhile longer; Araminta—or Matilda Jane—finished her ice-cream, leaned back in her chair, and fanned herself with a newspaper, which her companion had drawn from his pocket, and she had folded for the purpose. She had by this time, I suppose, perceived Crawford's singular interest in her person, and she appeared inclined to allow him every facility for the gratification of it. She turned herself about, placed her head in attitudes, stroked her glossy tresses, crooked her large little finger more than ever, and gazed with sturdy coquetry at her incongruous admirer. I, who did not admire her, at last, for a second time, proposed an adjournment; but, to my surprise, Crawford simply put out his hand in farewell, and said that he himself would remain. I looked at him hard; it seemed to me that there was a spark of excitement in his eye which I had not seen for many weeks. I made some little joke which might have been taxed with coarseness; but he received it with perfect gravity, and dismissed me with an impatient gesture. I had not walked more than half a block away when I remembered some last word—it has now passed out of my mind—that I wished to say to my friend. It had, I suppose, some importance, for I walked back to repair my omission. I re-entered the garden and

267

returned to the place where we had been sitting. It was vacant; Crawford had moved his chair, and was engaged in conversation with the young woman I have described. His back was turned to me and he was bending over, so that I could not see his face, and that I remained unseen by him. The lady herself was looking at him strangely; surprise, perplexity, pleasure, doubt as to whether "fashionable" manners required her to seem elated or offended at Crawford's overture, were mingled on her large, rosy face. Her companion appeared to have decided that his own dignity demanded of him grimly to ignore the intrusion; he had given his hat another cock, shouldered his stick like a musket, and fixed his eyes on the fiddlers. I stopped, embraced the group at a glance, and then quietly turned away and departed.

As a physician—as a physiologist—I had every excuse for taking what are called materialistic views of human conduct; but this little episode led me to make some reflections which, if they were not exactly melancholy, were at least tinged with the irony of the moralist. Men are all alike, I said, and the best is, at bottom, very little more delicate than the worst. If there was a man I should have called delicate, it had been Crawford; but he too was capable of seeking a vulgar compensation for an exquisite pain—he also was too weak to be faithful to a memory. Nevertheless I confess I was both amused and re-assured; a limit seemed set to the inward working of his resentment—he was going to take his trouble more easily and naturally. For the next few weeks I heard nothing from him; good friends as we were, we were poor correspondents, and as Crawford, moreover, had said about himself— What in the world had he to write about? I came back to town early in September, and on the evening after my return, called upon my friend. The servant who opened the door, and who showed me a new face, told me that Mr. Crawford had gone out an hour before. As I turned away from the house it suddenly occurred to me—I am quite unable to say why—that I might find him at the concert-garden to which we had gone together on the eve of my departure. The night was mild and beautiful, and—though I had not supposed that he had been in the interval a regular *habitué* of those tawdry bowers—a certain association of ideas directed my steps. I reached the garden and passed beneath the arch of paper lanterns which formed its glittering portal. The tables were all occupied, and I scanned the company in vain for Crawford's familiar face. Suddenly I perceived a countenance which, if less familiar, was, at least, vividly impressed upon my memory. The lady whom Crawford had ingeniously characterized as the daughter of the proprietress of a third-rate boarding-house was in possession of one of the tables where she was enthroned in assured pre-eminence. With a garland of flowers upon her bonnet, an azure scarf about her shoulders, and her hands flashing with splendid rings, she seemed a substantial proof that the Eighth avenue may, after all, be the road to fortune. As I stood observing her, her eyes met mine, and I saw that they were illumined with a sort of gross, good-humored felicity. I instinctively connected Crawford with her transfiguration, and concluded that he was effectually reconciled to worldly joys. In a moment I saw that she recognized me; after a very brief hesitation she gave me a familiar nod. Upon this hint I approached her.

"You have seen me before," she said. "You have not forgotten me."

"It's impossible to forget you," I answered, gallantly.

"It's a fact that no one ever does forget me?—I suppose I oughtn't to speak to you without being introduced. But wait a moment; there is a gentleman here who will introduce me. He has gone to get some cigars." And she pointed to a gayly bedizened stall on the other side of the garden, before which, in the act of quitting it, his purchase made, I saw Crawford.

Presently he came up to us—he had evidently recognized me from afar. This had given him a few moments. But what, in such a case, were a few moments? He smiled frankly and heartily, and gave my hand an affectionate grasp. I saw, however, that in spite of his smile he was a little pale. He glanced toward the woman at the table, and then, in a clear, serene voice: "You have made acquaintance?" he said.

"Oh, I know him," said the lady; "but I guess he don't know me! Introduce us."

He mentioned my name, ceremoniously, as if he had been presenting me to a duchess. The woman leaned forward and took my hand in her heavily begemmed fingers. "How d'ye do, Doctor?" she said.

Then Crawford paused a moment, looking at me. My eyes rested on his, which, for an instant, were strange and fixed; they seemed to defy me to see anything in them that he wished me not to see. "Allow me to present you," he said at last, in a tone I shall never forget—"allow me to present you to my wife."

I stood staring at him; the woman still grasped my hand. She gave it a violent shake and broke into a loud laugh. "He don't believe it! There's my wedding-ring!" And she thrust out the ample knuckles of her left hand.

A hundred thoughts passed in a flash through my mind, and a dozen exclamations—tragical, ironical, farcical—rose to my lips. But I happily suppressed them all; I simply remained portentously silent, and seated myself mechanically in the chair which Crawford pushed toward me. His face was inscrutable, but in its urbane blankness I found a reflection of the glaring hideousness of his situation. He had committed a monstrous folly. As I sat there, for the next half-hour—it seemed an eternity—I was able to take its full measure. But I was able also to resolve to accept it, to respect it, and to side with poor Crawford, so far as I might, against the consequences of his deed. I remember of that half-hour little beyond a general, rapidly deepening sense of horror. The woman was in talkative mood; I was the first of her husband's friends upon whom she had as yet been able to lay hands. She gave me much information—as to when they had been married (it was three weeks before), what she had had on, what her husband (she called him "Mr. Crawford") had given her, what she meant to do during the coming winter. "We are going to give a great ball," she said, "the biggest ever seen in New York. It will open the winter, and I shall be introduced to all his friends. They will want to see me, dreadfully, and there will be sure to be a crowd. I don't know whether they will come twice, but they will come once, I'll engage."

She complained of her husband refusing to take her on a wedding-tour—was ever a woman married like that before? "I'm not sure it's a good marriage, without a wedding-tour," she said. "I always thought that to be really man and wife, you had to go to Niagara, or Saratoga, or some such place. But he insists on sticking here in New York; he says he has his reasons. He gave me that to keep me here." And she made one of her rings twinkle.

Crawford listened to this, smiling, unflinching, unwinking. Before we separated—to say something—I asked Mrs. Crawford if she liked music? The fiddlers were scraping away. She turned her empty glass upside down, and with a thump on the table—"I like that!" she cried. It was most horrible. We rose, and Crawford tenderly offered her his arm; I looked at him with a kind of awe.

I went to see him repeatedly, during the ensuing weeks, and did my

270

best to behave as if nothing was altered. In himself, in fact, nothing was altered, and the really masterly manner in which he tacitly assumed that the change in his situation had been in a high degree for the better, might have furnished inspiration to my more bungling efforts. Never had incurably wounded pride forged itself a more consummately impenetrable mask; never had bravado achieved so triumphant an imitation of sincerity. In his wife's absence, Crawford never alluded to her; but, in her presence, he was an embodiment of deference and attentive civility. His habits underwent little change, and he was punctiliously faithful to his former pursuits. He studied—or at least he passed hours in his library. What he did—what he was—in solitude, heaven only knows; nothing, I am happy to say, ever revealed it to me. I never asked him a question about his wife; to feign a respectful interest in her would have been too monstrous a comedy. She herself, however, more than satisfied my curiosity, and treated me to a bold sketch of her life and adventures. Crawford had hit the nail on the head; she was veritably, at the time he made her acquaintance, residing at a boarding-house, not in the capacity of a boarder. She even told me the terms in which he had made his proposal. There had been no love-making, no nonsense, no flummery. "I have seven thousand dollars a year," he had said—all of a sudden;—"will you please to become my wife? You shall have four thousand for your own use." I have no desire to paint the poor woman who imparted to me these facts in blacker colors than she deserves; she was to be pitied certainly, for she had been lifted into a position in which her defects acquired a glaring intensity. She had made no overtures to Crawford; he had come and dragged her out of her friendly obscurity, and placed her unloveliness aloft upon the pedestal of his contrasted good-manners. She had simply taken what was offered her. But for all one's logic, nevertheless, she was a terrible creature. I tried to like her, I tried to find out her points. The best one seemed to be that her jewels and new dresses—her clothes were in atrocious taste—kept her, for the time, in loud good-humor. Might they never be wanting? I shuddered to think of what Crawford would find himself face to face with in case of their failing;—coarseness, vulgarity, ignorance, vanity, and, beneath all, something as hard and arid as dusty bricks. When I had left them, their union always seemed to me a monstrous fable, an evil dream; each time I saw them the miracle was freshly repeated.

People were still in a great measure in the country, and though it had begun to be rumored about that Crawford had taken a very strange wife, there was for some weeks no adequate appreciation of her strangeness. This came, however, with the advance of the autumn and those beautiful October days when all the world was in the streets. Crawford came forth with his terrible bride upon his arm, took every day a long walk, and ran the gauntlet of society's surprise. On Sundays, he marched into church with his incongruous consort, led her up the long aisle to the accompaniment of the opening organ-peals, and handed her solemnly into her pew. Mrs. Crawford's idiosyncrasies were not of the latent and lurking order, and, in the view of her fellow-worshipers of her own sex, surveying her from a distance, were sufficiently summarized in the composition of her bonnets. Many persons probably remember with a good deal of vividness the great festival to which, early in the winter, Crawford convoked all his friends. Not a person invited was absent, for it was a case in which friendliness and curiosity went most comfortably, hand in hand. Every one wished well to Crawford and was anxious to show it, but when they said they wouldn't for the world seem to turn their backs upon the poor fellow, what people really meant was that they would not for the world miss seeing how Mrs. Crawford would behave. The party was very splendid and made an era in New York, in the art of entertainment. Mrs. Crawford behaved very well, and I think people were a good deal disappointed and scandalized at the decency of her demeanor. But she looked deplorably, it was universally agreed, and her native vulgarity came out in the strange bedizenment of her too exuberant person. By the time supper was served, moreover, every one had gleaned an anecdote about her bad grammar, and the low level of her conversation. On all sides, people were putting their heads together, in threes and fours, and tittering over each other's stories. There is nothing like the bad manners of good society, and I, myself, acutely sensitive on Crawford's behalf, found it impossible, by the end of the evening, to endure the growing exhilaration of the assembly. The company had rendered its verdict; namely, that there were the vulgar people one could, at a pinch accept, and the vulgar people one couldn't, and that Mrs. Crawford belonged to the latter class. I was savage with every one who spoke to me. "Yes, she is as bad as you please," I said; "but you are worse!" But I might have spared my resentment, for Crawford, himself, in the midst of all this, was simply sublime. He was the genius of hospitality in person; no one had ever seen him so careless, so free, so charming. When I went to bid him good-night, as I took him by the hand—"You will carry it through!" I said. He looked at me, smiling vaguely, and not showing in the least that he understood me. Then I felt how deeply he was attached to the part he had undertaken to play; he had sacrificed our old good-fellowship to it. Even to me, his oldest friend, he would not raise a corner of the mask.

Mrs. Ingram and Elizabeth were, of course, not at the ball; but they had come back from Newport, bringing an ardent suitor in their train. The event had amply justified Mrs. Ingram's circumspection; she had captured a young Southern planter, whose estates were fabled to cover three-eighths of the State of Alabama. Elizabeth was more beautiful than ever, and the marriage was being hurried forward. Several times, in public, to my knowledge, Elizabeth and her mother, found themselves face to face with Crawford and his wife. What Crawford must have felt when he looked from the exquisite creature he had lost to the full-blown dowdy he had gained, is a matter it is well but to glance at and pass—the more so, as my story approaches its close. One morning, in my consulting-room, I had been giving some advice to a little old gentleman who was as sound as a winter-pippin, but, who used to come and see me once a month to tell me that he felt a hair on his tongue, or, that he had dreamed of a blue-dog, and to ask to be put upon a "diet" in consequence. The basis of a diet, in his view, was a daily pint of port wine. He had retired from business, he belonged to a club, and he used to go about peddling gossip. His wares, like those of most peddlers, were cheap, and usually, for my prescription, I could purchase the whole contents of his tray. On this occasion, as he was leaving me, he remarked that he supposed I had heard the news about our friend Crawford. I said that I had heard nothing. What was the news?

"He has lost every penny of his fortune," said my patient. "He is completely cleaned out." And, then, in answer to my exclamation of dismay, he proceeded to inform me that the New Amsterdam Bank had suspended payment, and would certainly never resume it. All the world knew that Crawford's funds were at the disposal of the bank, and that two or three months before, when things were looking squally, he had come most generously to the rescue. The squall had come, it had proved a hurricane, the bank had capsized, and Crawford's money had gone to the bottom. "It's not a surprise to me," said Mr. Niblett, "I suspected something a year ago. It's true, I am very sharp."

"Do you think any one else suspected anything?" I asked.

"I dare say not; people are so easily humbugged. And, then, what could have looked better, above board, than the New Amsterdam?"

"Nevertheless, here and there," I said, "an exceptionally sharp person may have been on the watch."

"Unquestionably—though I am told that they are going on to-day, down town, as if no bank had ever broken before."

"Do you know Mrs. Ingram?" I asked.

"Thoroughly! She is exceptionally sharp, if that is what you mean."

"Do you think it is possible that she foresaw this affair six months ago?"

"Very possible; she always has her nose in Wall street, and she knows more about stocks than the whole board of brokers."

"Well," said I, after a pause, "sharp as she is, I hope she will get nipped, yet!"

"Ah," said my old friend, "you allude to Crawford's affairs? But you shouldn't be a better royalist than the king. He has forgiven her —he has consoled himself. But what will console him now? Is it true his wife was a washerwoman? Perhaps she will not be sorry to know a trade."

I hoped with all my heart that Mr. Niblett's story was an exaggeration, and I repaired that evening to Crawford's house, to learn the real extent of his misfortune. He had seen me coming in, and he met me in the hall and drew me immediately into the library. He looked like a man who had been thrown by a vicious horse, but had picked himself up and resolved to go the rest of the way on foot.

"How bad is it?" I asked.

"I have about a thousand a year left. I shall get some work, and with careful economy we can live."

At this moment I heard a loud voice screaming from the top of the stairs. "Will *she* help you?" I asked.

He hesitated a moment, and then—"No!" he said simply. Immediately, as a commentary upon his answer, the door was thrown open and Mrs. Crawford swept in. I saw in an instant that her good-humor was in permanent eclipse; flushed, disheveled, inflamed, she was a perfect presentation of a vulgar fury. She advanced upon me with a truly formidable weight of wrath.

"Was it you that put him up to it?" she cried. "Was it you that put it into his head to marry me? I'm sure I never thought of him—he isn't the twentieth part of a man! I took him for his money—four thousand a year, clear; I never pretended it was for anything else. To-day, he comes and tells me that it was all a mistake—that we must get on as well as we can on twelve hundred. And he calls himself a gentleman—and so do you, I suppose! There are gentlemen in the State's prison for less. I have been cheated, insulted and ruined; but I'm not a woman you can play that sort of game upon. The money's mine, what is left of it, and he may go and get his fine friends to support him. There ain't a thing in the world he can do—except lie and cheat!"

Crawford, during this horrible explosion, stood with his eyes fixed upon the floor; and I felt that the peculiarly odious part of the scene was that his wife was literally in the right. She had been bitterly disappointed—she had been practically deceived. Crawford turned to me and put out his hand. "Good-bye," he said. "I must forego the pleasure of receiving you any more in my own house."

"I can't come again?" I exclaimed.

"I will take it as a favor that you should not."

I withdrew with an insupportable sense of helplessness. In the house he was then occupying, he, of course, very soon ceased to live; but for some time I was in ignorance of whither he had betaken himself. He had forbidden me to come and see him, and he was too much occupied in accommodating himself to his change of fortune to find time for making visits. At last I disinterred him in one of the upper streets, near the East River, in a small house of which he occupied but a single floor. I disobeyed him and went in, and as his wife was apparently absent, he allowed me to remain. He had kept his books, or most of them, and arranged a sort of library. He looked ten years older, but he neither made nor suffered me to make, an allusion to himself. He had obtained a place as clerk at a wholesale chemist's, and he received a salary of five hundred dollars. After this, I not infrequently saw him; we used often, on a Sunday, to take a long walk together. On our return we parted at his door; he never asked me to come in. He talked of his reading, of his scientific fancies, of public affairs, of our friends

275

—of everything, except his own troubles. He suffered, of course, most of his purely formal social relations to die out; but if he appeared not to cling to his friends, neither did he seem to avoid them. I remember a clever old lady saying to me at this time, in allusion to her having met him somewhere—"I used always to think Mr. Crawford the most agreeable man in the world, but I think now he has even improved!" One day—we had walked out into the country, and were sitting on a felled log by the roadside, to rest (for in those days New Yorkers could walk out into the country),—I said to him that I had a piece of news to tell him. It was not pleasing, but it was interesting.

"I told you six weeks ago," I said, "that Elizabeth Ingram had been seized with small-pox. She has recovered, and two or three people have seen her. Every ray of her beauty is gone. They say she is hideous."

"I don't believe it!" he said, simply.

"The young man who was to marry her does," I answered. "He has backed out—he has given her up—he has posted back to Alabama."

Crawford looked at me a moment, and then—"The idiot!" he exclaimed.

For myself, I felt the full bitterness of poor Elizabeth's lot; Mrs. Ingram had been "nipped," as I had ventured to express it, in a grimmer fashion than I hoped. Several months afterward, I saw the young girl, shrouded in a thick veil, beneath which I could just distinguish her absolutely blasted face. On either side of her walked her father and mother, each of them showing a visage almost as blighted as her own.

I saw Crawford for a time, as I have said, with a certain frequency; but there began to occur long intervals, during which he plunged into inscrutable gloom. I supposed in a general way, that his wife's temper gave him plenty of occupation at home; but a painful incident—which I need not repeat—at last informed me how much. Mrs. Crawford, it appeared, drank deep; she had resorted to liquor to console herself for her disappointments. During her periods of revelry, her husband was obliged to be in constant attendance upon her, to keep her from exposing herself. She had done so to me, hideously, and it was so that I learned the reason of her husband's fitful absences. After this, I expressed to Crawford my amazement that he should continue to live with her.

"It's very simple," he answered. "I have done her a great wrong, and I have forfeited the right to complain of any she may do to me."

"In heaven's name," I said, "make another fortune and pension her off."

He shook his head. "I shall never make a fortune. My working-power is not of a high value."

One day, not having seen him for several weeks, I went to his house. The door was opened by his wife, in curl-papers and a soiled dressing-gown. After what I can hardly call an exchange of greetings,—for she wasted no politeness upon me,—I asked for news of my friend.

"He's at the New York Hospital," she said.

"What in the world has happened to him?"

"He has broken his leg, and he went there to be taken care of—as if he hadn't a comfortable home of his own! But he's a deep one; that's a hit at me!"

I immediately announced my intention of going to see him, but as I was turning away she stopped me, laying her hand on my arm. She looked at me hard, almost menacingly. "If he tells you," she said, "that it was me that made him break his leg—that I came behind him, and pushed him down the steps of the back-yard, upon the flags, you needn't believe him. I could have done it; I'm strong enough"—and with a vigorous arm she gave a thump upon the door-post. "It would have served him right, too. But it's a lie!"

"He will not tell me," I said. "But you have done so!"

Crawford was in bed, in one of the great, dreary wards of the hospital, looking as a man looks who has been laid up for three weeks with a compound fracture of the knee. I had seen no small amount of physical misery, but I had never seen anything so poignant as the sight of my once brilliant friend in such a place, from such a cause. I told him I would not ask him how his misfortune occurred: I knew! We talked awhile, and at last I said, "Of course you will not go back to her!"

He turned away his head, and at this moment, the nurse came and said that I had made the poor gentleman talk enough.

Of course he did go back to her—at the end of a very long con-valescence. His leg was permanently injured; he was obliged to move about very slowly, and what he had called the value of his working-power was not thereby increased. This meant permanent poverty, and all the rest of it. It lasted ten years longer—until 185–, when Mrs. Crawford died of *delirium tremens.* I cannot say that this event restored his equanimity, for the excellent reason that to the eyes of the world —and my own most searching ones—he had never lost it.

THE GHOSTLY RENTAL

≈≈≈≈≈≈≈≈≈≈≈≈≈≈≈≈≈≈≈≈≈≈≈≈≈≈≈≈≈≈≈≈≈≈≈≈

The Ghostly Rental

〜〜〜〜〜〜〜〜〜〜〜〜〜〜〜〜〜〜〜〜〜〜〜〜〜〜〜

"The Ghostly Rental," twenty-eighth of Henry James's published tales and last of the fifteen uncollected stories, appeared in Scribner's Monthly, *September 1876. It has been lately reprinted in* The Ghostly Tales of Henry James *edited by Leon Edel (1948). Its inclusion here completes the collection in two volumes—Mordell's* Travelling Companions *is of course the other—of this very special group of his fictions.*

I WAS IN MY TWENTY-SECOND YEAR, AND I HAD JUST left college. I was at liberty to choose my career, and I chose it with much promptness. I afterward renounced it, in truth, with equal ardor, but I have never regretted those two youthful years of perplexed and excited, but also of agreeable and fruitful experiment. I had a taste for theology, and during my college term I had been an admiring reader of Dr. Channing. This was theology of a greatful and succulent savor; it seemed to offer one the rose of faith delightfully stripped of its thorns. And then (for I rather think this had something to do with it), I had taken a fancy to the old Divinity School. I have always had an eye to the back scene in the human drama, and it seemed to me that I might play my part with a fair chance of applause (from myself at least), in that detached and tranquil home of mild casuistry, with its respectable avenue on one side, and its prospect of green fields and contact with acres of woodland on the other. Cambridge, for the lovers of woods and fields, has changed for the worse since those days, and the precinct in question has forfeited much of its mingled pastoral and scholastic quietude. It was then a College-hall in the woods—a charming mixture. What it is now has nothing to do with my story; and I have no doubt that there are still doctrine-haunted young seniors who, as they stroll near it in the summer dusk, promise themselves, later, to taste of its fine leisurely quality. For myself, I was not disappointed. I established myself in a great square, low-browed room, with deep window-benches; I hung prints from Overbeck and Ary Scheffer on the walls; I arranged my books, with great refinement of classification, in the alcoves beside the high chimney-shelf, and I began to read Plotinus and St. Augustine. Among my companions were two or three men of ability and of good fellowship, with whom I occasionally brewed a fireside bowl; and with adventurous reading, deep discourse, potations conscientiously shallow, and long country walks, my initiation into the clerical mystery progressed agreeably enough.

With one of my comrades I formed an especial friendship, and we passed a great deal of time together. Unfortunately he had a chronic weakness of one of his knees, which compelled him to lead a very sedentary life, and as I was a methodical pedestrian, this made some difference in our habits. I used often to stretch away for my daily ramble, with no companion but the stick in my hand or the book in my pocket. But in the use of my legs and the sense of unstinted open air, I have always found company enough. I should, perhaps, add that in the enjoyment of a very sharp pair of eyes, I found something of a social pleasure. My eyes and I were on excellent terms; they were indefatigable observers of all wayside incidents, and so long as they were amused I was contented. It is, indeed, owing to their inquisitive habits that I came into possession of this remarkable story. Much of the country about the old college town is pretty now, but it was prettier thirty years ago. That multitudinous eruption of domiciliary pasteboard which now graces the landscape, in the direction of the low, blue Waltham Hills, had not yet taken place; there were no genteel cottages to put the shabby meadows and scrubby orchards to shame—a juxtaposition by which, in later years, neither element of the contrast has gained. Certain crooked crossroads, then, as I remember them, were more deeply and naturally rural, and the solitary dwellings on the long grassy slopes beside them, under the tall, customary elm that curved its foliage in mid-air like the outward dropping ears of a girdled wheat-sheaf, sat with their shingled hoods well pulled down on their ears, and no prescience whatever of the fashion of French roofs—weather-wrinkled old peasant women, as you might call them, quietly wearing the native coif, and never dreaming of mounting bonnets, and indecently exposing their venerable brows. That winter was what is called an "open" one; there was much cold, but little snow; the roads were firm and free, and I was rarely compelled by the weather to forego my exercise. One gray December afternoon I had sought it in the direction of the adjacent town of Medford, and I was retracing my steps at an even pace, and watching the pale, cold tints—the transparent amber and faded rose-color—which curtained, in wintry fashion, the western sky, and reminded me of a sceptical smile on the lips of a beautiful woman. I came, as dusk was falling, to a narrow road which I had never traversed and which I imagined offered me a short cut homeward. I was about three miles away; I was late, and would have been thankful to make them two. I diverged, walked some ten minutes, and then perceived that the road had a very unfrequented air. The wheel-ruts looked old; the stillness seemed peculiarly sensible. And yet down the road stood a house, so that it must in some degree have been a thoroughfare. On one side was a high, natural embankment, on the top of which was perched an apple-orchard, whose tangled boughs made a stretch of coarse black lace-work, hung across the coldly rosy west. In a short time I came to the house, and I immediately found myself interested in it. I stopped in front of it gazing hard, I hardly knew why, but with a vague mixture of curiosity and timidity. It was a house like most of the houses thereabouts, except that it was decidedly a handsome specimen of its class. It stood on a grassy slope, it had its tall, impartially drooping elm beside it, and its old black well-cover at its shoulder. But it was of very large proportions, and it had a striking look of solidity and stoutness of timber. It had lived to a good old age, too, for the woodwork on its doorway and under its eaves, carefully and abundantly carved, referred it to the middle, at the latest, of the last century. All this had once been painted white, but the broad back of time, leaning against the door-posts for a hundred years, had laid bare the grain of the wood. Behind the house stretched an orchard of apple-trees, more gnarled and fantastic than usual, and wearing, in the deepening dusk, a blighted and exhausted aspect. All the windows of the house had rusty shutters, without slats, and these were closely drawn. There was no sign of life about it; it looked blank, bare and vacant, and yet, as I

283

lingered near it, it seemed to have a familiar meaning—an audible eloquence. I have always thought of the impression made upon me at first sight, by that gray colonial dwelling, as a proof that induction may sometimes be near akin to divination; for after all, there was nothing on the face of the matter to warrant the very serious induction that I made. I fell back and crossed the road. The last red light of the sunset disengaged itself, as it was about to vanish, and rested faintly for a moment on the time-silvered front of the old house. It touched, with perfect regularity, the series of small panes in the fan-shaped window above the door, and twinkled there fantastically. Then it died away, and left the place more intensely somber. At this moment, I said to myself with the accent of profound conviction—"The house is simply haunted!"

Somehow, immediately, I believed it, and so long as I was not shut up inside, the idea gave me pleasure. It was implied in the aspect of the house, and it explained it. Half an hour before, if I had been asked, I would have said, as befitted a young man who was explicitly cultivating cheerful views of the supernatural, that there were no such things as haunted houses. But the dwelling before me gave a vivid meaning to the empty words; it had been spiritually blighted.

The longer I looked at it, the intenser seemed the secret that it held. I walked all round it, I tried to peep here and there, through a crevice in the shutters, and I took a puerile satisfaction in laying my hand on the door-knob and gently turning it. If the door had yielded, would I have gone in?—would I have penetrated the dusky stillness? My audacity, fortunately, was not put to the test. The portal was admirably solid, and I was unable even to shake it. At last I turned away, casting many looks behind me. I pursued my way, and, after a longer walk than I had bargained for, reached the high-road. At a certain distance below the point at which the long lane I have mentioned entered it, stood a comfortable, tidy dwelling, which might have offered itself as the model of the house which is in no sense haunted—which has no sinister secrets, and knows nothing but blooming prosperity. Its clean white paint stared placidly through the dusk, and its vine-covered porch had been dressed in straw for the winter. An old, one-horse chaise, freighted with two departing visitors, was leaving the door, and through the undraped windows, I saw the lamp-lit sitting-room, and the table spread with the early "tea," which had been improvised for the comfort of the guests. The mistress of the house had come to the gate with her friends; she lingered there after the chaise had wheeled creakingly away, half to watch them down the road, and half to give me, as I passed in the twilight, a questioning look. She was a comely, quick young woman, with a sharp, dark eye, and I ventured to stop and speak to her.

"That house down that side-road," I said, "about a mile from here—the only one—can you tell me whom it belongs to?"

She stared at me a moment, and, I thought, colored a little. "Our folks never go down that road," she said, briefly.

"But it's a short way to Medford," I answered.

She gave a little toss of her head. "Perhaps it would turn out a long way. At any rate, we don't use it."

This was interesting. A thrifty Yankee household must have good reasons for this scorn of time-saving processes. "But you know the house, at least?" I said.

"Well, I have seen it."

"And to whom does it belong?"

She gave a little laugh and looked away, as if she were aware that, to a stranger, her words might seem to savor of agricultural superstition. "I guess it belongs to them that are in it."

"But is there any one in it? It is completely closed."

"That makes no difference. They never come out, and no one ever goes in." And she turned away.

But I laid my hand on her arm, respectfully. "You mean," I said, "that the house is haunted?"

She drew herself away, colored, raised her finger to her lips, and hurried into the house, where, in a moment, the curtains were dropped over the windows.

For several days, I thought repeatedly of this little adventure, but I took some satisfaction in keeping it to myself. If the house was not haunted, it was useless to expose my imaginative whims, and if it was, it was agreeable to drain the cup of horror without assistance. I determined, of course, to pass that way again; and a week later—it was the last day of the year—I retraced my steps. I approached the house from the opposite direction, and found myself before it at about the same hour as before. The light was failing, the sky low and gray; the wind wailed along the hard, bare ground, and made slow eddies of the frost-blackened leaves. The melancholy mansion stood there, seeming to gather the winter twilight around it, and mask itself in it, inscrutably, I hardly knew on what errand I had come, but I had a vague feeling that if this time the door-knob were to turn and the door to open, I should take my heart in my hands, and let them close behind me. Who were the mysterious tenants to whom the good woman at the corner had alluded? What had been seen or heard—what was related? The door was as stubborn as before, and my impertinent fumblings with the latch caused no upper window to be thrown open, nor any strange, pale face to be thrust out. I ventured even to raise the rusty knocker and give it half-a-dozen raps, but they made a flat, dead sound, and aroused no echo. Familiarity breeds contempt; I don't know what I should have done next, if, in the distance, up the road (the same one I had followed), I had not seen a solitary figure advancing. I was unwilling to be observed hanging about this ill-famed dwelling, and I sought refuge among the dense shadows of a grove of pines near by, where I might peep forth, and yet remain invisible. Presently, the new-comer drew near, and I perceived that he was making straight for the house. He was a little, old man, the most striking feature of whose appearance was a voluminous cloak, of a sort of military cut. He carried a walking-stick, and advanced in a slow, painful, somewhat hobbling fashion, but with an air of extreme resolution. He turned off from the road, and followed the vague wheel-track, and within a few yards of the house he paused. He looked up at it, fixedly and searchingly, as if he were counting the windows, or noting certain familiar marks. Then he took off his hat, and bent over slowly and solemnly, as if he were performing an obeisance. As he stood uncovered, I had a good look at him. He was, as I have said, a diminutive old man, but it would have been hard to decide whether he belonged to this world or to the other. His head reminded me, vaguely, of the portraits of Andrew Jackson. He had a crop of grizzled hair, as stiff as a brush, a lean, pale, smooth-shaven face, and an eye of intense brilliancy, surmounted with thick brows, which had remained perfectly black. His face, as well as his cloak, seemed to belong to an old soldier; he looked like a retired military man of a modest rank; but he struck me as exceeding the classic privilege of even such a personage to be eccentric and grotesque. When he had finished his salute, he advanced to the door, fumbled in the folds of his cloak, which hung down much further in front than behind, and produced a key. This he slowly and carefully inserted into the lock, and then, apparently, he turned it. But the door did not immediately open; first he bent his head, turned his ear, and stood listening, and then he looked up and down the road. Satisfied or re-assured, he applied his aged shoulder to one of the deep-set panels, and pressed a moment. The door yielded—opening into perfect darkness. He stopped again on the threshold, and again removed his hat and made his bow. Then he went in, and carefully closed the door behind him.

Who in the world was he, and what was his errand? He might have been a figure out of one of Hoffmann's tales. Was he vision or a reality—an inmate of the house, or a familiar, friendly visitor? What had been the meaning, in either case, of his mystic genuflexions, and how did he propose to proceed, in that inner darkness? I emerged from my retirement, and observed narrowly, several of the windows. In each of them, at an interval, a ray of light became visible in the chink between the two leaves of the shutters. Evidently, he was lighting up; was he going to give a party—a ghostly revel? My curiosity grew intense, but I was quite at a loss how to satisfy it. For a moment I thought of rapping peremptorily at the door; but I dismissed this idea as unmannerly, and calculated to break the spell, if spell there was. I walked round the house and tried, without violence, to open one of the lower windows. It resisted, but I had better fortune, in a moment, with another. There was a risk, certainly, in the trick I was playing—a risk of being seen from within, or (worse) seeing, myself, something that I should repent of seeing. But curiosity, as I say, had become an inspiration, and the risk was highly agreeable. Through the parting of the shutters I looked into a lighted room—a room lighted by two candles in old brass flambeaux, placed upon the mantel-shelf. It was apparently a sort of back parlor, and it had retained all its furniture. This was of a homely, old-fashioned pattern, and consisted of hair-cloth chairs and sofas, spare mahogany tables, and framed samplers hung upon the walls. But although the room was furnished, it had a strangely uninhabited look; the tables and chairs were in rigid positions, and no small, familiar objects were visible. I could not see everything, and I could only guess at the existence, on my right, of a large folding-door. It was apparently open, and the light of the neighboring room passed through it. I waited for some time, but the room remained empty. At last I became conscious that a large shadow was projected upon the wall opposite the folding-door—the shadow, evidently, of a figure in the adjoining room. It was tall and grotesque, and seemed to represent a person sitting perfectly motionless, in profile. I thought I recognized the perpendicular bristles and far-arching nose of my little old man. There was a strange fixedness in his posture; he appeared to be seated, and looking intently at something. I watched the shadow a long time, but it never stirred. At last, however, just as my patience began to ebb, it moved slowly, rose to the ceiling, and became indistinct. I don't know what I should have seen next, but by an irresistible impulse, I closed the shutter. Was it delicacy?—was it pusillanimity? I can hardly say. I lingered, nevertheless, near the house, hoping that my friend would re-appear. I was not disappointed; for he at last emerged, looking just as when he had gone in, and taking his leave in the same ceremonious fashion. (The lights, I had already observed, had disappeared from the crevice of each of the windows.) He faced about before the door, took off his hat, and made an obsequious bow. As he turned away I had a hundred minds to speak to him, but I let him depart in peace. This, I may say, was pure delicacy; —you will answer, perhaps, that it came too late. It seemed to me that he had a right to resent my observation; though my own right to exercise it (if ghosts were in the question) struck me as equally positive. I continued to watch him as he hobbled softly down the bank, and along the lonely road. Then I musingly retreated in the opposite direction. I was tempted to follow him, at a distance, to see what became of him; but this, too, seemed indelicate; and I confess, moreover, that I felt the inclination to coquet a little, as it were, with my discovery —to pull apart the petals of the flower one by one.

I continued to smell the flower, from time to time, for its oddity of perfume had fascinated me. I passed by the house on the cross-road again, but never encountered the old man in the cloak, or any other wayfarer. It seemed to keep observers at a distance, and I was careful not to gossip about it: one inquirer, I said to myself, may edge his way into the secret, but there is no room for two. At the same time, of course, I would have been thankful for any chance side-light that might fall across the matter—though I could not well see whence it was to come. I hoped to meet the old man in the cloak elsewhere, but as the days passed by without his re-appearing, I ceased to expect it. And yet I reflected that he probably lived in that neighborhood, inasmuch as he had made his pilgrimage to the vacant house on foot. If he had come from a distance, he would have been sure to arrive in some old deep-hooded gig with yellow wheels—a vehicle as venerably grotesque as himself. One day I took a stroll in Mount Auburn cemetery—an institution at that period in its infancy, and full of a sylvan charm which it has now completely forfeited. It contained more maple and birch than willow and cypress, and the sleepers had ample elbow room. It was not a city of the dead, but at the most a village, and a meditative pedestrian might stroll there without too importunate reminder of the grotesque side of our claims to posthumous consideration. I had come out to enjoy the first foretaste of Spring— one of those mild days of late winter, when the torpid earth seems to draw the first long breath that marks the rupture of the spell of sleep. The sun was veiled in haze, and yet warm, and the frost was oozing from its deepest lurking-places. I had been treading for half an hour the winding ways of the cemetery, when suddenly I perceived a familiar figure seated on a bench against a southward-facing evergreen hedge. I call the figure familiar, because I had seen it often in memory and in fancy; in fact, I had beheld it but once. Its back was turned to me, but it wore a voluminous cloak, which there was no mistaking. Here, at last, was my fellow-visitor at the haunted house, and here was my chance, if I wished to approach him! I made a circuit, and came toward him from in front. He saw me, at the end of the alley, and sat motionless, with his hands on the head of his stick, watching me from under his black eyebrows as I drew near. At a distance these black eyebrows looked formidable; they were the only thing I saw in his face. But on a closer view I was re-assured, simply because I immediately felt that no man could really be as fantastically fierce as this poor old gentleman looked. His face was a kind of caricature of martial truculence. I stopped in front of him, and respectfully asked leave to sit and rest upon his bench. He granted it with a silent gesture, of much dignity, and I placed myself beside him. In this position I was able, covertly, to observe him. He was quite as much an oddity in the morning sunshine, as he had been in the dubious twilight. The lines in his face were as rigid as if they had been hacked out of a block by a clumsy woodcarver. His eyes were flamboyant, his nose terrific, his mouth implacable. And yet, after a while, when he slowly turned and looked at me, fixedly, I perceived that in spite of this portentous mask, he was a very mild old man. I was sure he even would have been glad to smile, but, evidently, his facial muscles were too stiff—they had taken a different fold, once for all. I wondered whether he was demented, but I dismissed the idea; the fixed glitter in his eye was not that of insanity. What his face really expressed was deep and simple sadness; his heart perhaps was broken, but his brain was intact. His dress was shabby but neat, and his old blue cloak had known half a century's brushing.

I hastened to make some observation upon the exceptional softness of the day, and he answered me in a gentle, mellow voice, which it was almost startling to hear proceed from such bellicose lips.

"This is a very comfortable place," he presently added.

"I am fond of walking in graveyards," I rejoined deliberately; flattering myself that I had struck a vein that might lead to something.

I was encouraged; he turned and fixed me with his duskily glowing eyes. Then very gravely—"Walking, yes. Take all your exercise now. Some day you will have to settle down in a graveyard in a fixed position."

"Very true," said I. "But you know there are some people who are said to take exercise even after that day."

He had been looking at me still; at this he looked away.

"You don't understand?" I said, gently.

He continued to gaze straight before him.

"Some people, you know, walk about after death," I went on.

At last he turned, and looked at me more portentously than ever. "You don't believe that," he said simply.

"How do you know I don't?"

"Because you are young and foolish." This was said without acerbity—even kindly; but in the tone of an old man whose consciousness of his own heavy experience made everything else seem light.

"I am certainly young," I answered; "but I don't think that, on the whole, I am foolish. But say I don't believe in ghosts—most people would be on my side."

"Most people are fools!" said the old man.

I let the question rest, and talked of other things. My companion seemed on his guard, he eyed me defiantly, and made brief answers to my remarks; but I nevertheless gathered an impression that our meeting was an agreeable thing to him, and even a social incident of some importance. He was evidently a lonely creature, and his opportunities for gossip were rare. He had had troubles, and they had detached him from the world, and driven him back upon himself; but the social chord in his antiquated soul was not entirely broken, and I was sure he was gratified to find that it could still feebly resound. At last, he began to ask questions himself; he inquired whether I was a student.

"I am a student of divinity," I answered.

"Of divinity?"

"Of theology. I am studying for the ministry."

At this he eyed me with peculiar intensity—after which his gaze wandered away again. "There are certain things you ought to know, then," he said at last.

"I have a great desire for knowledge," I answered. "What things do you mean?"

He looked at me again awhile, but without heeding my question.

"I like your appearance," he said. "You seem to me a sober lad."

"Oh, I am perfectly sober!" I exclaimed—yet departing for a moment from my soberness.

"I think you are fair-minded," he went on.

"I don't any longer strike you as foolish, then?" I asked.

"I stick to what I said about people who deny the power of departed spirits to return. They *are* fools!" And he rapped fiercely with his staff on the earth.

I hesitated a moment, and then, abruptly, "You have seen a ghost!" I said.

He appeared not at all startled.

"You are right, sir!" he answered with great dignity. "With me it's not a matter of cold theory—I have not had to pry into old books to learn what to believe. *I know!* With these eyes I have beheld the departed spirit standing before me as near as you are!" And his eyes, as he spoke, certainly looked as if they had rested upon strange things.

I was irresistibly impressed—I was touched with credulity.

"And was it very terrible?" I asked.

"I am an old soldier—I am not afraid!"

"When was it?—where was it?" I asked.

He looked at me mistrustfully, and I saw that I was going too fast.

"Excuse me from going into particulars," he said. "I am not at liberty to speak more fully. I have told you so much, because I cannot bear to hear this subject spoken of lightly. Remember in future, that you have seen a very honest old man who told you—on his honor— that he had seen a ghost!" And he got up, as if he thought he had said enough. Reserve, shyness, pride, the fear of being laughed at, the memory, possibly, of former strokes of sarcasm—all this, on one side, had its weight with him; but I suspected that on the other, his tongue was loosened by the garrulity of old age, the sense of solitude, and the need of sympathy—and perhaps, also, by the friendliness which he had been so good as to express toward myself. Evidently it would be unwise to press him, but I hoped to see him again.

"To give greater weight to my words," he added, "let me mention my name—Captain Diamond, sir. I have seen service."

"I hope I may have the pleasure of meeting you again," I said.

"The same to you, sir!" And brandishing his stick portentously— though with the friendliest intentions—he marched stiffly away.

I asked two or three persons—selected with discretion—whether they knew anything about Captain Diamond, but they were quite unable to enlighten me. At last, suddenly, I smote my forehead, and, dubbing myself a dolt, remembered that I was neglecting a source of informa- tion to which I had never applied in vain. The excellent person at whose table I habitually dined, and who dispensed hospitality to students at so much a week, had a sister as good as herself, and of conversational powers more varied. This sister, who was known as Miss Deborah, was an old maid in all the force of the term. She was deformed; and she never went out of the house; she sat all day at the window, between a bird-cage and a flower-pot, stitching small linen articles—mysterious bands and frills. She wielded, I was assured, an exquisite needle, and her work was highly prized. In spite of her deformity and her con- finement, she had a little, fresh, round face, and an imperturbable serenity of spirit. She had also a very quick little wit of her own, she was extremely observant, and she had a high relish for a friendly chat. Nothing pleased her so much as to have you—especially, I think, if you were a young divinity student—move your chair near her sunny window, and settle yourself for twenty minutes' "talk." "Well, sir," she used always to say, "what is the latest monstrosity in Biblical criticism?"—for she used to pretend to be horrified at the rationalistic tendency of the age. But she was an inexorable little philosopher, and I am convinced that she was a keener rationalist than any of us, and that, if she had chosen, she could have propounded questions that would have made the boldest of us wince. Her window commanded the whole town—or rather, the whole country. Knowledge came to her as she sat singing, with her little, cracked voice, in her low rocking-chair. She was the first to learn everything, and the last to forget it. She had the town gossip at her fingers' ends, and she knew everything about people she had never seen. When I asked her how she had acquired her learning, she said simply—"Oh, I observe!" "Observe closely enough," she once said, "and it doesn't matter where you are. You may be in a pitch-dark closet. All you want is something to start with; one thing leads to another, and all things are mixed up. Shut me up in a dark closet and I will observe after a while, that some places in it are darker than others. After that (give me time), and I will tell you what the President of the United States is going to have for dinner." Once I paid her a compliment. "Your observation," I said, "is as fine as your needle, and your statements are as true as your stitches."

Of course Miss Deborah had heard of Captain Diamond. He had been much talked about many years before, but he had survived the scandal that attached to his name.

"What was the scandal?" I asked.

"He killed his daughter."

"Killed her?" I cried; "how so?"

"Oh, not with a pistol, or a dagger, or a dose of arsenic! With his tongue. Talk of women's tongues! He cursed her—with some horrible oath—and she died!"

"What had she done?"

"She had received a visit from a young man who loved her, and whom he had forbidden the house."

"The house," I said—"ah yes! The house is out in the country, two or three miles from here, on a lonely cross-road."

Miss Deborah looked sharply at me, as she bit her thread.

"Ah, you know about the house?" she said.

"A little," I answered; "I have seen it. But I want you to tell me more."

293

But here Miss Deborah betrayed an incommunicativeness which was most unusual.

"You wouldn't call me superstitious, would you?" she asked.

"You?—you are the quintessence of pure reason."

"Well, every thread has its rotten place, and every needle its grain of rust. I would rather not talk about that house."

"You have no idea how you excite my curiosity!" I said.

"I can feel for you. But it would make me very nervous."

"What harm can come to you?" I asked.

"Some harm came to a friend of mine." And Miss Deborah gave a very positive nod.

"What had your friend done?"

"She had told me Captain Diamond's secret, which he had told her with a mighty mystery. She had been an old flame of his, and he took her into his confidence. He bade her tell no one, and assured her that if she did, something dreadful would happen to her."

"And what happened to her?"

"She died."

"Oh, we are all mortal!" I said. "Had she given him a promise?"

"She had not taken it seriously, she had not believed him. She repeated the story to me, and three days afterward, she was taken with inflammation of the lungs. A month afterward, here where I sit now, I was stitching her grave-clothes. Since then, I have never mentioned what she told me."

"Was it very strange?"

"It was strange, but it was ridiculous too. It is a thing to make you shudder and to make you laugh, both. But you can't worry it out of me. I am sure that if I were to tell you, I should immediately break a needle in my finger, and die the next week of lock-jaw."

I retired, and urged Miss Deborah no further; but every two or three days, after dinner, I came and sat down by her rocking-chair. I made no further allusion to Captain Diamond; I sat silent, clipping tape with her scissors. At last, one day, she told me I was looking poorly. I was pale.

"I am dying of curiosity," I said. "I have lost my appetite. I have eaten no dinner."

"Remember Bluebeard's wife!" said Miss Deborah.

"One may as well perish by the sword as by famine!" I answered.

Still she said nothing, and at last I rose with a melodramatic sigh and departed. As I reached the door she called me and pointed to the chair I had vacated. "I never was hard-hearted," she said. "Sit down, and if we are to perish, may we at least perish together." And then, in very few words, she communicated what she knew of Captain Diamond's secret. "He was a very high-tempered old man, and though he was very fond of his daughter, his will was law. He had picked out a husband for her, and given her due notice. Her mother was dead, and they lived alone together. The house had been Mrs. Diamond's own marriage portion; the Captain, I believe, hadn't a penny. After his marriage they had come to live there, and he had begun to work the farm. The poor girl's lover was a young man with whiskers from Boston. The Captain came in one evening and found them together; he collared the young man, and hurled a terrible curse at the poor girl. The young man cried that she was his wife, and he asked her if it was true. She said, No! Thereupon Captain Diamond, his fury growing fiercer, repeated his imprecation, ordered her out of the house, and disowned her forever. She swooned away, but her father went raging off and left her. Several hours later, he came back and found the house empty. On the table was a note from the young man telling him that he had killed his daughter, repeating the assurance that she was his own wife, and declaring that he himself claimed the sole right to commit her remains to earth. He had carried the body away in a gig! Captain Diamond wrote him a dreadful note in answer, saying that he didn't believe his daughter was dead, but that, whether or no, she was dead to him. A week later, in the middle of the night, he saw her ghost. Then, I suppose, he was convinced. The ghost reappeared several times, and finally began regularly to haunt the house. It made the old man very uncomfortable, for little by little his passion had passed away, and he was given up to grief. He determined at last to leave the place, and tried to sell it or rent it; but meanwhile the story had gone abroad, the ghost had been seen by other persons, the house had a bad name, and it was impossible to dispose of it. With the farm, it was the old man's only property, and his only means of subsistence; if he could neither live in it nor rent it he was beggared. But the ghost had no mercy, as he had had none. He struggled for six months, and at last he broke down. He put on his old blue cloak and took up his staff, and prepared to wander away and beg his bread. Then the ghost relented, and proposed a compromise. 'Leave the house to me!' it said; 'I have marked it for my own. Go off and live elsewhere. But to enable you to live, I will be your tenant, since you can find no other. I will hire the house of you and pay you a certain rent.' And the ghost named a sum. The old man consented, and he goes every quarter to collect his rent!"

I laughed at this recital, but I confess I shuddered too, for my own observation had exactly confirmed it. Had I not been witness of one of the Captain's quarterly visits, had I not all but seen him sit watching his spectral tenant count out the rent-money, and when he trudged away in the dark, had he not a little bag of strangely gotten coin hidden in the folds of his old blue cloak? I imparted none of these reflections to Miss Deborah, for I was determined that my observations should have a sequel, and I promised myself the pleasure of treating her to my story in its full maturity. "Captain Diamond," I asked, "has no other known means of subsistence?"

"None whatever. He toils not, neither does he spin—his ghost supports him. A haunted house is valuable property!"

"And in what coin does the ghost pay?"

"In good American gold and silver. It has only this peculiarity— that the pieces are all dated before the young girl's death. It's a strange mixture of matter and spirit!"

"And does the ghost do things handsomely; is the rent large?"

"The old man, I believe, lives decently, and has his pipe and his glass. He took a little house down by the river; the door is sidewise to the street, and there is a little garden before it. There he spends his days, and has an old colored woman to do for him. Some years ago, he used to wander about a good deal, he was a familiar figure in the town, and most people knew his legend. But of late he has drawn back into his shell; he sits over his fire, and curiosity has forgotten him. I suppose he is falling into his dotage. But I am sure, I trust," said Miss Deborah in conclusion, "that he won't outlive his faculties or his powers of locomotion, for, if I remember rightly, it was part of the bargain that he should come in person to collect his rent."

We neither of us seemed likely to suffer any especial penalty for Miss Deborah's indiscretion; I found her, day after day, singing over her work, neither more nor less active than usual. For myself, I boldly pursued my observations. I went again, more than once, to the great graveyard, but I was disappointed in my hope of finding Captain Diamond there. I had a prospect, however, which afforded me compensation. I shrewdly inferred that the old man's quarterly pilgrimages were made upon the last day of the old quarter. My first sight of him had been on the 31st of December, and it was probable that he would return to his haunted home on the last day of March. This was near at hand; at last it arrived. I betook myself late in the afternoon to the old house on the cross-road, supposing that the hour of twilight was the appointed season. I was not wrong. I had been hovering about for a short time, feeling very much like a restless ghost myself, when he appeared in the same manner as before, and wearing the same costume. I again concealed myself, and saw him enter the house with the ceremonial which he had used on the former occasion. A light appeared successively in the crevice of each pair of shutters, and I opened the window which had yielded to my importunity before. Again I saw the great shadow on the wall, motionless and solemn. But I saw nothing else. The old man re-appeared at last, made his fantastic salaam before the house, and crept away into the dusk.

One day, more than a month after this, I met him again at Mount Auburn. The air was full of the voice of spring; the birds had come back and were twittering over their winter's travels, and a mild west wind was making a thin murmur in the raw verdure. He was seated on a bench in the sun, still muffled in his enormous mantle, and he recognized me as soon as I approached him. He nodded at me as if he were an old Bashaw giving the signal for my decapitation, but it was apparent that he was pleased to see me.

"I have looked for you here more than once," I said. "You don't come often."

"What did you want of me?" he asked.

"I wanted to enjoy your conversation. I did so greatly when I met you here before."

"You found me amusing?"

"Interesting!" I said.

"You didn't think me cracked?"

"Cracked?—My dear sir—!" I protested.

"I'm the sanest man in the country. I know that is what insane people always say; but generally they can't prove it. I can!"

"I believe it," I said. "But I am curious to know how such a thing can be proved."

He was silent awhile.

"I will tell you. I once committed, unintentionally, a great crime. Now I pay the penalty. I give up my life to it. I don't shirk it; I face it squarely, knowing perfectly what it is. I haven't tried to bluff it off; I haven't begged off from it; I haven't run away from it. The penalty is terrible, but I have accepted it. I have been a philosopher!

"If I were a Catholic, I might have turned monk, and spent the rest of my life in fasting and praying. That is no penalty; that is an evasion. I might have blown my brains out—I might have gone mad. I wouldn't do either. I would simply face the music, take the consequences. As I say, they are awful! I take them on certain days, four times a year. So it has been these twenty years; so it will be as long as I last. It's my business; it's my avocation. That's the way I feel about it. I call that reasonable!"

"Admirably so!" I said. "But you fill me with curiosity and with compassion."

"Especially with curiosity," he said, cunningly.

"Why," I answered, "if I know exactly what you suffer I can pity you more."

"I'm much obliged. I don't want your pity; it won't help me. I'll tell you something, but it's not for myself; it's for your own sake." He paused a long time and looked all round him, as if for chance eavesdroppers. I anxiously awaited his revelation, but he disappointed me. "Are you still studying theology?" he asked.

"Oh, yes," I answered, perhaps with a shade of irritation. "It's a thing one can't learn in six months."

"I should think not, so long as you have nothing but your books. Do you know the proverb, 'A grain of experience is worth a pound of precept'? I'm a great theologian."

"Ah, you have had experience," I murmured sympathetically.

"You have read about the immortality of the soul; you have seen Jonathan Edwards and Dr. Hopkins chopping logic over it, and deciding, by chapter and verse, that it is true. But I have seen it with these eyes; I have touched it with these hands!" And the old man held up his rugged old fists and shook them portentously. "That's better!" he went on; "but I have bought it dearly. You had better

298

take it from the books—evidently you always will. You are a very good young man; you will never have a crime on your conscience."

I answered with some juvenile fatuity, that I certainly hoped I had my share of human passions, good young man and prospective Doctor of Divinity as I was.

"Ah, but you have a nice, quiet little temper," he said. "So have I—now! But once I was very brutal—very brutal. You ought to know that such things are. I killed my own child."

"Your own child?"

"I struck her down to the earth and left her to die. They could not hang me, for it was not with my hand I struck her. It was with foul and damnable words. That makes a difference; it's a grand law we live under! Well, sir, I can answer for it that *her* soul is immortal. We have an appointment to meet four times a year, and then I catch it!"

"She has never forgiven you?"

"She has forgiven me as the angels forgive! That's what I can't stand—the soft, quiet way she looks at me. I'd rather she twisted a knife about in my heart—O Lord, Lord, Lord!" and Captain Diamond bowed his head over his stick, and leaned his forehead on his crossed hands.

I was impressed and moved, and his attitude seemed for the moment a check to further questions. Before I ventured to ask him anything more, he slowly rose and pulled his old cloak around him. He was unused to talking about his troubles, and his memories overwhelmed him. "I must go my way," he said; "I must be creeping along."

"I shall perhaps meet you here again," I said.

"Oh, I'm a stiff-jointed old fellow," he answered, "and this is rather far for me to come. I have to reserve myself. I have sat sometimes a month at a time smoking my pipe in my chair. But I should like to see you again." And he stopped and looked at me, terribly and kindly. "Some day, perhaps, I shall be glad to be able to lay my hand on a young, unperverted soul. If a man can make a friend, it is always something gained. What is your name?"

I had in my pocket a small volume of Pascal's "Thoughts," on the fly-leaf of which were written my name and address. I took it out and offered it to my old friend. "Pray keep this little book," I said. "It is one I am very fond of, and it will tell you something about me."

He took it and turned it over slowly, then looking up at me with a scowl of gratitude, "I'm not much of a reader," he said; "but I won't refuse the first present I shall have received since—my troubles; and the last. Thank you, sir!" And with the little book in his hand he took his departure.

I was left to imagine him for some weeks after that sitting solitary in his arm-chair with his pipe. I had not another glimpse of him. But I was awaiting my chance, and on the last day of June, another quarter having elapsed, I deemed that it had come. The evening dusk in June falls late, and I was impatient for its coming. At last, toward the end of a lovely summer's day, I revisited Captain Diamond's property. Everything now was green around it save the blighted orchard in its rear, but its own immitigable grayness and sadness were as striking as when I had first beheld it beneath a December sky. As I drew near it, I saw that I was late for my purpose, for my purpose had simply been to step forward on Captain Diamond's arrival, and bravely ask him to let me go in with him. He had preceded me, and there were lights already in the windows. I was unwilling, of course, to disturb him during his ghostly interview, and I waited till he came forth. The lights disappeared in the course of time; then the door opened and Captain Diamond stole out. That evening he made no bow to the haunted house, for the first object he beheld was his fair-minded young friend planted, modestly but firmly, near the door-step. He stopped short, looking at me, and this time his terrible scowl was in keeping with the situation.

"I knew you were here," I said. "I came on purpose."

He seemed dismayed, and looked round at the house uneasily.

"I beg your pardon if I have ventured too far," I added, "but you know you have encouraged me."

"How did you know I was here?"

"I reasoned it out. You told me half your story, and I guessed the other half. I am a great observer, and I had noticed this house in passing. It seemed to me to have a mystery. When you kindly confided to me that you saw spirits, I was sure that it could only be here that you saw them."

"You are mighty clever," cried the old man. "And what brought you here this evening?"

I was obliged to evade this question.

"Oh, I often come; I like to look at the house—it fascinates me."

He turned and looked up at it himself. "It's nothing to look at outside." He was evidently quite unaware of its peculiar outward appearance, and this odd fact, communicated to me thus in the twilight, and under the very brow of the sinister dwelling, seemed to make his vision of the strange things within more real.

"I have been hoping," I said, "for a chance to see the inside. I thought I might find you here, and that you would let me go in with you. I should like to see what you see."

He seemed confounded by my boldness, but not altogether displeased. He laid his hand on my arm. "Do you know what I see?" he asked.

"How can I know, except as you said the other day, by experience? I want to have the experience. Pray, open the door and take me in."

Captain Diamond's brilliant eyes expanded beneath their dusky brows, and after holding his breath a moment, he indulged in the first and last apology for a laugh by which I was to see his solemn visage contorted. It was profoundly grotesque, but it was perfectly noiseless. "Take you in?" he softly growled. "I wouldn't go in again before my time's up for a thousand times that sum." And he thrust out his hand from the folds of his cloak and exhibited a small agglommeration of coin, knotted into the corner of an old silk pocket-handkerchief. "I stick to my bargain no less, but no more!"

"But you told me the first time I had the pleasure of talking with you that it was not so terrible."

"I don't say it's terrible—now. But it's damned disagreeable!"

This adjective was uttered with a force that made me hesitate and reflect. While I did so, I thought I heard a slight movement of one of the window-shutters above us. I looked up, but everything seemed motionless. Captain Diamond, too, had been thinking; suddenly he turned toward the house. "If you will go in alone," he said, "you are welcome."

"Will you wait for me here?"

"Yes, you will not stop long."

"But the house is pitch dark. When you go you have lights."

He thrust his hand into the depths of his cloak and produced some matches. "Take these," he said. "You will find two candlesticks with candles on the table in the hall. Light them, take one in each hand and go ahead."

301

"Where shall I go?"

"Anywhere—everywhere. You can trust the ghost to find you."

I will not pretend to deny that by this time my heart was beating. And yet I imagine I motioned the old man with a sufficiently dignified gesture to open the door. I had made up my mind that there was in fact a ghost. I had conceded the premise. Only I had assured myself that once the mind was prepared, and the thing was not a surprise, it was possible to keep cool. Captain Diamond turned the lock, flung open the door, and bowed low to me as I passed in. I stood in the darkness, and heard the door close behind me. For some moments, I stirred neither finger nor toe; I stared bravely into the impenetrable dusk. But I saw nothing and heard nothing, and at last I struck a match. On the table were two old brass candlesticks rusty from disuse. I lighted the candles and began my tour of exploration.

A wide staircase rose in front of me, guarded by an antique balustrade of that rigidly delicate carving which is found so often in old New England houses. I postponed ascending it, and turned into the room on my right. This was an old-fashioned parlor, meagerly furnished, and musty with the absence of human life. I raised my two lights aloft and saw nothing but its empty chairs and its blank walls. Behind it was the room into which I had peeped from without, and which, in fact, communicated with it, as I had supposed, by folding doors. Here, too, I found myself confronted by no menacing specter. I crossed the hall again, and visited the rooms on the other side; a diningroom in front, where I might have written my name with my finger in the deep dust of the great square table; a kitchen behind with its pots and pans eternally cold. All this was hard and grim, but it was not formidable. I came back into the hall, and walked to the foot of the staircase, holding up my candles; to ascend required a fresh effort, and I was scanning the gloom above. Suddenly, with an inexpressible sensation, I became aware that this gloom was animated; it seemed to move and gather itself together. Slowly—I say slowly, for to my tense expectancy the instants appeared ages—it took the shape of a large, definite figure, and this figure advanced and stood at the top of the stairs. I frankly confess that by this time I was conscious of a feeling to which I am in duty bound to apply the vulgar name of fear. I may poetize it and call it Dread, with a capital letter; it was at any rate the feeling that makes a man yield ground. I measured it as it grew, and it seemed perfectly irresistible; for it did not appear to come from within but from without, and to be embodied in the dark image at the head of the staircase. After a fashion I reasoned—I remember reasoning. I said to myself, "I had always thought ghosts were white and transparent; this is a thing of thick shadows, densely opaque." I reminded myself that the occasion was momentous, and that if fear were to overcome me I should gather all possible impressions while my wits remained. I stepped back, foot behind foot, with my eyes still on the figure and placed my candles on the table. I was perfectly conscious that the proper thing was to ascend the stairs resolutely, face to face with the image, but the soles of my shoes seemed suddenly to have been transformed into leaden weights. I had got what I wanted; I was seeing the ghost. I tried to look at the figure distinctly so that I could remember it, and fairly claim, afterward, not to have lost my self-possession. I even asked myself how long it was expected I should stand looking, and how soon I could honorably retire. All this, of course, passed through my mind with extreme rapidity, and it was checked by a further movement on the part of the figure. Two white hands appeared in the dark perpendicular mass, and were slowly raised to what seemed to be the level of the head. Here they were pressed together, over the region of the face, and then they were removed, and the face was disclosed. It was dim, white, strange, in every way ghostly. It looked down at me for an instant, after which one of the hands was raised again, slowly, and waved to and fro before it. There was something very singular in this gesture; it seemed to denote resentment and dismissal, and yet it had a sort of trivial, familiar motion. Familiarity on the part of the haunting Presence had not entered into my calculations, and did not strike me pleasantly. I agreed with Captain Diamond that it was "damned disagreeable." I was pervaded by an intense desire to make an orderly, and, if possible, a graceful retreat. I wished to do it gallantly, and it seemed to me that it would be gallant to blow out my candles. I turned and did so, punctiliously, and then I made my way to the door, groped a moment and opened it. The outer light, almost extinct as it was, entered for a moment, played over the dusty depths of the house and showed me the solid shadow.

Standing on the grass, bent over his stick, under the early glimmering stars, I found Captain Diamond. He looked up at me fixedly for a moment, but asked no questions, and then he went and locked the door. This duty performed, he discharged the other—made his obeisance like the priest before the altar—and then without heeding me further, took his departure.

A few days later, I suspended my studies and went off for the summer's vacation. I was absent for several weeks, during which I had plenty of leisure to analyze my impressions of the supernatural. I took some satisfaction in the reflection that I had not been ignobly terrified; I had not bolted nor swooned—I had proceeded with dignity. Nevertheless, I was certainly more comfortable when I had put thirty miles between me and the scene of my exploit, and I continued for many days to prefer the daylight to the dark. My nerves had been powerfully excited; of this I was particularly conscious when, under the influence of the drowsy air of the seaside, my excitement began slowly to ebb. As it disappeared, I attempted to take a sternly rational view of my experience. Certainly I had seen *something*—that was not fancy; but what had I seen? I regretted extremely now that I had not been bolder, that I had not gone nearer and inspected the apparition more minutely. But it was very well to talk; I had done as much as any man in the circumstances would have dared; it was indeed a physical impossibility that I should have advanced. Was not this paralyzation of my powers in itself a supernatural influence? Not necessarily, perhaps, for a sham ghost that one accepted might do as much execution as a real ghost. But why had I so easily accepted the sable phantom that waved its hand? Why had it so impressed itself? Unquestionably, true or false, it was a very clever phantom. I greatly preferred that it should have been true—in the first place because I did not care to have shivered and shaken for nothing, and in the second place because to have seen a well-authenticated goblin is, as things go, a feather in a quiet man's cap. I tried, therefore, to let my vision rest and to stop turning it over. But an impulse stronger than my will recurred at intervals and set a mocking question on my lips. Granted that the apparition was Captain Diamond's daughter; if it was she it certainly was her spirit. But was it not her spirit and something more?

The middle of September saw me again established among the theologic shades, but I made no haste to revisit the haunted house.

The last of the month approached—the term of another quarter with poor Captain Diamond—and found me indisposed to disturb his pilgrimage on this occasion; though I confess that I thought with a good deal of compassion of the feeble old man trudging away, lonely, in the autumn dusk, on his extraordinary errand. On the thirtieth of September, at noonday, I was drowsing over a heavy octavo, when I heard a feeble rap at my door. I replied with an invitation to enter, but as this produced no effect I repaired to the door and opened it. Before me stood an elderly negress with her head bound in a scarlet turban, and a white handkerchief folded across her bosom. She looked at me intently and in silence; she had that air of supreme gravity and decency which aged persons of her race so often wear. I stood interrogative, and at last, drawing her hand from her ample pocket, she held up a little book. It was the copy of Pascal's "Thoughts" that I had given to Captain Diamond.

"Please, sir," she said, very mildly, "do you know this book?"

"Perfectly," said I, "my name is on the fly-leaf."

"It is your name—no other?"

"I will write my name if you like, and you can compare them," I answered.

She was silent a moment and then, with dignity—"It would be useless, sir," she said, "I can't read. If you will give me your word that is enough. I come," she went on, "from the gentleman to whom you gave the book. He told me to carry it as a token—a token—that is what he called it. He is right down sick, and he wants to see you."

"Captain Diamond—sick?" I cried. "Is his illness serious?"

"He is bad—he is all gone."

I expressed my regret and sympathy, and offered to go to him immediately, if his sable messenger would show me the way. She assented deferentially, and in a few moments I was following her along the sunny streets, feeling very much like a personage in the Arabian Nights, led to a postern gate by an Ethiopian slave. My own conductress directed her steps toward the river and stopped at a decent little yellow house in one of the streets that descend to it. She quickly opened the door and led me in, and I very soon found myself in the presence of my old friend. He was in bed, in a darkened room, and evidently in a very feeble state. He lay back on his pillow staring before him, with his bristling hair more erect than ever, and his intensely dark and bright old eyes touched with the glitter of fever. His apartment was humble and scrupulously neat, and I could see that my dusky guide was a faithful servant. Captain Diamond, lying there rigid and pale on his white sheets, resembled some ruggedly carven figure on the lid of a Gothic tomb. He looked at me silently, and my companion withdrew and left us alone.

"Yes, it's you," he said, at last, "it's you, that good young man. There is no mistake, is there?"

"I hope not; I believe I'm a good young man. But I am very sorry you are ill. What can I do for you?"

"I am very bad, very bad; my poor old bones ache so!" and, groaning portentously, he tried to turn toward me.

I questioned him about the nature of his malady and the length of time he had been in bed, but he barely heeded me; he seemed impatient to speak of something else. He grasped my sleeve, pulled me toward him, and whispered quickly:

"You know my time's up!"

"Oh, I trust not," I said, mistaking his meaning. "I shall certainly see you on your legs again."

"God knows!" he cried. "But I don't mean I'm dying; not yet a bit. What I mean is, I'm due at the house. This is rent-day."

"Oh, exactly! But you can't go."

"I can't go. It's awful. I shall lose my money. If I am dying, I want it all the same. I want to pay the doctor. I want to be buried like a respectable man."

"It is this evening?" I asked.

"This evening at sunset, sharp."

He lay staring at me, and, as I looked at him in return, I suddenly understood his motive in sending for me. Morally, as it came into my thought, I winced. But, I suppose I looked unperturbed, for he continued in the same tone. "I can't lose my money. Someone else must go. I asked Belinda; but she won't hear of it."

"You believe the money will be paid to another person?"

"We can try, at least. I have never failed before and I don't know. But, if you say I'm as sick as a dog, that my old bones ache, that I'm dying, perhaps she'll trust you. She don't want me to starve!"

"You would like me to go in your place, then?"

"You have been there once; you know what it is. Are you afraid?"

I hesitated.

"Give me three minutes to reflect," I said, "and I will tell you."

My glance wandered over the room and rested on the various objects
that spoke of the threadbare, decent poverty of its occupant. There
seemed to be a mute appeal to my pity and my resolution in their
cracked and faded sparseness. Meanwhile Captain Diamond continued,
feebly:

"I think she'd trust you, as I have trusted you; she'll like your face;
she'll see there is no harm in you. It's a hundred and thirty-three dollars, exactly. Be sure you put them into a safe place."

"Yes," I said at last, "I will go, and, so far as it depends upon me,
you shall have the money by nine o'clock tonight."

He seemed greatly relieved; he took my hand and faintly pressed
it, and soon afterward I withdrew. I tried for the rest of the day
not to think of my evening's work, but, of course, I thought of nothing
else. I will not deny that I was nervous; I was, in fact, greatly excited,
and I spent my time in alternately hoping that the mystery should
prove less deep than it appeared, and yet fearing that it might prove
too shallow. The hours passed very slowly, but, as the afternoon began
to wane, I started on my mission. On the way, I stopped at Captain
Diamond's modest dwelling, to ask how he was doing, and to receive
such last instructions as he might desire to lay upon me. The old
negress, gravely and inscrutably placid, admitted me, and, in answer
to my inquiries, said that the Captain was very low; he had sunk since
the morning.

"You must be right smart," she said, "if you want to get back before
he drops off."

A glance assured me that she knew of my projected expedition,
though, in her own opaque black pupil, there was not a gleam of self-
betrayal.

"But why should Captain Diamond drop off?" I asked. "He certainly seems very weak; but I cannot make out that he has any definite
disease."

"His disease is old age," she said, sententiously.

"But he is not so old as that; sixty-seven or sixty-eight, at most."
She was silent a moment.

"He's worn out; he's used up; he can't stand it any longer."

"Can I see him a moment?" I asked; upon which she led me again
to his room.

He was lying in the same way as when I had left him, except that

307

his eyes were closed. But he seemed very "low," as she had said, and he had very little pulse. Nevertheless, I further learned the doctor had been there in the afternoon and professed himself satisfied. "He don't know what's been going on," said Belinda, curtly.

The old man stirred a little, opened his eyes, and after some time recognized me.

"I'm going, you know," I said. "I'm going for your money. Have you anything more to say?" He raised himself slowly, and with a painful effort, against his pillows; but he seemed hardly to understand me. "The house, you know," I said. "Your daughter."

He rubbed his forehead, slowly, awhile, and at last, his comprehension awoke. "Ah, yes," he murmured, "I trust you. A hundred and thirty-three dollars. In old pieces—all in old pieces." Then he added more vigorously, and with a brightening eye: "Be very respectful—be very polite. If not—if not—" and his voice failed again.

"Oh, I certainly shall be," I said, with a rather forced smile. "But, if not?"

"If not, I shall know it!" he said, very gravely. And with this, his eyes closed and he sunk down again.

I took my departure and pursued my journey with a sufficiently resolute step. When I reached the house, I made a propitiatory bow in front of it, in emulation of Captain Diamond. I had timed my walk so as to be able to enter without delay; night had already fallen. I turned the key, opened the door and shut it behind me. Then I struck a light, and found the two candlesticks I had used before, standing on the tables in the entry. I applied a match to both of them, took them up and went into the parlor. It was empty, and though I waited awhile, it remained empty. I passed then into the other rooms on the same floor, and no dark image rose before me to check my steps. At last, I came out into the hall again, and stood weighing the question of going upstairs. The staircase had been the scene of my discomfiture before, and I approached it with profound mistrust. At the foot, I paused, looking up, with my hand on the balustrade. I was acutely expectant, and my expectation was justified. Slowly, in the darkness above, the black figure that I had seen before took shape. It was not an illusion; it was a figure, and the same. I gave it time to define itself, and watched it stand and look down at me with its hidden face. Then, deliberately, I lifted up my voice and spoke.

"I have come in place of Captain Diamond, at his request," I said. "He is very ill; he is unable to leave his bed. He earnestly begs that you will pay the money to me; I will immediately carry it to him." The figure stood motionless, giving no sign. "Captain Diamond would have come if he were able to move," I added, in a moment, appealingly; "but, he is utterly unable."

At this the figure slowly unveiled its face and showed me a dim, white mask; then it began slowly to descend the stairs. Instinctively I fell back before it, retreating to the door of the front sitting-room. With my eyes still fixed on it, I moved backward across the threshold; then I stopped in the middle of the room and set down my lights. The figure advanced; it seemed to be that of a tall woman, dressed in vaporous black crape. As it drew near, I saw that it had a perfectly human face, though it looked extremely pale and sad. We stood gazing at each other; my agitation had completely vanished; I was only deeply interested.

"Is my father dangerously ill?" said the apparition.

At the sound of its voice—gentle, tremulous, and perfectly human—I started forward; I felt a rebound of excitement. I drew a long breath, I gave a sort of cry, for what I saw before me was not a disembodied spirit, but a beautiful woman, an audacious actress. Instinctively, irresistibly, by the force of reaction against my credulity, I stretched out my hand and seized the long veil that muffled her head. I gave it a violent jerk, dragged it nearly off, and stood staring at a large fair person, of about five-and-thirty. I comprehended her at a glance; her long black dress, her pale, sorrow-worn face, painted to look paler, her very fine eyes—the color of her father's—and her sense of outrage at my movement.

"My father, I suppose," she cried, "did not send you here to insult me!" and she turned away rapidly, took up one of the candles and moved toward the door. Here she paused, looked at me again, hesitated, and then drew a purse from her pocket and flung it down on the floor. "There is your money!" she said, majestically.

I stood there, wavering between amazement and shame, and saw her pass out into the hall. Then I picked up the purse. The next moment, I heard a loud shriek and a crash of something dropping, and she came staggering back into the room without her light.

"My father—my father!" she cried; and with parted lips and dilated eyes, she rushed toward me.

"Your father—where?" I demanded.

"In the hall, at the foot of the stairs."

I stepped forward to go out, but she seized my arm.

"He is in white," she cried, "in his shirt. It's not he!"

"Why, your father is in his house, in his bed, extremely ill," I answered.

She looked at me fixedly, with searching eyes.

"Dying?"

"I hope not," I stuttered.

She gave a long moan and covered her face with her hands.

"Oh, heavens, I have seen his ghost!" she cried.

She still held my arm; she seemed too terrified to release it. "His ghost!" I echoed, wondering.

"It's the punishment of my long folly!" she went on.

"Ah," said I, "it's the punishment of my indiscretion—of my violence!"

"Take me away, take me away!" she cried, still clinging to my arm. "Not there"—as I was turning toward the hall and the front door— "not there, for pity's sake! By this door—the back entrance." And snatching the other candles from the table, she led me through the neighboring room into the back part of the house. Here was a door opening from a sort of scullery into the orchard. I turned the rusty lock and we passed out and stood in the cool air, beneath the stars. Here my companion gathered her black drapery about her, and stood for a moment, hesitating. I had been infinitely flurried, but my curiosity touching her was uppermost. Agitated, pale, picturesque, she looked, in the early evening light, very beautiful.

"You have been playing all these years a most extraordinary game," I said.

She looked at me somberly, and seemed disinclined to reply. "I came in perfect good faith," I went on. "The last time—three months ago—you remember?—you greatly frightened me."

"Of course it was an extraordinary game," she answered at last. "But it was the only way."

"Had he not forgiven you?"

"So long as he thought me dead, yes. There have been things in my life he could not forgive."

I hesitated and then—"And where is your husband?" I asked.

"I have no husband—I have never had a husband."

She made a gesture which checked further questions, and moved rapidly away. I walked with her round the house to the road, and she kept murmuring—"It was he—it was he!" When we reached the road she stopped, and asked me which way I was going. I pointed to the road by which I had come, and she said—"I take the other. You are going to my father's?" she added.

"Directly," I said.

"Will you let me know to-morrow what you have found?"

"With pleasure. But how shall I communicate with you?"

She seemed at a loss, and looked about her. "Write a few words," she said, "and put them under that stone." And she pointed to one of the lava slabs that bordered the old well. I gave her my promise to comply, and she turned away. "I know my road," she said. "Everything is arranged. It's an old story."

She left me with a rapid step, and as she receded into the darkness, resumed, with the dark flowing lines of her drapery, the phantasmal appearance with which she had at first appeared to me. I watched her till she became invisible, and then I took my own leave of the place. I returned to town at a swinging pace, and marched straight to the little yellow house near the river. I took the liberty of entering without a knock, and, encountering no interruption, made my way to Captain Diamond's room. Outside the door, on a low bench, with folded arms, sat the sable Belinda.

"How is he?" I asked.

"He's gone to glory."

"Dead?" I cried.

She rose with a sort of tragic chuckle.

"He's as big a ghost as any of them now!"

I passed into the room and found the old man lying there irredeemably rigid and still. I wrote that evening a few lines which I proposed on the morrow to place beneath the stone, near the well; but my promise was not destined to be executed. I slept that night very ill—it was natural—and in my restlessness left my bed to walk about the room. As I did so I caught sight, in passing my window, of a red glow in the

311

north-western sky. A house was on fire in the country, and evidently burning fast. It lay in the same direction as the scene of my evening's adventures, and as I stood watching the crimson horizon I was startled by a sharp memory. I had blown out the candle which lighted me, with my companion, to the door through which we escaped, but I had not accounted for the other light, which she had carried into the hall and dropped—heaven knew where—in her consternation. The next day I walked out with my folded letter and turned into the familiar cross-road. The haunted house was a mass of charred beams and smoldering ashes; the well-cover had been pulled off, in quest of water, by the few neighbors who had had the audacity to contest what they must have regarded as a demon-kindled blaze, the loose stones were completely displaced, and the earth had been trampled into puddles.

Chronological List of the First Twenty-Eight Tales

(Including first book publication dates, and a few more accessible reprintings.)

Year	Month	Journal	Title	Reprinting	Date
1865	Mar.	*Atlantic*	"The Story of a Year"	*American Novels and Stories*	1947
				Eight Uncollected Tales	1950
1866	Feb.	*Atlantic*	"A Landscape Painter"	*Stories Revived*, Vol. II	1885
				A Landscape Painter	1919
	Jun. 15	*Galaxy*	"A Day of Days"	*Stories Revived*, Vol. I	1885
				A Landscape Painter	1919
1867	Mar.	*Atlantic*	"My Friend Bingham"	*Eight Uncollected Tales*	1950
	Jun.-Aug.	*Atlantic*	"Poor Richard"	*Stories Revived*, Vol. III	1885
				A Landscape Painter	1919
1868	Jan.-Feb.	*Galaxy*	"The Story of a Masterpiece"	*Eight Uncollected Tales*	1950
	Feb.	*Atlantic*	"The Romance of Certain Old Clothes"	*A Passionate Pilgrim*	1875
				Stories Revived, Vol. III	1885
				Novels and Stories, Vol. XXVI	1923
	Apr.	*Atlantic*	"A Most Extraordinary Case"	*Stories Revived*, Vol. III	1885
				A Landscape Painter	1919
	Jun.	*Galaxy*	"A Problem"	*Eight Uncollected Tales*	1950
	Jul.	*Atlantic*	"De Grey: A Romance"	*Travelling Companions*	1919
	Jul.	*Galaxy*	"Osborne's Revenge"	*Eight Uncollected Tales*	1950
1869	Jul.	*Galaxy*	"A Light Man"	*Stories Revived*, Vol. I	1885
				Master Eustace	1920
	Jul.-Sept.	*Atlantic*	"Gabrielle de Bergerac"	*Gabrielle de Bergerac*	1918
				Eight Uncollected Tales	1950

Year	Month	Magazine	Title	Collection	Date
1870	Nov.-Dec.	*Atlantic*	"Travelling Companions"	*Travelling Companions*	1919
1871	Mar.-Apr.	*Atlantic*	"A Passionate Pilgrim"	*A Passionate Pilgrim* *Stories Revived*, Vol. II *N. Y. Edition*, Vol. XIII	1875 1885 1908
	Aug.	*Atlantic*	"At Isella"	*Travelling Companions*	1919
	Nov.	*Galaxy*	"Master Eustace"	*Stories Revived*, Vol. III *Master Eustace*	1885 1920
1872	Oct.-Nov.	*Atlantic*	"Guest's Confession"	*Travelling Companions*	1919
1873	Mar.	*Atlantic*	"The Madonna of the Future"	*A Passionate Pilgrim* *N. Y. Edition*, Vol. XIII	1875 1908
	Jun.	*Galaxy*	"The Sweetheart of M. Briseux"	*Travelling Companions*	1919
1874	Jan.	*Atlantic*	"The Last of the Valerii"	*A Passionate Pilgrim* *Stories Revived*, Vol. III *Novels and Stories*, Vol. XXVI	1875 1885 1923
	Feb.-Mar.	*Galaxy*	"Madame de Mauves"	*A Passionate Pilgrim* *N. Y. Edition*, Vol. XIII	1875 1908
	May-Jun.	*Scribner's Monthly*	"Adina"	*Travelling Companions*	1919
	Aug.	*Galaxy*	"Professor Fargo"	*Travelling Companions*	1919
	Oct.-Nov.	*Atlantic*	"Eugene Pickering"	*A Passionate Pilgrim* *Novels and Stories*, Vol. XXIV	1875 1923
1875	Aug.	*Galaxy*	"Benvolio"	*The Madonna of the Future*, Vol. II *Master Eustace*	1879 1920
1876	Aug.	*Scribner's Monthly*	"Crawford's Consistency"	*Eight Uncollected Tales*	1950
	Sept.	*Scribner's Monthly*	"The Ghostly Rental"	*The Ghostly Tales of Henry James* *Eight Uncollected Tales*	1948 1950